Another banner day. It isn't enough that flying terrifies me, let's add the WORST HAIR DAY on record. Throw in being late to the airport and now me and the extra 30 pounds of junk in my trunk are squeezed in next to THE HOTTEST GUY EVER. Funny, he doesn't look that thrilled to see me. 🌼

On days like today there's only ONE thing you can do—smile and put on your . . .

big girl panties

K.

By Stephanie Evanovich

BIG GIRL PANTIES

And in Hardcover

THE SWEET SPOT

STEPHANIE EVANOVICH

big girl panties

AVON

An Imprint of HarperCollinsPublishers

AVON BOOKS
An Imprint of HarperCollins*Publishers*
195 Broadway
New York, New York 10007

Copyright © 2013 by Stephanie Evanovich
Excerpt from *The Sweet Spot* copyright © 2014 by Stephanie Evanovich
ISBN 978-0-06-232548-8
www.avonromance.com

First Avon Books mass market printing: October 2014
First William Morrow paperback printing: February 2014
First William Morrow paperback international printing: July 2013
First William Morrow hardcover printing: July 2013
First William Morrow paperback special printing: June 2013

For the Boyz of 1900,
who have been making my dreams come true
since 1986, 1989, and 1992. Love you guys.

Acknowledgments

It is with sincere affection and admiration that I'd like to thank the following:

Bob Podrasky—for telling me to "just finish the thing!" and that he'd help me. And then he did.

Andrea Cirillo—for taking Bob's call. And then taking a hundred of mine.

Meg Ruley—for suggesting a title that still makes me giggle.

Rachel Kahan—for being the best editor a writer could have. And for always making me laugh.

Liate Stehlik—for making it look easy. And by "it," I mean "everything."

Michael Morrison—for revving up his e-reader.

The team at HarperCollins/William Morrow—Trish Daly, Kathy Gordon, Heidi Richter, Jen Hart, Megan Traynor, Lynne Grady, Tavia Kowalchuk, Shelby Meizlik, Doug Jones, Rachel Levenberg, Virginia Stanley, Erin Gorham, Lorie Young, Julia Meltzer, Jamie Kerner, Mary Schuck, and Andrea Rosen—for all their hard work and dedication.

Amy Parratt Coswell—for being my partner in crime in too many adventures to count, this being one of them.

Caroline Murphy—for knowing just how to talk a girl off a ledge.

Joe Palamara—for being the smartest personal trainer in the business today. For his knowledge and wisdom on the topic of what makes a body tick. And for the last time, dude, this book is not about you.

big girl panties

Chapter One

"I'M SORRY, MR. MONTGOMERY," THE PRETTY EMPLOYEE behind the counter said apologetically, "but for the next flight out, it's the best I can offer."

Logan Montgomery rarely hated anything, but flying coach was an exception. He thought he had left those days behind long ago. Even with two seats side by side, there was never enough room. He could've waited until the middle of the night and flown first class, but Logan chose to get home sooner. Not only was he ready for a night in his own bed, he simply had too much to do on the other end of his flight.

Logan was booked solid for the next three days, thanks to the shuffling he had to do to accommodate this trip. Football season was gearing up, basketball was winding down, and baseball was in full swing, and if it had been anyone but Chase Walker who'd asked him to fly from New York to Toronto on the spur of the moment, he would've begged off.

Chase was first baseman for the New York Kings, and while the Kings had extremely qualified trainers on staff, Chase wouldn't settle for anyone but Logan. And, what an overpaid baseball player and best friend wants, he gets. Logan had stretched Chase out for two days and then worked him out earlier that morning, and the Golden Boy was ready to go. Logan really couldn't complain. The cost for such spontaneous, unparalleled services was premium; the money was already in Logan's account.

Logan slid into his seat, long legs wedging up against the seat in front of him. He tried in vain to sit up straighter, attempting to somehow create more room, then took a deep breath. He closed his eyes, filtering out the external noise, the passengers filing in around him, their accompanying scuffles with the overhead compartments. A toddler fussed, refusing to sit down, insisting on remaining in her mother's lap. Logan exhaled a silent Zen mantra of gratitude for his window seat and relatively short flight. Satisfied that mind had overcome matter, Logan clicked his seat belt into place. That's when he looked up and saw her.

Oh, please don't let her sit next to me, he silently begged, watching her make her way down the aisle, her thick thighs rubbing together and her ample hips bumping into seats as she passed them. Her auburn hair was disheveled in ten different directions. She counted the rows and stopped right in front of Logan, giving him a quick glance. *Why do I always get the old lady, the drunk guy, or the fat chick?* Logan thought. *God, I hate coach.* His mantra transformed quickly into moping.

Perfect, Holly thought, withholding the maniacal laughter she knew would have the flight crew calling for security. It wasn't enough that she hated to fly. It wasn't even enough that she had to give up her original same-day flight and stay in Toronto overnight after what felt like twelve rounds with the Mike Tyson of corporate raiders. She even managed to maintain her sanity after mistaking the hotel's tiny bottle of body wash for shampoo and lathering her already overgrown hair into an unmanageable, flowery-smelling mop. Blow-drying only made it worse. She couldn't even find a rubber band to pull it back with. The waistband of her pants felt like a tourniquet due to the weight she'd gained in recent months. She could feel her bra strap cutting painfully into her right shoulder. And now she had to spend the next two hours squishing Adonis himself.

Holly could almost feel his disgust toward her radiating out of him, as if the irritated expression on his handsome face wasn't enough of an indicator. Another round of her pissing someone off just by showing up. She gritted her teeth and stuffed a large, brown, worn-out-looking satchel under the seat in front of her and ran her fingers hurriedly through the rat's nest on her head before sitting in it. In an effort to create some extra room for herself, she moved the armrest up. Trying to appear casual, she took a deep breath, sucked in her stomach as best she could, and buckled herself in.

At least she doesn't need the seat belt extension, Logan mused. He was a little afraid to inhale, recalling a fat woman he sat next to some years ago who smelled of hard-boiled eggs and rotten cheese. Tentatively, he drew in a breath. She smelled like baby powder and lavender, distinctly lavender. He relaxed a bit, giving a small nod in her direction.

He couldn't help but notice how white her knuckles got on takeoff. Her fists were clenched so tight against the seat. Curiously, she showed no other outward signs of fright. At least she didn't start wailing or get the vapors or do absurd tricks to take her to her "happy place." But with a second glance, Logan realized she wasn't just gripping her armrest. She wasn't moving. At all. He took a quick look at her face to make sure she wasn't turning blue. She was staring straight ahead, eyes wide open, fixated on some focal point in the front of the aircraft.

"Breathe, girl," Logan found himself saying.

Holly blinked once, her face pale, and tried to inhale, which to Logan sounded more like a gasp. "I'm not so good at takeoff," she responded on an exhaled whoosh of air.

"You're doing fine," he told her confidently, and opened a magazine.

Thanks, Superman, she thought, feeling the plane start to level off. *Easy for you to say. I'll bet you can actually fly and are just on vacation.*

Once they were safely in the air and Holly's panic passed, she noticed how perfectly groomed he was. He probably got a haircut every four weeks without fail. His eyelashes were longer than hers, and he even managed to make a green polo shirt and jeans look dressy. His broad shoulders vied for space much the same way her hips and thighs did, only where he was defined muscle, Holly was just mass. She glanced down at the magazine he was casually thumbing through. *Health and Fitness.* Its pages showcased dozens of toned, firm bodies, much like his. The fitness models wore skimpy garments that appeared painted onto their flawless tan skin. They flashed gloriously white teeth as they stretched and posed before backdrops of waterfalls, pools, and cliffs overlooking warm, sunny beaches. There were pictures of people in that magazine who looked like Holly, too—all with the word "before" in big bold letters underneath. She couldn't swear to it, but they looked like they were taken in front of grocery stores. Holly felt the sweat start to bead on her upper lip.

A female flight attendant, looking strikingly like the model on page twenty-five, stopped at their row with the refreshment cart and turned on the charm. It was all Holly could do not to give a loud snort. But then he spoke. No longer in the throes of takeoff anxiety, she could actually listen to him. Even his voice was like velvet, level and silky with a touch of a sexy drawl. He flirted with the flight attendant briefly before requesting bottled water, then passed on the food. Holly did the same, dead sure she was robbing them both of some cruel, prejudicial satisfaction by not saying, "I'll take everything you've got." Holly turned to Logan as the cart rolled away and gave half a laugh.

"Nothing like the fit of an airplane seat to ruin an appetite. I'll bet this plane was used to transport munchkins out of Oz." Holly liked to get right to the point—taking on the six-hundred-pound gorilla in the room—but felt like kicking herself. Why the hell did she feel the need to validate this specimen of masculine vanity? But she knew exactly why. She was going to be spending an hour sitting next to him and she knew she didn't make the grade on his first-impression meter. If she didn't want to spend the flight sitting like a statue in an effort not to embarrass herself by occasionally rubbing against him, she'd have to win him over.

He actually smiled, confirming the existence of his magazine-worthy pearly whites, and gave a small shrug. He had grown accustomed to other people's feeling intimidated by his looks. "Airline food stinks anyway." He was being sincere and his smile said so. Logan believed in karma.

She had sensed his original reaction when he first laid eyes on her—Logan could tell. And Logan didn't want to be thought of as the sort of guy who deliberately made others feel bad about themselves. He was just a busy guy, a temporarily stressed guy. A guy too big to fly coach on a packed flight, and he felt bad for having thought the worst of the woman next to him right away. Especially about the way she smelled. Only lavender lingered, mostly from her hair. He'd always liked lavender. "I'm Logan," he said.

"Holly." She extended a soft, unmanicured hand, which he shook. He had a strong, manly hand, not callused and gnarled from manual labor, but not the limp-wristed softness of a coddled pretty boy, either. "Holly Brennan. Nice to meet you. Sorry if I'm squishing you a bit. They didn't have any room in first class."

So, she was in the same boat as he. But by the looks of her, he imagined it would've taken quite a bite out of her pocketbook to buy the extra space. "I know. I got bumped out, too. Heard some guy hit a big lottery and is flying in his extended family so they can climb the Statue of Liberty or throw pennies off the Empire State Building," he said, then added, "Go figure."

Of course he'd been bumped. After all, why would a Greek god willingly choose to mingle with mere mortals? Around a guy like this, it was impossible not to take inventory of all your own flaws. He looked like he belonged on his own private jet, sipping Patrón, or whatever the ultrachic were currently imbibing. He didn't look like he was accustomed to being jammed in like a sardine in coach. Now he was stuck having to make small talk with the likes of her.

Holly stumbled through conversation, hating the words as they rushed forth. "I never realized there was that big a difference between coach and first class. Almost like night and day. Of course, ever since my butt grew a twin, I notice."

It was the second time she'd tried to make direct reference to her size, but Logan again refused to join her in the joke. He understood Holly's tactic, though: laugh at yourself before others get the chance. Classic defense mechanism.

From a professional point of view, Logan couldn't help wondering what type of body Holly Brennan had under all her self-esteem issues. Bodies were his business. Holly had sparkly green eyes and a sweet smile, despite the fact it came with a double chin and self-inflicted insults. The red hair, in its current state at least, could have passed for a three-alarm fire. Her clothes were wrinkled like she'd slept in them, and not comfortably. It was a look that would have made anyone else appear insane. But Holly Brennan didn't look crazy. She just looked worn out.

Logan didn't want Holly to feel he was judging her, so he let her off the hook. "Keeping in shape is an everyday battle," he said. He also knew the key to learning something about a person was to make them feel safe enough to open up. He wanted to make Holly comfortable, so maybe she'd stop all the jawing and cut to the truth.

"Watching somebody die is an everyday battle, too," she mumbled, her round face scrunching up.

"Pardon me?" Logan hadn't expected to hear anything so tragic, and the shock showed on his face.

"I was never thin," Holly blurted, suddenly feeling even more closed in by her surroundings, "but when my late husband was diagnosed, it seemed like food was the one thing I could always count on being there, you know?"

In his mind's eye, Logan saw himself thumping his fist against his own forehead.

"I'm really sorry, I didn't mean to pry. You look too young to have lost . . ." *Smooth,* he thought, the words trailing off. Widowing and loss in general have no age limit. Where the hell was his composure all of a sudden? Probably in first class with a hot towel being applied to it.

"It's all right." She hated the pity. But what she hated

even more was the fact that she'd just used her status as a widow to make this man feel as uncomfortable as she did. Besides, it probably wasn't his fault he was a total buck—the silver-spoon variety, the type nothing bad ever happens to. She hurried through the rest of her speech, sorry she even brought it up. "He was thirty-two. We met in college. He stayed home 'til . . . eighteen months. Then after—" Holly paused, aware that her wall was weakening, something she refused to let happen in front of a total stranger. She had already said more than she intended to. "Well, after"— she shrugged, mentally replacing the bricks—"I don't know. Doesn't really matter, does it?"

No. It didn't matter. "I'm sorry," Logan repeated, not willing to risk becoming tongue-tied again.

They sat in awkward silence, the word "sorry" swirling thick in the air around them. He was sorry for her situation. She was sorry for herself.

Exhausted from depression and self-loathing, Holly folded her hands in her lap, an unconscious effort to hide her muffin top. She flashed back to the customer-service counter at the airport no more than two hours ago and the uncomfortable way the airline rep looked her over as she booked Holly into one of the last remaining seats on the flight, and the rep's not-so-gentle suggestion that Holly might want to wait for another flight to keep her first-class seat—a reservation Holly had made to avoid the embarrassment of being forced to buy two seats in coach. The victory that resulted after the stare-down and subsequent judgment that one seat would suffice felt hollow. Holly shifted in her chair, and with that movement, shifted her thoughts as well—to all she'd lost in the past three years, and how fast those years had passed. Logan studied her discreetly. She'd laid it all out in front of him on a flight from Toronto to Newark. Had she done it because of his initial reaction, one that maybe he hadn't been so good at hiding? Would he have been so quick to judge her if they were seated together in first class? Would he even have taken a second look? Would he have extended his hand, started a conversation, if his own comfort zone hadn't been violated? In the spirit of karmic exploration, he decided it might be worth learning more.

Logan regrouped and started over. "So. Are you coming or going? I'm on my way back. I live in New Jersey. Englewood."

"Coincidence," she replied politely, turning her head in his direction, the frown back in place. "I live in Englewood Cliffs. My husband had an account in Toronto that needed to be settled."

The sense of karma returned like a wave crashing down upon him. It was a chance to right a wrong, to reach out to another person and at the same time bring himself back into balance. Logan waited a moment, wanting to choose his words carefully.

"You've been through a real rough stretch, I know. It's easy to let yourself go when you're focused on someone else. But the fact is, you're still here, very much alive, and far too young to hang it up. I could help you break some bad habits. Might even make you feel better."

"And just how might you be able to do that?" She

gave him a skeptical sideways glance, intrigued by the fact that he'd turned on the charm for her.

"I'm a personal trainer," he told her, "primarily for athletes. We live so close to each other, I could get a program going for you with no trouble."

She bristled. "Do I look like an athlete to you? Hate to break it to you, but the last time I played any sports, Billie Jean King was smack-talking Bobby Riggs."

His smile grew wide. "Somehow I doubt that. That happened in the seventies. You probably weren't even born yet. And besides, I said 'primarily.'"

She didn't bother smiling back. "I appreciate your charity, but it won't be necessary. Thanks anyway."

But Logan was feeling caught up in a rush of inspiration he hadn't felt in years, an idea beginning to take root. He threw his head back and laughed. "Who said anything about charity? I'm just trying to drum up business. Occupational hazard, I guess."

He was sure she would never be able to afford his five-hundred-dollar-an-hour price tag, and he needed new business like a hole in his head. But besides wanting to make up for acting like a shallow ass, Logan was suddenly hit with the overwhelming feeling that a real opportunity was presenting itself. His job often bordered on mundane now. Lately he felt like little more than a glorified counter of repetitions, a naysayer to the latest in fad drugs and metabolism boosters. This would be a break from his normal slog.

When Logan first started training—long before working with Chase Walker, Eli Manning, and other professional ballplayers—he'd felt a real sense of accomplishment in showing a beginner all they were capable of. There was a real high in pushing someone to their limit, watching them transform, especially with women. The female body in motion was an entirely different animal. It had so much more natural balance, so much more grace. Logan thought about how it responded to weight training in a totally different and noticeable way. It had been too long since he'd enjoyed the challenge of showing a woman her true potential. And Holly was in no way Logan's type, so the sexual tension would be minimal. In the early stages of his career, that had often been a stumbling block when it came to female clients. He had long since acknowledged this unprofessional shortcoming with only a modicum of dishonor. Something about his testosterone and their estrogen, mixed with an endorphin rush, was sometimes more than he could resist. Adding fuel to that fire was the fact that most of the women he took on as customers were women he found attractive to begin with. He refused to feel bad about it. It was a problem that solved itself quite naturally as his client list grew long with the teammates of his most prestigious customers instead of attractive women. But with Holly, there would be no problem keeping it professional. She would be the perfect project. He could help her get back in the game of her own life and enjoy watching her transformation in the process.

Logan came up with a lowball figure and Holly stopped frowning, seeming to consider his offer. It was an offer presented to her by an extremely attractive stranger with dark skin, even darker hair, and big chocolate eyes. *Everyone likes chocolate,* she thought to her own amusement. He reminded her of a Saint Bernard puppy, the very type of dog whose job it was to come to the rescue of desperate people. A Saint Bernard puppy with lovely broad shoulders and bulging biceps. Maybe he wasn't such a bad guy after all. Or maybe he was, in which case it would serve him right to be saddled with her several times a week for a couple of months. Either way, what could it hurt? It had been so long since she kept company with anybody, there were probably worse places she could start.

For the rest of the flight, neither of them said any more about his proposal. Logan entertained Holly with stories of his time in Brazil, training in martial arts, hoping to distract her as the plane descended. And it worked—he kept her fully engaged and she barely noticed the plane touching down. They landed and made their way together to the parking lot. Before they parted ways, Holly asked him for his card, telling him she would take up his gauntlet and be in touch.

"Make the appointment now." He jumped on the opportunity, not wanting to give her too long to think about it and come up with excuses. Without waiting for her to answer, he reached into his knapsack, handed her his card, pulled out his BlackBerry, and requested her cell phone number. "How's Thursday, six P.M.?"

She briefly looked down at his business card and wasted no time accepting. "You're on, Logan Montgomery."

Chapter Two

LOGAN SHUT THE FRONT DOOR TO HIS TENTH-FLOOR luxury condo with his foot, balancing his knapsack, his duffel bag, the mail, and his keys. He reached for the wall switch with his elbow to turn on the lights, then made his way to the dining room table and began absently sorting through the mail, once again amazed at how much stuff could accumulate in just a few days. Bill, check from client, bill, magazine, check, advertising flyer, fitness merchandise catalog, bill, magazine, check from client.

He paused. He'd just taken on a new client, a spontaneous gesture made out of a combination of zeal and self-reproach. A client so far out of the realm of his current level of programs, the experience would practically make him a novice as well. He couldn't remember the last time he had a client starting from square one.

He would have to bone up on his beginner's manual. It wouldn't hurt him to reinforce his own education. He went back to the sorting and stopped when the doorbell rang. He tossed the mail on the table, glanced at the clock on the wall, and crossed back to the door. It was pretty late for a haphazard stop-by. He opened the door and a lazy grin spread across his face.

She was long and lean, with delicate bone structure. Blond, perfectly styled hair, glossy pink lips, round doelike eyes. The hip-hugging jeans, blue satin camisole, and white leather jacket made her the perfect combination of waif and sizzling seductress. It was a look that had graced hundreds of magazine layouts and made Natalie Kimball a star.

"When you didn't answer my text, I figured you were out of town," he drawled, moving out of the way for her to enter.

"Now, what sort of surprise would that be?" Natalie gave his cheek an affectionate pinch as she flounced past him and into his living room. She was feisty and he liked it. He followed behind her, appreciating the sweet breeze of her perfume.

"I just got home. Good timing; you'd make a great stalker," Logan teased, joining her in the living room, where she stopped short and rounded on him, obviously disgruntled with his joke.

"I fly almost two hundred days a year," she huffed. "I know how to look up a flight schedule. Don't flatter yourself, Logan, you're not that special."

But he was that special, Natalie hated to admit, especially to herself. Logan Montgomery was a great catch and it hadn't taken her long to figure it out. He was everything a girl could want. He made his own successful living; he had famous friends. He was confident and gorgeous and charming, adapting to every situation with an ease he could have only been born with. He never told her how to handle her own affairs, unless she specifically asked his advice. He was easygoing yet smart about business. He never talked down to her, always appreciating her intelligence. And the *sex*. Logan made love to her like making women orgasm was his sole purpose in life and she was the only woman on the planet.

There was just one problem. Logan was so nonchalant outside the bedroom, bordering on aloof. Like he could stop seeing her tomorrow and he wouldn't lose one step. He was never the least bit disappointed when she had to turn him down. He never interrogated her as to her whereabouts or even seemed particularly interested in them aside from polite inquiries. He charmingly evaded any hint of commitment. He never showed a bit of jealousy at other men's attentions and outright advances. He wasn't overanxious to touch her in public when they went to events, though he occasionally did. It had been a welcome challenge in the early stages of their four-month relationship, but now she wanted to make a change—a change she couldn't seem to get him to endorse. It was beginning to drive her mad. She had been waiting in the parking lot of his building for an hour after receiving the suggestive text message saying that he was boarding a flight for home.

"Hey, beautiful," he said, quick to make amends,

and closed the distance between them. "I was just kidding you. You are positively a sight for sore eyes, and I wish you had been waiting at the door"—he reached beneath her hair with both hands and pulled her in for a sound kiss; she was sweet and flushed and instantly yielded to his affection—"wearing nothing but a bow," he breathed into her ear when they both came up for air. Satisfied he had quelled the beginnings of a fit, he set her back and swiped at her lower lip with his thumb to remove smeared gloss.

"Oh, if only that were true." She sighed dramatically, searching his face. "I would wear nothing but a bow for the rest of my life." She tried to match his casual demeanor. "But instead I'll be on a plane first thing tomorrow to Cali for the Reebok spread."

"How long you staying this time?" he asked, his gaze focused solely on her mouth. Without even looking into her eyes, he could make her heart start racing. His eyes were already conveying the need, the desire, to taste her again. And more. It triggered the need in her.

"Maybe two weeks." Natalie sighed again, already feeling weak in the knees. Her lips came together in a well-practiced adorable pout. "The agency lined up some other appointments to make the most of the trip. It might be longer if any of those pan out."

"Then we better not waste any time." Logan kissed her again, deeper, his strong arms peeling off her jacket and tossing it aside before pulling her in close again. His fingertips toyed with and then dipped slightly into the waistband of her jeans at the small of her back.

"I guess I'd look like a real dick if I took you right

here without even offering you something to drink." He reluctantly withdrew from her and, grabbing her hand, led her toward the kitchen. "Thirsty?"

"Oh yeah, I'm thirsty," she purred, and tugged him right past the refrigerator and down the short hall to his bedroom. Once there, she jumped into his arms, wrapping her long legs around him and planting her lips back on his. Logan easily carried her over to the bed and deposited her there, quickly shedding his clothes. She waited, hungrily watching him, knowing from experience that taking off hers was something he thoroughly enjoyed. He finished and stood before her, naked and magnificent, deciding what he wanted to remove on her first. She got tired of waiting. She reached out, and with one smooth touch, she watched his sex rise to full attention. Before she could do it again, he made his decision.

He grabbed Natalie's camisole and pulled it over her head, exposing unencumbered jutting breasts. Augmented, to be sure, but who cares? Cupping them, he kissed each one in worship, massaging the soft perky flesh, his tongue darting out, flicking around her nipple. A passion-filled push sent her tumbling backward and he pulled off her shoes, one at a time, tossing them over his shoulder. He unbuttoned her jeans and with an even quicker motion removed them, deliberately leaving behind her panties. He spread her legs, and going down to his knees, he kissed them, dead center, a thin layer of silk the only thing between his lips and her rapidly moistening mound. He ran his tongue along where her panties met her inner thigh and dipped it behind them, teasing her. He hooked his thumbs around the strings at her hips and pulled the panties off, kissing her there again. Moan after throaty moan escaped her as Logan danced his tongue around her folds, taking time with every pass at her clit. He lingered there, enjoying the sounds she made. When he had his fill, content that she was wet and manic, he picked Natalie up and, taking a seat on the edge of the bed, straddled her on his knees. He reached over to his nightstand and opened the drawer. Reaching in, he retrieved a condom.

"We wanna play it safe tonight, baby. I don't know where I've been." Logan teased with his standard line. With them settled back on the bed, he held the foil packet out to her, holding on to one end.

"Make a wish." He smiled devilishly at her.

I wish we didn't need these, she thought. She placed her fingers right next to his on the condom and they tore it open. Logan caught it and rolled it on quickly before impaling her on his throbbing erection.

They groaned in unison. His hands firmly on her hips, Logan effortlessly glided her up and down until she found his rhythm on her own. She tightened her arms around his neck and rode him. And then, with a deep-throated moan, she dug into his shoulder with her long smooth fingernails and purposefully dragged.

"Watch the claws, kitten," he murmured, deliberately arching away.

Insistently, Natalie continued to dig into his shoulder. She kissed his cheek, swirled her tongue around and into his ear, and then ventured to his throat. Kiss after kiss, and then teeth.

"No no no." His voice husky with passion, he lifted her off his neck as soon as he felt it. "No biting," he said, admonishing her with a slight shake. They had been at this juncture before. He liked her aggressiveness but loathed her unrelenting attempts to mark him. Her persistent choice of target was his neck—an attempt to send some sort of message that proclaimed he was taken. He wanted no part of it.

"Sorry," she replied with feigned embarrassment, an effort to appear caught up in the moment. She pulled herself nearly off his shaft and then thrust herself fully onto him again, her muscles squeezing when their pelvises met. She heard him exhale in pleasure and repeated the action until she was sure he was caught back up in the ecstasy her movements created. And then she returned to the base of his neck. Trying to make her move resemble more of a kiss, she sucked in as she pulled her lips away. Successful in the strategy, she continued with it. The third time she did it, her mouth was too wet and the resulting suction noise was unmistakable.

"Natalie. What did I say?" He chided her and stood up, wasting no time separating them. He threw her back on the bed face-first, then quickly pulled her up. Before her knees could make contact with the mattress, he deftly drove himself into her from behind, scarcely missing a stroke. His whole approach changed. No longer generous and leisurely, he fucked her hard, grinding his hips with every thrust, ensuring he made contact with her most sensitive spot.

"Logan," she groaned. He was so touchy about the

love scars. Holding her unyieldingly around her waist, he filled her deliciously, faster and harder, working up to his own release. She tried unsuccessfully to resent the familiar tingle that was starting to build at her core as he masterfully ground into her again and again, in a way more punishing than pampering. The tingle began to flourish and spread until there was no other feeling besides it. Her hands clenched into fists and pounded the bed as she gave in. His legs stiffened and his grip tightened. She screamed his name into the bedspread as she came.

THEY LAY AMONG THE RUMPLED HEAPS OF BEDDING. Natalie was nestled into the crook of his welcoming arm, her head resting on his chest. He pulled the sheet up over them both, to protect them from the chill air on their spent, damp bodies. Any hint of prior anger was forgotten with their mutual orgasms. *He even likes to cuddle,* she mused wordlessly, snuggling up to him. He was like a lovemaking demigod.

"Damn, girl." Logan rolled his neck and shoulders against the pillow at the headboard, bringing out the sting of the fresh scratches on his back. "I think I'm going to need some Neosporin. It feels like you shanked me."

Natalie giggled, not the least bit inclined to move. Her head rolled along with the rippling that came with his muscles flexing. It was like riding a pectoral wave, pure exhilaration. "Oh come on," she teased when they settled back down, "I thought you were a tough guy. But I'll be more than happy to rub you down with whatever you need to prevent infection. Want to check my nails for rust? Are you up to date on all your shots?" She held up a hand in front of him.

"Very funny," he laughed, playfully swatting down her hand with one of his own before rubbing her back. Then he remembered. "You realize if I find a hickey when I look in the mirror, I'm going to be seriously pissed."

She picked up her head for a quick inspection and debated whether or not to say anything. She could see a faint outline of her overbite and maybe a touch of bruising in the dim light cast from the hallway. With her luck, it would be gone by morning. Natalie wrinkled her nose, conceding that she should have just bitten him harder the first time, when she had the chance—before his guard went up. She could have handled his wrath if she had gotten the job done. It was certainly low enough on his neck that it wouldn't be seen if he needed to dress up. She was hopeful she could keep him in bed for several more hours and spare them both the confrontation. She settled back down on his chest, her hand drifting down his solid belly, maybe to take his mind off the topic at hand.

"So wear a shirt with a collar. I don't see what the big deal is." The words slipped out despite her best intentions and her wandering hand stopped just short of his groin.

"The big deal," he replied, "is that I don't appreciate having my sex life tattooed all over me."

"You know," she said, a mixture of sulk and condescension, irritated by his deliberate use of the word "sex" instead of "love" when describing their bedroom activities, "there are men out there who would be showing off that sort of thing from me."

"Then maybe you should be sleeping with them," Logan immediately replied, his easygoing nature starting to feel the strain. Why did she have to constantly remind him of her attractiveness? It was so covertly needy. When she wasn't throwing her desirability in his face, he had to remind her of just how beautiful she was. Or worse yet, had to listen to her voice her dissatisfaction with herself. She was a model for Christ's sake; her whole paycheck was based on what she looked like.

Logan liked Natalie from the minute he met her in Las Vegas, at the sports expo. She was doing modeling work and he was attending. He never made an attempt at hiding his appreciation of her firm, nubile body. In the beginning she was mysterious and alluring. Her life was much like his, busy and exciting. She was bright and witty, which added to her appeal. Every time they got together was a hurricane. Each moment of the obligatory "going out" part of the evening was spent in anticipation of when they could get behind closed doors. Logan reflected on how Natalie turned from a seemingly shy little sex kitten into a tigress with a few well-placed strokes of his hand, how she always left him wanting more. But the last few weeks had felt more like a boring game of seesaw. He could understand the occasional day when a woman felt unattractive or insecure and needed to go fishing for a compliment, something he was always ready and willing to supply. But lately all their conversations led in the same direction and ended up in the same place. It was a place he was getting tired of avoiding.

Natalie tried one more time to find his jealousy nerve. "Maybe I already am sleeping with them."

"Will I be able to figure out who he is by a hickey or a scratch?" Logan made one more attempt at levity.

"You know what, Logan? Sometimes you're a real jerk-off." She drew back the sheet, wrapped it loosely around herself toga-style, and rose. Angrily, she began the hunt around the room to gather her discarded clothing. Logan propped himself up on a bent elbow, resting his head on his hand, and watched her—the fact that she had taken the time to cover up, even in the nearly dark room, did not go unnoticed.

"Come on, Nat," he finally said softly, patting the spot she had vacated moments before with his free hand. "You don't have to leave. It's late. I don't want you to go. Come back to bed. I'll drive you to the airport tomorrow."

She stopped her search, turned on the light, and stared at him lying nude and stretched out before her. He was so striking it almost hurt to look at him. He sounded so sincere and she wanted to believe him. But his last sentence was the giveaway; he knew he would be rid of her in the morning. He probably already knew that a car supplied by her agency would be picking her up. There was no way he would put off his morning clients to drive her to the airport. He'd just made the offer so he wouldn't look like the bad guy. Logan was never the bad guy; he was just the no-strings-attached guy. She could forget about any heartfelt declaration of feelings. She knew there would not be one forthcoming.

His coaxing broke her reverie. "Look at you, standing there all wrapped up and pissed off. Like I don't know just how hot the body under that sheet is. Your hair's all tousled, making you look sexy as hell. Come back here and let me show you just how much you turn me on."

"When are you going to tell me my wish came true and I can stop opening condoms?" she asked point-blank, suddenly willing to force his hand and deal with the consequences.

"Back to that again, are we?" He fell back onto the bed muttering, all traces of playfulness and affection fully evaporated.

Natalie resumed the search for her clothing, now stomping across the room to recover her camisole and positively seething. "You sound like I'm asking you to make some sort of outrageous sacrifice. I realize having a whore at your disposal must be terribly convenient, but for me it's getting kind of old."

"I never treated you like a whore." He sighed at the ceiling. "If for no other reason than I never paid you."

"I wish you had paid me," she hissed back. "At least then I would've had a clear understanding of where I stood and not wasted my time considering you an option."

This was the last time Logan intended to have this particular exchange. It had grown tiresome, maneuvering through this verbal minefield just for the sake of some hot sex. Sex certainly wasn't something Logan had to worry about. He could get it anytime, and with very little effort. What eluded him was the answer to why he stayed on this mental merry-go-round with Natalie. He wasn't particularly interested in owning anybody, and he certainly wasn't into being owned.

Logan rose off the bed, not bothering to say anything more or cover up as he headed into the kitchen to pour a much-needed glass of water. Maybe Natalie would cool off, too.

Left alone in the bedroom, thoroughly dismissed, Natalie quickly dressed. Intending to leave without so much as another glance at Logan, she walked briskly past him where he leaned against his kitchen counter and rushed toward the exit. Only his voice stopped her when she reached the living room.

"Isn't it enough that you have dozens of men at your disposal? Why are you pushing this so hard, Natalie? Why do you want to mess up a good thing?"

"And committing to me would be messing up a good thing?" she asked incredulously, turning back to the voice coming from the next room, grateful she had a moment to steel herself against the exquisite beauty of its owner. She was determined not to be taken in.

Logan was not about to let the conversation be reduced to a screaming match. He wasn't the screaming kind to begin with, but he was well aware that she could be. He calmly emptied the contents of his glass, set it down, and came out of the kitchen to join her. "We've only been seeing each other a couple of months," he replied evenly.

"Not a couple. Four. Four months. Almost five," she

said, correcting him, the hurt evident in her voice and on her face.

"Half of them spent with you running all over the country," he replied gently.

"I only have another year and a half on my contract."

He cut her off, shaking his head. "It's not about your job. It's about moving too fast. We're in good places in our lives right now, doing good things. We knew going into this relationship that we were busy people with lots of commitments, to ourselves and to others. I just don't feel like that's changed. Yet." Logan knew it sounded insensitive, though that wasn't his intention. He tried to soften the sting with a backhanded compliment. "Besides, I think the only reason you even care is because I'm being the least bit hesitant. If it was *me* asking *you* to commit, you'd be avoiding me like the plague."

"Not true," she said emphatically, no longer concerned about looking like the desperate, clingy one. "I knew there was something special about you the night we met. Didn't you see it? For heaven's sake, didn't you *feel* it?"

"What I felt was amazingly lucky that someone like you would go out of her way to spend some of her free time with me," Logan replied earnestly, though he was unwilling to hurt her further by telling her he didn't feel the same way. He had never felt something special about any woman, ever. It had never really dawned on him that he was supposed to. He wasn't currently seeing anybody else, but he also was never convinced it was ever the right time to close the door on the wealth of possibilities. He didn't usually date multiple women, but he recognized the fact that he couldn't make a relationship last. They didn't end badly most of the time—just fizzled. Women wandered in and out of his life after realizing he didn't make sacrifices to accommodate them. He never led anyone on or stood anyone up, and he was always forthcoming about the fact that there just wasn't much of his time to spare. He worked long hours, by choice. Then he had to fit in his own workouts. The only time left was his man-cave time and the other main perk of his profession: tickets to every single sporting event he could ever want to attend. He wasn't ready to see man-cave time disappear yet, at least not on a permanent basis. And with Natalie, when push came to shove, he knew deep down he couldn't put up with being the boy toy of an insecure, scratch-happy hellcat. He didn't want to lose her, but he also wasn't willing to lie to her, or himself, to make her stay.

Logan hesitantly reached out, and when she made no move to recoil, he gently took her by her shoulders. "Besides, seriously, Nat, I don't think either one of us is ready to take it to that level. Having to talk every day and tell each other our whereabouts twenty-four/ seven. So wrapped up in each other that we have to feel funny if we spend any time at all with someone else of the opposite sex, when we're apart for weeks at a time. Wasn't it you that wanted to keep things from getting too serious, something about a 'sassy single' image you wanted to maintain?"

How convenient for him, she miserably thought. She remembered making those very same statements on their first date, because she made them often. It was the sort of mindless chatter most people threw out before they knew whether or not there was any chemistry. Maybe not about having a public persona to take into consideration, but about not wanting to seem too eager. Logan never had to say it; she had done it for him. She'd never considered that it could be so easily and readily used against her. And she never believed she could be the kind of person who would resort to deliberate biting and lurking and waiting with bated breath for the phone to ring. Natalie closed her eyes against the warmth of his touch, wishing he would pull her back into his embrace instead of keeping her at arm's length. His unconscious action spoke volumes, and she was finally listening.

"Image? Just whose image are you interested in, seriously?" She opened her eyes and settled them on his perfect face, praying for some sort of sign that he cared she was getting ready to walk out the door.

"I don't have an image," he responded, running a hand through her hair and giving an affectionate tug on her earlobe. "I'm just a guy who owns a couple of gyms."

"Gyms whose clientele are the rich and famous," she retorted weakly, tired of the tricks, his as well as her own. "It makes you one of them by association. Please stop acting like I'm the one with everything to lose and you are so gallantly trying to protect my interests. It only makes me feel more of a fool."

"You're not a fool, kitten." The corners of his mouth turned up in what she could only construe as a sardonic smile. "But sometimes you really do act foolish."

So that was it. One more veiled insult neatly wrapped up and packaged to look like a term of endearment. Maybe it was time she stopped chasing him and let them see what, if anything, they really meant to each other.

She twisted out of his grasp, retrieved her bag from his coffee table and her jacket from the floor, and made her way to the door. She opened it and, with all the righteous indignation she could muster, took one more heartbroken look at him, standing before her in all his naked glory.

"Fuck you," she told him dejectedly, and walked out, slamming the door behind her.

Logan casually followed in her wake to lock the door and turn out the lights before heading back to bed. Catching himself with a quick glance in an oval-shaped mirror mounted in the hallway, he stopped short. He moved nearer to his reflection, looked closely, and let loose a sigh of annoyance. He looked back to the front door and announced to his empty home:

"That's gonna leave a mark."

Chapter Three

HOLLY WAS SITTING ON THE COUCH IN HER LIVING room. In one hand she held the television remote. In the other, a liter bottle of Coke. A bag of Funyuns sat wedged between her legs. She surfed the channels aimlessly from one program to another.

It should have been just another night, when the only thing to come alive was her television. On a normal night, she could hide within the countless sitcoms depicting the hapless antics of mismatched couples falling in love despite their foibles. She could uncover murder plots along with glamorous women who looked like they'd stepped out of magazines, not grubby police stations. They busted thugs with the help of unbelievably attractive male partners who found them irresistible, despite the danger and the call of duty. Holly could be picking apart reality TV, snickering at the fools who willingly set their dignity aside for the sake of being in front of a camera. But this wasn't just another night. It was the night before her first training session. She felt anxious. In less than twenty-four hours, she would be the one looking like a fool. Holly needed a diversion. She wished she could find the infomercial of Tony Little pushing his Gazelle. Even when Bruce was rapidly deteriorating, Tony Little was a good for a much-needed laugh as she watched his long Fabio hair trying to keep up with his frenzied pseudo-leaping as he shouted inspirational mumbo jumbo.

Holly stopped on a show about hoarders. The people featured looked more like her but were living neck-deep in garbage and broken keepsakes. She watched in horrified fascination as teams of well-meaning, hazmat-suited cleaners came to the hoarders' rescue. They scooped the trash up off the floors while doctors asked the hoarders how they felt about discovering a twenty-five-year-old blanket full of holes and covered in rodent droppings, or a petrified fruitcake they got from a neighbor back in 1996. Within the hour, their homes were set right and their problems solved. She knew it wasn't that easy.

The show was interspersed with endless commercials of what a person could take or use to make themselves better. This lotion will give you skin that shimmers and begs to be touched. That shampoo will make you a man magnet. Drug companies hawked pharmaceuticals with lists of side effects that sounded worse than the diseases themselves. *Sure, you may become suicidal, but at least you can say you quit smoking.* And then there was the never-ending parade of diet ads. Celebrities who'd had, in Holly's opinion, perfectly acceptable figures to begin with were transformed into skin and bones, and *now* they were living the life they always dreamed of. What the hell was wrong with their lives to begin with? Holly grimaced through one more commercial, her favorite. The one about the pill that sheds the pounds magically and in record time but should only be taken by those who "seriously need to lose body fat." Even the way the spokeswoman said the word "fat" was a comical overpronouncement of the three letters, stretching them out for full effect, emphasizing the gravity of the situation. Holly pointed the remote at the television and turned it off.

She could see her reflection in the now-dark plasma screen, a distorted mirror image of Holly sitting on the couch. She stared into it. The image on the screen was an amorphous blob. Flesh stacked upon more flesh oozing all over the couch. The neon yellow and green from the top of the Funyuns bag between her legs was reflected with unsettling clarity. She squeezed her thighs together tightly and heard the crunching sound of the Funyuns being pulverized. Holly leaned her head back on the couch and sighed. *Tomorrow, all this will change,* she told herself. Tomorrow she would become the disciple of Logan Montgomery, the tallest, darkest, handsomest stranger she'd ever met. A man who was not only convinced she needed saving but was confident he could save her. She took a deep breath, trying to quell the mounting panic that accompanied the thought. What if he wasn't as nice as he seemed that day on the plane and was really Attila the Trainer? What if he was all looks and no knowledge and ended up snapping something she needed, like her spine? What if she farted while trying to do a sit-up?

The phone rang and Holly reeled in her fright. She threw the Funyuns on the table in front of her and took a quick sip from the Coke. She reached across to the other side of the couch to pull the handset from its cradle.

"Hey, girlfriend," the cheery voice said. "How you holding up?"

Tina Abbott had known Holly longer than anyone. Tina was a hometown girl who'd married her high school sweetheart and became Mrs. Tommy Blake. They had three kids and never left Fairview, Oregon, but the friendship between Tina and Holly had remained through the years and across the miles. Tina had the bubbly, energetic personality Holly had always longed for and an overactive metabolism to match. While in junior high, she and Holly acquired the nicknames Stick and Stone because they were always together. Tina was Stick—tall and thin and dark. Holly was Stone—short and round. Holly never found the name particularly flattering but tried to embrace it anyway. She found it amusingly ironic since there were times she was sure Tommy would have liked to skip her across a lake. She had been a third wheel way too often for Tommy's liking and she could tell he was relieved when Holly left for college. Tina was pregnant before Holly's first semester was over.

Holly greeted her childhood friend. "Hi, Tina. Hanging in there. How's tricks?"

"Same as it ever was. I meant to call you earlier, but the baby has a cold. The cough is horrendous. And you should see the stuff that's coming out of her nose. She's like some sort of snot machine." Tina laughed.

"Sounds appetizing," Holly quipped, ignoring the pang of sadness that always came with the word "baby." She and Bruce had talked about it, but he was diagnosed before they really started trying. After that, it was just a downward spiral. Holly told herself it wasn't meant to be. She could never decide if in the end it was a good or bad thing. She couldn't imagine being a single parent with the added burden of seeing a child through the sort of grief she'd endured.

Tina continued. "Since Monday all she's done is cling to me, the poor thing. I feel like I haven't slept in days. How did it go in Toronto?"

"Pretty much like I expected. They worked me over, trying to tell me I didn't have the proxy, but in the end they sold at the original price. I just kept saying, 'I don't understand,' a lot, looking horribly perplexed and showing them the letter they originally sent. I did say, 'Maybe I should call a lawyer?' a bunch of times, too. After a while I think they just wanted to get rid of me."

"Bruce would've been proud of you," Tina told her. "What are you going to do with your newfound wealth?"

"It's really not all that much," Holly replied, not bothering to tell her friend that the money meant nothing to her. It didn't seem appropriate. Tina and Tommy were struggling and money was always tight. Tina stayed at home raising the children while Tommy worked his job at a lumberyard. They were too proud to take money from Holly when she offered it, so Holly settled for sending expensive Visa gift cards for every occasion. "I did have a weird experience on the plane home though."

"Oh no." Holly could hear the concern in Tina's voice. "You didn't freak out on the plane, did you? Did you take the Xanax like I told you?"

"No, I didn't take Xanax," Holly said, regretting having told Tina about the prescription she got after Bruce's funeral. "I didn't freak out either. I met a guy."

"You did?" Holly could picture Tina sitting down on a chair and tucking her feet under her, getting ready to interrogate her. "Do tell!"

Holly was quick to clarify. "Not that much to tell. Although he is awfully easy on the eyes. He's a personal trainer. I'm going to start working with him. My first session is tomorrow."

"Holy shit!" Tina squealed with delight. "Is he coming to the house? Like in *Desperate Housewives*?"

Holly thought about the business card still in her wallet. "No. He gave me a card with an address on it. He probably works out of Planet Fitness or Crunch. They're both in that area."

"You nervous?" Tina asked.

"Hell yes I'm nervous! I don't think he intentionally wants to kill me, but he may end up doing it accidentally. He's in pretty good shape. Honestly, I've never seen anything like him in person. I thought dudes like him were all Photoshopped."

"Holy shit," Tina repeated. "He knows you've been sitting on the couch for the last year and a half, right?"

"I think he can probably tell that just by looking at me." Holly's gaze drifted back to her reflection in the television screen and she quickly closed her eyes, shaking her head. What had she gotten herself into? "I figure I'm just going to show up and focus on staying alive. But I'm going to give him your number in the event of an emergency just in case, okay?"

"No problem."

"Remember, I don't want to be kept alive on machines." Holly shuddered, the memory of Bruce at the end still painfully etched in her mind.

"Don't even kid about that. You're going to be fine. I'm sure he knows what he's doing," Tina said before asking, just to verify, "So he's cute?"

"Disgustingly."

"Like Bob Harper–and-Dolvett-from–*Biggest Loser* cute?"

"Cuter," Holly said without hesitation. "I can't believe you even watch that show. What could you possibly find appealing in it? You weigh a hundred pounds soaking wet."

"It's inspirational," Tina replied.

"It's television. Did you ever notice that when they get to that ranch and weigh in, they get to wear next to nothing? There they are, feeling like total pieces of crap, and they have to let the whole world know they weigh four hundred pounds wearing nothing but a pair of shorts and a sports bra. Then by the end, when their skin is still all floppy and saggy, they're all wearing tank tops and pants made of so much spandex they're practically girdles. The only thing inspiring is seeing them being able to put some clothes on. Don't even get me started on how they work out for eight hours a day and a week later have only lost three pounds. What kind of bullshit is that?" Holly ranted. The thought of Tina watching that show grated on Holly's nerves like sandpaper. It only fueled her friend's misguided notions about Holly's lifelong struggle with her weight.

Tina continued unaffected by the rant and still fully engrossed. "I wonder if this guy is going to scream in your face and make you cry and have a breakdown to get to all your issues?"

"You're not helping with the nervousness, you know," Holly said. "Besides, I don't think this guy is that invested in my situation. I think he pretty much just took pity on me."

"Or he wants to make some money." Tina laughed again.

"Probably both," Holly replied.

"Please tell me you at least went out and bought some fancy new workout clothes."

"I did buy some sneakers," Holly admitted. "I'm not really into the fashion-show aspect of this. Plus I don't think there's enough spandex out there to fool him. I thought I would worry about the important stuff, like breathing and staying conscious."

"It's not about fooling anyone, Holly. It's about setting the stage for success."

"Did you just throw a Weight Watchers ad at me?" Holly asked suspiciously.

"Probably, and since you brought it up, did you check

out those pills I was telling you about? The ones to help you lose weight?"

Holly could feel her teeth start to grind. She knew Tina was only trying to be helpful. She also knew Tina had a particular fondness for miracle cures, in addition to being clueless on the subject. Every now and then, much to Holly's dismay, Tina would stumble onto some crackpot weight-loss scheme, usually involving a pill, which she just had to share. "Yeah, I checked it out," Holly said hesitantly.

Tina expertly quoted the commercial. " 'For every two pounds you lose, it helps you with the third.' "

"Yeah," Holly said slowly. "I read that on the box. You know what else it does? It makes your ass leak. I read that on the box, too."

"Oh," Tina said, giggling nervously. "It does?"

"They refer to it as 'oily stools that could be hard to control,' which, I have to admit, makes it sound more enchanting. They recommend you wear dark-colored clothes so no one will notice when it happens. They don't really mention how to handle the smell." Holly tried not to sound annoyed.

"I didn't know that," Tina said, crestfallen. "That's gross."

"Glad you see it my way," Holly replied, colder than she intended.

"I'm just trying to help," Tina said defensively.

Holly softened. "I know you are."

"I guess I need to remember what you always tell me. That if it sounds too good to be true, it usually is," Tina said, lightening up as well.

"How could you know? You haven't had to worry about weight a day in your life. It's like me trying to give you advice on parenting."

"Good point. You know I love you and just want you to be happy again."

"I love you, too," Holly told her, deliberately leaving out that she didn't think she would know happiness if it came up and bit her. "But why don't you let me worry about my weight?"

"You just need to take that first baby step," Tina told her optimistically.

"I just wrote a check to a personal trainer. I feel like I'm stepping off a cliff. That's not big enough for you?"

Chapter Four

LOGAN WASN'T SURE THE WOMAN WHO SHOWED UP was the same Holly Brennan he'd met on the plane. The Holly standing before him appeared youthful and much less stressed. She wore black sweatpants, an oversized pink T-shirt, and the latest in cross-trainers. Her dark red hair looked finally tamed, pulled neatly back in a ponytail. She even carried with her a two-liter bottle of water. While he never really thought she would bail out, he was secretly impressed to see that she'd come ready to get down to business.

"Hi, Holly." He gave her a wave, walking over to her as she entered his studio. The khaki shorts exposing his defined calves and the yellow T-shirt that pulled across his expansive torso before tucking itself in at his trim waist were nothing short of jaw-dropping. "Nice to see you again. I just need to get a couple signatures from you. Standard contract waiver sorts of things. You ready to get to work?"

"As ready as I'll ever be." Holly smiled, taking the pen. She didn't know whether to be scared to death or psyched as hell, but she had come this far, and now there was no turning back. That opportunity had come and gone in the fifteen minutes she spent loitering on the sidewalk. The client with the time slot before hers had drifted out the door, a monster of a man she was sure was a professional basketball player. He smiled knowingly and asked if she was lost. She shook her head and said, "No, thanks."

Holly had assumed Logan worked out of a gym, but once inside his studio she realized she'd completely miscalculated. This was exclusively his space, and she was going to receive his full attention. He really was a personal trainer, with an emphasis on "personal." In the spacious room stood Logan, Holly, and every piece of exercise equipment known to the workout world. The place was orderly, pristine, and didn't smell like a locker room. Happy pop music drummed in the background. Holly started leaning toward scared. There would be no one here to hear her screams. She calmed herself with the thought that even someone as strong as he was would have trouble disposing of her body.

The next thing he did was weigh her. Holly's smile instantly faded and the urge to scream bordered on overwhelming as he led her to an old-fashioned balance-beam scale, the only piece of equipment that didn't look like it came from the space age. *He probably uses it to make sure people stay face-to-face with*

*their misery as long as humanly possible. The begin-
nings of his wearing you down and tearing you down
until you're so weak from humiliation and degradation
that he can sneak in and finish you off, assassin style.*

"Didn't anyone tell you these things come in digital
now?" she said under her breath, thinking that at least
a digital scale would be more like ripping off a Band-
Aid. A few seconds and *bang!* The horrifying number
slaps you in the face like an icy-cold mackerel. Holly
bent down, beginning to untie her sneakers. *Every
ounce counts.*

"These medical-type scales are much more reliable
and easier to calibrate," Logan told her calmly. "Not to
mention, I don't need a magnifying glass to read them.
You can keep the shoes on; it's not going to make that
much difference." Ouch.

"Maybe the digital ones are harder to read because
what they say is none of your freaking business," Holly
grumbled, standing back up. Still, she got on the scale,
shaking her head in dissatisfaction the whole time,
mostly at herself.

"Everyone hates this part," Logan said, trying to
settle her as he nudged the needle farther and farther
to the right. "But we need a starting point. It's only a
number, kid, it's only a number. But if it makes you feel
better, take a good look at it; it's the last time you will
ever see it."

Holly was seventy-eight pounds from the highest
number considered acceptable, even to her.

"Happy now?" She couldn't keep the sarcasm from
her voice. She hadn't stepped on a scale in years and

now she remembered why. What did she expect? That she was somehow fooling him and herself into thinking she wasn't obese? That the scale was going to read one hundred and thirty pounds and they could both go home? A nervous laugh bubbled out of her, echoing throughout the room. A hundred and thirty pounds? Maybe if someone dug up her bones six months after she was dead and weighed them. She hadn't seen one hundred and thirty since she was in junior high. "Guess you have your work cut out for you. I think I saw the term 'no refunds' in that thing you just made me sign. That goes for you, too, you know."

He continued, seemingly oblivious to her sarcasm, which only made her crankier. He wrote her weight down in her file. She refused to give in to the little voice in her head urging her to grab his pen and stab him with it.

"Do you have any physical ailments I need to consider?" He looked up from the folder in his hands.

"Yeah. I'm really fat."

"Do you smoke?"

"Only when I'm on fire."

"Drink?"

"Whenever I'm thirsty." For emphasis, Holly opened her bottle of water and demonstrated, some water leaking out and dribbling down her chin onto her shirt.

"Are you on drugs?"

"I'm on the pill; does that count?" Holly felt the heat rise up to her cheeks, grateful he was too busy writing in her file to see it. A widow on the pill; it sounded like an announcement that she was open for business. "You know, to regulate my cycles. And your question sounds rhetorical. Are you going to pump me full of steroids?"

"Maybe if you tell me you're going to become an Ultimate Fighter, but one step at a time, okay?" He tossed down her file and gave her a wink, figuring it was time to try a different approach. Holly found his wink adorable but was still supremely uncomfortable with his overly personal line of questioning.

"As long as you don't shoot me up with weird stuff that makes me all blotchy, like whatever happened to your neck," Holly remarked caustically, anxious to draw the attention away from herself, even if only for a moment and at his expense. She knew exactly what had caused the mark on his neck, although she couldn't recall having seen one since Tommy first started dating Tina.

Logan's hand immediately shot up, as it had countless times during the week, to cover the faint remnants of his last encounter with Natalie. Holly had seen it. Hell, everyone for the last three days had seen it, except she was the only one ballsy enough to say something. Thank goodness he had a shirt on. He shuddered to think what she might have come up with if she saw that his back still looked like something out of a Freddy Krueger movie.

"That's very clever," he replied offhandedly. "People usually wait until *after* the workout before trying to antagonize me." He smiled at just how wide her eyes got and how quickly she shut her mouth. Score one for Hickey Man.

They started out slow, strolling on twin treadmills.

Casually, they talked of simple things, all the while Logan observing her stance, her breathing, just how in or out of shape she really was. He smiled to himself. She was relaxed, lucid; she was going to be fine. He stopped his walking, turning his focus solely on her. He gradually kicked up the intensity and her treadmill's incline until he saw the sweat start to bead around her neck and her breathing become labored. He wound the treadmill back down and she rehydrated. Then he moved on with some weight lifting on machines that had pulleys, which seemed innocuously easy to Holly. They threw around a medicine ball, and by the time they were done, almost an hour later, she was sweating clear through her shirt and her hair was all but dripping. He handed her a towel and a fresh bottle of cold water he pulled out of a nearby refrigerator.

"You did good, kid. Have I scared you away?"

She took a huge gulp and a deep breath. "Do I look scared? I can't wait to try those." She pointed to the row of free-weight curling dumbbells and barbells racked along a mirrored wall.

"You look soaked," he replied, feeling the rush that came with seeing a client through a good workout, appreciative that she wasn't the type to give a thought to what she looked like. That would only rob her of the focus she needed to get into the zone. He, of course, hadn't even broken a sweat. "We have an extra ten minutes before your session's over. I was going to cool you down. If you like, we can do some dead lifts and skull crushers instead."

"Hell, why stop with dead lifts and skull crushers?

Let's add some vein rippers and lung collapsers while we're at it," she said, smirking. "What's with all the scary names?"

Holly Brennan was a real smart-ass. *This might be fun,* Logan thought, and smiled with satisfaction. "It's only going to get harder."

Holly held up her water bottle in a toast, subtly looking him up and down. "Here's to hoping."

"Come with me." Logan took a step away from all the equipment, waving his arm for her to follow. He walked over to a small alcove in the corner of the gym where thick blue cushy mats replaced the black waffled rubber carpet designed to absorb impact. When she joined him, he took her towel and pointed to the mats.

"Lie down," he said. "On your back."

"Beg your pardon?"

"I'm going to stretch you out," he told her.

"For a minute there I thought we were taking this relationship to another level." Holly laughed uncomfortably. She wasn't sure what he was talking about, but it sounded like something that happened in a dungeon and involved a rack.

"I'm waiting." He settled his hands on his hips, all business.

"I'm all sweaty and smelly," she said uneasily. She couldn't think of anything she wanted less than for him to touch her.

"I know. I got you that way. And I'm still waiting."

"That's okay. I don't need you to stretch me. I'm fine."

"Who's the expert here? Now you're fine. You won't be tomorrow when all your muscles are screaming.

Now lie down," he repeated tersely, holding out his hand for her water bottle.

"You don't need to go all tyrant. I was trying to do you a favor," she mumbled, doing as he told her.

"Thanks for thinking of me," he replied, having clearly heard her.

Once she was settled on the mats, he spread her legs, and straddling one leg, he took hold of the other. Placing one hand on the heel of her sneaker and the other on her calf, he slowly began to raise her leg. When her leg was perpendicular to the floor, the hand that was previously on her foot moved lower to her calf. The hand that was on her calf moved and now rested on the back of her thigh. And then he increased the pressure.

Holly wanted to remain unaffected. But he was towering over her, seemed all around her.

"Try to relax. It won't feel as uncomfortable if you don't fight against it," Logan said, feeling her tension.

Relax? Holly thought. *What is he, crazy?* She hadn't been touched by anyone in almost two years. Now Zeus was climbing all over her like she was Mount Olympus. His legs were firmly pressed up against both sides of her thigh to keep her leg on the mat from moving. His hand was an inch away from her backside. And her backside was mere inches away from her front side. She was still hot, but now in a completely different way. Fresh sweat broke out on her forehead. He gently pushed her leg farther.

"Breathe into it," he told her.

She didn't even know she was holding her breath. He pushed a fraction of an inch more with the hand on her thigh. It was uncomfortable, but nothing compared to the feeling of the pure electricity emanating from his splayed fingers.

"Breathe, girl," he ordered with a smile. "Like during takeoffs."

Holly took one look at the perfect dimples his smile created on his cheeks and let out all her pent-up air. He pushed a tiny bit farther, holding it for a few seconds. How the hell did he remember that? Those were the first words he ever said to her.

"I have a great memory." He read her mind as he stood. Then he bent her leg and, moving his hand to the bottom of her sneaker, pushed her knee toward her chest. "Damn, you're flexible," he remarked, pushing her knee up farther.

"You sound surprised." She tried to sound casual. The sight of his exposed biceps flexing to maintain the pressure was making it next to impossible.

"More like impressed," he replied before asking, "You okay? Tell me if anything hurts."

"Sure. I'm fine." She lied. Nothing actually hurt, but she couldn't have been farther from okay.

"Your face is red," he said. "Keep breathing."

He took her bent knee and, after kneeling down next to her, shifted it over her other leg. He placed a hand on her shoulder. Applying equal pressure, Logan held her shoulder in place and pushed her bent leg downward toward the mat, stretching the entire side of her body. Holly thought she might perish from how wonderful it felt. She fought back the urge to squirm in ecstasy beneath him. He was so very close, masterfully holding her down from above. She could smell his skin, clean with a hint of expensive cologne. He looked down from his position over her and the dimples reappeared.

"This one is a crowd favorite," Logan said.

She was both disappointed and grateful when it ended and he laid her leg back flat on the mat.

Oh thank God, Holly thought, *I don't know how much more of that I could stand.* She congratulated herself on maintaining her composure.

And then he straddled the leg he was done with, he grabbed her other leg, and the exquisite torture began all over again.

She managed to withstand his repeating the process by thinking of nothing but breathing and refusing to look directly at him. It bordered on hopeless. His being invaded every one of her senses with every one of his. He softly murmured words of encouragement and support, and his hands overran all her nerve endings. She was certain if she actually looked into his face and he smiled at her again, she would liquefy. She didn't see how it could get any worse. Until he sat her up, knelt behind her, and began to massage her shoulders. His strong powerful hands were surprisingly gentle. He moved her ponytail to the side to gain better access. She could feel his breath warm on the back of her neck. He was completely unconcerned with her drenched condition. His warm hands sensually kneaded; his thumbs pressed into her shoulder blades and rubbed. She wanted to scream, she wanted to moan. She felt as languid as if she'd just been made love to. He finally rose. He moved in front of her and, bracing his feet, held out his hands. She automatically put her hands in his and planted her own feet on the floor. He exhaled and easily hauled her up until she was standing beside him.

"Fantastic job." He looked down on her, beaming.

You took the words right out of my mouth, she thought.

Chapter Five

THEY SAW EACH OTHER THREE TIMES A WEEK. HOLLY was always on time, ready to go, with her sweatpants, her baggy washed-out T-shirts, and her wisecracks. She always entered his gym with a calm yet steadfast determination that rivaled the attitude of any of his more notably competitive clients. She had a self-deprecating sense of humor that Logan came to enjoy, once he realized it wasn't real malice aimed at herself. It was refreshing not to have to spend half their time together stroking her ego. At times he wondered if she even had one. It wasn't the way she went to great lengths to avoid catching a glimpse of herself in any of the mirrors that lined a full wall of the gym—that didn't surprise him. It was more in the way that when it was time to work, she dug in, with total focus and concentration, until the set was over. Then, as she recovered, she delivered

the occasional punch line. She had no concern for the
rolls of fat around her midsection that became exposed
as her shirt hiked up when she lifted weights above
her head or bent over. She ignored the wedgies created
when she lunged. She wordlessly got into every single
uncomfortable and sometimes graceless position he
told her to assume. And she would sweat, even more
than she did that first day. So much so that she began
to bring her own towels, although he specifically told
her he had more than enough to meet her every need.
He was thoroughly amused when he learned why she
was doing it. She would bring beach-sized towels and
lay them over the weight benches or any other piece of
equipment that had a seat. She had read somewhere it
was the polite thing to do so she wouldn't "skunk it up."

"It's not that kind of gym," he laughingly told her.
He wasn't offended. He knew his places were lavish,
immaculate, and state-of-the-art.

"I know," Holly quickly said, looking down and pretending to examine her fingernails before continuing,
her face flushed with embarrassment. "But I'm leaving
. . . I'm leaving . . . snail trails."

"Snail trails?" He laughed again, fully appreciating
the visual.

"Oh good grief." She snapped her head back up at
him and pressed on, still embarrassed but now aggra-
vated as well. "Yeah, I'm sweating between my legs.
I'm leaving a mess at anything and everything my ass
touches!"

He realized it undoubtedly was something that was
truly bothering her and he swallowed one more laugh.

"Holly, I clean all the equipment that's used before the next client arrives. It comes with the territory. You aren't the only person that happens to, although you're probably the first to give it such a colorful name. I'm guessing that explains why you're bathing in CK One before you arrive."

"No," she said, trying to stay irritated but smiling in spite of herself. "I do that because I don't want to smell like a dirty sneaker. It's too much?"

"It smells nice," he said, returning her smile with a rakish one of his own and giving her a friendly rub on the shoulder. He took her towel and laid it on a nearby incline bench. "And a welcome change from all the swamp ass I've gotten used to."

"Oh my God, *swamp ass*." Holly giggled lying down on the bench and towel while Logan retrieved a barbell. "I bet we could make up an entire dictionary of grody gym terms."

He handed over the forty-pound barbell. "I'm all for it, but right now the only term you need to worry about now is 'whoop your ass.' Come on, give me fifteen chest presses. Now."

He began ordering beach-sized towels to accommodate her. And she continued to sweat for him in buckets.

Holly spoke little about her past, her present, her future, and Logan never asked, chalking it up to awkwardness at the differences in their lifestyles. It was something he admired about her, but it also left him intrigued. It wasn't uncommon for his clients to go above and beyond in telling him about their personal lives, at times making him feel more like a therapist than a personal trainer. He was made confidant to secrets about everything from wives and lovers to children and parents, coworkers and teammates. He kept people motivated through divorces and addictions and scandals. He had become a master at taking the energy generated by an emotional rant and transferring it into a successful workout. But with Holly, it was all about business and innocuous witticisms. Be here now; it's time to work, not play *This Is Your Life*. She was paying him money that in all likelihood was hard for her to come by; they owed it to each other to get the most out of every session.

As time passed, however, Logan's curiosity grew and he had to hold himself back from asking. Her late husband's name was Bruce. That was it, the only outside information he became privy to. He only discovered it when she mentioned it in passing. She'd been talking about how they used to hike. It came up when Logan commented on Holly's exceptional cardiovascular endurance—not because she wanted to chat.

Instead of trying to feed his curiosity, Logan worked Holly hard, sometimes harder than he would any other client. She was a quick learner. If ever she became frustrated, he never heard her complain. In fact, she seemed to thrive on the impossibility of a chore. Sometimes he would hear her sincerely groan just before falling short of finishing a task he'd set before her, and almost always after. She understood his mission was to constantly raise the bar and set her up to fail. She knew if it ever actually became easy, it meant he wasn't doing his job.

Each time he weighed her, which was once a week, Holly thought up a new way to maim him—and kept it to herself. Her favorite fantasies usually ended with Logan being shoved down the stairs at the entrance to the building. The very same stairs she climbed to get to him.

"Let's talk about your diet," he said to her one day, out of the blue, about a month into her training. She was warming up on an elliptical machine.

"Let's not," she instantly replied. *Geez, it isn't even a weigh day,* she internally lamented. Why did he want to take an unnecessary, internal-organ-rupturing tumble? "I'd rather do lunges." There was nothing Holly detested more than leg lunges. Dragging around her own carcass was excruciating, especially when she was in a room full of nifty-looking weight machines. He made her do hundreds of them during every session.

"Not an option, kid, but I'll be happy to oblige on the lunges," he retorted smoothly. He knew she didn't want to have the conversation. But the time for it had come, whether she wanted to have it or not.

"I like to eat. End of story." She scowled, getting off the cardio equipment and trying to think of how to get them both closer to the stairway. Maybe she could crack him upside his head with a dumbbell instead. A ten-pounder would certainly do the trick, if she got in a good wind-up with it.

He smiled and crossed his arms over his chest. "Do you really think you got to your current weight because you like to eat? Most people like to eat. It's been reported that it's even necessary for survival. Have you had your thyroid checked?"

"Yes," she puffed out at him. "Right after Bruce died I went to the doctor for a full physical. Unfortunately, I'm fine internally. Oh yeah, he did mention I was too fat."

"There is no denying genetics play a role in a person's body type. People are predisposed to six-pack abs just like they are to having blue eyes. But any time a person is carrying excessive fat, there is usually something deeper going on. There are generally two common types of eating disorders suffered by the obese." He continued in his maddening clinical way to ignore her reluctance to delve into precisely what she didn't want to talk about. As he talked, he went about gathering all the weights she would be using during her session. "One is compulsive overeating. In layman's terms, an addiction to food. Using food and eating to hide from emotion. To fill a void and cope with stress and the problems that occur in everyday life. Compulsive overeaters are most times fully aware that their eating habits aren't normal but get little support, other than being told to get some willpower and go on a diet. It's just as damaging to their self-esteem as telling an anorexic to just eat."

"Who would have thought?" Holly burst out laughing. "I have something in common with an anorexic."

"Sort of," Logan answered, "with the exception of the stereotyping that overweight people have no control. And that's a big misnomer. It's totally about control. Many of them are specifically using their bodies as would-be blockades against the very people they feel are judging them. They want everyone to like them but are using food to cope with feelings of not being good enough, which only perpetuates the problem, and usually makes it worse. It's a vicious cycle of eating as a way to forget the pain of needing acceptance."

"I don't care if people like me," she told him.

"Oh, come on," Logan replied. He was determined not to let her one-liner herself out of the conversation, no matter how badly she might want to. "I don't believe you don't care if people like you. Everyone wants to be liked, at least a little bit. And despite your best efforts at being surly, you are really quite likeable. That's why it's also important to remember that most eating disorders have emotional aspects."

"Okay then, so what's the other train of thought on what ails me?" Holly asked him, trying to minimize the sarcasm, feeling flattered that he called her likeable.

Logan went on, encouraged by her willingness to listen and not just shut him down. "The other culprit is binge eating. Binge eaters usually suffer a combination of symptoms similar to compulsive overeaters, only with bulimia added in."

"I'm not bulimic." She snickered.

"Obviously," he retorted.

"I have thought about taking it up once or twice," she added, snickering again.

"Please don't," he told her seriously.

She immediately apologized. "Sorry. I realize you're only trying to help."

"Good girl." He smiled at her again and continued.

"What bingers do that is different from compulsives is consume large quantities of food in a short period of time, usually two hours or less. They eat uncontrollably, even after becoming uncomfortably full. They'll sometimes eat things they don't even particularly like just for the sake of eating. But unlike bulimics, they don't purge after an episode. They also have an extremely difficult time losing weight and maintaining a healthy weight."

"Sounds like you're entering my territory," she said, and Logan had trouble deciding whether she was joking or not. Given that survival itself was probably a struggle for her since losing her husband, he couldn't shake the vision of her at home, full of cheap processed foods that were high in fat, sugar, and calories and with no nutritional value.

"Actually, my dear complicated little grasshopper, I think you are probably a combination of both."

"Figures," she said scathingly.

"I never said you didn't have your work cut out for you," Logan told her truthfully.

"So what's the solution, Einstein?" She pressed him, suddenly anxious to end the conversation and get to lifting.

Logan took note of the switch in her demeanor. He was getting too close and she was getting ready to put her wall back up. He decided it was best to finish the tutorial for now, but not before he covered the most important part of the topic. "Look, it's too soon to tell what sort of body you are going to end up with when we're done here. If what you told me when we met is true, odds are you're not going to end up looking like Jennifer Aniston, no matter how much time you spend in a gym working at it. And that's just something that you need to come to terms with. It's about getting you healthy. But this I want you to know, and I want it to sink in: there are five specific factors that determine fitness; you are in firm possession of four of them."

"Really?" She stopped fidgeting and gave him back her full attention.

"Absolutely," he told her enthusiastically. "The criteria break down into cardiovascular fitness, muscular strength, muscular endurance, flexibility, and body composition, which is the clinical term for your body-fat-to-mass ratio."

She interrupted with a snort. "I can see you saved the best for last. Let me take a crack at the one I'm falling short on."

"Hey." Logan promptly cut her off and pointed a stern finger in her direction. "I'm not going to tolerate the wisecracks on this one. Do you realize just what a special gift you've actually been given? From the first day you walked in here, I've been impressed with not only your cardio endurance but your muscular strength and flexibility. You don't get that stuff from just having a good attitude. Athletes bust ass for months to get what you had naturally from the get-go."

"I feel a lecture coming on," she murmured, beginning to chew on a fingernail.

He relented. "If that's what you needed, I would surely provide it. But I don't want to lecture you. I just want you to be aware of how much you have going for you. For when it gets tough. And make no mistake, it's going to."

"Tougher than an eating disorder and subjecting myself to your torture? You don't think I'm going to be able to make it, do you?" She sounded dejected for the first time since he made her get on the scale.

"Holly," he said, softening just a little while remaining firm. "You've been giving a hundred percent since day one and your body is responding to it. But eventually, it's going to adjust to the new routine. The eating is the thing that's going to challenge you, probably for the rest of your life. I just want to make sure you've taken stock of your arsenal for when you're feeling weak and out of control. So that you can get past it and make the sort of changes that take root and last. It's no accident that ninety-five percent of people who take off weight put it back on. They get discouraged and their old habits are the comfortable and familiar ones. I don't want that to happen to you. Getting in control of eating addiction isn't like kicking smoking or drugs or alcohol. Those are addictions that you give up completely, and once you get through the withdrawal you win the war by abstaining. Your battle is so tricky. You're always going to need food. You're going to have to get to a point where you coexist with it and it's not the crutch you fall back on."

"I guess now would be a bad time to tell you I've taken up smoking?" Holly tried to bring some flippancy to the situation. The attempt was unsuccessful and she saw his eyes flash with genuine anger.

"If I thought you were the least bit serious, I would actually think about throttling you."

"Geez. Lighten up. I'm having enough trouble with one addiction, thank you very much. I'm just trying to stop the shakedown here."

He didn't want to shake her down, force her into talking about the things that she might not be ready to admit. He watched her silently continue to bite her nails, absorbing the information he had given her. She heard him, and for now that would have to be sufficient. He wanted her back into the proper head space before they fully got into her session.

"One thing is certain: the most common denominator in both compulsive eating and binging is the cycle of food replacing emotion. Depression is an emotion that ranks high on that list and is something that has been in the forefront of your life the last couple years, no matter how hard you might try to suppress it. Have you thought about seeing your doctor for it? Maybe a therapist?"

"Oh, sure." Holly made no attempt to mask her disdain. "Let me go blather my problems and take advice from someone who in all probability is crazier than I am. Yeah, no thanks."

"Don't be so quick to assume there's anyone out there crazier than you," he teased. "But for the sake of argument, how about just calling your regular doctor? Surely any doctor worth his salt would recognize the depression that comes with becoming a widow."

"Why?" she asked him heatedly. "So they can start mixing drug cocktails to keep me from feeling anything at all? Or better yet, they give me some great new drug they didn't bother to fully test and I wake up six months later growing a tail?"

"Okay. I get it." He was quick to try to defuse her anger, attributing it to the fact that running to see a doctor for something that wasn't outwardly hurting her was something she probably couldn't afford. Especially considering that he was taking up a chunk of her cash flow. Plus she did have a point. "And by 'get it,' I mean that I totally understand and in many ways agree. I'm always in favor of trying holistic means before running to the pharmacy, definitely in cases like this. And you're in luck for employing other tactics. Endorphins are natural chemicals in the body that fight depression. They release during physical outputs of energy, and you're certainly doing plenty of those."

"You think?" she asked him, the sarcasm fully back in place. It was uncomfortable knowing he obviously had spent a lot of time thinking about her, or at least her situation. With her situation being that she was an out-of-control, nonstop-munching, gluttonous freak.

"Holly, I want you to do me a favor. I want you to start writing down what you eat. Every morsel of anything you put in your mouth. It's not a test or even something I want you to share with me, unless of course you want to. This is strictly something I want you to do for you. And if you're feeling stressed or depressed, I want you to note what you're feeling while you eat. Can you do that?"

"You're never going to ask to see it?" she asked him

STEPHANIE EVANOVICH

skeptically, grabbing a towel off the shelf where he kept them.

"Nope," Logan said, taking the towel from her and laying it flat on a weight bench before pointing at it, the unspoken command for her to get into position for a set. He added before going to get the final piece of equipment they would need, "Just by doing it, you'll feel like you have more control and can see when your peak stress-eating times are. Then you can make adjustments from there. You can see when you are or aren't getting enough fruits and vegetables, when you're eating too much junk or not getting enough water. You'll start getting a clearer picture of the patterns you might want to work on changing. And when you notice depressed feelings coming on, you can try to head them off by doing something else, even if it's something simple like taking a walk. Hell, you can come here to do cardio whenever you like, even if I have another client here. Just give me a call with a heads-up. Remember, the rules are simple. For every calorie you take in beyond the minimum your body needs to function, you want to burn one out with exercise. The more intense the workout, the more calories you'll continue to burn after you're done. And as far as the food journal goes, I'll always be willing to look at it if you want to tweak it, but I promise I will never ask."

Holly left that session with a surge of new motivation. Much of the conversation was about not what was wrong with her but what was right with her. Logan hadn't laid judgments on her, just presented clinical

64

facts. But he had also done his homework. He gave her suggestions for things to do that were within her control. There were no gimmicks involved, just hard steady work. She didn't really see what would be so helpful about writing her food intake down, but it sounded simple enough. Plus the competitive side of her hated the prospect of coming up short if Logan went back on his promise and asked to see it. She decided to give it a try.

Logan told her she needed an arsenal. Having gotten used to eating mostly takeout, she started with a fruit bowl. Bananas and pears were her weapons of choice. Soon grapes and apples joined in. She began perusing salad bars like she was shopping for fine antiques. She made her goal variety. Once a week, she tried a new food. She tried to pick ones she'd always turned her nose up at in the past, like salmon and tofu and hummus. Sometimes she was pleasantly surprised, other times she still felt like barfing.

It didn't take her long to figure out that if she wrote down what she was going to eat before she ate it, she made better choices. The entire plan was wildly successful for several weeks, until the "Milky Way Malady" struck.

Holly wanted a Milky Way. It should have been simple enough; she ate them all the time. But when she bought it, she realized her journal was at home. Not willing to deviate from her strategy of "write first, eat second," she dropped the candy bar in her purse and waited until she got back to the house. The scrumptious candy bar consumed her every thought on the drive home. It virtually called to her from inside the confines of her purse. She salivated at the thought of creamy caramel and nougat wrapped up in chocolaty goodness. She got home and made straight for the kitchen. She pulled out the candy, opened the food diary, and grabbed the pen.

And then Holly saw all the other entries within the journal. All the healthy eating logged within the pages of her budding success story. She just couldn't bring herself to write down what she was sure would be the beginning of her downfall. The pages began to blur. She slammed the journal closed and pushed herself away from the counter. Without even realizing, she began to pace back and forth in the kitchen.

"You're just a stupid candy bar!" Holly yelled at the Milky Way.

The Milky Way sat on the counter, in between the fruit bowl and the journal, an innocent candy bar representing caloric catastrophe. She could almost feel the bananas giving her the evil eye.

"I just won't write it down," she rambled out loud. "I don't have to write it down. I'm only doing all this to show up Logan in case he asks. And he's never going to ask. And why do I have to do everything he says, anyway? I'm the one writing the checks." Satisfied with her logic, she opened the Milky Way and took a big bite. And then another.

The first two bites were everything she thought they would be. Chocolaty goodness and heavenly sweetness danced around her mouth. By the end of it, she was sick to her stomach. It was nearly choking her. All the joy of the first bites was gone, lost in the guilt of failure.

She skipped dinner that night, an attempt to recoup the calories consumed in her fit of confectionery rage. She went to bed early, hungry and defeated. She tossed and turned. For hours, sleep refused to claim her. Logan's words replayed like a broken record in her head. She knew what she had to do. Getting out of bed, she wearily padded downstairs and flipped the light on in the kitchen. Taking the pen, she opened the journal to the last entry. Pressing down so hard with the pen it nearly tore the paper, she wrote:

MILKY WAY—FEELING?—INSANE.

Holly dragged herself back upstairs. Once in her room, she sat on the bed and laid her head in her hands. *It shouldn't have to be this hard,* she thought. *A candy bar shouldn't have the authority to ruin someone's day.* She was terrified this was going to end like it always did in the years of candy-bar consumption before it, with a mindless three-day feeding frenzy. She wished there was someone she could talk to. It was too late to call Tina, not that Holly really wanted to anyway. She didn't even know how to put into words what her problem was, other than that a candy bar had her on the verge of a nervous breakdown. Tina would never understand what was going on in her head right now. No matter what stance Tina took, whether supportive or disappointed, Holly knew it would be the wrong one.

It was time for her security blanket.

It wasn't really a blanket. It was Bruce's favorite old green flannel shirt. She couldn't wear it; she hadn't been able to fit into any of Bruce's shirts for years. But when all other coping mechanisms failed and all the food couldn't fill the hole in her soul, Holly would pull it from the closet, fold it up, and lie with it under her cheek. When he first died, she slept with it, taking comfort in everything about it. It had well-worn softness and the scent of Bruce that remained secure within its fibers. It tricked her momentarily into thinking he was still there. She got up and went to his closet, where all his clothes still remained. She pulled it off the hanger and held it in her hands. And then, without knowing why, she stuck her arm in the shirt's sleeve. Then she did the same with her other arm. With her thin cotton nightgown on underneath, the shirt accepted her intrusion. She pulled the front of it closed and, with excited shaking fingers, began to button it. And then she raced to the mirror.

The shirt wasn't loose on her by any means, but it wasn't about to rip either. Her breasts were unforgiving and the button at the center of her chest strained. She quickly unbuttoned that one. But the rest of the buttons were all secure, and while the shirt was snug, it showed no signs of stress. She stared at herself in the mirror for several long moments with tears building up in her eyes. She hadn't really looked at herself in the mirror in a long time, with the exception of brushing her teeth in the morning. Now she was staring into the reflection of herself wearing a shirt deemed too small for as long as she could remember. The shirt was giving her a hug. She tilted her face up toward the heavens.

"Thanks, Bruce," Holly whispered through her tear-filled smile.

She took the shirt off, folded it up, and got in bed. With the shirt securely under her cheek, she fell asleep.

Chapter Six

LOGAN KEPT HIS WORD AND NEVER ASKED ABOUT Holly's food journal, but he was certain she'd made some alterations, because three months into training she was down forty pounds. It was a healthy weight loss, indicative of lifestyle changes and not drastic measures. Her curves were not yet obvious, but her round face started showing high cheekbones he hadn't noticed before. The double chin was receding and she positively glowed. She didn't get overly excited by her evolution, consistently referring to each pound as "just a drop in the bucket," nor was she ever outwardly critical or discouraged by her progress. She maintained the same focused determination she'd had since she started. It was a winning combination and Logan couldn't help patting himself on the back. Sure enough, his duckling was well on her way to becoming a swan.

Holly thrived on Logan's encouragement. His positive energy started accompanying her wherever she went. His upbeat catchphrases would come to her like the lyrics to her favorite songs. She never told him about the night with the Milky Way but tried to look at it as a turning point. She hadn't crumbled and turned into a rampant eating machine. She woke up the next morning and got right back on track.

It probably didn't hurt that she had a training session the following day. As soon as she walked into his building, the candy bar was all but forgotten.

Holly began to look at herself in the mirror more. She would strip down to her underwear and pose in front of it, as if in a weight-lifting competition. She marveled at the way her muscles popped out when she flexed them. She could feel her ribs beneath her skin. Her collarbone started showing prominently. There was still plenty of flesh around her midsection, her bottom, and her legs, but it was tighter. She could contract it and it would respond.

She looked strong. She felt strong. She was strong. Logan confirmed it every time he saw her. His warm bedroom eyes held the truth of his conviction. His easy smile communicated his relentless enthusiasm. She couldn't help but believe it. They had a partnership, each of them with different reasons for the same goal. She wanted to make him as proud of her as she was grateful to him.

She was changing, both physically and mentally. She felt braver and ready to take risks.

She knew where she wanted to start.

WITH HIS CELL PHONE ON THE NIGHTSTAND CHIRPING HAP-
pily, Logan opened one eye and looked at the clock:
1:42 A.M. He reached out blindly toward the glow of
the phone, thinking that if the person on the other end
wasn't one step from death, he or she soon would be.
He didn't recognize the number. When he mumbled a
sleepy hello and heard nothing on the other end, he was
tempted to throw the phone across the room and out
into the hallway. Just before he drew it away from his
ear to push the OFF button, he heard a little rush of air.

"Logan?" A tiny voice. It sounded muffled, wavering.

"This is he. Who is this?" he grumbled. Whoever she
was, he wasn't in the mood.

"It's Holly." She released an uneasy giggle. "I'm on
my home phone. You said I could call anytime."

He immediately sat up, swinging his legs over the
edge of the bed, rubbing his face. "Holly? What's up?
Everything all right?"

There was another long moment of silence followed
by a shaky, "Actually, no. I'm in trouble. I think I'm
about to do something stupid."

As soon as he heard the word "trouble," the rest of
her words became gibberish. Without asking any more
questions, he confirmed that he had Holly's address in
his BlackBerry and told her to stay put. He threw on
a pair of basketball shorts and a T-shirt, jumped into
his black Navigator, and plugged her information into
his GPS. It wasn't until he was halfway across town
that it dawned on him—he hadn't even found out what
was wrong. For her to have called him at all, much less
in the middle of the night, could only mean an emer-

gency. Was she hurt? Was she in danger? Had she been robbed or assaulted? Logan found that with each question, his foot pressed harder on the accelerator. He flew recklessly through quiet streets, his alarm increasing with the speedometer. His GPS's mechanical voice instructed him to turn onto her street. Even in the dark he became aware of the change in scenery. Trees lined the road and huge houses sat atop manicured hills. He saw the house number she'd given him illuminated on a sign stationed near a mailbox just as his GPS instructed him to turn into a long drive. The landscaped lawn stretched to a rather impressive modified colonial. A white sporty BMW convertible was parked in front of the circular driveway. He looked at the address again. This girl was chock full of surprises. As he pulled up next to her car, she opened the front door of the house, appearing to be completely unharmed and in her usual state of dress, sweatpants and ratty tee, though he hadn't seen the fuzzy pink bedroom slippers before. She stepped outside.

"Holly. What's going on? Are you all right?" He jumped out of his car and rushed to her side, not sure if he was talking about her crisis or the suddenly obvious fact that she wasn't a destitute widow.

"I'm fine. And I'm really sorry to have bothered you, Logan. You didn't have to come here. We probably could have handled this on the phone. But please, come in."

They walked through the spacious foyer, the house fully lit. When they got to the kitchen, she let out a heave of disgust and threw her arms in the direction of the granite-topped kitchen island. "This is what's going on."

She flung herself into a chair, unwilling to meet his eye. Logan looked at the island and grimaced. On display, right next to the meticulously kept notebook that served as her food diary and a bowl of fresh fruit, was a Sara Lee Coconut Crème Pie, a box of Twinkies, a two-liter bottle of Coke, bags of both Lay's Sour Cream and Onion potato chips and M&M's, and a pint of Ben & Jerry's ice cream. *She called me in the middle of the night because she was on the brink of a binge?* He didn't know what annoyed him more—the fact that he had just become the food police, or the painfully apparent fact that she could've paid full price for his services after all. She wanted his help? She'd get it.

"Get your running shoes on," he ordered abruptly, then began systematically returning the contents of the kitchen island to the freezer and random cupboards while she did so.

Logan took Holly outside and they walked briskly down her driveway. Neither of them spoke. The only sound besides their footsteps was the late-summer crickets getting in what would soon be their final songs of the season. Then Logan started to jog, taking every uphill route he could find. It took Holly real effort to keep up. After twenty minutes of trying to match every one of his long strides with two shorter strides of her own, Holly came to a grinding halt.

"Enough. Uncle. You win." She slowed down to a walk, and so did he.

Logan was peeved, but he didn't want to admit it. He wanted answers but wasn't even sure what questions needed asking. He felt out of the loop. He felt taken, though he could never once recall being lied to. How could he have been so stupid? She told him she lived in Englewood Cliffs, a town that prided itself on its exclusive multimillion-dollar McMansions. What did he think, she was living in a cardboard box in front of one? He had made the assumption she was flat broke because of her haggard appearance and her reluctance to ever divulge any information about herself. He childishly took comfort in one thing though: while he was barely out of breath, Holly was huffing and puffing.

"What's really going on here, Holly?" he demanded. "Who are you?"

"What do you mean? I was in total danger of eating all that crap." She tried to inhale without involuntarily shuddering. "Do you think I'm kidding you? You'd want me to call if I was going to put a bullet in my head, wouldn't you?"

Logan was caught off guard, all thoughts of the mystery surrounding her momentarily suspended. He stopped walking. She seemed really serious. Would she really have eaten all that food in one sitting after all the hard work she had put in over the last four months?

"You really would have eaten all that junk? At once?" He didn't bother to mask his awe, or his anger. Why was she so willing to get in the way of her own success? Settling his hands on his hips, he scolded her. "What could have driven you to do something like that in the middle of the night?"

Even in the light of nothing but the moon, he could see her eyes growing glassy, reflecting its beams when she peered up at him.

"Cleaning closets." She tried to add a sad little smile and failed miserably.

Logan instantly understood. His heart gave a loud thud. She had been packing up the last remnants of her husband.

"I just thought it was time, I guess," she added wistfully. "Maybe I was wrong."

Abandoning his initial harshness, Logan turned to his professional expertise. "Maybe it is time, and you just have to rise to the challenge. Your endorphins should be raging right about now, and you look like you'd rather vomit than eat. I could stay awhile and help you with the closet."

Holly gave him a genuine smile he could see through the darkness. "It's almost done. I'm down to the nitty-gritty. The stuff I can't see being recycled." The smile slowly faded.

"Come on; let's get it done," Logan said, doing his best to sound encouraging. They walked at a more relaxed pace back to the house. He followed her up the stairs and down the hallway toward her bedroom.

Glancing into another room, he stopped short. "Holly? What about this one?"

The room was unlike any of the others he'd passed. This room was stark, sanitary, and sterile. From the plain white walls to the barren wood floor, the only contents of this room were a hospital bed and some medical equipment. There were oxygen tanks and monitors, all wheeled into one corner with the cords wrapped neatly around them. The bed was nothing but a mattress lying flat inside its adjustable frame with chrome half rails on each side. He stepped inside the room and instantly felt its sacredness. On one wall, the wall opposite the blindless windows, was the only decoration that adorned the room. It was a huge framed photograph of mountains; snow covered them at the top, and a refreshing lake at their base mirrored them. The backdrop sky was perfectly blue with the exception of a few puffy white clouds in the distance. It took up nearly the entire wall. Logan felt his chest start to tighten. Was this the last thing her husband saw before he died? He looked at Holly standing in the doorway.

"This is a beautiful picture," he told her somberly.

"Isn't it?" Holly said from her spot in the hallway. She hadn't been in this room in almost a year. After the funeral, when everyone returned to their own lives, she'd spent days in it. She would sit on the rented hospital bed and think, *This was the last place Bruce was alive.* Surely his spirit would linger, freed from the confines of pain, she told herself, even if only long enough to point her in the right direction. Ignoring the hospice's calls to arrange a pickup, she kept paying the bill on all the equipment in the room and waited for a sign that would tell her what to do next. Days turned into weeks and weeks into months. The instructions never came, the hopelessness mounted, and she walked out of the room and into despair. She never shut the door to it though, just in case. To see Logan in the room was both amazing and unsettling. The ultimate positive life force was standing in the middle of the death room.

"Holly," Logan asked her gently, breaking into her thoughts, "maybe you want to put this stuff in storage?"

"I don't own it," she replied, devoid of any emotion.

"Is it included in the things being picked up tomorrow?"

"No."

"Would you like it to be?" His voice was soothing, his eyes full of compassion.

It only took one look at his face, and Holly knew the answer he hoped she would give. She wordlessly nodded her head, maintaining the same blank expression.

"Do you own any tools?" he asked in the same comforting tone.

"Tools?" she repeated, confused.

"Screwdrivers, wrenches, stuff like that?"

"There's a box in the garage," she said from the doorway. She watched Logan walk across the room to grab a monitor in each hand before joining her.

"Let's go get it," he said pragmatically. "They'll never be able to get this bed out the door without removing the rails and the legs. Who needs a couple of goofballs in here scratching up your hardwood floors and banging into your walls? We'll put everything together downstairs and it'll all be in one spot for when it gets picked up."

She took one of the monitors he was holding and he followed her back downstairs. They dropped off the monitors in the dining room and she took him to the garage. He made casual chatter that she didn't hear a word of. To acknowledge she heard him would require responses on her part. She wasn't capable of coherent responses; she was one step from a blathering mess. She wanted to be numb and focused and not bother him with further drama. She had done too much of that already. He didn't seem to mind her being distracted. He wasn't disapproving of the fact that she had effectively put off this horrid chore for well over a year. He picked up the toolbox; she got a Ziploc bag for the nuts, bolts, and screws; and they went back upstairs.

"I've got this," he told her before going back into the bedroom, "if you want to finish up someplace else."

She felt the look of relief spreading over her face. He knew. It was like he could feel her agony. She nodded mutely at him and retreated to the safety of her own room. An empty box waited for her and automatically she began to fill it with Bruce's most personal effects. She started with the bathroom and his toiletry kit, which contained his electric razor, his deodorant, and the cologne she occasionally got him to wear. She removed all his prescription bottles, many half full, making a mental note to dispose of them properly. Holly pulled his toothbrush out of the holder, where it was stationed beside hers. She looked at her own toothbrush, now alone in the holder, and swallowed the lump in her throat. It seemed so final now. A toothbrush that hadn't been used in almost two years had the power to create such a void. Holly quickly left the bathroom.

She could hear Logan down the hall. There was the metallic clanging from pieces of the bed being taken apart. There were also sporadic grunts as he tried to get stubborn screws and bolts to cooperate.

There was only one drawer left in her bedroom to do: Bruce's underwear drawer. It wasn't just filled with her husband's boxers and T-shirts. It was where he kept his most treasured possessions. At the bottom of the drawer was the Saint Christopher pendant his grandmother had given him when he made his confirmation. And the science award medal he'd won in sixth grade, when he created a tiny car that ran on water and baking soda. Maybe she would send the award to his parents and the pendant back to his grandmother; she had disconnected from them in her grief. His class ring from Brown was there. He'd insisted she keep it and not bury it with him, because it was eighteen-karat gold and would be worth something. There was his favorite pair of sunglasses, secure in their case. And there was also a picture of Holly and Bruce at a Mexican restaurant in Toronto, taken with an old Polaroid instant camera. It had been his twenty-fourth birthday, his first after she arrived in Canada. Despite his protests, Holly had alerted the restaurant staff to the occasion. They presented Bruce with their celebratory gigantic sombrero and, with Holly's full support, forced him to wear it. She remembered Bruce fretting that it could give him lice, but he put it on anyway. With Holly's head easily fitting under the brim as well, the waiter snapped the picture and gave it to them. Holly had no idea Bruce had kept it. He even had a hint of a smile, and he rarely smiled in pictures. She wasn't aware how long she touched and inspected each artifact. Time once again had no relevance. She finally took them all and stuck them in her jewelry box. With shaking hands and a heavy heart, she emptied the contents of Bruce's final drawer. And then she went to her own closet and retrieved Bruce's green flannel shirt. She placed it in the box. If she was to have any hope of making it through this night, it would have to go. If for no other reason than she wasn't willing to go through this hurt ever again. She had all the mementos she needed.

Logan was nearly finished dismantling the bed when she passed the room he was working in. She stopped. Suddenly she wanted to be in there. She wanted to be near the person who had taken on her wretched task as his own, and in the middle of the night no less. Setting the box down, Holly took a seat on the floor, leaning her back up against the wall. The pieces he had already taken apart were neatly stacked against the wall near the door, as was the mattress. All the hardware used to connect the bed was safely in the Ziploc bag.

"You look pale," Logan told her.

"You look like this bed is giving you a run for your money." She tried to sound lighthearted.

"I have yet to meet the bolt I couldn't persuade to turn," he said. "You all done?"

"I am." Holly looked at the box beside her. "I don't know what to do with this stuff. It feels wrong to just throw it away. Do people want someone's old underwear and electric razor and toothbrush?"

Logan took a moment before answering. "I don't think the toothbrush will be of any use to anyone, but poor people need underwear and razors, too. As long as it's not full of holes and it's clean, I'll bet you can donate it. Not to mention, when charities have to do this unpleasant task, I'm almost positive they take everything and respectfully dispose of what they can't use. I think you should do whatever feels right."

"Thanks, Logan." She smiled at him. He always seemed to know just what to say.

Logan stood up and reached for her hand, helping her to rise. "We're almost done. Let's bring this all downstairs."

They worked side by side in silence, until one side of the dining room contained the majority of the contents of the nearly empty sickroom. When they went back to take the mattress down together, Holly looked at the picture.

"I have no clue what to do with that," she said, pointing to it.

"When the time is right, you will," he instantly replied. "You don't have to get rid of it at all if you don't want to. It's a great piece of artwork."

"Maybe Sloan-Kettering would like it?"

Logan smiled at her. "It would be a lovely tribute. But you don't need to decide that tonight."

Holly nodded her agreement and together they took hold of the mattress and brought it downstairs.

"You want something to drink?" Holly asked after they leaned the mattress up against a wall.

"Sounds great."

Holly left Logan alone in the dining room. He glanced around at the boxes of men's clothes. Cloth garment bags full of suits, jackets, and dress shirts were lying over several chairs. They were packed so carefully, stacked so neatly, as if their owner was just transporting them from one locale to another. But no; he shook his head. She was getting ready to say good-bye to them. Logan was confident Holly had given her husband the same level of attention.

He meandered back into the warmly decorated living room. Right before taking a seat on the cream-colored leather sectional, he spied it. It was on the mantel above the stone fireplace. A wedding photo of Bruce Brennan and his bride. Logan strolled over to get a better look, picking the photograph up. Bruce was, in a word, average. He appeared to be standard height, not too fat, not too thin. Hair wasn't too long or too short. Logan would have called it brownish. He had green eyes. Not like Holly's emerald green, but more of an indecisive hazel. Bruce didn't have any distinctions or disfigurements, with the exception of some horn-rimmed glasses. He was handsome in a nondescript sort of way. His tuxedo fit well, always a plus in Logan's book. Bruce looked happy enough, although more content than ecstatic.

Logan went on to study Holly in the photograph. She was beaming, radiant, beautiful, everything a bride should be. And she had been right. Even on her wedding day, she wasn't thin. Present were the pudgy round cheeks Logan had come to know, the full upper arms, the thicker torso he had become so familiar with. But she looked healthy. There was also no denying the fire in her eyes. The sort of inherent brightness that indicates an inner life force, the life force he had begun to see in her, in his gym.

He made a quick scan of the rest of room, looking for other photos, but there were none. It seemed the gigantic house held only a single framed eight-by-ten as evidence of its inhabitants. Logan's interest returned to the photograph in his hand. Why couldn't he get a solid read on this girl? Why was she so unwilling to talk, leaving him with nothing to make but misguided assumptions? How was it that just when he thought he had her figured out, she seemed to take him in a different direction again? He looked up, unaware that she'd come back into the room. She was looking at the photo, too, and when Logan met her eyes, he knew right away that this time, she couldn't hold back the tears.

"God, this is all so hard." Her voice cracked and her fists clenched around the two bottles of water she was carrying.

"Come here." Logan put down the picture and held out his arms, taking a step toward her.

Holly walked into them without hesitation and he took the unopened bottles from her and tossed them on the couch before wrapping his arms around her. Her tension began to ease. She felt so protected, small even. She couldn't remember the last time she felt so small. There was nothing untoward about the hug, and finally she felt the freedom to cry. Someone much stronger was holding her up, somebody sturdy and in control. Logan said very little, just the occasional "Yes, I know," all the while rubbing her shoulders reassuringly as she released all the pent-up pain that had become her constant companion. When she seemed all cried out, he guided her to the couch and he sat down. She flopped.

"Don't you wish," she said as she ran her hands from her forehead downward, trying to dry her face, "that when people you love died, all their stuff would just disappear, too? Just completely vanish?"

He gave her a tender smile. "I think it's an important part of the grieving process. You'll be glad you did it. Just not right now."

"You're right, you know." Her hands moved up through her hair and she sighed in exasperation. "Jesus, don't you ever get tired of being right?"

"Holly," Logan asked gently, "where is everyone, your family and friends? People to help you get through all this shit?"

She hastened to get up and pull herself together, suddenly flustered. "I'm so sorry, Logan. I didn't mean to bother you with this. Thanks so much for coming."

There was at least one question he was going to get answered about her. With two hands, he sat her back down. "Oh no you don't, young lady. I'm not bothered, and if I was, it's too late anyway. I'm here. And I'm sorry if the next ten minutes hurt, but you are going to answer me. I've been training you for nearly four months, and in that time I've learned nothing about you. Zero. Zilch. Nada."

"That's not true, I talk all the time," Holly said quickly. "You're always telling me to focus." It was a feeble attempt at diverting attention from the topic.

Logan shot her a look that spoke of extreme tolerance mixed with fatherly reproach. "Telling me I set the incline of a treadmill on Mount Kilimanjaro is not talking. Asking me if I can see the baby's head yet when you're doing abdominal crunches is not meaningful conversation."

She couldn't help the giggle she released and he joined her with a small chuckle of his own before taking a more serious tone and asking her again.

"Stop dodging me. Where is everyone, Holly?"

She cleared her throat and took an unsteady breath. "There is no one."

"No one," he repeated. "You're an orphan?"

"Not exactly." She took another breath, this one a wind-up for the story she figured he deserved to know. "My family is very much alive and, last I heard, living in Oregon, where I grew up. Bruce was a U.S. citizen with a Canadian mother who had connections to the DCC."

"DCC?" Logan politely asked.

"Defense Construction Canada. Think troop support and homeland security."

"Gotcha."

"When he graduated from Brown, he was offered a position with a technology firm in Toronto. Developing some secret stuff. Bruce loved Canada, loved the prospect of being involved in something so cutting-edge. They even offered me a job there, in the accounting department, when I graduated the following year." Holly's words trailed off. She was becoming increasingly uncomfortable.

Logan patiently waited, watching Holly begin to bite her fingernails, the sign he had gotten used to seeing when she was nervous or unsure. How could she possibly tell him her history without sounding selfish and rotten?

"Holly, whatever it is, you can tell me."

"I was a change-of-life baby," Holly finally said. "My mother was almost forty-four when I was born, my father nearly fifty. They were already set in their ways by the time I came along. And they were already old."

"Fifty isn't all that old," Logan said.

Holly pursed her lips together, her mouth forming a thin line. "It is when it comes to changing diapers and chasing after a toddler full-time. Especially when you don't particularly want to. It didn't take me long to figure out that I was little more than a nuisance."

Logan wanted to tell her there was no way that could possibly be true but held his tongue.

Holly continued. "My parents weren't actually abusive, but they were strict and stifling. They wanted quiet, they wanted to be left alone. Like I said, they were set in their ways. Those ways did not include carting a kid to soccer or ballet."

Logan nodded, the picture starting to get clearer. Food doesn't move.

"They were also hoarders," Holly said, just above a whisper, her eyes growing wide at the confession.

"Hoarders?" Logan repeated, his eyes getting bigger as well.

"Not like filthy, dead-cats-crushed-under-piles-of-moldy-food hoarders," Holly said quickly, trying to clarify, before adding, sadly, "Mostly books and magazines and clothes piled up. It didn't leave much room for toys, or even moving around."

"I see," Logan said grimly.

"By the time I was a teenager, I realized they were really sick, the kind of sick that couldn't be helped, not unless they wanted it. But they didn't think they had a problem. They thought of themselves as history collectors. Trying to make sense of their mess was exhausting and they resented the effort. All I could think about was getting out of there. I could tell they wanted me to."

"Seriously?" Logan said quietly, astounded she could talk about it so casually. In all the time they had spent together, Holly had never once burdened Logan with an old-fashioned bitch fest about feeling rejected. It took him a minute to wrap his head around it. He didn't know much about hoarding, other than it was a mental disorder that was difficult to treat, even when the patient was willing. It was hard to think of Holly as a child, surrounded by trash and unable to move, feeling like a burden to her parents. His own parents had always been his biggest advocates and it was only because of their encouragement that he was willing to take his most challenging risks. "I'm so sorry, Holly."

"It sounds much worse than it actually was." Holly nodded and continued with such enthusiasm; Logan could tell she was stepping back to a happier time. "Brown gave me a great scholarship; student loans took care of the rest. I met Bruce my sophomore year, when he was a junior. He was already settled by the time I joined him. I loved Canada. *We* loved Canada. We hiked, we skied. We loved camping. There is just so much beauty up there. Up north, with Bruce, I was able to breathe. We didn't have many friends but didn't care. We had each other. Bruce and I were doing fine on our own. We had eight wonderful years. Perfect, really." Her voice trailed off, hardened. "But pancreatic cancer doesn't have a great survival rate. He felt he had the best chance of beating it with doctors in New York. So we packed it up and moved here. And he died here. It was just so bad from the moment they found it and spread to his liver and spine so quickly. My parents did come for the funeral and they tried to talk me into going back with them. But I couldn't be sure of their motives and so much time had passed, you know? I realized they didn't have a clue who I was. And worse yet, I felt like I didn't know them anymore. It was like I was talking to strangers about other strangers. I don't think they knew just how conscientious Bruce really was. I thought he was paranoid at the time. Not only was he an expert in saving and investing, he was insured to the max. Probably overinsured, but I think he wanted me taken care of in case something bad happened to him. Little did he know. Anyway, when I told my parents I was going to stay here in New Jersey, a decision I made mostly out of grief and laziness, I couldn't tell if they were relieved or angry. So basically Martin and Agnes Busch wished me luck, and I haven't seen or heard from them since. I'm sure I'm nothing but a memory."

Logan was dumbfounded and took a minute to digest all he'd been given. It was becoming increasingly clear where Holly's emotional eating was coming from. He was just about to comment on how impressed he was that she'd attended Brown when it hit him. "Wait a tick. Did you just tell me your maiden name was Busch?"

She raised her chin a fraction higher and looked him right in the eye before nodding. "And not the rich, presidential, or Anheuser good kind of Busch, either."

"You spent your entire childhood with the name Holly Busch?" he said in disbelief.

She nodded again.

"You're kidding me. I don't believe you. Who does that?" he kept asking, not caring if she thought he considered her parents demented.

"Who does it? Quirky folks with a jaded sense of humor, obviously," she replied. "When I would complain about it to them, they used to tell me it would build character. You should meet my sister, Azalea."

"What the fuck?!" Logan gasped, horrified.

"I'm teasing," she quickly told him, startled by his immediate and adverse reaction.

"Thank God." He exhaled and shook his head.

"I don't have a sister, just an older brother, the crown prince of the Busch family. Prince Albert. And no, they never kept him in a can."

"Holly, please stop with the shtick. It's too early in the morning and you're scrambling my brain." He was on the verge of pleading.

"Sorry. Force of habit. I really do have a brother named Albert. He's fifteen years older than me and just like them. I guess it could have been worse. They didn't name me Rose."

"Yeah, I guess that would be worse." Logan was flummoxed, wishing he could find the positive spin on what sounded like a completely dismal childhood. "Why did you say you weren't sure of your family's motives before?"

"Because Albert is one sneaky bastard. He got married and moved away to start stockpiling shit in his own house. But he also put the idea in my parents' heads that after college I could return to take care of them as they got older. The three of them hatched the plan like they were doing me a favor. After all, I was fat and awkward; nobody was going to want me anyway. The day they told me it was expected of me, I felt like I had just been handed a death sentence."

"I'm speechless," he said, frowning.

"It's okay. I got the last laugh, sort of. I did manage to land a husband, but they were in no position to pay for a wedding. So we paid for it ourselves. By then they had pretty much become hermits, so they didn't even attend. They only were willing to travel after Bruce died because Albert was with them, telling them the reward of getting me to go back there would be worth it to them. I could go on with a hundred more examples, but not only don't I want to bore you, by the look on your face, I don't think you can take it."

"I think you're right," he readily admitted.

"Long story short, instead of character, what they really ended up building in me was a deep resentment that made it very easy to turn my back on them. The day I took the name Brennan was easily the happiest day of my life. I even got to keep my initials. Bonus."

He was almost afraid to continue inquiring. "No friends?"

"A few. Not many from my childhood. I developed a pretty thick skin. I probably harbored a lot of jealousy. Other kids all had normal names and tidy parents and pleasant lives. There was a real sense of accomplishment when I walked away from my past." She said, after pausing a moment and shrugging dismissively, "My best friend is still there. She's the only person I ever told about what was going on behind closed doors at my house. I think that's why they thought I had no friends, although it was really the shame of anyone seeing how I lived that kept me from inviting people over. Most of my friends are Canadian, people Bruce and I worked with. We e-mail. Some of them came to the funeral."

"But why such a huge house if there were only the two of you? This house is hardly representative of the term 'no one.'" Logan looked around the living room with its twenty-foot cathedral ceiling, rich hardwood floors, and general opulence. It was clean and completely devoid of any clutter, almost like Holly was intent on going in the other direction from how she was raised.

"Bruce bought the house out of foreclosure for maybe half its original value the day after he was diagnosed. I don't think it hurt that the timing really cooperated. The U.S. economy was starting to tank and the Canadian dollar was getting stronger. He bought it with the intention of my being able to sell it after he was gone. You know, appreciating assets and all that other terminology. I pretty much left that stuff to him, although he did try to educate me. I told you he was an investing genius. Besides, he couldn't stand the thought of living on top of other people. He really liked his space. You should have seen our house in Canada. You had to go a quarter mile just to get to the mailbox."

"This is an awful lot of house for one person," Logan commented.

"I know," Holly admitted pensively. "But I'm not quite ready to let it go. Or him. I know we were only here a short time, and it sure isn't filled with happy memories, but sometimes I can still feel him, and until that feeling is gone, I won't leave him here alone. I was hoping that getting rid of his things might help that process along."

"One foot in front of the other." He quoted one of his favorite phrases, then added, "Holly, you are amazing."

"Hardly." She laughed. "From the day he died, I was a hot mess. I didn't give a damn about anything or anyone. Getting out of bed was a chore. Fortunately—or unfortunately, depending on who you ask," she said, rolling her eyes, "every take-out joint in a twenty-mile radius delivers. That day I met you? On the plane? I had just finished closing a deal on some stock options Bruce had left over, options I almost had to forfeit to the company's new president because I waited too long. For a while there, I couldn't even be bothered with opening the mail. But Bruce would have haunted me forever if I'd let that asshole have his stock. Bruce really didn't like that guy."

Logan joined in with a laugh of his own, satisfied that he had finally uncovered some of her secrets, impressed by her ability to keep them to herself for so long. Clearly she no longer needed to, and Logan felt free to get caught up in the recovery of her seemingly ever-present sense of humor. He also had a much clearer picture of just how far back her eating disorder was rooted.

"That's why I think you're amazing," Logan said with

conviction before reaching out to meaningfully pat her knee. Then he stood up and made his way to the kitchen. He couldn't change what had happened to Holly in the past, but he could see to it that she felt his support for her future. "Now, listen here, you," he called in to where she was sitting. "There is something we have to get settled before I leave here tonight."

"I guess you're going to start charging me your going rate?" He could practically hear her smirking.

"Not even close," he responded from the kitchen. "But that's not a bad idea."

Holly could hear him rustling about, the sound of drawers opening and closing. "I promise never to call you in the middle of the night again?" she called back to him. She was only half-teasing.

He returned. "Oh, forget that, but thank you in advance." He sat down with a spoon and the pint of ice cream. He took off the lid and tossed it on the coffee table in front of them before jamming the spoon in it and giving her a significant look. He held the pint of ice cream up in front of her. "This is not the enemy. There is absolutely nothing wrong with rewarding yourself with some treats now and again, in either celebration or even self-pity. What is *not* okay is going outside the box and looking at the treat as a failure and thereby giving yourself license to keep failing. This is not the enemy!" he repeated with mock severity. "This is ice cream. Karamel Sutra, to be exact. Sounds sexy." He scooped a spoonful of ice cream and put it in his mouth. "What else don't I know about you? Holy shit, this stuff really is delicious." He looked at the container again before taking another spoonful and holding it out to her. "Come on, tough girl, join me in this before I eat it all myself."

I should have told him about the Milky Way was Holly's first thought. Logan would have really been able to put that sucker into perspective.

He brought the spoon to her lips, and as she opened her mouth, her second thought began to emerge. She began mentally composing a letter to the chubby girl's version of *Penthouse Forum,* starting with *The most handsome man in the world has a penchant for feeding me ice cream . . . while naked.* Her smile got wide. So did his. For entirely different reasons, she was sure. They ate the whole pint, giggling.

"See?" he said, licking the spoon for the last time and dropping it back into the now-empty container. "No harm, no foul. A little ice cream never hurt anyone, except maybe the lactose intolerant. Like I told you before, it's about coexisting. Just remember, when you eat those calories, you just have to work a little harder the next day to burn them off. I already put the rest of the food away. If you're smart, you'll wake up tomorrow and throw it all out. But don't let me find out they shared a table for one again, or there'll be hell to pay, got me?"

She blushed, feeling naughty and contented at the same time. She gave him a stiff-armed military salute. "Understood. But what's fair is fair. I just spilled my guts. Now, what's *your* life story, or did Zeus just throw down a thunderbolt and you landed on Nordhoff Place?"

"Well," he said, grinning with pride, "he would have had to throw down two. Don't forget about my location on West Thirty-fifth." Logan kept a fully equipped facility in the city, for clients who were city dwellers. He didn't generally make house calls, although most of his clients had their own fully equipped spaces. It was a short ride through the Lincoln Tunnel and he booked about a third of his sessions there. "I much prefer the Englewood location though. The air just seems cleaner, the vibe a little less hectic. I'm a pretty simple guy. I grew up with an insanely average life in Danbury, Connecticut. My dad's an accountant, my mom a fourth-grade schoolteacher. I have a sister named Joanna, JoJo for short. She's three years older and a school psychologist up near where my folks live. She's married and has three kids of her own. I grew up loving baseball, played a lot in school, and ended up getting a scholarship to the University of California at Irvine, where I found out I liked sports physiology better. That turned out to be a good move. I realized how mediocre my baseball skills were when I became a small fish in a very big pond."

"Yeah, right," she said skeptically, unwilling to believe he was second-rate at anything.

"No. It's true," he confessed without malice. "It probably didn't hurt that I was rooming with a guy who was going to become one of the greatest players in modern history." Logan waited a moment to see if she would inquire as to whom, and when she showed no interest, he continued. "I used to help him with strains and sprains and before I knew it, I found myself fascinated with the human body on the whole. With just what it's capable of enduring, how it operates and adapts under the stress of extreme physical outputs. With how important a part the mind really plays in all of it." He tapped his finger on the side of his temple.

Holly couldn't help staring. Even in his self-indulgent years, he had turned his own personal negatives into a positive. Effortlessly. As if he just naturally fell onto the path of what was best for him. And he was fascinated with the human body, even hers. She wasn't sure exactly how she should feel about that. After all, even the Elephant Man's body held fascination.

"You never wanted to become a doctor?" she asked, wanting to sound merely interested and not in awe.

"Nah." Logan was quick in his reply and with a grin. "All that extra schooling and having to be on call—where's the fun in that?" He waited a minute and his grin got wider. "Although I seemed to have been on call tonight and it wasn't so bad. At least for me it wasn't, watching you trying to keep up about ten minutes into that run. You can't really try those sorts of tactics on someone who needs a kidney transplant or has pneumonia." He stopped abruptly, aware that he was venturing into sensitive subject matter. There was no doctor in the world that could save what Holly had lost. Just because he personally never knew Bruce Brennan didn't mean he never existed. The painful proof that he did was all in the adjoining room.

"I'm sorry, Holly," he told her soberly. "I didn't mean to come off like that. If my being a doctor could have saved your husband, I would have become one in a heartbeat."

She said nothing and instead hurriedly took the empty ice cream container and the spoon back to the kitchen, afraid that Logan would get a good look at her and be able to read her thoughts. Not only had he come at a moment's notice, an act she never expected, but he genuinely cared.

She had never connected Logan's being or not being a doctor with her late husband. But he certainly did. This whole night was becoming less about Bruce and more about Logan, and it was invigorating. She wasn't supposed to be invigorated; she was supposed to be miserable. Being miserable went hand in hand with respecting the memory of her husband, didn't it? She was supposed to be miserable a while longer.

Holly stalled in the kitchen a few more moments to gather her scattered thoughts back together. She had called Logan because there was no one else to turn to. He came because she had called him, depressed and desperate. He would have done it for anybody. There was nothing to read into and she didn't want to analyze anymore. Not herself. Not how a widow should or shouldn't act or feel. Not her human Saint Bernard sitting in the next room. She only knew one thing for certain: the last twenty-four hours had left her mentally and physically exhausted. She threw the ice cream container in the garbage and the spoon in the sink.

"I'm proud of you, you know," Logan told her when she returned, and patted the spot on the couch beside him, encouraging her to make contact with him. She needed human contact after all she had been through tonight. He recognized the signs that came with catharsis, and she had certainly had one. She tentatively curled up next to him, leaning her head on his shoulder, and they sat in comfortable silence for a few moments before he continued. "You work so hard. You're willing to try anything. I've never once had to deal with you having a bad hair day or breaking a nail. To find out what you've had to endure, well, I feel like it's an honor to call you my friend." He began to yawn and close his eyes. She had fallen asleep minutes before.

Chapter Seven

LOGAN AWOKE WITH A START. THE SUN WAS ALREADY up. Not a good sign. He checked the time on his phone. Six forty-five. Shit. He had clients at seven. Luckily, all his appointments for the day were in Jersey. He'd have to split and head right to the gym, and might be late anyway. Holly was still on his shoulder, her breathing deep and even. He stood slowly, laying her back down on the couch. She barely stirred as he covered her with a nearby blanket. *Probably her first real sleep in days,* he mused, and hurried out the door, making sure it was locked behind him.

Chase and Amanda Walker were already warming up on the treadmills when Logan got there. Chase had had his own set of keys since the day Logan opened. He and Logan had been friends since they were freshman roommates at UC Irvine. They'd been two scared kids miles away from home, feeling homesick and in over their heads but too stubborn to show it, except in small glimpses to each other.

Even once Chase's athletic star began to shine, their bond remained strong. They roomed together all four years, and after Logan's interest became more about training and less about baseball, Chase began taking Logan's advice on everything from nutrition to how to get more power out of his swing. Chase went so far as to use part of his signing bonus with the Kings to finance Logan's master's degree in sports physiology at William Paterson University in New Jersey. He encouraged Logan to take the plunge and start his own business, doing his part by floating him a hefty loan, becoming his first client, and spreading the word.

Sticking with Chase Walker turned out to be the wildest of rides. Chase was permanently etched in the annals of baseball history as the Golden Boy, a title earned for his Midwestern, corn-fed, boyish good looks, plus his uncanny ability to smash baseballs into neighboring counties and throw them just as far. He was humble, generous personally as well as publicly, and virtuous. Those characteristics made him an endorsement seeker's dream. Simply put, Chase Walker lived up to his name and everything he touched turned to gold.

But more recently, Chase had expanded his place in history with a bona fide sex scandal. The truth was Chase Walker loved to spank naughty women. He felt it was his duty to protect, cherish, and serve discipline. It was a secret fetish he managed to keep to himself for years, even from his friend and college roommate—not that Logan felt it was really any of his business. Looking back, all the signs had been there. Chase used the word "behave" a lot. He had a suggestively domineering approach to women that seemed to act as a magnet instead of a turnoff. He was never too emotionally attached to any one girl, even before making the pros, yet his exes would seemingly melt in his presence when they encountered him again. Chase, in turn, would be genuinely happy to see them.

Amanda Cole, a beautiful, self-assured business owner, found Chase's dominant side very romantically appealing, much to her own initial surprise. They met four years into Chase's ten-year deal with the Kings and within weeks they became exclusive, each intent on bringing the other into line. Thanks to an inconveniently placed security camera in a Kings Stadium tunnel, a shady employee, and a slow news week, Chase and Amanda were unwittingly exposed in a harmless game of naughty-girl foreplay, and Chase's secret, *their* secret, was uncovered.

Mortified at first, Amanda took to going underground. Chase, however, faced the public with the same rakish charm he'd won them over with in the first place. If the media wanted to scandalize what amounted to nothing more than a silly private moment between two consenting single adults, there really wasn't much he could do about it. He followed that up with the standing offer that if any media outlet found they had too much dead air on their hands or pages that needed filling, he would happily spare the time to do a story on any of the numerous and unsung charities he participated in. He backed that up with a week of sending TMZ his itinerary. The story quickly faded and the Golden Boy stayed golden. And it freed him from the only skeleton that would ever fall out of his closet. He no longer had to concern himself with the slim chance of a past partner coming out of the woodwork to blackmail him about his sex life, not that he'd actually spent much time worrying about it to begin with. And a few women did come out to tell their tales, eager to claim their fifteen minutes of fame at his expense, as the media briefly debated whether or not he had crossed some politically correct line. But even Chase's would-be accusers came off sounding more worshipful of him than tarnishing. It earned him another title—the "Sexiest Who's Your Daddy." That brought Amanda out of hiding in record time, with a jealous fury that left Chase even more enchanted with her. It was as if he'd tapped into an underground trend just itching to come to life. Any lingering interest in the topic was met with Chase flashing his eighty-five-million-dollar-a-year smile, maintaining that a gentleman would never kiss and tell, and the subject was dropped—whether or not anyone else wanted it that way.

With her deep-blue angel eyes and voluptuous curves, Amanda put a spell on Chase from the moment they met and gave him quite a run for his money to boot. But she would never love another, and if in exchange she had to give up some of her privacy, he was, without question, worth it. She trusted that he would protect her and he did. Their private life stayed relatively private. One was rarely seen without the other nearby. She learned to adapt and go with the flow.

Now Amanda was the one thing she'd sworn she would never be: a trophy wife. And it felt great. After all, *he* was *her* trophy husband. They were inseparable. While others were betting the relationship wouldn't last, that Chase and Amanda would burn themselves out on each other, those who knew them well knew better.

Logan was in the know.

Logan never had a real problem with Amanda's joining Chase on his workouts. She stuck mostly to the treadmill and elliptical machines, unless it was her turn to train, since she had become a part-time client as well. Amanda and Chase worked out at completely different levels. Chase worked out hard-core, sometimes never making with the small talk at all, depending on what time of the year it was and how his performance stats were looking. Amanda, on the other hand, looked at her training sessions as more like social events, considering her personal appointments were scheduled while her husband wasn't available, even to her. Logan had the distinct impression that his role was that of a diversion for Amanda and a glorified babysitter in Chase's absence, something he surely wouldn't have chosen, but he knew there was little he could do about it. Refusing to accommodate his best friend and the man who'd helped him on the road to success wasn't an option, so Logan did his best to entertain Amanda while at the same time improve her fitness level. It worked about 50 percent of the time. Logan could get her to concentrate during the actual exercises, but in between sets she could be counted on for a running commentary on everything from current events to analyzing the most intimate details of Logan's private life. Being attracted to Amanda was never even remotely an issue, but wanting to apply duct tape over her mouth was. She was relentless in her sisterly pestering. She said that Logan was getting too old to be a player and would never find true happiness until he had someone to share his life with. She would cite countless examples of how her happy-go-lucky husband had found peace because he had someone to call his own. It was both endearing and infuriating, mostly because it had a ring of truth to it, not that Logan would ever admit it. Once Chase Walker found something he loved as much as baseball, he really did seem complete, dragging Amanda with him wherever he went, whenever he could. The only part of having them in the gym together that bothered Logan was how damn mushy they were all the time. Whenever Chase took a break and she was within arm's reach, he kissed her, touched her cheek, or patted her bottom. And her timing for being within reach was impeccable. It was enough to send a diabetic running for insulin. Logan had stopped telling them to "get a room" months ago. It did no good anyway; they barely heard him. When Logan went out with them socially, it was just as bad. But they all knew Chase's body was his career, so when it was time to work, they all got down to business, trying to curtail the public displays of affection during baseball season.

Chase and Amanda looked at Logan as he burst through the door. The treadmills stopped.

"Rough night?" Chase did a halfhearted double take while jumping onto the gym floor. Amanda was infinitely more interested and turned around, leaning against her treadmill. Logan looked a wreck. He had bags under his eyes and a slight case of bed head. His shirt showed evidence of dried sweat. He didn't smell so hot, either.

"Sorry I'm late. Let's get to work." Logan held up his hand, a preemptive strike. "Amanda, nothing further, if you would be so kind."

"Oh, I think not," she teased, her arms crossing over her chest. It was so rare for him to have a hair out of place, much less oversleep. She gave Chase a meaningful glance. "What could have Logan so backward today?"

"A client. Let's get to work." Logan jerked a thumb toward the leg press.

"A client who keeps you out all night? And just what sort of program is *she* on? Is that ice cream on your shirt?"

"Amanda," Chase broke in, tapping his watch several times while Logan examined his shirt, "there's batting practice at ten. I have to be out of here by eight thirty. Playoffs, dear, playoffs."

"I guess it's safe to assume this is a new client?" Amanda declared, pretending she didn't hear her husband. The playoffs were months away.

"Don't get your hopes up, Amanda. It's not what you're thinking, although as always, I appreciate your enthusiasm. Yes, it's a new client," Logan told her, while trying to scratch out the offending stain that graced the center of his shirt.

"A new client?" Amanda repeated deliberately, taking a quick look at her husband before going back to Logan. "Where are you squeezing her . . ."—she held the long, drawn-out pause for full effect—" . . . in? And why are we just hearing about her now? It's probably also safe to assume that now that she's kept you out all night, she won't be writing you any more checks?"

"The reason you're hearing about her now is because I was trying to spare myself the exchange we're currently having. I know nothing brightens your day more than the prospect of becoming my wedding planner. This is nothing like that." He gave up on the shirt and, taking it off, walked hurriedly to his small office in the back of the gym to pull out one of the extra tees he kept in his desk before calling back at them, "She's a recent widow."

"Why am I having trouble picturing a seventy-year-old?" Amanda mused impishly to her husband, though she made the comment loud enough for Logan to hear.

"Maybe because she isn't seventy?" Chase said while doing several warm-up lunges and then touching his toes. "I'm willing to bet she's not even thirty."

"It's true, she's not seventy. Not every woman I come in contact with is a potential booty call," Logan told them both reprovingly as he returned, not bothering to tuck the new shirt into his shorts. "And she is, too, over thirty. She's just having a really hard time."

"Hard time?" Amanda let out a giggle. "Helped her out with that, now, did you?"

"You have to go there, don't you? I'd like to think that even I'm not enough of a dog to take advantage of a grieving widow."

"It has nothing to do with your being a dog, Logan. I just know how much you like your sleep. There's usually only one thing you let interrupt it," Amanda told him, not unkindly.

"Sleep is as important as exercise," Logan said in agreement. "But this was a bit of a crisis. Besides, she's not my type."

"This one is less than six feet tall? Can't fit through a straw? Has a brain? Doesn't bite? Come on, she has to fall into one of those categories somewhere." Amanda continued the unrelenting probe, taking full advantage of yet another slip.

Chase was beginning to shift impatiently from one foot to the other but still managed a snicker. Logan looked to him, imploring. "Help me out here, Chase. I'm too tired to play with her today."

Unfortunately Logan's fluster had raised a red flag. Logan was being way too protective about the circumstances behind his lateness. Chase was now curious. Normally, Logan never had a problem talking about any woman. "I have to admit, you are acting a bit strange—I would even go as far as to say a tad defensive—about this new secret client of yours. I'm probably going to hate myself for this, but . . . if you're not looking to get her naked, what gives?"

Logan realized that once Chase sided with his wife, Logan had no choice but to comply or the inquisition would go full throttle. So he rushed through what he hoped would be enough to satisfy them. "I was seated next to her on an airplane, on the way back from nursing you in Toronto, you big baby."

"Excuse me, but that was a career-threatening injury." Chase tried to sound sympathetic and then promptly abandoned the tactic. "And I was bored as shit." Amanda had been forced to stay in New Jersey for that trip, with her father having knee surgery. The Blue Jays were also decimated with injuries and in last place with little hope of getting out of the basement any time during the season. Since they were going to rest him anyway to make sure he didn't aggravate the muscle, Chase saw it as the perfect opportunity to pal around Toronto with his closest friend during the four-game road trip.

"Wait a minute," Amanda said giddily. "You met her on the plane back from *that* ridiculous excursion?"

Logan thought it best to ignore them both and continued. "We got to talking. She's a nice girl. Way overweight. Out of shape. Had some rough breaks. She lives nearby. I'm helping her make some changes. That's *it*."

"Ah." Chase read between the lines, his conclusion reached. "A new Frankenstein's monster for you, I see. It has been a while."

"That's cold," Logan said, feeling a bit outwitted. "You want to talk about Frankenstein's monsters? It didn't even take you a New York minute to turn a savvy businesswoman like Amanda into a total spoiled brat. Besides, I prefer to think of it more like the story of the ugly duckling. Women are all beautiful once they realize their potential and live up to it."

"That analogy is *so* much better," Amanda said, chiming in sarcastically, not the least bit offended by the brat reference and more intrigued than ever. "But I don't think I'm buying it."

Logan thought about Holly's ashen face as she sat on the floor in a room full of rented medical equipment that should have been returned over a year ago. He thought about her all alone for nearly two years in an oversized house still full of her dead husband's belongings. He wasn't sure he knew how to share what happened last night with the friends he knew lived such a charmed life. He was troubled by it himself. "This one is different, guys. This one really needed a friend."

It was plain to see the change in Logan's posture. He sounded worried. Amanda could tell right away this was not a normal Logan condition.

"Do you think she could use another one?" Amanda asked sincerely.

"Another friend? I'm not sure she's ready for the likes of you," Logan teased her affectionately.

"None of us were," Chase chimed in, winking at his wife.

Amanda wrinkled her nose in mock annoyance at her husband before turning back to Logan. "Look, if you say she's a recent widow, surely she could use a bit of fun. Why don't you let us give her the royal treatment at Kings Stadium for the night? You usually take in a game when the Red Sox are in town; why don't you bring her along? We'll show her a good time."

Logan considered it for a moment. The Walkers were excellent hosts. And it could serve a dual purpose. Once Amanda met Holly, she would abandon all efforts at trying to see the situation as anything more than what it actually was. Leaving Amanda to let her imagination run wild and come to her own conclusions could end up making him miserable. Besides, Holly could use the opportunity to break free from the confines of that house for a while. "I think it's a great idea. Thanks for the offer."

Amanda quickly turned back to Chase. "Pick a night."

"Saturday," Chase replied, sounding more impatient.

"Oh, and just for the record, one of the last women I dated had a PhD," Logan added.

"More like a Ph *double* D." Amanda couldn't resist one more dig. "And maybe after the game we can do dinner or drinks or something. What do you think, honey?"

Chase had his questions answered and had hit his limit of husbandly indulgence. He needed to pump some iron. He made his way over to the leg press, where Logan was waiting, while switching into borderline-disciplinarian mode. "Fine. Whatever. Logan, tickets will be at the will-call window. Amanda, if you don't stop talking, I'm going to drag you over a weight bench, and it won't be to spot me." After giving her loving husband a tiny smirk, Amanda turned back to the treadmill and kicked it up to a jog. He would have to catch her first. And later on that night, she would make sure he did.

Chapter Eight

LOGAN WAS WAITING FOR HOLLY RIGHT WHERE HE said he would be, outside the stadium entrance nearest the will-call window. He had offered to pick her up, but she told him not to bother. It gave her more time to come to grips with the fact that she was really going out, being social. She wasn't even sure she knew how to do that anymore, not that she was ever really all that good at it to begin with. And she wasn't just going to be social; she was going to be front-and-center, hanging-with-the-in-crowd social. Just the thought was overwhelming and her first instinct had been to politely refuse. But when Logan explained that the invitation was issued because he was late to his most famous client's appointment after falling asleep on her couch, she really didn't see where she had much of a choice. She had woken up the next morning to find herself covered up and alone, convinced she had dreamed the whole night, until she saw she was still wearing her sneakers and found the ice cream spoon in her sink. The memory came flooding back. She had told him nearly every single detail of her sad, pathetic life, short of the most pathetic secret of all. She hadn't married Bruce Brennan because she was deeply in love. She married him because he was the first person who asked, the only person who showed any interest in her at all, and because it enabled her to make her escape. He had been an acceptable means to an end. He was kind and considerate but quirky and a bit of a loner, much like she was. Bruce was a classic left-brained overanalyzer, supremely logical and willing to believe only what he could calculate to a successful conclusion. Even the way he proposed was more like a complex equation of vectors and variables than any heartfelt declaration of love and devotion. When she accepted, it felt like she had just completed a business transaction, but she entered into the binding agreement telling herself they were kindred spirits who would get stronger by leaning on each other. He wasn't overly emotional when he found out about her parents, calmly telling her that her past wasn't nearly as important as their future. When her parents didn't attend their wedding, he married Holly and whisked her away, never mentioning them again unless Holly did, only to remind her that what was ahead of her certainly couldn't be worse than what she'd left behind.

They stumbled awkwardly through life in the beginning but learned to trust, and she could honestly say that love did grow. Maybe not the white-hot, passionate love she read about and saw in the movies, but more of a mild-mannered, dependable coupling. Bruce conducted sex the same way he did everything else—carefully programmed. It was always in bed, always at night, and always a predictable routine that started with several quick openmouthed kisses. What followed was a pattern of synchronized touching; mounting, with a few pants from her and the occasional grunt from him; then release. An underlying sound track of porno music wouldn't have made it exciting.

But they had a steady, respectful, mutual caring that surely would have endured the test of time. However, they weren't afforded the opportunity to put that theory to the test. Instead, he withered and died before Holly's eyes, refusing to leave his care to anyone but her. She would take it to her grave that near the end of his life, she resented Bruce Brennan. Resented him for convincing her that as long as they had each other, they would never need anyone else—then leaving her, more alone than when she started. She resented him for having made her assume the role of his nurse, with all the nonstop mess and anguish that came with it. For lingering on the brink of death as long as he did after he no longer recognized her, having left her behind in the haze of a hospice-approved morphine drip weeks before. She began to blame him. That his illness had resulted in the very things she ran away from—caregiving, death, and having to clean up afterward. The only thing worse was the guilt over the resentment after he was gone.

The internal battle of grief versus guilt raged within her for countless months to follow, allowing her to come to terms with neither. The presence in her house that prevented her from selling it was his ghost, languishing and all-knowing of her inner struggle, reminding her of how she'd failed him. His spirit refused to help her because it knew the truth.

Logan had called her amazing the night he came to her house to save her from eating herself into a coma. Holly wondered just how amazing Logan Montgomery would think she was if he knew those cold hard facts. He would likely tell her that she had received the ul-timate payback for consenting to marry a man under false pretenses and then emotionally deserting him in his final hours. And he'd be right. Karma had bitten her on her big fat ass. She swallowed the tears of self-pity that threatened and shook herself as she walked through the Kings Stadium parking lot.

Holly slowed her pace when she caught sight of him, taking a minute to privately watch him from afar. Logan was wearing carpenter-style jean shorts and a blindingly white hoodie with what she assumed was a Kings T-shirt underneath, and spotless white sneak-ers to match. Of course he wasn't wearing a cap, she mused. It would be unheard of for him to muss up his hair. All in all, he reminded her more of an Abercrom-bie and Fitch model than a guy going to a ball game. *How the hell does he do it?* she wondered. *How the hell does he manage to always look like a million bucks, no matter how casually he's dressed?* The singular adjec-tive that kept popping into Holly's mind was "beautiful." Logan was actually beautiful while remaining wholly masculine.

He was standing on the sidewalk, casually playing with his BlackBerry, the late-afternoon sun glinting off his shiny thick hair. While his head was down, the outline of his profile was nothing short of incredible, with his straight nose and square chin. Holly counted no less than five women who openly gaped as they neared him, several unable to resist looking back after they passed in the hopes he would look up. Several men did, too. Logan was oblivious to it all and kept his attention on his phone, with the occasional scout-around to see if she was coming. When he spied her, he grinned, and with one more push of a button on his phone, he stuck it into one of his pockets. It was showtime.

"I can't believe I'm doing this." She smiled up at him as she approached.

"Come on, let's go have some fun," he replied, grinning back. "I already picked up the tickets."

They casually made their way through the stadium's front gates and began weaving through the maze of fans toward the field level. The Walkers had purchased both an indoor and an outdoor box, so that when their families came to watch, they didn't have to worry about the weather. Chase also enjoyed hosting the families of some of the special-needs children from his favorite charities. Amanda disliked sitting in the seats designated for the players' wives or girlfriends. When they were dating, Chase was sure she was doing it just to tick him off, until he found out she was also a not-so-secret Bleacher Creature and had two foul balls to prove it. Although she alluded to it, he could never get her to confirm if one of those balls was hit by him. She rarely sat upstairs in the luxury suite, and since it was a beautifully cool midsummer evening, Logan wasn't surprised to find that the tickets waiting for him were ten rows up from the first-base line.

Once the surprise at seeing Holly wore off, Amanda liked her immediately. Logan had been right when he said Holly wasn't his type, and that was okay with her. Amanda had gotten used to trying to make conversation with Logan's dates. They were always long, tall drinks of water, phony high-maintenance types who tried too hard to ingratiate themselves to Amanda. They giggled too much, wore too little, and bragged too often. And blond—they were nearly always blondes.

Holly wore almost no makeup, save a little mascara and lip balm. Her dark red hair was pulled back with a headband and she wore jeans with a cotton button-down shirt and loafers. It was painfully obvious Holly hadn't bothered to buy any new clothes since her now forty-five-pound weight loss, so it was hard to discern the details of her shape with her shirt practically swallowing her. Amanda felt like jumping for joy. Surely it meant something that this woman had entered Logan's life.

It took Holly a while to get comfortable with Amanda. After all, Amanda was a pseudocelebrity, and her husband was a bona fide one. Amanda confirmed the superstar wouldn't be meeting up with them until after the game. That was a good thing. It would give Holly some time to get acclimated to the situation. Luckily Amanda was laid-back and cheerful, and instead of inundating Holly with questions, she opted for teaching Holly all about baseball. Holly already knew the basics but took advantage of the opportunity to sit back and let Amanda do all the talking. Amanda was down-to-earth, without any of the pretentiousness Holly had been afraid she might encounter. She refrained from name-dropping and ignored the fact that half the people in the stadium were wearing her last name on the backs of their jerseys and T-shirts. The only indication of who Amanda really was came right before her husband was introduced and ran onto the field. Seated between Amanda and Logan, Holly noticed Amanda suddenly stop her chatter, and with a shy smile, she turned her attention to the field. And then they announced his name and the nearly packed stadium broke out into a deafening roar.

Seeing Chase Walker in person for the first time, there were two things that instantly came to Holly's mind. One: that Chase looked like an adorable little boy, with eyes so piercing and bright, she could see them clearly from her seat. It was impossible not to see them when the first thing he did after high-fiving his fellow Kings players and taking his place was to look in the direction of his wife and smile at her. Two: he was a giant, dwarfing most of the men who stood in line with him as the introductions continued. He was muscle on muscle, with a barrel chest and stocky thighs that reminded her of her own, only his didn't jiggle when he ran. It was an intriguing combination, and Holly found it impossible to look away from him.

He was an imposing figure to say the least, even with his seemingly perpetual easygoing smile. As soon as "The Star-Spangled Banner" was over and the teams went into their respective dugouts, Amanda went back to telling Holly all the ins and outs of the game. Between them, they had a great time watching, even keeping up and filling out the scorecard—all but ignoring Logan, which seemed fine by him. They stopped keeping the book when it became apparent that the Kings were going to lose, even though Chase didn't have a bad outing. When it was over, the three of them waited in the clubhouse for Chase to join them, and he appeared a half hour later. The little boy was gone, replaced by a sandy-haired, perfectly groomed, exceptionally handsome gentleman.

Immediately after kissing his wife and greeting Logan, Chase extended his monstrous and multiskilled hand to Holly and thanked her for coming. He apologized for not making her first Kings experience a winning one. Luckily, he was pulled away by a reporter and Holly was spared having to respond.

When Chase returned several minutes later, Amanda suggested they go out for a bite to eat, someplace quieter, away from the baseball crowd.

Chase instantly admitted he was starving.

They ended up at a local sushi bar, and Holly actually had a good time, once she got past the intimidation of meeting the Golden Boy and the flood of attention that followed them as soon as he was recognized. And to Chase's credit, he made sure she did get past it, showing a genuine interest in her. He knew Toronto, courtesy of the countless road trips the Kings took there, and asked Holly to expand on some of the things he knew about her old hometown. He even complimented the color of her hair, referring to it exotically as "cinnamon" and making her blush.

This didn't go unnoticed by Logan. He felt a pang of something he refused to label as jealousy, which only made him more uneasy. There was just no need for it, no matter how much blushing Holly did. Chase had always been a notorious charmer and had been making women blush since the day Logan met him, including most of Logan's previous girlfriends. It also was no secret that Walker preferred his women with meat on their bones. But he was only interested in his wife's bones, and despite the charisma he couldn't turn off, he had no desire to stray. Besides, Logan had no stake in Holly, other than a professional one. In the end, Logan decided what he was feeling wasn't jealousy at all, but indigestion from a hot dog he consumed during the third inning.

The more relaxed Holly got, the chattier she became. Conversation flowed freely and heated up when Amanda and Holly took the opportunity to gang up on Logan about what a rigid borderline-dictator he was on the job.

"Oh my gosh," Amanda giggled, practically bouncing up and down in her chair with energy. "Do you ever check out his face while he counts your reps? So intense and serious. He looks like a math professor!"

"It's called focus, Amanda. You should try it sometime," Logan shot back.

Holly chimed in. "Amanda, how about when you're just finishing a set, and he sort of yells, 'You got this!'? He usually does it when I'm on an incline bench doing a chest press with a forty-pound barbell over my head. Thank God he's spotting, 'cause it's so startling I almost drop the weight onto my throat."

"*Et tu,* Brute?" Logan sighed at Holly, smiling and shaking his head.

Amanda continued. "Ever tell him something hurts? After he calls you a wimp, he makes sure every exercise incorporates just the part of the body you had the nerve to complain about."

"Holly never complains. That distinction is entirely yours, Mrs. Walker," Logan replied. "And quite frankly, even I'm not sure how to work around the body part called 'everything.'"

"I don't know what either one of you is talking about. Dude is a total punk. After I'm done working out with him, I feel like I've just taken a nap," Chase commented drily, in macho loyalty.

Logan threw his head back and laughed. He was proud to take the ribbing. "I'll remember that next time I hear your hamstring pop."

When they parted ways at the end of the night, Holly thanked everyone for a wonderful time and Amanda immediately invited her to another game as her guest. Holly eagerly accepted and they exchanged numbers. Logan's lips formed a tight line. He had the nagging feeling Amanda was not convinced that Holly was just a client. He worried he may have made a colossal mistake in introducing them. And if Amanda was making plans to take it to the next level, he didn't know where the hell that level was, or worse yet, how to stifle it. Still, he said nothing.

"HOLLY'S ONE STEP FROM DELIGHTFUL, DON'T YOU THINK?" It was really more of a statement than a question.

"It isn't going to work, you know." Chase got right to the point, hours later, exhausted from postplay with his wife in addition to the game itself. He pulled her to him, her naked back snug against his torso, and wrapped his arm around her.

"What do you mean?" Amanda asked, sounding remarkably innocent.

"You know very well what I mean. Stop meddling." His baritone rumbled a stern warning next to her ear, and a chill went up her spine.

"You're starting to sound like Ricky Ricardo. What's next? I'm going to have some esplainin' to do?" She wiggled in against his thighs, fitting to his mold. "Don't worry, Ricky, I won't try to get into the show."

Chase ran his large hand the length of Amanda's thigh to a still-warm round globe and caressed. "That's pretty funny. I remember that show. That Lucy would do some wacky stuff. And we both know what happened to her when Ricky had enough of her nonsense." He gave her a halfhearted, loving smack and she gave him an enchanting giggle before he returned to his point. "The girl is very nice, cute even," Chase said. "But if you insist on doing this, someone is going to get hurt. And it's going to be her. This one's a client for Logan, nothing more."

But Amanda was unfazed and gave Chase a little *tsk-tsk* from her half of his pillow.

"Am I going to have to explain about vehicles to you again?"

"What the hell are you talking about, woman?" Chase yawned, losing interest as soon as she used the word "explain."

"You don't see it. Logan doesn't see it, although he certainly should. He and I believe in a lot of the same principles when it comes to cosmic wheels and karma and such; you know that. Holly probably doesn't even see it. But I do. Oh, I do. All the women he's ever introduced us to have been these walking, talking carbon-copy bombshells. He exchanges them as soon as he tires of them, which I assume is right after he sleeps with them, or once they manage to string a sentence together."

"You were the one who made him bring her along. And you sound almost jealous. Is there something I need to worry about?" Chase possessively tightened his arm around her, more out of habit than concern.

"Of course not, silly. I'm just trying to illustrate for you the higher forces at work here. He meets her on a plane coming back from a trip he didn't really need to be on. He just happens to take her on as a client, even though last I heard, he's been turning down new clients for a year, no matter what your name is or what team you play for. Not to mention, I can't even remember the last time he entertained the thought of training a woman, yet suddenly he's running to her house in the middle of the night on a phone call. He calls her his 'ugly duckling' and somehow makes it sound like a term of endearment."

"He calls all the women he trains ugly ducklings." Chase yawned again, unmoved and unimpressed.

Amanda's eyes grew wide. "I beg your pardon? He called *me* an ugly duckling?" she demanded hotly.

Chase released a small chuckle and kissed the top of her head, deliberately neglecting to outright confirm or deny. "Well now, that would be lunacy. It's a stupid figure of speech, a motivator. Not the best, I'll be the first to admit. He likes to get to the swan part. He's got a thing about birds, I guess. He used to tell me I was a phoenix rising from the ashes. Can we get some sleep now, please?"

"There is a huge difference between those two comparisons, don't you think? One is a mythical sacred firebird, the other an ostracized misfit." She stiffened in his arms, becoming increasingly bothered with each justification her husband made. If Chase thought she was going to let him go to sleep at this particular juncture, he needed to think again.

"He once called Roger Clemens a penguin." Chase yawned again and made the effort to appease her. "That's hardly flattering. Or was it a lemming? That's not even a bird, is it? I can't believe we're having this conversation. I told you I agree that it's stupid."

"You're damn right it's stupid. But even if he does say it, does believe it, what in heaven's name is he waiting for? To start showing her off, I mean. You saw her tonight. Her clothes don't even fit. And I'm not even talking about just a little loose. It looked like two of her could've fit in those jeans."

"Now he's supposed to be her personal shopper?" Chase retorted.

"No, of course not. But he should be encouraging her to unveil herself. Unless of course he has some hidden reason for wanting her to stay all covered up. Especially if, as he says and as you agree, he has no personal stake in any of this. Wouldn't it help her self-esteem and his own cause to show the world how much she's progressed? For crying out loud, did you see that shirt? You couldn't even tell if she had boobs hiding under there."

"There were definitely boobs," was the sleepy burble. "She's probably not thin enough for him yet. Good night, love."

"Excuse me? What the fuck do you mean by that?" Amanda sat up now, fully awake and completely perturbed. She didn't want to believe her friend would deny chemistry on that basis alone. And that her husband would so casually condone it. Chase opened both eyes but remained on his pillow, his tone now humorless.

"Amanda Walker, what's gotten into you? You know I hate the F-word. You're a lady, not a sailor on shore leave. And you are getting way too involved in this. It's none of our business what type of women Logan likes or the fashion statements his clients make. Now, I am bushed, and I really want to get some sleep. Come back here."

But Amanda refused to lie back down, incensed that somehow her own fuller figure might be viewed as substandard by Logan or anyone else. Crossing her arms, she continued to fume. "I can't believe you and I would be friends with someone who refers to women in terms of ugly birds until he waves his magic wand over them. Not thin enough? What a hateful thing to say. Forget *me*. Why would *you* be friends with someone so superficial—"

"That's it." Chase growled and sat up, giving no further warning. Taking his wife's arm, he sent her over his lap with a forceful tug. Despite her one word of protest—"No!"—his strong square hand came down, initiating her second spanking of the night, only this one was for the sake of his sanity and not their mutual pleasure. Amanda felt the difference in his delivery immediately as he peppered her bottom with firm, well-placed swats, indicating he meant business. He fired off a quick scolding—he was no longer interested in analyzing the shortcomings of his friends and was tired of her fussing. As soon as he heard her frustrated acquiescence and tearful plea for him to stop, he helped her sit up beside him. She promptly lay back down, presented him with her back, and scooted over to her side of the king-sized bed, indulging in an offended pout.

Chase quickly followed, turned her around to face him, and silenced any further protest by lowering his lips breathtakingly onto hers, an act that even in her chagrin she responded to with fervor. Minutes later, as he tore his lips away from hers, he shook a weary finger at her. "We don't go to sleep angry. I know you mean well, angel. If you are right about Logan and this girl, then nothing you can do will help or hinder their getting together. Right or wrong?"

"Yes," she begrudgingly admitted, her thoroughly kiss-swollen lower lip still protruding.

"You wouldn't have wanted someone getting this involved in *our* affairs, now, would you?" Chase asked with a worn-out but still fiendishly roguish smile, tracing his thumb across her cheek to check for any stray tears.

"No," Amanda huffed, refusing a total surrender by turning back around, yet allowing him to reposition her into the very spot where their conversation started, snug and secure against him. She murmured under her breath, "But a little push never hurts."

As Chase drifted off to sleep, the last thing he remembered, after thinking his wife had way too much time on her hands, was to tell her, "If anyone knows about pushing, it's you."

Chapter Nine

HOLLY LAY IN BED THAT NIGHT, STARING AT THE ceiling with fingers tightly intertwined across her stomach, a position she had assumed a thousand times before, throughout her childhood and adolescence. When in the darkness, she would pray to God. She would pray to feel the love of the detached unyielding people who created her. She prayed to be understood and appreciated and given a chance to succeed, even if she didn't exactly know what her definition of success was. And daily, without fail, she would ask God to please let her be thin. Not forever, she would pray, just for a few days. Just long enough so that she might know what it's like to bare her midriff, shop for a bikini. To look forward to attending the sort of event that required a sleeveless clingy little black dress, after receiving the countless invitations that were sure to accompany her new willowy figure. To show off her legs in a tight miniskirt with stiletto heels and not look like a moose trying to ice-skate. To have lecherous jerks gawk and stare, not because they were snickering at her rolls of fat, but because they were marveling at her beauty as she gracefully breezed by them without so much as a backward glance. To feel light on her feet as opposed to like a bull in a china shop, lumbering instead of walking. For one stinking day to not have to give a second thought to clothes and scales and judgments. It wasn't too much to ask, and she would give anything back in return.

She knew that prayer by heart, although it had been a long time since she called upon it. Once she married she had been free to abandon it, secure that she had someone by her side who accepted her and then loved her, in spite of and even because of her socially perceived shortcomings. Bruce had never bothered with and was likely incapable of eloquent pronouncements about beauty or desire, but he did tell her he loved her every day with sincere affection. For Holly that was more than enough, and her prayers became ones of gratitude and thankfulness. About three seconds after they lowered him into the ground, she stopped praying altogether.

Thank God she was no longer the praying kind, she thought. After tonight, she wouldn't even know what the hell to ask for.

Holly tried to reconcile the events of the evening. The way things were changing was too radical. Or was it that she'd been living in a state of suspended animation since Bruce's death? Eight years ago, she had been living in the woods in Ontario and could count her social circle on one hand. Twenty months ago, she was virtually alone watching the man she pledged to stand by forever take his last breath. Now she was dining with baseball heroes. A week ago, she didn't even know what a Chase Walker was, and if she'd had to venture a guess, she would have said it was some new fitness craze for geriatrics or a funky alcoholic beverage involving a shot and a beer. She thought back to sitting at the table in the restaurant, how surreal it all seemed. How surreal her life had become since getting on that plane and sitting down next to that man. How Logan was able to make her *feel* again, even if that feeling was intimidation and caution that morphed into admiration. And now she could add disconcertment. There were too many variables she just hadn't counted on.

Originally, Holly thought "personal trainer" was just a polite term for "drill sergeant," a mean-spirited taskmaster whose only goal in life was to try to kill you in the most wretched yet civilized ways possible. It was only your hatred for him that sustained you. When she accepted Logan's proposal, she had been more than willing to hate him. Holly only excelled at hating herself. When she first met Logan, she was sure he would fill the role of hate magnet nicely. It would be like a mutual-torture society. He could hate her imperfections for her, and she could hate everything else. Sure, he was charming and hotter than Lucifer's loincloth. She could consider that a bonus, for the days when she didn't particularly feel like hating anybody.

So he was good-looking. Big deal. Good-looking she could handle. Anyone willing to take out a loan could achieve beauty. Tuck this, suck that, take a bit off here. Change colors on a whim. But character? It had no price tag; no amount of money could buy it. When Logan turned out to be a genuine human being and an all-around nice guy, Holly felt like she'd maybe turned a corner and possibly even made a friend. All he expected of her was that she participate in her own life. She had made the conscious decision when she started training that her best course of action was to just show up, refuse to whine, and focus on staying alive, no matter what atrocities he forced her to endure.

And the simple approach worked better than she ever imagined. Holly learned that she loved the feel of her strength bursting out of her. To have a totally different kind of pain, the kind that, after she gritted her teeth and got through it, would stop. He knew just how to create that pain and at the same time confirm to her that it was worth it. But she hadn't counted on all the touching.

Sweet Jesus, the *touching*. So subtle at first, the strong encouraging hands over hers to help her pump out the last few repetitions in a set, when fatigue began to set in. His hands weren't really pushing the weight for her, but instead, there was almost a transfer of energy from him to her, to help her get it accomplished. He adjusted her shoulders, arms, legs, and sometimes hips to make sure her form was perfect, helping her attain the maximum benefit from the exercises and minimize risk of injury. Holly understood the science behind it. She also understood that it had been a long time since she'd felt a man's touch, and Logan's touch was becoming more and more electrifying. She worked harder and harder to keep her efforts from requiring his assistance. She began to growl and snap when he even pretended he was going to help her finish her set. She tried doing it in a way that sent the message that she was digging down deep for more energy to do it herself, and it usually worked.

There was no way, however, to escape *the stretch*. And after all this time, she still hadn't gotten used to it. In fact, they seemed to last longer, had become more intimate. He never rushed; he would not rest until he was satisfied that Holly's every muscle was given the best chance for a full recovery. It had become the most exquisite torment. The only thing she considered worse than the touching was the stopping of it. He was the meanest drill sergeant Holly had ever met. She endured this agony three times a week and tried like hell not to arrive too early.

She was becoming more and more dependent on his company, no matter how much she fought the touch, an uncomfortable feeling at best. Sitting at that restaurant table tonight, the odd man out at a mini-convention of genetic miracles, was more than she'd bargained for.

Feeling too wound up to sleep, Holly got out of bed and retrieved her laptop. As she got back in bed and powered it up, she tried to remember the last time she'd even turned it on. It had to have been over a week. She was trying to rein in her habit of playing Café World on Facebook. Holly had joined the popular networking site when one of her Canadian friends from work e-mailed her that it was a great way to keep in touch. When Holly stumbled across the virtual restaurant she could create and man, it nearly became an obsession. All the delicious food she could prepare and serve to imaginary patrons held so much appeal. She spent days setting up her perfect little café with just the right ambiance. When she almost missed her gynecologist appointment because she was waiting for her onion soup to finish, she knew she had a borderline problem. She did enjoy keeping up with all her friends back in Toronto though. Maybe she'd spend some time writing a few e-mails. It would be a refreshing change of pace to be able to report some good news. She could tell Tina she had dinner with Chase Walker, with the added benefit of Tina's being unable to overwhelm her with a thousand questions all at once.

Just one peek at the café first. Maybe set up a dish on her stoves that would take several days to cook.

Holly was totally unprepared for what popped up when she logged in to her Facebook account.

She had a friend request. It was from Logan Montgomery. Her gasp was audible.

She was shocked. Why had he even bothered to look her up?

"He probably adds all his clients," Holly said, rationalizing out loud. Still, she hesitated to confirm his invitation. The opportunity to get another glimpse into Logan's personal life was appealing yet dangerous. He was already consuming way too much of her gray matter when she was alone.

Holly clicked on CONFIRM and then went straight to his page.

She was greeted by the familiar smiling face in his profile picture, taken at some sort of party or night-club. He was wearing a navy blue suit, a look she had never seen on him before. She hungrily stared at it, not having to worry that he would catch her marveling at his chiseled perfection. His toffee eyes were so warm they could melt a girl if he kept them on her too long. His dazzling smile was a testament to his never-ending enthusiasm, beckoning for her to join him in it. She already knew she would never build up an adequate immunity to his dimples.

The statuses he posted were all upbeat and encourag-ing, full of self-improvement tips and Zen-like sayings. There was no self-absorbed bragging or blowing of his own horn. None of that was necessary. His wall was teeming with posts from hundreds of "friends" who obviously held him in the highest regard. Athletes ex-pressed gratitude to him for various issues he'd helped see them through; charity leaders thanked him for either time or money donated. Women gushed about how great it was to see him, nearly begging him to "get together again." Each and every post was politely answered by him, graciously confirming that it was his pleasure to be a part of something so worthwhile. That he was glad he could help. That he had a won-derful time as well. That he looked forward to seeing so-and-so again, without ever actually committing to when that would be. She went into his information section and an inadvertent sigh of relief escaped her when it made no mention of any significant relationship status. His religion was "spiritual." His politics were "liberal leaning toward Democrat." He liked popular music and action movies, with a few comedies thrown in. He didn't watch much television. He was well-read, with his favorite books either classics or self-help. She couldn't contain her glee at the discovery that one of his favorite books was *Brave New World*. Jesus, it could have been written about him, with its World State of Alphas and eternal peacefulness and everyone happy. Of course, the similarity ended with the use of soma, as Logan held a clear disdain for any mind-altering drugs in general. Even Holly knew that. Suddenly, it felt like he was in the room with her. Logan Montgomery had successfully entered her bedroom, without even setting foot in it.

With shaking hands, she opened his photo albums and was immediately thankful she was sitting down. With one click of her mouse, she was launched into a plethora of masculine excellence. All stages of Logan were represented. The at-work Logan, as she knew him best. The social Logan, at parties and holidays and sporting events, dressed both casually and in black tie. Lots of the photos had him standing beside celebrities and professional athletes. Holly felt a pang of stalker's guilt when she opened an album of him on vacation in Fiji.

"Holy moly." She exhaled loudly. "That's what's hiding under his clothes?!"

She shamelessly ogled pictures of him on the beach wearing nothing more than a pair of board shorts. For the first and probably only time in her life, she wished a man was wearing a Speedo. She had little doubt Logan would be able to pull off a banana hammock with ease. He was bronze and glistening and defined, with an expansive, smooth chest and clear-cut abs that fed into what Holly just knew was a perfect package. In fact, the way his obliques separated at his hips, it was practically an advertisement leading her to make the assumption. At least that was what Holly told herself to assuage her vulgar musings. Holly's staring began to resemble a game—trying to find one single flaw. Maybe some scar from a booster shot gone bad, some hideous mole with hair growing out of it, a crooked toe, anything to bring him down to her level. There was nothing. She would have to be content believing he had a hairy ass or a testicle that hadn't dropped.

Chase and Amanda were in some of the photos of Fiji as well. Chase looked equally impressive, a few inches taller than Logan and beefier. Amanda, while not exactly thin and covered up a bit more in a one-piece bathing suit with matching sarong, still managed to look like she'd stepped out of *Vogue*. Her long black locks, haphazardly pulled back, only enhanced her heart-shaped face and cobalt eyes.

And then there was the woman.

Holly felt her throat tighten.

She was stunning. Tan, tiny bikini, not an ounce of fat on her, a mane of flaxen flowing hair, round baby-blue eyes. She was Logan's ideal counterpart. They were sitting poolside at a swim-up bar, sharing one of those tropical drinks, the kind that arrives in a giant glass and uses two straws. They looked so perfect together, all smiles and dimples, like they could have been taking the picture for a Sandals beach resort brochure. Holly couldn't even recall the last time she bought a bathing suit. There were pictures of them dressed up at a fancy restaurant, the blond woman's tiny white sequined dress leaving little to the imagination, except maybe how many miles her legs went on for. Logan's unforgettable, tuxedoed handsomeness would encourage any woman's imagination to run wild.

Holly leaned back against her pillows, frowning. Penguin suits were for weddings and awards shows. *Who wears a tuxedo to dinner on vacation? People like Logan Montgomery do.* It probably wasn't even a rental, but tailored to meet his numerous fancy-schmancy needs. But even that wasn't the worst part; she came to the stark realization after she left that photo album and continued to look at his other pictures. There were other women as well, much to her disappointment. Not many, but all with several striking similarities. First, there was enough blond hair represented in the photos to make Holly want to consider a stock purchase in peroxide. But even more unsettling was that all of these blondes were tall and thin and busty. Worse yet, they were as unblemished as Logan was. Except for the would-be supermodel who appeared to have some sort of zit on her chin that her makeup just wasn't covering enough. Probably had PMS and was back to being perfect in a week. Some of the women Holly vaguely remembered seeing somewhere before.

Holly felt her teeth tearing into her lower lip and then

chastised herself. It wasn't fair to be comparing herself to any of these women; no one had asked her to. Not one of her companions tonight had made her feel inferior, especially her friend Logan. The man who always stayed positive, unruffled, who told her she could do anything in a way that made her believe it, that made her feel alive.

Unfortunately, he was also the man who had begun to invade her dreams. And no matter how many times he came running to her in the middle of the night for a hug and a pint of ice cream, he was the man who would never be returning her desire. They were *friends*. It would have to be enough. Holly swallowed the lump in her throat and closed the lid to her computer. She readjusted the pillows and crawled back under the covers. She tried to close her eyes.

Someone to *hate*? Talk about your all-time backfires.

Chapter Ten

TWO DAYS LATER, CHASE SHOWED UP AT LOGAN'S TO train. Amanda was conspicuously absent.

Chase rolled his eyes, mentioned something about a coffee date, and dove right into his workout. Logan didn't push it, but he had a pretty good idea of who could pull Amanda away from her adoring husband. Logan sighed inwardly. Amanda was on a mission. As he spotted for Chase, Logan silently applauded the man. *Next time you have her across your knees, give her one for me,* he wordlessly requested.

AMANDA AND HOLLY WERE SITTING OUTSIDE AT A SMALL wrought-iron table. Without her husband, Amanda received a few passing glances as other people tried unsuccessfully to place her, but their coffee date remained uninterrupted. There was a genuine sincerity to Holly that Amanda was not only comfortable with but drawn to. Holly had a dry wit that made Amanda laugh out loud, and Holly certainly couldn't be accused of trying too hard. In fact, to Amanda, it would appear Holly wasn't trying at all.

But it didn't take Holly long to get caught up in the excitement that surrounded Amanda in everything she did. It seemed Amanda had the perfect life and was smart enough to appreciate it. And she wasn't skin and bones. Amanda's figure was one step past robust. While it couldn't be denied that she was beautiful, there was a natural grace that came from the total acceptance she had of herself. Holly wondered if it was something Amanda always had or if it was a recent development. Chase Walker sweeping you off your feet would be enough to give any woman confidence, for sure, but didn't you need confidence in the first place to attract a man like Chase Walker? It was like the self-esteem version of the question "Which came first, the chicken or the egg?"

Holly and Amanda had met at a local Starbucks and talked awhile, about everything from Bruce to Chase and the leaked video that revealed the Walkers as spanking enthusiasts. Holly had seen the tape, but only a few days earlier, when she followed a link to YouTube and without any fanfare became a voyeur looking into a couple's personal life. It wasn't just a pat or two, but more than a dozen meaningful swats to Amanda's upturned denim-clad backside. It started with their walking into view, Amanda purposefully nudging him with her shoulder as they strode. Chase lurched forward exaggeratedly, as if she had launched him with the strength of an Amazon, and he turned back to her, wagging a playful finger in her direction. Amanda returned the gesture by grabbing the offending finger in one hand and poking him in the chest with the other while laughing. Chase took a quick look around and in the next instant, he grabbed her. Bending her at the waist and pulling her neatly to his side, he suspended her several inches in the air and effectively rendered his sentence. Without any sound and with Amanda's feet swaying, it could have been interpreted as an assault. Until he returned her to the ground and she stood back up. The only thing violent after that was the way she grabbed the lapels of his jacket to yank him to her as he leaned her up against the wall in the empty but brightly lit underground tunnel. There was nothing even remotely resembling violence in the way Chase automatically placed his hand between Amanda's head and the concrete wall to protect her before the force of his kiss jolted them both. The minute-and-forty-five-second-long tape concluded with Chase's abruptly drawing away, grabbing her hand, and taking one of those big meaningful steps toward the nearest exit. He was stopped by a gentle pull in the opposing direction as Amanda rose on her tiptoes to bring her lips to his again. He kissed her one more time and they practically ran out of camera view. It was innocent and honest and heart-meltingly sincere. Holly watched it multiple times, spellbound, and feeling guilty for wishing she could have heard the dialogue. In the end she was convinced it couldn't have been filmed better for a movie. All the elements were there. Chase: the dashing, larger-than-life would-be hero. So comfortable in his own skin, confident in taking charge, but immediately yielding to her subtlest of urges. Amanda: the beautiful damsel who obviously reveled in Chase's attention and boldly maneuvered the situation to escalate it to its ultimate ending. There was indisputable adoration evident on both of their faces as they went from playful to passionate. The emotions displayed during the whole exchange were palpable. All caught on tape by a nondescript, tiny black ball on the wall next to a sprinkler. It was distributed by a creep working the night shift who wanted to make a little quick cash. Even the quality and lighting and angles were perfect. It was as if it was meant to be.

"Of course they tried to edit out everything past the spanking, in the name of journalism. More like ratings," Amanda huffed with an indignant wave of her hand, sitting straight up in her chair and leaning forward, closer to Holly. She had never really spoken about the incident at length with anyone, beyond what she was programmed to say by public relations advisers on retainer. But with Holly, Amanda felt safe. Holly was getting to know Amanda now, after Amanda had lived through it and grown from it. Everyone else had witnessed the meltdown, and since then, Amanda had spent the majority of her time with Chase.

"But people found it so damn romantic; it sort of took on a life of its own. We got a lot of mail saying that folks were tired of being force-fed scandals. That Chase had never been anything but a perfect role model to kids and grown-ups alike, and it was a disgrace that people were trying to make him look like a batterer at worst and a pervert at best. We got a lot of support, even if we are a little kinky. That's why we don't fight so hard to get it pulled off the Internet." Amanda couldn't hold back the subsequent giggle. "And it was awfully romantic. Seeing it, you know? Not that I thought it at the time. Chase really has a romantic streak a mile long. He also just happens to be one of those old-fashioned Neanderthal types who really enjoys whacking ass. But he even does that in this romantic, I-care-about-you-so-much way. No one was more surprised than me. He tapped into a part of my sexuality I didn't even know existed. I'm not sure I can explain it. The feel of him getting turned on while I'm over his lap squirming and wiggling is a total rush. My only regret was taking off, leaving him to clean the mess up alone." Amanda paused, thoughtful, and then sighed. "I was just so ashamed, not by Chase per se, but by the violation of our privacy, something I felt he should have been more careful to protect. I mean, I was nobody. The only reason it was news was because it was Chase. I wanted to blame him for not knowing we were someplace where we could be seen. I couldn't bear the thought of people judging me. Of making a twisted joke out of a relationship I was just getting used to navigating. He told me he would take care of it, and he did. I should have just trusted him."

"But it wasn't about him and you at that point," Holly reminded her. "You said yourself, it had taken on a life of its own. I read some of the comments on that

YouTube clip, and most of those folks were downright creepy."

Amanda leaned back into her chair, shrugging. "That's what helped me get over it actually. Have you ever seen some of the shit you can find on the Web? Don't even get me started on all the women who began to harass Chase about their willingness to take my place. He got e-mails and offers that made him sick to his stomach. And he's hardly a choirboy. Chicks wanting him to do the most outlandish and perverse things to them. Once I realized the broad spectrum of depravity out there, I figured we were actually pretty normal and tame. That is, after I got over the horror of thinking strangers were going to point at me and laugh."

Getting laughed at. I feel like that all the time, Holly thought, secretly amazed and relieved that she really did have something in common with someone like Amanda. Of course, that was where the similarities ended. From just watching that video, it was easy to see that Amanda knew passion, in every sense of the word, something that was as foreign to Holly as attractiveness. She would have loved to learn more, but to question the woman on her sex life would be tacky, regardless of how willing Amanda was to talk about it.

"Still, it had to have been hard," Holly said slowly. "I felt intimidated just by the people looking at us having dinner the other night, and I knew they weren't looking at me. But then again, I'm not much of a people person to begin with. Eventually I may have to make some changes and at least find some work, for mental health reasons if not financial ones. Luckily, I have the luxury of some time, and I plan on taking more of it. Not that I really have much of a choice. I can't see anyone hiring me any time soon. I've been out of the work loop for a long time, not to mention my social graces are sorely lacking."

"Don't sell yourself short, Holly," Amanda told her with sincere empathy. "I've never experienced such a loss; just the thought of something happening to Chase could throw me into a panic. You don't bounce back from something so awful overnight."

"I appreciate your compassion, but I should probably tell you, I gave up on people after I became a widow."

"That's a bunch of crap," Amanda replied, waving her hand again. "I would never find myself so at ease with a social leper. You're recovering from a horrible life-altering experience. It takes time. And you're not running for office or in a popularity contest, so why should you go one step out of your way to make jerks like you? We're a lot alike, you know. Choosy about who we let in. There's nothing wrong with it. I just have to put up a better front of friendliness because of my husband. I only have a few real friends. Once I let Chase win me over, a lot of my friends wandered off. Some were jealous; some just got on with their own lives."

"And some people just suck," Holly added.

"True enough!" Amanda laughed and then casually segued to the next topic. "But even Chase is careful about who he lets get really close to him. Sure, he's outgoing and a team player and has a lot of people who answer to him, but he's been burned a few times. Aside from me and our families, the only person he really trusts is Logan."

Holly's posture changed. Her eyes widened and she looked down at her own hand, nervously playing with the plastic lid on her coffee cup. Bingo.

The mere mention of his name started giving Holly butterflies. Deep down inside, in places she'd never had them before. Places she never knew existed. She had no business having butterflies anywhere when it came to the likes of Logan. But Holly didn't want to pretend she felt nothing about Logan anymore. She wanted to explore the crush, learn everything there was to know about him. Even the things that would hurt to find out, like his obvious preference for tall skinny blondes. She wanted to share the giddy rush she got just hearing his name spoken out loud. And if anyone could shed some light on the man who was boggling her mind, it was Amanda. But could Amanda be trusted, or would she demolish the fantasy by telling Holly she should set her sights elsewhere?

"He really is a great trainer." Holly's inadvertent sigh of longing escaped, poorly hidden in a statement that had no bearing on the conversation.

Amanda pretended she didn't notice. "He's the best out there. He continues learning. He's forgotten more than most trainers will ever know. He's got this holistic approach that athletes just thrive on. He could be booked twenty-four hours a day if he wanted to be. He must have really seen something in you if he took you on. He hasn't been willing to fit in a new client in forever!"

"Really?" Holly asked, a bit bewildered yet unable to stop a smile from forming at the thought that Logan actually may have lied to her to get her to work with him. "When I met him and he offered up his service, he told me he was trying to drum up business."

"Drum up business? He hasn't had to solicit new business in years!" Amanda practically squealed with amusement. "See? Like I said, he must have really seen something in you. And he must have been right by the looks of you. At least I'm guessing he's right. I mean, no offense, but your clothes look like you stole them off a hobo. They don't even look like they belong to you."

"I-I know," Holly stammered, looking down again, but this time at her old worn-out clothes. "I didn't think it was worth getting new stuff yet. I still have so much farther to go."

"That may be true, but guess what, Holly? We're all works in progress. You should be willing to reward yourself for your effort *today*. What are you waiting for? Besides, you're paying good money for all this training; it's almost an insult to both you and Logan to not show off the results."

"I don't even know where to start," Holly confessed sheepishly, unwilling to tell Amanda her latest shopping trip was to Target, where she spent twenty-five dollars on a T-shirt and gym pants and thirty-five dollars on paper goods. "I don't think I'm even used to this body yet."

Amanda smiled, satisfied her plan had come together so nicely with almost no effort. "Well, that's the good thing about shopping. You can keep doing it 'til you get it right. Come to think of it, I could use a bit of practice myself."

Holly returned the smile. Amanda was right; the time had come. And who better to spend the day shopping with? Amanda had great style and was hardly so skinny that she'd look good in *everything*. She could help Holly take her new figure out for a spin.

Holly was ready for the change. Unfortunately, Logan was not.

When Holly came into the gym the next day, not only was she sporting a new bobbed haircut, but the sweatpants and too-big T-shirt were gone, replaced by the latest workout clothes. The flared spandex pants hugged her waist and behind; the form-fitting white Nike tee commanded JUST DO IT in neon green and revealed an impressive bust. Where she was once shapeless and undefined, an hourglass figure had begun to take its place. He was momentarily taken aback. Then he had to keep himself from becoming engrossed in it.

"Excuse me, miss," he teased when she bounded through the door and jumped on a treadmill after dropping a duffel bag on the floor, "but this is a private gym and I already have a client in this time slot."

"Knock it off, Logan," she told him, flushing with discomfort and feeling more idiotic than attractive. She turned on the treadmill to begin a quick warm-up.

"What are you talking about?" he responded energetically, making a concerted effort to keep eye contact and failing, his gaze drifting back to her chest. "Holly, you look spectacular, although I really pictured you as more of an Adidas girl. I like the new hair. What's with the bag? Are we going to have another towel debate?"

"I'm going to shower real quick here tonight, if that's all right. Amanda and I are going to the stadium to catch the game. It'll save me a few minutes."

"Of course it's fine," he said, more churlish than he would have liked, although she didn't notice.

Logan was miffed and couldn't for the life of him figure out why. Sure, he knew his program would pay off. He had seen the results on the scale every week. Still, he was taken off guard by the change. Maybe because he hadn't authorized the upgrade. Maybe because he had a pretty good idea of who was behind it. Odds were it wasn't Holly.

But this was *his* job, *his* objective being achieved. Why should he care who encouraged Holly to branch out and fully embrace the fruits of her labor? Still, it took real effort for him to not show any outward disgruntlement.

Logan never dreamed Holly's session would slowly turn into his own personal hell. It wasn't just because of her now prominently displayed breasts. Without the benefit of the oversized sweats and shirt, each time Holly moved, he watched seemingly placid flesh twitch as distinctive muscle took its place. She was wonderfully proportioned, something the T-shirts and sweatpants had successfully camouflaged. Her backside was tantalizing and heart shaped.

Holly pulled and stretched and grunted, her focus completely on the exercises he put before her, ignorant to his newfound fascination with her. The guttural sounds that escaped from deep within Holly as she summoned the strength to lift weights in a set now began sounding more sensual. Sweat soaked through the shirt, down her back, and between her legs. Hair that was no longer concealed in a ponytail fell free in dampened disarray.

It was worse than any aphrodisiac. Reacting to Holly was unexpected. He would have to get his testosterone in check.

Still, he couldn't help but be proud of her. This was a victory they had every right to share, wasn't it?

When Amanda came into the gym near the end of Holly's workout, Logan felt himself becoming annoyed all over again. He took a quick look at the clock on the wall.

"You want a stretch? I can see your date is here," he said to Holly, nodding his head in the direction of the door. They both looked to the entrance and waved at Amanda.

"I feel pretty good," Holly replied, grabbing her bag off the floor and heading toward the changing room. "I can stretch myself out tomorrow. I'll be right out," she called over her shoulder.

Logan felt his jaw start to clench, deliberating whether he was pissed off at Holly's cavalier departure from an important element of her workout or relieved that she would be leaving that much quicker and he wouldn't have to touch her.

"Doesn't Holly look great, Logan?" Amanda remarked as the door closed, forcing him to end his internal debate before its final conclusion.

He narrowed his eyes in Amanda's direction. "If you work the program, the program works, Amanda. You know that."

"You know, you really do have a phrase for everything," she laughingly replied, and then added, "I know you're a professional and all that, but I really expected you to show a bit more enthusiasm. You have to admit, the haircut alone is pretty astounding. You should have seen the glee on the face of my hairdresser when he started hacking off all those dead ends. Care to join us?"

"I can't take in a game tonight," he told her, starting to return all the weights Holly used during her session to their designated spots. "I have another client tonight and a six o'clock tomorrow morning."

Amanda didn't bother to mask her disappointment. "Come on, we'll have you home by midnight. We won't even go out to eat, I promise."

"I just told you, I have another client in fifteen minutes," he said curtly.

"You can meet up with us after."

"Sorry, kid, I can't tonight," he told her testily, grabbing the towels and cleaner spray bottle from where he kept them and beginning to wipe down the equipment Holly had used.

"If you insist," Amanda said with a sigh, then tried a different tactic. "Maybe we'll go out after with one of the guys from the team."

"Just remember," Logan said, pointing to the door, "your new friend in there isn't used to being the center of attention. You may not want to throw her into the deep end too quickly."

He had reacted and she didn't miss it. Amanda smiled sweetly. "Oh, Logan, don't be silly. I'm not going to throw her anywhere. I just want to introduce her to some of the guys on the team. Unless, of course, you think that's a bad idea. Or you mind."

"Why would I mind?" Logan said a little too quickly. "Unless you're really up to something."

"What would I be up to?" Amanda asked, following behind him as he saw to his task.

"Oh, I don't know, trying to make me jealous maybe?" he stated simply, spraying a weight bench with disinfectant and promptly wiping it clean.

"You're not the jealous type, remember?"

Logan stopped what he was doing and took a quick look at the changing-room door to make sure Holly was still securely inside. He took a step closer to Amanda, his voice lowering. "Maybe because of the not-so-subtle makeover attempt?"

Amanda managed to look aghast but was secretly overjoyed. He had noticed. "That almost sounds like this is about you. Sorry to rain on your *My Fair Lady* parade, but you'd have to agree—it's time for Holly to start living again in the real world, and I just thought the sooner the better. And what makeover? Some gym clothes that fit, and a much-needed haircut?"

Logan went back to what he was doing, afraid she was getting too close to the truth. "You forget. I know you. It's something you would do hoping to get a reaction out of me."

"Did it work?" she asked, blatantly hopeful.

Logan went back to cleaning weight equipment. If

Amanda even sensed his recent inner turmoil there would be no stopping her.

"I just don't want you filling her head with ideas that aren't going to happen," he said, refusing to answer the question.

"Thanks for the clarification. My mistake. I'm glad you won't mind," Amanda said, going over to the closed door and giving it a loud knock. "Come on, Holly! If we get out of here soon we can wander around near the field during the batting warm-ups!"

"Why would I mind?" he muttered, realizing he was repeating himself. He tried to cover it up with an overly casual, "Just do us all a favor: please keep her away from Aaron McAllister. He's got more notches on his bedpost than Hugh Hefner. I don't want to see her hurt, or needing a round of penicillin."

"Eww. That's so weird, Chase said the same thing. Not that either one of you had to. You can read 'creeper' written all over Aaron's face from the minute he says hello. I was thinking more along the lines of Troy Miller. Recently divorced, kind of shy and reserved. He's terribly cute, and if I remember correctly, his ex-wife was the crunchy-granola-earth-mother type."

"Which is the nice way of saying she isn't a super-model. Ever think maybe that's *why* he's divorced?" Logan said with a jeer. "Maybe Troy realized he could trade up."

It was Amanda's turn to narrow her eyes. "And you realize how shallow that sounds, right, Logan? I'm going to pretend you didn't say it and attribute your bad manners to my badgering you. Or maybe you realize that Troy might actually be interested in someone like Holly and you're just trying to convince yourself that Holly isn't really all that attractive."

He had the decency to look ashamed. "Go with door number one and consider yourself on my last nerve. It was a rotten thing to say. I admit it. But I'm starting to feel smothered by your best intentions. Holly's my friend. Why can't that be enough for you?"

"Because deep down inside, I know it's not enough for you," Amanda told him, supremely confident. "You're just too stubborn to admit it."

"I'm stubborn? I guess I should take your word for it. You are the walking definition," Logan said, hating that for all intents and purposes, her plan had worked. The last hour was the proof. "I realize you think you're helping me here, but please, Amanda, I'm begging you. Just let it be."

The answer to his plea came with the opening of the changing-room door. Holly stepped out, wearing white jeans with a lilac-colored baby-doll shirt and strappy wedge sandals. The pants were snug, clinging to her thighs and hips without gaps or bulges or panty lines. The shirt, with its little puffs at the shoulders, exposed her now well-toned arms and encased and enhanced her ample breasts before cutting in just below them and flaring out over her newly indented waistline. The familiar scent of CK One that normally surrounded her was replaced with an expensive perfume that was lighter, fresher, and sexier and seemed to magically waft from where she was standing to his nostrils in record time. Her newly cut bob was gelled back and still wet-looking, making her eyes look like shiny emeralds. Her pretty lips glistened with a touch of gloss. She gave Amanda and Logan a shaky smile. "I'm ready to go."

Logan swallowed hard, tried to ignore the movement in his groin, and mentally ran through the list of women's numbers in his BlackBerry he'd start calling as soon as his last client left.

He told them to have a good time.

Chapter Eleven

AMANDA WAS RELENTLESS. SHE THREW HOLLY AND Logan together whenever she could. Kings games, dinners, the theater. Logan decided early on that as long as he didn't pick Holly up, pay her tab every time, and take her home or kiss her good night, it wasn't a date.

And truth be told, Holly was an excellent companion. She even broke up the tedium of Chase and Amanda's public displays of affection, often joining him in covert grumblings of shared irritation at their sappiness. But the more Amanda worked her angle, the more Logan found himself acting as chauffeur, and the more he did pay the bill. And the more he thought about what it would be like to end the evenings with his lips locked on Holly's.

Logan started calling out of the blue to invite Holly to movies and walks and sometimes just to check in on how her day went. It seemed so natural, the ebb and flow of their daily routines meshing together around their common goal. Holly was always happy to hear from him and she never burdened him with drama or endless transparent flirtations. She didn't really know much about sports, other than her limited knowledge of the Kings, but she didn't mind learning about them either. She did know quite a bit about hockey, citing that an appreciation of ice hockey was any good Canadian's duty. She was willing to experience anything he suggested with a childlike wonder. It was like having a guy friend, except every now and then, he thought about what it would be like to have sex with her, since by the end of her training sessions he had begun to picture her naked. It was taking more of his concentration to get through her stretches. As soon as she obediently got down onto the mat, he could almost hear her body, firmer now and better proportioned, warm and glistening from her exertions, calling out for his touch.

Her sweat-saturated hair began to paint a picture in his imagination of how she might look after having been voraciously sexed up or just getting out of the shower. It became a struggle to keep his eyes from wandering to the perfectly shaped triangle of moisture that had built up between her legs and now seemed to invite him to bury his face there.

The rationale to his unprofessionalism and obsession was simple, Logan told himself. Holly was the first woman he'd allowed into his life who didn't want him, sexually or otherwise. There were no catches or hidden agendas. She was perfectly content with his mentoring and friendship. And it was a friendship that he thoroughly enjoyed, although he wasn't used to it. It added an allure to her that he was sure he could learn to ignore. He just had to wait it out.

It was a Thursday night in early September. Chase was enjoying a night off and invited Logan to join him and Amanda at a local pub near their home to shoot some pool and have a few beers. The tavern was small and intimate, with an outdated pinball machine in the corner and a jukebox filled with songs that spanned decades beside it. A well-worn dartboard hung on a wall. A pool table took up nearly half the space in the tavern. There were five small tables just beyond the entrance and a bar with about twenty stools that ran along it. Although clean and tidy, there was no mistaking it: McDuff's was a dive that always carried with it the faint scent of a keg having recently been dumped over and mopped up. The Walkers had been going there since stumbling across it by accident after moving into the mansion Chase had custom-built three years ago. A scouting expedition, as Chase would call them, the random, destinationless drives he would take whenever he had a few days in a new town. He would rent a car and forgo the use of a GPS, get in it, and drive, satisfying his wanderlust and occasional need for solitude. In his car he was guaranteed the privacy he sometimes craved but couldn't always attain. Once Amanda began to join him on the road, she would ride shotgun and together they would venture out to explore all the tucked-away nooks and crannies the world had to offer. When they found McDuff's after pulling into its empty parking lot one evening to escape a sudden torrential downpour, it was like discovering an oasis. He and Amanda spent several hours that night chatting up the owner, who remained tight-lipped about their sudden appearance, except to strongly suggest to his regulars that they do the same. It became the go-to place where they could escape Chase's celebrity status and still go out and relax.

If Chase was terribly surprised when Logan came through the door with Holly in tow, he didn't show it. He looked briefly to his wife, who bestowed on him a gloating smile.

"Well, that just saved me a phone call," Amanda whispered to Chase as they approached, confident he wouldn't be able to reprimand her before Logan and Holly joined them.

"Don't start," Chase mouthed in reply before smiling at the couple. "There he is. Hi, Holly, he talked you into slumming it tonight?"

"Oh, I don't know," Holly responded, setting her purse on the bar and taking a quick look around, liking what she saw. "This place has a down-home feeling I could learn to love."

Amanda seized the moment immediately. "See, Logan? Not every girl needs to be stepping out of a limo in the high-rent district."

"Yes, Amanda." Logan sighed and threw in an exaggerated look heavenward. "You prove it to me time and time again. And just when I thought the last perfect girl was taken. To think, there I was, getting ready to ask Chase if we could have you cloned."

"Not on your life, dude." Chase wrapped an overprotective arm around his wife's shoulder and pulled her to him, planting a kiss on her forehead. "There are just some things that are one of a kind and aren't meant to be shared."

"Right back at you, babe," Amanda replied, leaning into him.

"Not to mention, I can barely keep up with the antics of one; can you imagine the kind of havoc a carbon copy of her would create?" Chase added, kissing her again.

Amanda playfully slapped her husband in his midsection. "You would somehow find a way to marry us both."

"She's right, you know," Logan said in agreement, looking to Holly. "It would probably kill him, but he would find a way."

Chase finally relinquished his grip on his wife and reached for his beer. "But what a way to go, my friends, what a way to go."

"I think if you took them both to Utah, you might be able to make it happen," Holly said, feeling like the fourth wheel on a tricycle but wanting to say something. Once again she had been reminded that even though Logan had a perfectly good woman accompanying him, he'd rather create a clone more in keeping with his good taste.

Nervous laughter followed by uncomfortable silence hung heavy in the air.

"Logan? You up for looking stupid at pool?" Amanda said, sensing the general discomfort. "Holly, you play? We could play doubles."

"I don't," Holly admitted. "I mean, I'll try, but I'm really more of a liability."

"That settles that," Chase said gallantly, smiling furtively at his wife. "I'm going to sit this one out, too. But I'll take winner."

Amanda blinked up at him, wide-eyed and innocent-looking; returned his smile with a coy one of her own; and leaned into him to place her lips on his. "Keep an eye on him, Holly," she said after pulling back, never taking her eyes off her husband's. Amanda gave Chase a little wink before turning and sashaying her way across the room. Logan rolled his eyes briefly at Holly and mimicked the motion of sticking his finger down his throat at yet another public display of affection that they were forced to bear witness to. He turned to join Amanda at the pool table.

Holly and Chase were left at the end of the bar. A few other patrons were scattered about, but all of them knew Chase as a regular and after having greeted him upon his arrival, were inclined to give him some space. Chase and Holly leaned against the bar, watching Logan and Amanda try to psych each other out as she racked the balls on the pool table and he chalked up a pool stick.

"It's all going to be okay, you know," Chase said quietly, seemingly to no one in particular.

"Oh, I know," Holly turned her head and told him quickly, wishing they could drop the conversation before it even started, afraid of even taking a guess as to the underlying meaning of Chase's vague statement.

Chase continued in the same quiet tone, outwardly

fixated on the game taking place twenty feet away. "I see the way you look at him now. When you're sure he isn't watching."

"Is it that obvious?" she asked, her face clouding over with trepidation. What he was talking about became crystal clear and a new, much bigger problem presented itself. She was now more worried that if Chase could tell so easily, she was no longer any good at hiding it.

He turned to her and smiled, piercing sea-green eyes alight with knowing. "It is to me. So different from the girl I first met last summer. But then again, that girl is different in a lot of ways now, isn't she?"

Holly felt herself blushing under his warm gaze and was thankful for the bar's dim lighting. Chase was so handsome yet different from Logan. It was an approachable attractiveness that in the beginning Holly was able to work up a resistance to after her initial curiosity with him. It would have been easy for him to be conceited, but she was surprised to find he was gentle and unassuming, conscious of everything going on around him. She had spent so much time in his presence these last several months, and she had been careful never to view him as anything more than her new friend's adoring husband, but now, with Chase's focus and attention solely on her, Holly had no choice but to acknowledge him. And with his appealing, knowing smile came a stark realization. He wasn't just making small talk and he wasn't trying to pry; he just totally understood her predicament. Everything she had heard from Amanda and read and witnessed from a safe distance was true. Chase was open-minded, caring, and a true romantic at heart. That if Holly lied to him about where he wanted to take this conversation, he would be disappointed with her. And for reasons she couldn't even fathom, she didn't want to disappoint him.

"But change is good, isn't it?" She tried to sound confident, bringing her beer up to her mouth.

"Of course, especially when it comes to doing something for your health." Chase willingly agreed, turning his attention back to the pool table for a moment just as Amanda was calling an across-the-table shot. He watched her bend over to line up her aim, her generous round backside in his direct line of view. As if she felt his gaze upon her, Amanda gave a discreet look over her shoulder, made eye contact with him, and with the tiniest upturn of her full lips, pulled back the cue. As soon as Amanda neatly made the shot, Chase turned his attention back to Holly, his patented boyish grin in place. "Sorry about that. She knows watching her play pool makes me crazy. She is so in for it when I get her home."

Holly felt a new warmth rise to her cheeks, but this one from his direct implication. Holly wasn't sure if he meant Amanda would later find herself across his knees, or thoroughly ravished, or both. It was still a strange feeling to Holly, knowing such a detail about Chase and Amanda's private life, despite the fact that he seemed to have no trouble casually referencing it. Holly wondered if the comment was Chase's way of making sure that his current personal interest in Holly was in no way a blurring of boundaries. And if she was correct, she could certainly see the reasoning behind it.

Chase probably had someone falling in love with him a hundred times a day; his natural way of caring about people combined with his good looks was easy to misconstrue. But it was obvious that Chase Walker was a one-woman man. Holly felt a twinge of envy. Amanda had this man openly confessing that she drove him to the brink of insanity.

"The only person I ever managed to make crazy was myself," Holly murmured.

Chase let loose a laugh. "Good one. Amanda keeps telling me you're hilarious."

"What has Logan told you?" she blurted out, her eyes darting briefly to the pool table and back. She figured that if the proverbial jig was already up, she could drop the whole nonchalance routine.

Chase stopped laughing but his smile remained. He crossed his arms against his hulking chest.

"Ah. Yes. Logan. What has Logan told me? I guess the real question would have to be, what hasn't he told me?" he wondered aloud.

Holly immediately regretted asking the question and attempted to take her words back. "I don't mean to stick you in an awkward position, Chase. He's your friend. You have no loyalty to me. Forget I asked."

"Now, hold on a minute, little lady. You're not even letting me answer the question," Chase drawled, turning his back on the game, sitting down on a stool, and leaning his elbows on the bar. Holly followed suit and Chase gave a quick wave of his bottle to Glen, the bartender, indicating they were ready for fresh beers. Glen was a mild-mannered, pleasant-looking blue-collar type in his early thirties, sporting several tattoos and friendly blue eyes. He took care of the Walkers and Logan for their tips, not for their celebrity status. It was only a matter of seconds before four fresh bottles were set down in front of them.

"I'll leave these other two unopened, Chase," Glen told them, opening two of the bottles and making direct eye contact with Holly, giving her a smile and a nod. "In case they get warm before Amanda and Logan are ready for them and you want to switch them out."

"Thanks, Glen," Chase replied, laying a fifty on the bar.

"I've known Logan for almost half my life," Chase said thoughtfully after the bartender brought over his change and wandered away from earshot. He took a sip out of his new bottle. "Certainly the best parts. Not sure if I could have gone the distance without him. We have a lot in common. We enjoy seeing the results that come with hard work. We know we've been blessed in our lives and that we're the only ones who can be responsible for our own happiness."

"That's a good way to be," Holly replied, taking a swig of her beer, thinking how easy that way of thinking must be when everything goes your way.

"Of course, it's easy to take that approach when you have a lot of good luck," Chase said, appearing to have read her mind. "But I'm not totally convinced that one doesn't automatically follow the other. If you're willing to roll with the punches, you find you get punched less."

"What is it with all you overachievers and your inspirational phrases?" Holly asked impulsively after taking another long swallow from her beer. She had never been big on alcohol, food always having been her vice of choice. It didn't take much to make her feel bolder.

"Uh-oh." Chase laughed, taking note of her now-half-empty bottle and her newly found cynicism. "Are we going to have to worry about you growing a pair of whiskey muscles and throwing down?"

"No." Holly drained the bottle and set it on the bar, fighting the painful belch that drinking the brew so fast created. "I just think you two must have spent a great deal of time reading Deepak Chopra or Tony Robbins."

"Well, Logan and I did take a philosophy course together at UCI, but I didn't really think I was paying all that much attention," Chase mused.

"What happened, you jocks needed a few liberal arts credits?"

"Actually, I think I lost a bet. Or he dared me to become enlightened. Maybe both. At any rate, I'm pretty sure I aced the course, probably with his help. My approach to life has always been a lot simpler than Logan's. I've always been a 'go big or go home' sort of guy. See it, identify it, and deal with it. He's always been a bit more cerebral." He pointed to one of the unopened bottles on the bar, and not bothering to wait for Holly's response, he twisted the cap off and set the bottle in front of her.

"Now, that I believe," she remarked, making no move to reach for the bottle.

"Except for the 'no pain, no gain' theory," Chase said, finishing off his beer and opening the other bottle left on the bar for himself. "We're both subscribers to that one."

"That one doesn't surprise me either," Holly told him drily.

"I like to think we strike a good balance with each other."

"And I always figured you two were cut from the same cloth." Holly reached for her fresh beer. She had said too much, the result of trying too hard, and was one snarky comment away from insulting the man. Her only hope was to blame being drunk.

But Chase didn't appear on the verge of being offended. He looked at her kindly for a minute and then said, "About some things, maybe. Not everything."

"Like what?" Holly asked. She wanted to know.

"Like women." He smiled at her again. "And that's probably half your problem."

"I don't understand," she told him, confident they were getting to the meat-and-potatoes part of their conversation. All the things she didn't think she could bear hearing. She resisted the sudden urge to start guzzling her beer.

Chase paused, and Holly could tell he was giving some thought to what he was going to say. "Before I met Amanda, I was with a lot of women. I figured it was expected of me, sort of like it came with the job."

And that's so different from Logan, she thought sarcastically, remembering the various beauties she saw in Logan's Facebook pictures. Not that her memory had to go into overdrive—she had been visiting his page daily to torture herself and knew every single one of his pictures by heart.

Chase continued. "But each woman I met, or hooked

up with, had a unique specialness. It wasn't always about instant attraction. Of course, I had to be attracted in some way, but the definition of that was broad. She didn't have to look a particular way, fit a certain mold."

"I think the word you're looking for is 'type.' It's okay, Chase, you can say it," Holly told him, feeling an awful grinding in her stomach. It wasn't from alcohol.

"Okay. Type. I didn't have one. The only type that mattered to me was the type of mood I was in. Logan? Not so much. It was always a certain type of look that caught his attention, and for as long as I've known him, he hasn't strayed from it."

"And I'm not it," Holly said sadly, beginning to pick at the label on her Coors Light.

"No. You're not," Chase told her gently, and then said, "But it's that very fact that has me so curious."

"Really?" She stopped toying with the bottle and looked back up at Chase, hopeful. "How so?"

"You're here, aren't you?" he asked her meaning-fully. "I certainly didn't tell him to bring you. I just called a friend and asked if he wanted to join us for a beer. Not that your company isn't always a welcome addition," Chase added with a grin.

"And you think that means something?" Holly couldn't help grinning back, brightening. Logan *had* called her on the spur of the moment, asking her if she'd like to tag along. It wasn't like they already had a plan.

"I'm not really sure," he told her truthfully. "I know how fond Amanda's become of you, and that a lot of the times we've gone out have been with her orchestra-tion. But times like tonight do leave me wondering."

"That's not much help," Holly mumbled under her breath, deflated. "I figured it was something like that, Amanda coercing Logan all along. Not much to wonder about there."

"This much I do know: Logan has always been a bit of a scoundrel and getting attached to a woman has never been part of his plan. He's never stayed with any woman for long. It's like he recognizes what he looks like and thinks that he's supposed to be this playboy. Remember what I mentioned before about what I thought was expected of me? It's almost like he's doing something that he feels is expected of him. We don't spend much time getting into each other's business, but I don't need to be a rocket scientist to figure out his rotation of girls either."

"Why are you telling me all of this, Chase?" she whispered, more dismayed than encouraged.

"Because of the way you sound right now," he whispered back.

"Why do you even care?" She looked up at him with a sadness she knew reached her eyes.

"Because I think you deserve to be happy, even if it's not with Logan."

Holly blinked, swallowing hard, and nodded.

Chase continued sympathetically. "And I'm thinking that having him so close is probably getting rough. He's getting all the perks of this friendship, completely ignorant that your feelings have changed. You're playing along because you're not willing to risk exposing yourself and losing him. It appears to be a no-win situation. But you know, sometimes not getting what you want is getting exactly what you need."

Holly knew there was no point in confirming what Chase already knew and instead rolled her eyes, trying to smile. "Here we go again. More Dalai Lama–isms."

Chase chuckled. "I think the Rolling Stones would get the credit for that one. I also think you're strong, probably even stronger than you give yourself credit for. I've watched you do a complete turnaround with sheer will and determination, even if Logan had a hand in making that happen. And even if this relationship with Logan doesn't go exactly in the direction you want it to, it doesn't mean that it isn't worth it. He's a good guy to have on your side. His lack of interest doesn't mean you're not worthy. Or that you aren't a damn sexy woman."

She blinked at him again, this time smiling with no effort before shyly looking down at the bar. "Thanks, Chase."

"There is so much potential in you. It's as plain as the nose on my face. You remember that. Just because you may not be right for my single-minded friend, it doesn't mean there aren't plenty of men out there who'd fall in love with you in a heartbeat."

She stared at him, speechless. Never in her whole life had anyone spoken to her like that, not even Logan. Certainly not Bruce. Forget about her parents. It didn't even matter that the words came from someone completely uninterested in her. They were sincere. And then she saw it, even in the minimal lighting of the bar, amazed she had never noticed it before.

"You have a scar," she said in disbelief.

Chase took note of where she was looking, reached

up, and automatically touched a spot above his left eyebrow, his fingertips tracing across the inch and a half of rough raised skin. "This thing? Yeah, I got hit with a foul ball that ricocheted off the corner of a dugout back in college. A one-in-a-million shot. Never even saw it coming. If you look real close, you can see it actually looks like the stitching of the baseball. That thing was like a missile. Logan said I was lucky; it hit the hardest part of my head. I never was sure if he meant it as an insult."

It didn't really mar him in any way. In fact, it only enhanced his ruggedness. But somehow, that tiny mark made him real, and she was comforted by it. She had been surrounded by people she felt she didn't measure up to since her journey began, searching for the confirmation that any one of them would have a clue what it was like to be her. All along, the imperfection was right in front of her, and in the most unlikely candidate. Chase Walker was totally human, she mused. And in that moment, Holly became his greatest fan.

"Holly," Chase said, gently but insistently, "about what I said to you before. Tell me you understand."

"Understand what?" Amanda broke into the conversation, having finished with the pool table.

Chase sat up and casually rotated himself on his bar stool, creating a space between his legs. Pulling his wife by her waist, he settled her there. "Understand how impolite it is to eavesdrop." His answer sounded like an affectionate mix of teasing and scolding.

"Who's eavesdropping?" Amanda immediately responded. "I'm not hiding behind a curtain or anything.

It's not my fault you were so deep in conversation you didn't hear me tell you it was your turn."

"I'm guessing you lost?" Chase asked, his hand drifting slightly from her waist to settle on her hip. He glanced over to the pool table, where Logan was re-racking the balls.

"Yes, I did." Amanda sulked, more for her husband's enjoyment than from any bitterness at losing a game of billiards. "And don't change the subject."

"And what exactly was the subject again?" Chase asked innocently, deliberately trying to rile her.

Amanda gave an exasperated harrumph before turning directly to Holly. "Holly, what are you supposed to understand?"

"Um . . . I . . . well," Holly stammered. Chase was being evasive. But she realized what he was really doing was saving her from having to admit she had spent the last several months acting the fool.

Chase smoothly redirected the conversation, saving Holly from further stuttering. "I was simply reminding Holly that she needs to be wary of scoundrels out there looking to take advantage of young attractive widows with a few dollars in their pockets."

Wow, Holly thought, *this guy is good.* It was a tiny white lie wrapped in all sorts of truth. She did need to be wary, but only of one scoundrel in particular, and the only thing he had stolen was her heart.

Amanda seemed satisfied with his explanation. She turned back to Holly. "He's right, you know."

"I also wanted her to know there are lots of genuinely nice guys out there and she should work on recognizing the difference," Chase added, smiling supportively in Holly's direction. "For when she's ready to get back into the dating circuit, that is."

A momentary look of abject horror passed over Amanda's face and then quickly faded. She took several steps away from Chase's bar stool and his grasp, smiling absently at Holly. Then Amanda slowly turned her head back in the direction of her husband, leveled a cold stare at him, and through a forced smile said, "Oh he did, did he?"

Chase met his wife's fiery gaze, one that was shielded from Holly's view, with an amused eyebrow raised and an overly tolerant yet emphatic, "I sure did."

"Did what?" Logan, tired of waiting for Chase at the pool table, had returned to the bar to catch the tail end of the exchange. Taking note of all the empty bottles, he called out to the bartender, "Hey, Glen, can we get another round?"

Amanda was more than happy to furnish Logan with the answer to his question after passing another disgruntled look at her husband. "Chase here was just telling Holly about all the nice guys out there, for when she's ready to get back into the *dating circuit.*"

"Really?" Logan replied offhandedly while secretly wanting to advise his friend in no uncertain terms to mind his own business. He jammed his hand in his pocket to pull out some money and cover the round. "I'm curious: just how would a thoroughly married man and recovered man-whore qualify as an expert on that subject?"

"Did you just refer to my husband as a man-whore?"

Amanda asked, torn between getting defensive and laughing her ass off.

Logan shrugged. "Man-whore, baseball player, same difference."

Holly's mouth dropped open, and she felt the undercurrent of something strange taking place that she couldn't put her finger on. Suddenly everybody seemed so animated and it appeared they were all speaking in double entendres. But she was sure about one thing: she certainly didn't consider the term "man-whore" one of endearment.

Chase's amusement was unmistakable. "You haven't called me that in years. Are you drunk?"

Logan responded with the standard inside joke from their college days. "Not yet." No matter how drunk they actually were back then, "Not yet" would always be the answer to that question, even if it was being said while leaning face-first into a toilet bowl. He reached for one of the four fresh beers that Glen placed on the bar and took a long swallow, satisfied that he had avoided raising suspicion.

"Is that on the agenda?" Holly asked, excited by the prospect of seeing Logan sloshed, a huge departure from his ever-present control.

Logan shook his head, a small grin playing at his lips. "I don't think so."

"Pity," Amanda replied, temporarily sidetracked from her annoyance with her husband. "I don't think I've ever seen him drunk."

"You haven't," Logan said as Glen returned with the change from his twenty. "Keep it."

"Thanks, man," the bartender told him, leaning on the bar, and asked jokingly, "Did I hear the word 'drunk'? Does anyone need me to call a cab?"

"No, Glen, we're good," Chase said good-naturedly, shaking his head. "My wife and her friend here were just hoping to see Logan get that way. What they don't know is that a drunken Logan, while good for endless punch lines, is a god-awful sight."

"Why would a guy want to get drunk anyway when he's got a pretty lady to take home and impress?" Glen mused aloud.

"Oh, he doesn't have to impress me," Holly said, quick to clarify, hoping to save herself and Logan any embarrassment. "I'm already impressed with him. Besides, we're just friends."

Glen promptly stood back up. "Hold up, wait a sec. Logan, this isn't your girlfriend?"

"No," all four of them replied at once, each voice in a distinctly different tone.

Glen laid both his hands on the bar, taking in the widely varied expressions on all four faces before resting his gaze on Holly and smiling. "Well well well," he said slowly. "Ain't that something?"

Chase was the only one who actually smiled back. "Yes. Yes it is."

THE SILENCE ON THE CAR RIDE HOME WAS DEAFENING. Holly wasn't used to it; they always had something to talk about. Logan didn't even put the radio on, as he usually did. And there was such an edge to his mood that she didn't feel comfortable putting the radio on either. It was the first time they had done any drinking together, not that she considered his two beers actually drinking. She had gone way beyond that and it left her feeling at a disadvantage.

"Everything all right?" Holly finally asked.

"Of course," he replied brusquely. "Why do you ask?"

"No reason. You just seem sort of quiet."

"It's been a long day," he said quickly, staring straight ahead. "I'm pretty tired."

"We could have left earlier."

"And ruin your good time?" Logan said with a hint of sarcasm. "I wouldn't hear of it."

Was she drunk and acting sloppy or was he just tired and she was reading into it? Holly concentrated on not slurring. "I wasn't having that good a time. Don't ever jack up your schedule on my account."

Holly leaned her head back against the headrest and closed her eyes. The silence resumed for several more minutes before Logan finally broke it.

"So the bartender certainly took an interest in you," he said casually.

She straightened back up. "Glen? Yeah. He's nice."

"You two looked like you were getting pretty chummy."

"Why? Because he bought me a shot of . . . what was that stuff called again?"

"Goldschläger."

"Yeah. Goldschläger. It was yummy. You know it has real flakes of gold in it?" Holly recalled the sweet cinnamon schnapps that went down smooth and then set her insides on fire.

"It's also like ninety proof," Logan replied. "Let's see how much you like it tomorrow when I'm whooping your ass all around that gym."

"He bought us all one," she said, ignoring his comment about how she would pay for it in the morning.

"We tip him like fifty bucks every time we're in there. This was the first night he ever did anything like that. I can only assume it was to impress *you*."

"I guess that explains why you refused yours?"

"I'm driving," he said, his voice bordering on reproach, as if she should have known. "It was nice of you to drink mine for me."

The silence resumed again. So what? She had a couple of shots. And three beers. Holly stole sideways glances at Logan as he concentrated on the road. Sweet Jesus, his profile was just incredible. Why did he have to be so damn perfect? Always so self-controlled. Why couldn't he have let down his guard, gotten drunk, maybe even made a pass at her that they could both regret later? Instead, they were having a conversation like none they'd ever had before. It almost seemed as if he was accusing her of something, or worse yet, disapproving of her. And it hurt.

"Guess you'll be seeing him again?" Logan tried to sound indifferent.

"What makes you say that?" she immediately asked.

"Well, you took his phone number."

"He offered it to me. I didn't want to be rude," Holly explained.

"And you don't think it's rude to take a guy's phone number and then not call him?"

"Are you saying I'm rude?" Holly snapped, the hurt beginning to fade and indignation taking its place.

"I just think if the guy felt comfortable enough to give it to you, he must've thought there was a chance you'd use it."

"Or he's a horn dog who gives his number to every girl he meets." She laughed.

"True." He laughed along with her nervously. "I guess the real question then becomes, how many horn dogs' phone numbers will you be collecting?"

"Wow. That sort of makes me sound like a slut," she said, her hurt having reappeared.

"I just think you're new at this and you need to be careful, or guys might get the wrong impression."

"Now you're really making me sound like one," Holly said defensively.

"Sorry. That's not my intention." Logan tried to backtrack, knowing that he was failing at coming to grips with just why he was so antagonistic.

"I can't tell if you're concerned or just insulting me."

He tried to clarify. "I'm just saying, guys don't usually give their phone number out unless they think they stand a chance of seeing some action."

"You did," she was quick to reply.

"That's completely different. You and I have a business arrangement. Besides, this guy totally isn't your type."

"I don't have a type," she replied, muttering under her breath, "Unlike some people."

"Somehow I can't picture you on the back of a Harley with Glen the tattoo-loving bartender."

"Well, when you put it like that, maybe I will call him, because that sounds like fun. And what's your problem with tattoos?" she responded with sarcasm of her own.

"No problems here. Whatever floats your boat." He strived to go back to casual, knowing it wasn't working.

"Geez. Tired and beer makes Logan really bad tempered," she said jokingly, trying to follow his lead and lighten up the exchange.

They went back to awkward silence. Holly wished that if she had done something wrong, Logan would just come out and tell her. At least Chase was nice about it. By the time he pulled into her driveway, she only knew one thing. She needed to put some distance between them, at least until she sobered up. She was on the verge of doing something she was going to regret, and regret alone.

"I'll see you tomorrow," he reminded her as she got out of the car.

She made sure the door was closed before releasing her pent-up frustration and snapping, "Unfortunately."

Chapter Twelve

CHASE UNLOCKED THE FRONT DOOR AND HELD IT OPEN, resisting the urge to usher Amanda in with a firm hand applied smartly to her backside. She walked stiffly past him, maintaining the same brooding silence that had greeted his attempts at polite conversation since they left the bar. She crossed hurriedly through the foyer and directly to the elaborate winding staircase, while Chase waved off the security guards who picked them and his car up. When she was in the middle of her climb up the mountainous stairs, she heard the front door shut. She stopped short, turned back to Chase, and glared down at him.

"Sometimes you just don't know when to shut up," she told him frostily before turning back around, picking up her pace, and making her way to the top. Then she disappeared into the hall. By the time Chase reached the first step to pursue her, he heard the reverberation of their bedroom door slamming.

Amanda Walker was in the first phase of a tantrum.

Chase recognized the signs. Women had been throwing temper tantrums at him for as long as he could remember, often specifically for his benefit. His wife, however, wasn't prone to them, at least not genuine ones. He could pinpoint the moment that ignited the flare-up. Chase was positive that the bar napkin with Glen's phone number on it had everything to do with it.

Amanda went from sensual to surly as soon as she heard Chase had given Holly advice, and only became more so as the evening progressed. By the time they left the bar and the flirtatious repartee between Holly and Glen had resulted in the exchange of digits, Chase could feel her seething. It was the kind of irrational anger she reserved only for him, setting the stage for his favorite kind of altercation. Interested and already turned on, Chase followed Amanda up the stairs and down the long hallway to their room. He reached for the doorknob and turned. It wouldn't budge. The door was locked. He knocked lightly.

"Come on, Mandy, open up. Let's talk this out."

His request was met with more stony silence. After waiting a few moments, he knocked again with a bit more force and issued a stern warning. "Amanda Walker, unlock this door this instant, before I lose my sense of humor."

This time he heard fiddling with the knob and the door opened. His pillow came flying out to land in the hallway. The door slammed again and was quickly re-locked.

How symbolic, he said to himself. They had six fully furnished bedrooms. He looked at his pillow on the plush carpet at his feet and remained outside the locked room for a minute, trying to decide how best to handle the increasingly unpleasant turn of events.

Relationships like theirs had rules. Important rules, many of them unspoken, that needed to be adhered to, for the sake of both partners, or the relationship would not only cease to flourish but would be destined to fail. If Amanda had disappointed him or, worse yet, disobeyed him, his response would be easy. He would inform her that a spanking was in order and she would accept it, knowing the requirements of the life they chose together. Chase would then become methodical, almost dispassionate. Tip her, bare her, spank her . . . soundly. More times than not, she would purposefully set out to fulfill that very scenario, seeking the excite-ment of his reaction and craving the domination. It was a playful scene they often acted out. She wasn't really naughty and he wasn't really punishing her. There was usually a great deal of banter and plenty of threats, and it was all about choice.

But what was happening now was woefully unfa-miliar. If she was truly angry with him, that meant hands off. It didn't matter if he thought her anger was misplaced or not. It was a boundary he had to respect. There could be no misunderstandings between them when he put her over his knee, ever. And he didn't find it the least bit appealing to imagine Amanda being submissive to the point of never speaking her mind with confidence. The only decision he had left to make was whether or not she was really angry with him. He could count the times they'd actually fought on one hand, each of them disturbing and soul wrenching. He loved her to the point of going out of his way to make her needs paramount, and she reciprocated those feelings. What did either of them have to be miserable about? He was living a fairy tale and she was the appointed princess within it. Every now and then the demands that came with the position would frustrate her and she would need to be reminded that he was a package deal and the good that came from the lives they'd been blessed with certainly outweighed the bad. But times like that were never more than a blip, usually brought on by fatigue, and her sunny disposition soon returned.

Luck had once again been on his side when he met and fell in love with her. She wasn't spoiled or temperamental. The more he gave her, the less she wanted. She was sophisticated and refined, never failing him when they appeared publicly. She shared his values, realizing the importance of giving, always participating with gusto in any charity he chose to represent. To the outside world, she was the epitome of graciousness. Until he got her alone and she became his delightful brat, capable of erotically enraging him beyond his wildest imagination. She entertained his fetish like no woman had before her, making it as much about his needs as her own, and never making him feel guilty for it. And he couldn't recall one instance since they were married when she'd ever shut him out.

No sound came from behind the still securely locked door. Chase stared at it. Here there was no premeditated disrespect or childish display designed to elicit his trigger response. No indication, not even a hint, that she wanted his company or his attention at all. Suddenly Chase Walker felt like having a tantrum of his own.

"We don't go to bed angry!" he shouted lamely at the door. Dejected, he picked up his pillow and tucked it under his arm, then retreated into the guest bedroom closest to where Amanda had isolated herself. Feeling uncomfortable and disconnected, he tossed the pillow on the bed and left, heading back downstairs.

He aimlessly wandered from room to room in his twelve-thousand-square-foot castle, the forlorn prince longing for company other than his own. He turned on lights that were already on timers, only to turn them off again. He made a point of checking that all the potential points of entry were secure, despite the extensive alarm system that was monitored by his security team twenty-four hours a day. While passing the den, he debated watching some TV. Maybe he could find his way to the screening room and watch a movie instead. Deciding against both, he continued on. He stalled in the game room, considering a few rounds of pinball, maybe a game of Pac-Man or any of the other full-size arcade games he owned. Then he spied the pool table, the stark reminder of how the whole rotten night started. A night that started out like most others, with teasing and innuendo and such promise. He turned off the lights and left the games behind. He pondered a workout when he reached his gym, maybe just a quick exhausting run to release the anxiety brought on by Amanda's sudden fury and withdrawal. From the sliding glass doors that ran along the outside wall of the gym, he caught sight of the light reflecting off the pool. Perhaps a swim? Maybe a run, then a swim?

He stepped outside onto the patio that surrounded the pool and looked into the depths of the crystal-blue water. He listened to the waterfall that cascaded freely from the ornate pool's deepest end, a sound that usually brought with it the feeling of peace and serenity but now was bringing neither. The nights had turned cooler, but the pool's heating system would counterbalance that if he chose to dive in. There was always the hot tub. He took a few steps in its direction and frowned. The hot tub was no fun without his nearly naked—sometimes completely naked—wife in there with him. The same could be said for the pool. Shaking his head, he went inside the house and resumed his roaming, the overwhelming feeling of forced solitude daunting his every step. Every sound he made echoed throughout the silent house, reminding him of his seclusion. He stopped in the kitchen, opened and closed the refrigerator door several times, trolled the cupboards for a possible snack. He threw some ice in a glass and added some water even though he wasn't particularly thirsty. He could take most things in stride, but Amanda's being pissed at him was downright unsettling. It left him scattered and indecisive, characteristics he wasn't used to and didn't even know what to do with. And so much anger, for such a tiny infraction! Maybe he'd read it all wrong and was supposed to come crashing through the door to take her in hand? No, she would have joined him by now, to either make amends or egg him on.

Not bothering to take a sip from his freshly poured drink, he took it with him and headed back upstairs. He stood outside the silent closed door that his wife was behind a minute more before returning to the lonely guest bedroom where his pillow waited. He placed the glass on the nightstand, stripped off his clothes, and got into the bed. A bed half the size of the one in his master bedroom, but it suddenly seemed too big, even as his feet dangled off the edge in front. He closed his eyes and heaved a sigh of discontent before drifting off into a restless sleep.

Less than an hour later, Chase was awakened by a single sniffle. He opened his bleary eyes and saw her silhouette in the doorway. The light shining from the hall glowed behind her, and she reminded him of an angel. His beautiful, maddeningly headstrong angel.

"Come to bed, baby," he said softly, uncertain that she was really there and not just the wishful figment of the fitful sleep he had finally given in to. He lifted the blankets up in invitation. Not bothering to turn off the light in the hall, Amanda closed the door halfway and dashed over to the bed, climbing in beside him. Without a sound, he wrapped the blankets and himself around her, enfolding her. She snuggled in until she was flush against his sturdy muscle-bound frame and sniffled again, her face still damp with tears. He brushed his lips lightly over hers, tentative and unsure, until he felt her sensual touch travel up his steely arms.

Feathery-soft fingertips against iron crept from his biceps to his neck, where they settled, then tightened. Her mouth sweetly covered his and she breathed new life into him. His reaction was instantaneous and amorous despite the few remaining cobwebs of grogginess. Impatiently, he pulled the T-shirt she was wearing over her head, then hugged her tightly to him again. Her nipples responded to the smattering of hair that covered his chest, exciting them both further. She kissed him again, her own mouth open and delicately probing. He grabbed her bottom to shift her center into line with his pulsating shaft and felt the fabric of her panties, the same fabric that would hinder his access to her. Tearing his lips away from hers and easily maneuvering around her in spite of his bulk, he reached for the tiny piece of cloth with both strong, determined hands. He insistently tugged at the fragile lace while she wriggled in haste, as eager as he was to see them removed. Pulling them off completely and away from her, he discarded them haphazardly over the side of the bed. His large hand passed over her sex and his fingers dipped inside her wetness, rubbing, teasing, and enticing. She released a small moan of appreciation at his invasion and wiggled into it but said nothing more. Touching her wasn't enough, would never be enough. He was anxious to become part of her. He brought his hands back up to both sides of her face and tilted it up to his, placing another tender kiss on her lips. Chase entered her slowly as they still lay side by side and heard himself groaning as her body welcomed him. He was home. Wordlessly, he moved slowly within her, so that she might fully comprehend the way she affected him. He lovingly took his time with every single thrust in adoration of her until she could no longer stand it. Her breath turned into short mindless gasps and he could feel her muscles begin to involuntarily squeeze around him as her grip on him tightened. Amanda teetered on the brink of rapture and her gasps turned into little mews of breathless pleasure. Holding her tight within his embrace, he rolled her beneath him and precisely finished her off. She wrapped her limbs around him and he joined her.

"I HATE IT WHEN YOU'RE MAD AT ME," CHASE CONFESSED, breaking the silence some time later. They were still side by side, pressed together, in the too-small bed of the guest room. Light from the hallway spilled in from the half-open door. Each of them, spent and sated, was reluctant to move and leave the touch of the other.

He sounded despondent. The complexity of the man was amazing. He was so strong, to the point of sometimes being an overbearing brute. And she was able to reduce him to a pile of emotional rubble with nothing more than her displeasure.

She apologized without hesitation. "I'm sorry. I overreacted."

"Mind telling me what I did to set you off?" he asked, smiling. He already knew the answer.

"Nothing. I'm just in a mood," she reluctantly told him, burying her forehead against his chest. "I said I'm sorry."

"Amanda, are you lying to me?" Chase softly chided

her, having none of it. He crooked a finger under her chin and gently lifted it.

She allowed him to pull her head up before placing it on the pillow beside his. "Are you lying to me, pretending you don't know why I'm mad?"

"Touché," he said, bringing a hand up and tucking a stray lock of her hair behind her ear. His eyes searched hers. "This whole thing is getting out of hand, don't you think?"

He was giving her the look. The one she loved and hated at the same time. The look came so naturally to him, and even in a room that wasn't fully lit, he had gotten it across. It was the indulgent yet authoritative stare that always left her feeling like a combination of woman and child, probably because of what usually followed it.

"I don't know." She pouted, feeding into it. "Probably. But things were going along swimmingly before you stuck your big nose in."

"What did I do? I encouraged a single woman to take the phone number of a perfectly nice bartender," he said with feigned innocence.

"What you encouraged her to do is start dating," Amanda retorted.

"Which is what everyone should be encouraging her to do, you included," he reminded her.

She sighed in vexation. "Why do you think I keep taking her to your games?"

"You and I both know you aren't taking her to my games to get her involved with any of the guys from the team. Besides, she doesn't need a baseball player.

She needs a nice average guy who can be there for her."

Her temper resurfaced, and she became disinclined to continue matching wits with him. "Oh! You are impossible. What she needs, and wants, is Logan, and he's about to crack. Can't you see that?"

"And can't you see that it's starting to take its toll on her? You've been on this crusade for months and it's making everyone miserable, including us. I know him. He's not going to change. He would've made his move already. And did it ever dawn on you that what they have right now, a solid friendship, may be even better than what you so desperately wish for them?"

"I think you're wrong." She made a timid attempt at self-righteous bravado, knowing it was futile.

Chase waited for her eyes to lock back on to his.

"And I think this business ends today. As of right now, your illustrious matchmaking career is over. Am I making myself clear?" he told her, hoping but doubtful that she was going to follow his order. His lips were on hers before she could answer.

They settled back down and silence resumed. The comfortable kind, signifying that harmony had been restored. She was lying on his chest, her ear over his heart. She listened to it beating, steady and solid. His hand absently stroked up and down her back as he waited for sleep to reclaim him.

"Chase?" she asked with an edge of apprehension.

"Hmm?" he replied drowsily.

"Am I getting . . . you know." He was going to make her ask for it and win the ultimate battle of control. Her body slightly tensed.

His hand on her back stopped rubbing. He opened his eyes and smiled, thoroughly pleased. He delighted in her sometimes bashful inability to say the word, as if she was somehow embarrassed by its mere suggestion. It never happened when she was using it as a tool to excite him. It always occurred when she needed it most or felt she deserved it. He finished the question for her.

"Spanked?"

Her voice was a tiny squeak of anticipation. "Yes."

He released a masculine sigh, his hand drifting downward to rest possessively on her behind. "No, baby, not tonight. It doesn't feel right. I just want to hold you. Besides, I can't think of any better punishment for your behavior this evening than to deny you exactly what you want."

Chapter Thirteen

CHASE WALKER, UNBEKNOWNST TO ANY OF THEM, HAD inadvertently created a monster.

Amanda did follow Chase's order and stopped the push of nonstop invites, but only because she realized she no longer needed to extend them. Holly had become a permanent fixture in all of their lives, but Logan's in particular.

Holly had taken her conversation with Chase to heart and decided to heed his advice. If Chase was right, and by all accounts he was, what good would it do her to pine after Logan? It was a losing proposition no matter how she looked at it.

After the night at McDuff's, Holly knew throwing herself at Logan was out of the question. She knew nothing about seduction. And he certainly didn't show any interest. If anything, he was like an overprotective big brother. At best it would be an awkward, bungled attempt that could only end in disaster, even if by some chance it was successful. And she had no intention of putting in jeopardy the kind of friendship that had created such an amazing bond between them. It was time to get her house in order.

Chase's approval and support was like a tonic, and Holly was eager to find other sources. After the night at the bar, Holly felt empowered. When she took Glen's phone number, she knew she would never call him, but it was of little consequence. With the bartender's interest came a feeling of desirability, something that was all new to her. She began to view herself differently, as well as the world around her. Her smile came easily. She had a newfound pride in her appearance and eagerly began searching out ways to explore and enhance her femininity. She wanted to learn about fashion and develop her own style, and with Amanda's help, she did so. She shopped with the intention of learning how to exploit her hard-won assets. She would never have Amanda's exotic beauty, so she opted for well-put-together cuteness. Her clothing became sassy, colorful, and carefree. She went to one of cosmetics counters at the local Macy's and let them spend hours playing with her face, leaving the store with every single product they applied and tips on how to achieve the look herself. She felt the overwhelming desire to charm, and given her quick wit, being charming came relatively easily.

Without having Amanda to fight against, Logan hoped to resume the comfortable camaraderie that he and Holly had previously enjoyed. He was still preoccupied with her, but it had a new dimension. He relished the new positive aura that surrounded her as each day brought with it the promise of the new and interesting things she would discover about the person he had helped her become. He wanted to be caught up in the rush of her realizing all she had accomplished.

But Logan was also having trouble accepting the attention Holly had begun receiving from other men. Her new self-esteem drew people to her. He was quick to tell her all the reasons every man wasn't right for her. Her response to his mostly unwarranted assessments was to become defensive. With Holly not willing to tell him how she really felt and Logan not willing to acknowledge he felt anything at all, they unintentionally started to build a battlefield.

Holly had developed a giggle Logan knew was false. She batted her eyelashes at men who admired the view. She engaged in playful conversation with would-be suitors, even when Logan was standing right next to her, never failing to mention that Logan was nothing more than a friend. She wouldn't give out her phone number, but she took a few, determined to prove to him that she knew how to handle her own life, with the added pleasure of seeing how much it irked him. All of Logan's attempts to get Holly to tone it down were met with the shrill, bogus, silly laugh he was rapidly learning to despise.

But worst of all, she began to back-talk him while she trained. She questioned his judgment, debated his choices. She chatted more, and it took the focus away from getting what he wanted done in time. It quickly soured any sense of accomplishment he felt on her behalf. He was so frustrated with the whole mess, he unintentionally complained to Chase one day, right before the playoffs. To his total surprise, Chase was less than sympathetic, an attitude only made worse by the fact that Amanda had once again forsaken him in favor of spending time with Holly.

"Project hit the skids, Logan?" Chase snickered. "Not working out the way you planned?"

"Not exactly," Logan admitted reluctantly.

Chase chuckled sarcastically. "And you're surprised by this? Logan, I gotta tell ya, you're a tool sometimes, a full-on tool."

They'd been friends a long time, and Logan owed Chase a lot. But this was getting personal. "Care to explain that?" Logan tried to keep from sounding as angry as he felt.

Chase released the bar from the lateral pull-down machine, the weights banging together with a loud clang. He grabbed his water. "You want it both ways, man, and you just keep getting farther and farther away from either of them." When Logan clenched his jaw and pursed his lips together, Chase took a deep breath. "You are so adamant about how she's not your type, how you're just doing your good deed for the day, yet you've spent more time with her than with your last five girls combined. Saying no to spending time with her never enters your mind. It's like you don't want her, but you don't want anyone else to want her either. What exactly are you looking to accomplish here?

Want to see what you can get her down to? Waiting for her to become anorexic? The perfectly formed Stepford model, perhaps? So far from a real, feeling person that she eats, sleeps, and lives at your gym? So you can show her off to your friends and say, 'Behold my creation'? Oh, and one last thing: the look on your face when she flirts with anyone else, guys who don't care about that extra twenty pounds . . . *priceless*."

Logan opened his mouth to protest, and Chase held up his hand. "And don't blame Amanda. You and Amanda both created this mess, and I only know one thing. I want my wife back."

Logan gave a disgusted bark. "I wasn't even going to say that! I was going to say how proud I am of her and how I feel like this is somehow my fault! So why don't you just shut the hell up and take your wife back? Don't you have ways of getting her to cooperate? Isn't there a paddle or a riding crop somewhere with her name on it?" Logan only marginally regretted his words, even though he knew the blow would be considered low. Yes, the Walkers' extracurricular activities were common knowledge, and even sometimes around him they were playful. Those activities were also private and usually not up for discussion, not even with Logan. But Chase had struck a nerve. When exactly *did* Holly become such a touchy subject? Probably around the same time Logan started recalling some joke she told, hours after the fact, and laughing again. That would have been right around the same time he began noticing the faint scent of her sweat mixed with CK One, even when she hadn't been at the gym all day. When he would smile just thinking about the little things she did that were so damn delightful, like the way she would worry her lower lip as he explained something new that they were going to try that sounded extreme. Or the way she would silently bitch out a weight machine with hands waving and fingers pointing when his back was turned, completely unaware he was watching the whole scene taking place in a mirror. The same mirror where he caught her pretending to maniacally stab him multiple times in the back with an imaginary knife while he was picking up the weights he was going to hand her next. That was the same day he admitted that he just enjoyed working more on the days when she was training, or at least he had up until recently, before she became a stark raving vixen. Or maybe, just maybe, it was the same time he stopped wanting to see other girls, opting instead to fantasize about what it would be like to feel Holly writhing and moaning beneath him, wrapping her legs around him while he took her over and over again. One thing was certain: it was time to admit he was in trouble when it came to Holly Brennan. But when Logan returned his attention to his friend, ready to issue an apology, Chase was merely stroking his chin, as if examining his options.

"Paddling her into submission would never work. That's the one thing I didn't consider when I married her. The fact that she likes it almost more than I do. How the hell am I supposed to stay ahead of that?" Chase gave Logan a grin and they both relaxed.

"I hate that fucking giggle. It's like Holly knows it

pisses me off," Logan griped, returning to the original matter.

Chase joined in with a gripe of his own. "My wife is right, isn't she? This isn't just a game for you anymore. You *do* have a serious thing for her, don't you? Damn. I hate it when she's right. She's never going to let me hear the end of it."

"And the way she talks to me when she trains now," Logan said, truly injured. "She read a couple of books and suddenly she's an expert on fitness. Everything's a debate. You know I hate that shit. I went to school for six years. I have a master's, for Christ's sake!"

Then a lightbulb went off above Chase's head.

"You need to spank her."

Logan laughed so hard he nearly choked, appalled by his friend's audacity. "Are you crazy?" he said scathingly. "That caveman approach might work for you, but all it'll get me is a ride in a police car."

Chase shook his head. "I'm not talking about beating the woman here. But Holly's only doing all these shenanigans to get your attention. I say, give her some. Plus it'll serve as a small reminder of just what happens to little girls who insist on messing with the big boys."

Logan shook his head as well. "She's not so little. And you're making her sound like a child who needs to be controlled."

Chase smiled and raised an eyebrow. "Well, she is sort of acting like one, now, isn't she?"

"Maybe it's from all the time she's spending with your wife."

"Maybe, and heaven help you if that's true; Amanda

has it down to a science. But either way, the brat in her is now present and accounted for. And you sound like you're running out of options. If you don't get a handle on this soon, she's going to walk all over you."

"You make it sound so reasonable," Logan said, slightly awed. "And that is actually frightening. I really liked you better before you were liberated, by the way. When you kept all this shit to yourself."

"You know," Chase remarked casually, as if Logan hadn't even spoken, "the way you are when it comes to self-discipline and all that crap, I always thought you'd be a natural at convincing a naughty girl she wants to behave. You are totally missing out."

"I'm not sure this is such a good idea," Logan said, far from convinced but presuming that seducing Holly wasn't such a good one either.

"I guarantee, after it's over, you'll both feel better," Chase told him reassuringly.

"I've never spanked a woman in my entire life, Chase."

"Trust me. You're going to love it. And who knows, maybe she will, too."

Chapter Fourteen

WHO WAS IT WHO SAID THE DUMBEST PLANS ARE hatched from the most reckless of decisions? If it wasn't Logan, it should have been. By the time Holly showed up for her next workout, he was so pumped up by Chase, he had to hold back from grabbing her as soon as she walked through the door. He assumed the stance of a lion getting ready to spring, waiting for his prey to make its final mistake.

She made that mistake within the first ten minutes.

After Holly's warm-up, Logan retrieved eight-pound dumbbells from the rack and brought them over to where she was standing. "Okay, let's start with some alternating lunges combined with hammer curls."

"You have what, a million dollars' worth of equipment here, and you have me doing more lunges again?"

Holly commented drily. "And not for nothing, but I can really handle ten-pounders."

Logan said nothing and instead dropped the weights and grabbed her arm. He swiftly sat on the nearest bench and, tugging, sent her sprawling over his knees. Before she had an inkling of what was happening, he began spanking, never speaking a word, then stood up, taking her with him, and set her back on her feet.

Promptly, Holly slapped his face.

Shocked puppy eyes met livid green ones. She didn't look turned on or even particularly chastised. She looked mad as hell. She reached around to rub her stinging backside. "Are you nuts? What was *that* about?"

Mortified, Logan rubbed his cheek, her handprint clear against his clean-shaven face. "Guess I didn't do it hard enough." He tried ruefully to laugh it off.

"If you did it any harder, the only reason you'd be touching your face would be to help you spit your balls out."

He was grateful she was willing to make light of what was easily one of the most embarrassing moments of his life. The next time Logan saw Chase, he was going to deck him.

Logan decided that at this point, honesty was the best policy. At least partial honesty. Having just manhandled the woman, he figured it probably wasn't the best time to tell her he found her attractive.

"You've been driving me crazy. If you want to start a man collection, I can't do anything about that. But you've been questioning my authority in this gym non-stop for weeks. And not even the usual wise-guy stuff. You're condescending, like I'm one step from being your pool boy. You may be new and improved, but that doesn't make you the educated expert. Even though I technically work for you, when you come through these doors, I am the boss."

All the anger left her. She had been so busy trying to get him to notice her; she never realized she was turning into the kind of person she herself would get annoyed with. But worse than that, she was making him feel second-rate at his job after all he had helped see her through. It was unacceptable. Her shoulders slumped. "I just wanted to show you how strong I was getting. How grateful I am for all our hard work. I'm really sorry. I never meant to make you feel like that. I was just kidding around." The gloomy little voice was back, and Logan felt like he'd just been slapped again. He did what he knew he did best: he opened his arms.

"Come here."

She was hesitant to go to him, for more than one reason. Not only had he just assaulted her, but she wasn't sure a hug from him would be enough. She didn't want this friendship anymore; it wasn't working. She had never counted on becoming addicted to his touch, his very presence. All the attention from other men meant nothing to her, regardless of her pretended interest in it. They were just a measuring tool to compare against. And her being "new and improved" didn't mean anything to him. Holly was finally willing to acknowledge that she'd been doing this all for him—and all he'd been doing was his job. He told her she was driving him crazy, but not the kind of crazy that Amanda made Chase. The way Holly made Logan crazy was akin to her being a nuisance.

With her head down and feet that felt made of lead, Holly took the few steps over to him, filled with embarrassment and shame. As soon as she was wrapped in his arms, heard his heartbeat through his shirt, and smelled his Drakkar Noir, she started to cry. Logan held her tight as she struggled with the fact that she could never express to him precisely why he was the cause of her tears. Like a good friend, he'd kept his promise. He'd helped her break some bad habits. But who the hell was going to break her of *him*? She had to get ahold of herself. When he heard her hiccup several minutes later, he chuckled.

"Guess I can't charge you for this session, can I?"

She laughed weakly and looked up at him. "Guess not. But I'm sure there's something I could see you charged *for*."

He cupped her face in his hands and tilted it up before smoothing the hair away from it. "I'm really sorry, Holly. I'm not sure when or how this got so out of hand, but I was out of line. Look, I'll make you a deal. No more challenging me during a session. Unless something is hurting you, you do what I say. In turn, if you want to try something new, you tell me before we get started. If it fits in with the plan, we try it. If it doesn't, I'll see if I can work it into your program for the next time." He added as an afterthought, grabbing the side of his jaw, "And I say we implement a 'hands-off' policy, because I think you may have shaken a tooth loose."

Through her tear-filled eyes, Holly giggled. He knew that giggle. It was real.

"We have a deal?" He smiled at her.

"Deal," she told him, her voice still shaky.

Logan looked down at her, her freckled upturned nose, her green eyes sparkling, lashes still wet. Then his gaze settled on her full rose-colored lips, parted ever so slightly to catch her breath until her stuffy nose cleared. He did the only thing he could think of, the thing he'd wanted to do for way too long. He kissed her.

His warm lips, so tenderly placed on hers, at first were a surprise to Holly, and her mouth formed a tiny "oh" before opening wider to receive his, and the kiss deepened. Her heart accelerated as he aggressively required more, his tongue darting across the corners of her mouth before delving inside, his hands working their way down her back to pull her closer. She allowed his tongue full access to her mouth before gently sucking at his lower lip, her hands looping around his neck, tightening, and without thinking she began to grind against him. He pulled away long enough to smile at her pout and take her hand, leading her over to the blue cushy mats, her heartbeat drumming louder in her ears with every step.

Then his lips returned to the soft skin of her cheek, her ear, her neck. Her hands began an exploration of their own, running from his shoulders down cut lats and delts to his taut buttocks and back again, increasingly daunted by the encumbrance of his clothing. She wanted to touch each and every inch of him, taste every part of him, cherish every moment of him. Impatient, Holly pulled the T-shirt from the waistband of his shorts in an effort to get to his skin.

Logan brought his mouth back to hers, having missed her kiss and wishing he had more than one set of lips. He grabbed the neckline of her T-shirt and gave a forceful tug, ripping it nearly in half.

"You can have mine," Logan murmured into her mouth, and pulled again, ripping her shirt completely off. Her bra quickly followed.

"I'll take it," Holly whispered back, leaving his lips just long enough to pull his shirt over his head, exposing his washboard abs, and triumphantly resuming her discovery of the spectacular physique that had obsessed her since she first saw it in his Facebook picture. His skin was smooth and warm, his mouth delicious.

Forcibly he brought them both to their knees and then laid Holly down, swooping his mouth onto hers one more time before making his way to the valley between her ample breasts, his thumb and forefinger toying with already hardened nipples, his hands gently squeezing the lush swells. He suckled, and her sigh bubbled over from his temperate nipping, her fingers traveling up his triceps and reflexively digging in.

He pulled himself away from her and stood. Holly watched, tingling with rapidly escalating arousal, as he pulled off her shoes and sent them flying through the air, landing somewhere in the main gym, before he kicked off his own and removed his shorts. She took in a breath and held it. He was superb, everything she'd ever envisioned, his thick sex already starting to spring up. He stared down at her and licked his lips. Her statue of David had come to life before her and its eyes were burning with desire.

Joining her on the mats, he laid her back down, hooking his fingers into the waistband of her spandex pants. Cool air rushed across an already damp mound as he pulled them off.

She lay before him, exposed and unabashed. Mindless of her imperfections, so consumed by sensations reawakening within her combined with her need to be touched by him again, he was able to explore her freely. Unfamiliar with intimacy combined with extra flesh, he caressed muscle over bones with soft cushioning to protect them, curves leading to valleys of supple, sweet-smelling skin. He felt his control start to fail, eager to taste her, his lips and tongue following where his hands led. Her womanly moans of gratification only pushed at that control, left him wanting more. When he reached the junction of her thighs, she drew her breath in sharply as he pulled back and with his fingers, mercilessly toyed around the velvety rim of what seemed to be her very existence. He inserted two digits inside her, his thumb remaining to tease the sensitive bud hidden just inside her folds. Holly's legs spread wide, her back arched, and her hands pounded on the mat where she lay as his strong manly fingers built a rhythm of slow, sure strokes and measured rubbing until it was clear she was about to come undone.

And then he watched. And felt. Her body stiffened and then lurched, she convulsed around his hand, and his name became an ongoing chant, two syllables on separate heaving breaths. She gave herself to the pleasure without inhibition, not caring that they were on a mat in a gym. She didn't care that the door was unlocked and that they could be interrupted at any moment. She didn't even care that she had stretch marks and love handles and cellulite—he was welcome to witness it all. When she said his name for the last time, in a languorous, spent coo, he felt his erection get painful. He straddled her at the legs, making his way up her rounded body with lavish kisses to her neck, feeling her fingers running through his hair and then coming to rest carelessly on his shoulders.

"Logan?" she said dreamily, vaguely recollecting where she was and what he had just done. "I think I may need some clarification on the hands-off policy."

"Clarification?" he asked incredulously before capturing her mouth again with his own and spreading her legs with his knee. He picked his head up to look down at her face while driving forcefully into her. "Any questions?"

Chapter Fifteen

Found it!" Logan exclaimed as he pulled Holly's sneaker from under the weight bench, wondering how it managed to roll that far. He strolled back to the stretching room and stopped in the doorway. Holly was still on the mats, pulling his shirt over her head. His clothes looked good on her. His hands had looked good on her, too. When she didn't respond, he tossed the sneaker onto the mat beside her. "You're not going to believe where I found it. I don't think I've made a throw like that since I played baseball. I guess I should be lucky I didn't break a window."

"Thanks" was all she said, deliberately avoiding his eye, grateful he hadn't arrived a moment sooner to catch her smelling his clothing, a schoolgirl-like attempt to fix in her memory an experience she knew could never be forgotten anyway. She picked up the sneaker and began putting it on, appearing as if it took all of her concentration to complete the menial task.

Where was her witty retort or playful comeback? She was all but ignoring him. Not bothering to look for another shirt of his own, Logan leaned against the door frame and folded his arms across his broad naked chest, smiling.

"Hey," he called to her softly. "Look at me." He waited for her to meet his gaze, which she did with hesitation. "Why suddenly shy?"

Holly felt the flush creep up to her cheeks. He was so damn handsome, so damn charming, and too damn comfortable with all of this. She itched to slap the lazy grin off his face.

"I was just trying to remember if I read anything in our contract about this sort of thing."

"It's in the fine print." Logan grinned at her. "Check the back."

"I'll bet," she retorted acerbically, returning to re-aligning her shoelaces by yanking on them. "Glad to see you cover all your bases."

"Holly," he crooned to her, fully aware of the sudden and drastic change in her disposition. He walked over and sat down beside her, giving her shoulder a nudge with his own. "This is not the same woman who ten minutes ago was gasping my name. What do you think is going on here?"

"Nothing at all," Holly told her sneakers as she tied them, refusing to be taken in by his charisma and what she presumed was the smarmy gym equivalent of pillow talk. "Just don't think I'm going to pay more for this kind of service."

"Excuse me, young lady," he said sternly while reaching out his hand to cover hers, forcing her to stop what she was doing, "but this has gone beyond punny. Are you regretting what just happened?"

"Are you?" she quickly spat back, her eyes snapping up to meet his.

"I try not to do anything I'll regret. And at the risk of making one more horrible pun, I certainly don't regret doing you." He nudged her again.

"Do you say this to all your clients?"

Logan smiled. So her green eyes did hold a little bit of the monster.

"Only the men." He caught her off guard and laughed at her look of utter astonishment. Then he continued sincerely. "I won't lie to you, kid. I have, on occasion, slept with a female client. But what just happened here? This was different, special. I wanted it, badly. I've watched it slowly build for weeks, even tried to fight it. Trying to ignore it only made it worse. Oh yeah, I wanted it." He looked around before settling his gaze on her again, one filled with mirth and affection. "I didn't exactly picture it like this. But I've really come to care about you. I hope this is only the beginning of something. I hope we get another chance."

She stared into his face for a long moment before cautiously reaching out to run her fingers down his granite bicep, as if to confirm the whole occurrence hadn't been one of her dreams. As if to make sure all the sweet, warm words she'd just heard really did come from this living, breathing, walking piece of perfect man candy. When she reached his forearm, he grabbed her hand and kissed it before standing up. He reached out to her, and taking both her hands, he pulled her up beside him for a quick solid hug.

"But I'm not sure how many shirts I have here, and my next client is due in five minutes. So it's probably best to wait before we go another round."

Holly left the gym, thankful she had escaped before his next client arrived. She was sure what she had done was written all over her now-sexed-up face. She drove home, her mind awash in confusion. If her life was a screenplay, this would have been the part where the sentimental uplifting music would play, the credits would start to roll, and everyone would get up out of their seats and leave the theater, all warm and gushy.

But her life wasn't a romantic movie and she certainly wasn't a movie star, although her costar certainly looked like one. Time had stood still, and for a few fleeting minutes she had become the ingénue to a real-life idol. What was she supposed to do now? She'd let her guard down and the result was getting seduced by the kind of man she had only dreamed about. It was impossible to believe that thanks to an exercise regimen, a haircut, and some new threads, she had transformed into an irresistible beauty. Sweet Jesus, she wasn't even blond! Obviously, the man had taken some momentary leave of his senses or had been overcome with the urge to pity-fuck. All the lovely things he said afterward, including the confession that he had wanted her for weeks and had fought it, were probably said in the effort to keep her from freaking out in his gym and possibly even keep her as a client with no hard feelings.

But worse yet, if he did mean them, that would pose a much bigger dilemma. How on earth was she supposed to continually hold the attention of a man like Logan Montgomery? Holly wasn't sure she had the intestinal fortitude to keep up with his high-profile lifestyle or fend off every woman who wanted a piece of him. And then she realized she probably wouldn't have to. His parting words were talk of him fucking her again, not taking her out for dinner or home to meet his parents.

As she waited at a stoplight, her fingers unconsciously ran over her lips as if trying to feel for remnants of his kiss, one that was like no other. A kiss so warm and enticing, it could have been considered obscene. It was a catalyst to every repressed and tucked-away feeling she ever knew she could have. It unlocked her desire to throw caution to the wind and give herself over to those feelings. She giggled, thinking that if he actually had taken leave of his senses, she had been more than willing to join him. In a blur of hands and tongues and mouths, he took her to the sort of climax she never thought possible. From the moment he ripped off her shirt, she had become effortlessly motivated to behave like every sexpot she'd ever read about. Holly flushed anew and squirmed a little in her car seat at the flashback of the whole encounter. She shivered with the memory of his fingers inside her, the way they commanded that she bring that climax forth, the way she literally came into his palm, only to find he was able to make her do it again. The light changed to green and the car behind her honked its horn. She came back to the present and with one more giggle returned her focus to the road.

By the time Holly turned into her driveway, the sun had fully set on one of the most tumultuous days in her recent memory, and she had decided on her best course of action. No matter what the reason, whether pity or arousal, Logan had done her a tremendous favor. He had made her realize that she was once again a full feeling woman, only now complete with sexuality and chemistry and desire. It was yet another thing she could be grateful to him for. He didn't force himself on her; she had been a more than willing participant in what had turned out to be a revitalization of monumental proportions. She would go back into his gym on her next training day and make like nothing out of the ordinary had happened. She would let him off the hook without making him feel guilty for his indiscretion.

As she showered, acutely aware that she was washing off all the intimate and sensitive places his hands and mouth had been, she practiced how she would remain unaffected in his presence, although at first it wouldn't be easy. She would concentrate on keeping her focus on her exercises, just as she did in the beginning. She would let him touch her and stretch her without melting or sighing or being catapulted back in time to just a few hours ago, when his touching her had elicited a manic escapade of wanton passion. She would prove to him that she was mature and fully evolved, perfectly capable of handling a one-night stand without falling apart and becoming a psycho stalking bitch. Further-more, she would start calling some of the numbers of the interesting, attractive men she'd met who wanted to take her out. She would take Chase's advice and date. She might even actively pursue some of the Kings play-ers that Amanda went out of her way to throw at her. She would make it her goal to start enjoying all the lust and sex that was out there for the offering, secure in the knowledge that if she could excite a man like Logan, she could make a lesser man fall all over to electrify her. She never knew sex could be so spontaneous and explosive, demanding her body's response. Those weren't words that could have been used to describe Bruce when it came to sex. The mere possibility of someone else making her feel that again was euphoric.

She was in the kitchen, finishing an apple that was quartered and spread with peanut butter, when the doorbell rang. She made her way to the door and cau-tiously looked through the peephole.

On her doorstep was Logan Montgomery.

She pulled away from the peephole and, with her hand covering her mouth, shook her head. What the hell was he doing here? It was too soon. She wasn't ready yet. The memory was still too fresh from their previous encounter. Taking a deep breath, she squared her shoulders and unlocked the dead bolt.

She opened the door and tried not to sigh. "I was going to wash your shirt before bringing it back to you," she lied. He was never getting that souvenir returned.

He smiled, leaning up against the door frame. "I'm not here for the shirt. Can I come in?"

She held open the door and he entered, striding through the foyer and into her living room before stopping and turning around to face her, his hands planted on his hips, speaking in a clipped, serious tone. "I wanted to apologize for what happened before."

"It's—it's okay," she sputtered nervously after closing the door and joining him, but maintaining a safe distance. She began to wring her hands. "All that slapping and weeping going on, it was enough to make anyone act out of character. It was just such a nice kiss. I don't know what came over me. I should probably be thanking you. It was . . . fun."

He tilted his head to one side, smiling again. He dropped his hands and, after taking a deep breath, took a step closer to her. "I think we may be having a miscommunication. Yes, it was fun, but that's not what I'm talking about."

"It's not?" Holly's eyes grew wide and her mouth, while still open, was unable to produce a suitable retort.

Logan took another step, closer still. "No. It's not," he said, slowly shaking his head, his stare fixed on her full lips. He moved another few steps until he was right next to her before looking back up and into her eyes, his voice pure velvet. "I wanted to apologize for the ungentlemanly way I took you on my gym floor. Not very well done of me and certainly not my intention. I think I may have mentioned that before."

"O-oh, that," she stammered, swallowing hard. He was so close, his meltingly hot stare threatening to take her very breath away, his voice sultry and hypnotic. "Think nothing of it. You could have taken me anywhere."

He released a single chuckle and, reaching out, gently placed his finger over her mouth to silence her. "Thank you for that very kind offer, but I was thinking more along the lines of someplace a little more private, a bedroom maybe?"

She nodded mutely, unable to tear herself away from his smoldering eyes. He brought his head in, ever so slowly, and softly kissed her. "I really only meant to kiss you before," he whispered as he took his lips off hers. "Like that." He repeated the whisper and the action, only this time with his hands creeping up around her waist, pulling her closer to him. "But you lit me up like a firecracker." He breathed into her mouth, warm and gentle. "I know I mentioned a second chance. Another go-round, if you will. But this time we take our time." He moved his lips to her ear, the whisper becoming huskier. "Do it right."

"Right," she repeated breathlessly, allowing herself to be enveloped fully within his embrace, her head falling back to give him better access to the column of her throat as his mouth began to drift in that direction. His hands glided down her back and up again to settle just below her rib cage before groping upward. The same hands that were usually so precise and thorough now seemed to be everywhere in a frenzy to try to touch all of her at once. She felt the bulge in his shorts press against her. It was hard and full, and all in reaction to her. He wanted her as badly as she wanted him. It sent a fresh rush of passion coursing through her.

Logan roughly pulled at the knot in her robe before none-too-gently pushing her onto the couch. He had arrived at her house with the sole purpose of taking his time, allowing them both to fully experience each other through erotic foreplay. He wanted to fondle her slowly, find and memorize all the spots she had that were the most responsive, the most sensitive to his mouth and his hands. He wanted to become familiar with a body that until a few hours ago he'd known by heart but wasn't at all used to, one with womanly curves and muscle and substance. A body with breasts and a bottom that filled his hands with some to spare, a body whose newness made him ache with an undefined agitation. A body he'd created. To hell with taking his time. With her innocent excitement came the overwhelming urge to bury himself deep inside her again. His ears longed to hear her soft gasps at his invasion. He already knew she was hot and tight, and it was a discovery that shook him to his core. He dropped his khaki shorts, removed his shirt, and pulled off her panties. He ran his hand over the tuft of hair on her mound. Not overly waxed and hairless, but with soft curly fur that would soon be glistening with a wetness he'd produced. Thirsty for it, he kissed her there. Single-minded passes with his strong lips and rough tongue insistently probed until she was both breathless and witless. He lifted her legs and placed them on his shoulders, tilting her upward to bring her in line with him.

With supreme effort, he forced himself to enter her slowly, watching as inch by inch his rock-hard member disappeared within her willing, wet cavern. He felt her thigh muscles tighten when he reached his hilt, and she began to writhe beneath him. She reached out, desperate to touch him, feel him, pull him closer, and she moaned as he held her in position, denying her unspoken demand. Unable to, and with no desire to, escape, she dropped her hands and dug her nails into the couch's leather. He watched himself start to withdraw from her and drove into her again, this time quicker, with more purpose. She moaned again.

"Tell me, Holly," he commanded from above her, moving his gaze from her luscious junction, where he was still fully sheathed, up to her flushed face, holding her legs securely against him. "Tell me what you want."

"I want you, Logan," she responded feverishly. "Harder."

He thrust into her with vigor, watching her bite into her lower lip.

"Faster." She swooned, her head shaking from side to side.

He began moving within her, faster and persistently, to fulfill her request.

"All of you." She began to speak in breathy broken sentences. "I want you," she repeated on a sob as with orchestrated movement he drove into her repeatedly and brought her to the brink of ecstasy, and then neatly pushed her over it.

She cried out his name one final time before incoherent cries took its place and she began to stiffen and then shudder uncontrollably. He held her legs tightly as she wildly bucked against him, firmly entrenched in the sweet creaminess that was her essence. Before she was finished, his own unavoidable release spewed forth and he held fast as he climaxed, reluctant to leave her until no other option was possible.

He exhaustedly joined her on the couch, shifting her so that she lay directly on his torso and his arm rested on her back, his fingertips gently massaging her soft shoulder. They sat in silence for several long moments until their heart rates and breathing returned to normal.

"At least we don't have to worry about someone walking in on us," he finally remarked, astounded that the woman in his arms could make him deviate from his plan of leisurely exploration so efficiently, and with no effort. He'd pounced on her right in her living room like some high schooler with only minutes before her parents got home.

"And I will say this much," she told him languidly, loving the feel of his warm muscles pressed up against her. "You are getting us closer to the bedroom."

"The night is still young, sweetness," he rumbled suggestively into her ear, then tightened his arm around her and looked down at her flushed, smiling face. "And I'm just getting started."

Chapter Sixteen

HOLLY WOKE UP THE NEXT MORNING ALONE. SAFELY nestled in her bed, like countless mornings before, she patiently waited for wakefulness to fully take hold. She rubbed her face, then glanced at the clock. It was late, after nine. She had overslept. It wasn't until she stretched that she began to remember . . . vividly. She struggled to sit up, her aching muscles voicing their protest, and looked at the pillow next to hers. A faint indent on the pillow remained, signifying that indeed someone had been sleeping beside her. It was the same someone she vaguely remembered kissing her forehead and tucking the covers around her when leaving just before dawn.

Logan Montgomery had made love to her, literally all night long.

She was sore everywhere. She had done things with

him she had only read about. Positions she was sure only yoga masters were privy to. She was sore down *there,* from his insatiable desire to ravage her. And when he wasn't inside her, he held her, closely. They giggled and teased each other until the wee hours of the morning before finally drifting off into sated slumber.

"Wow. He certainly got me to the bedroom," Holly said out loud, falling back onto the bed. She briefly debated staying there all day, pretending the night hadn't ended. She rolled over and grabbed the pillow he used, bringing it up to her nose. His scent faintly remained. It was an intoxicating mixture of his sweat and hair gel plus the slight remnants of his cologne. She breathed it in and sighed. Last night was every dream she'd ever had come to life. She felt sexy and beautiful and even a little bit dirty. He brought all those feelings out in her, the minute his lips touched hers.

And then Holly's mind began racing. What happens now? Logan was not the kind to make commitments; that was abundantly clear. Certainly he would've had his fill of her after a night like that. But how was she supposed to forget about all the things he did to her, the intimacy they shared? How would she ever be able to remain unaffected by him once she saw him again? She'd have to. She was grateful she wouldn't have to see him until tomorrow, her next training day. What if he told her he couldn't train her anymore, citing some breach of contract? The "Naked Pretzel Clause," perhaps?

The phone rang beside her bed, making Holly jolt. She stared at the phone as if touching it would poison her. What if it was Logan calling to break the bad news, give her the brush-off after the wham-bam-thank-you-ma'am? He never called her house phone, always opting for calling her cell. Maybe it was Amanda. Holly could use talking to Amanda now, even if she didn't know exactly what to say.

Holly looked at the caller ID. It was Tina. She hurriedly picked up the receiver.

"Perfect timing," Holly said into the phone.

"Morning," Tina replied before saying their standard, "How's tricks?"

"How's tricks? I'll tell you how tricks are. I just spent the night having wild sex with my trainer." Holly tried to sound cool, but excitement prevailed.

There was a long pause, followed by a disbelieving, "No way."

Not the reaction Holly had hoped for. "Oh yes way."

There was another pause. "You had sex with that guy from the picture?" While she didn't have actual access to Logan's Facebook page, Tina was able to see Logan's profile picture in Holly's friend list. From that moment on, Tina had called him "that guy."

"Yes."

"I want details," Tina said flippantly.

"I'm not giving you details." Holly giggled, feeling the afterglow wash over her again. "But I will say this . . . holy shit, it was amazing. I'm not sure I'm going to be able to walk today."

"Well, that didn't take long. I guess what they say about trainers is true. Holly, how could you let this happen?" Tina's voice rang with reproach.

Holly felt the sting of it. "I don't even know how it

happened. And what do you mean by that? Forget it, don't answer that. I don't want to know. But you know what? I thought you'd have the decency to be happy for me, if for no other reason than I got the cobwebs cleaned out of my fun place."

"I am happy for you, if this is what you want. But you just went to that place you can't get back from."

"Who says I'm not ready to keep moving forward? I didn't throw myself at him, you know," Holly said defensively. "Whose side are you on here?"

"I'm on your side. But guys like that . . ." Tina's words trailed off.

"Guys like that *what*?" Holly demanded. "Don't go for girls like me?"

"They're single for a reason." The response was flat and monotone.

"I can't believe you just said that," Holly snapped. "We've been spending a lot of time together. He told me he's been attracted to me for a while. Why are you trying to make me feel so lousy? Unless you think he's lying or I don't deserve him?"

"No. I think it's all great. But I've heard about this stuff. Why wouldn't he want to see how far you'd go? You've been his trained seal for months," Tina said, her words measured and deliberate. "But I also don't think you should get carried away. You had sex; that's it. I just think if you're looking at this as having a future, you're heading for trouble. You've told me all about the crowd this guy runs with."

"I never said anything about a future. I'm not stupid. And he has a name." Holly swiped at the tears of exhaustion and disappointment that appeared in her eyes. "It's Logan."

"Okay. Logan. You've told me all about Logan and all his überfamous friends. How he's been taking you to ball games and fancy dinners. How you're practically joined at the hip with Amanda Walker. Now that he's gotten what he wanted, just don't be surprised if all that comes to an end."

"I'm already operating under that assumption, but thanks for the vote of confidence." Holly tried to make the comment sound like a joke. "And you're wrong about Amanda."

"What's next, you're going to trade in your loafers for stilettos?"

"That would be a stretch, even for me, but so what if I am?"

"Don't you think it's all a bit out of your realm?" There was an infuriating edge to Tina's tone that Holly had no choice but to recognize.

"How would you know? All your relationship knowledge comes from reality TV. What are you, jealous?" Holly asked. "Am I having too much fun for you? Not quite depressed enough for you anymore?"

"Jealous?" Tina's laugh was harsh. "Jealous of what? Jealous that you just got used up by a horny personal trainer? How very ethical of him. He's a real class act."

"You don't even know him!" Holly was close to shouting.

"I don't need to know him," Tina responded with surprising calm. "But I know you. You're not the one-night-stand sort of girl and just not the caliber this guy is used to. He's going to hurt you, and it's going to piss me off, and you're too far away for me to do anything about it."

Holly brought her tone down to match Tina's, only with an underlying coolness to try to mask the hurt. "There's nothing for you to do, Tina. I'm not always a problem that needs fixing. You're always saying you want me to be happy, and the morning I am, you shoot it all down."

"I know the truth hurts and I'm sorry. I have a rotten feeling about this, like he somehow took advantage of you. What else do you want me to say? 'I promise not to rub it in your face when he breaks your heart'?"

"You won't have to worry about that. Thanks for nothing. I have to go." Holly quickly pushed the OFF button on the telephone and threw it on the bed.

It wasn't the first, last, or only time Holly and Tina angrily hung up on each other, although it had been years. There was little doubt in Holly's mind that Tina was lashing out at least partially in envy. Tina had never liked when Holly got too much attention, even when they were in school. Not that Tina ever had to worry about it much back then. Holly always seemed to be in the background while Tina soaked up her position as the extroverted popular girl. As long as Holly wasn't too happy, Tina could act as her biggest supporter. Holly had repressed that realization, reminding herself that no one was perfect and afraid of losing the only real friend she ever had besides Bruce. However, this felt different. Whether Tina liked it or not, Holly was changing, and she had no intention of going back to the place she came from. Holly had begun to look at life as an adventure again. She wanted Tina to be happy for her, even if she was heading for disaster. Holly lay back on the bed and hugged Logan's pillow to her again. Holly had felt the resentment building up in Tina from the moment Holly told her about that first baseball game Logan took her to, although Holly downplayed it. Tina was always peevish and quick to point out that Holly and people like Logan and the Walkers were worlds apart and that she couldn't understand what Holly had in common with any of them. Eventually, Holly had stopped talking about her new life altogether. But last night had changed that. Holly needed her friend, and her friend had failed her.

But Holly couldn't ignore the nagging feeling that there was truth behind Tina's words either. Whether Tina had just zeroed in on Holly's weakness and exploited it, Holly couldn't be sure. She was certain of one thing though. What happened last night was likely nothing more than temptation overruling common sense. Holly would have to be careful to navigate her way through the aftermath of her night with Logan. She already felt like she'd lost a friend. The thought of his completely leaving her life was upsetting.

Holly went downstairs and found her cell phone on the kitchen counter. When she saw the text from Logan suggesting she come into the gym later for some cardio, she smiled with relief. He was right back to the status quo. She put down the phone and went back to bed.

She was taking the day off from Logan Montgomery.

THE NEXT DAY, HOLLY FOUND HERSELF STALLING OUTSIDE
of the building, much like the very first day she entered
it. The nervousness felt the same but the reasons behind
it couldn't have been more different. Once again, she
didn't know what awaited her at the top of the stairs.
But she knew who was waiting, and now she knew him
in a biblical sense. She hadn't heard anything more
from Logan after his single text. No flirtatious follow-
ups or sexy pillow talk. He didn't even call her to see
how she was doing. Convincing herself that their relationship would return to business as usual, Holly tried
to curb the disappointment that accompanied the conclusion. She wasn't so sure she would be able to hold up
her end of that bargain. Damn him for being every bit
as wonderful in bed as she thought he'd be. Not wanting to be late and refusing to give in to her fears, she
opened the door and began the climb to the unknown.

Logan was in his small office on the phone, casually leaning on his desk, his back to the door. Not un-
usual. He never answered any calls while training and
often used the time in between sessions to conduct a
few minutes of business. As soon as Holly saw him,
heard his baritone in muffled conversation, she felt her
knees grow weak. She tried switching to automatic
pilot, dropping her car keys in the holder next to the
door and got onto a treadmill to begin her warm-up.
Concentrating on the music was an epic fail. All she
could hear was the bass throbbing, pulsating in time
with her now-pounding heart.

The next thing she knew, he was standing beside her,
placing a bottle of water in the treadmill's cup holder.

"Hey there." Logan greeted her with a small grin and checked how much time she had left on her warm-up.

"Hey yourself," she replied, striving for nonchalance, and attempted to take her hands off the sides of the treadmill, now more concerned with experiencing cardiac arrest.

"I was surprised I didn't see you yesterday. I sent you a text to come cardio."

"I was pretty sore yesterday," Holly said without thinking, and then cringed.

Logan raised an eyebrow and the killer dimples appeared. "Really now?"

"I had cramps," she blurted, wishing her water bottle contained arsenic. It was like telling him she had her period. At least he'd be relieved, although he already knew she was on the pill.

He tilted his head slightly to one side, clearly amused. "Sorry to hear that."

"In my legs! I was mowing the lawn." Perfect. She could cross becoming a poker player off her list.

Logan nodded, keeping a straight face. "That certainly would qualify as cardio; you have a lot of grass. I'll bet your landscaper will really appreciate it."

"I—I mean I was tired," she stammered, giving up and feeling her cheeks flaming.

"Perfectly understandable," he replied easily, pushing the stop button on the treadmill. "You should be all rested up for today. Or in five minutes, your quads will seize up. Let's work out."

He seemed perfectly normal, professional as always. Holly was relieved and not surprised. If nothing else, he was intending to keep her as a client. As long as she shut up and didn't start prattling about how splendid he looked nude or how positively delicious he tasted. Following his lead, she met him at the chest press. He had already placed a towel over it. She sat down, and her session began.

Neither of them spoke, aside from his gruffly telling her what exercise she was doing next. After a while, it became unnerving. Logan seemed intent on behaving as if nothing had happened between them. Holly fought it by channeling it into extreme focus, and the end result was strength she didn't even know she possessed. Adrenaline poured out of her like sweat and fatigue never seemed to set in.

"Guess all that rest paid off, or the grass cutting," Logan finally mused after she pumped out the third set of box squats with a forty-pound barbell balanced across her shoulders. "Nicely done."

He took the barbell, then handed her two ten-pound dumbbells.

"Alternate lunges and bicep curls," he ordered.

"Lunges?" Holly immediately groaned out of habit. His eyes narrowed in warning and she swiftly closed her mouth. She bit back a smirk. Leg lunges were what started this whole mess in the first place. She began the exercise per his instructions.

"Lower," Logan commanded after a moment. "Spread your legs apart wider."

Holly tried to comply, but his voice had started to give her shivers. The same wording he always used suddenly sounded like innuendo. Of course, he hadn't told her to spread her legs wider the other night; he simply did it for her. It was maddening, trying to decide what was worse, his silence or his now-sex-charged instructions.

"Holly." Logan's stern voice broke into her thoughts. "I said lower. Knee to the floor."

And then he did it. He touched her. His hand shot out, playfully swatting her bottom.

Holly felt like she had been electrocuted. Her head snapped in his direction.

He was smiling innocently and gave her a wink. "You want to loosen up those sore muscles, don't you?"

Holly's knee went to the floor and everything after that was a blur.

And then he pointed to the Balzac.

Oh no, not the Balzac! Holly felt dizzy with despair. They hadn't used the Balzac in weeks. He really wasn't playing fair! The Balzac was another one of their definitions in the Groody Training Terminology Dictionary. It was really a free-standing lateral pulldown machine without a bench, and had a different attachment from the standard bar. That attachment was a hook with two foot-long lengths of heavy rope. Knotted at the ends of the ropes were two heavy round . . . well . . . balls. The exercise was designed to work the triceps and consisted of standing in front of the ropes, grabbing the balls and pulling them past the waist, while separating the ropes as far as possible then returning them to the original position. From beginning to end, it was the most phallic thing Holly had ever seen. Even the way it hung on the hook looked like a pair of testicles. She had started calling it the "ball sac" under her breath for her own amusement, but it slipped out one day by accident. Logan overheard it and pestered her until she gave a full explanation. After a hearty laugh and accusing her of being twisted, he suggested calling it something a little more polite. He recommended the spin on the nineteenth-century French novelist and the exercise was the Balzac ever since.

But if that wasn't enough to take Holly to all the wrong places mentally, there was one other thing, something far more sinister about the Balzac. The single most important part of the exercise is keeping your elbows completely at your sides to isolate the tricep muscle, which is virtually impossible.

Sweet Jesus, he was going to touch her. And not just touch her. *Really* touch her. It was one of those exercises where he touched her every time. It was brutal on her nerve endings long before he took touching to a whole new level. It was easily as bad as a stretch, probably worse because of the intimate unknown variable. She wouldn't have been surprised to find out that they hadn't used it in weeks because it was too erotic for him as well. Now that he was sated, he could go back to torturing her. She walked over to where he waited, trying to appear focused, but her nerves were tighter than guitar strings.

She took her place in front of the Balzac and he took his spot right behind her. And as she grabbed onto the two balls to give them a controlled tug down, his hands pinned her elbows to her sides. He masterfully restrained her so that the only movement available to her was yanking those balls up and down and apart to pull the weight. And he wasn't going anywhere until the set was over. There was no way to tell whether he was a foot or an inch behind her. If she leaned back, just a bit, would she bump into all the best parts of him at once with his arms already halfway around her? Could she make those parts react the same way they did the other night? She could feel his breath on the back of her neck; it felt like a blow torch. When she started going too fast in the effort to get it over with, his grip on her tightened.

"Slow it down, girl. It isn't a race." He breathed in her ear and she thought her heart actually stopped. No matter how close he was, it was too close.

Somehow Holly made it through the rest of her workout. Logan went back to being all business and she thought about getting her teeth cleaned. She tried to make up a grocery list. She considered purchasing a lizard to rid her house of unwanted bugs—anything to detach herself from her current situation. By the time he stretched her, she was like jelly, weak and spent from fending off his presence. He remained silent as he worked, pulling her legs in much the same way he had two nights before, giving little more than the occasional glance down at her to make sure she was still breathing. No witty comments or small talk was exchanged. With his hands impassively all over her and with her unable to do anything but lie there, sadness settled in Holly. He had already moved on, completely comfortable resuming their relationship where it left off. He wasn't even going to give her the courtesy of telling her he'd had a great time. And why would he? What did she know about the art of making love? She could practically have reclaimed her status as a virgin, at least before he'd gotten hold of her. She fought back the urge to cry, reminding herself that if she had known the outcome beforehand, she still would have jumped at the chance to have him, even if only for one night. He had been her fantasy fulfilled. She wouldn't disrespect it, no matter how much it hurt. When it was finally over, he reached for her hand and pulled her up off the mats in the same manner he always did.

Once she was on her feet beside him, Logan gave her the obligatory, "Great job."

Holly nodded in a daze and wiped the sweat off her upper lip with the sleeve of her T-shirt, ignoring the towel in his hand. Not knowing what else to do, she took the first two steps in the direction of the front door.

Then she felt his hand on her hip. Dipping his fingers into the waistband of her pants, Logan purposefully pulled her back until she was flush against his iron chest. He wrapped his arms around her.

"Thank God that's over with." He exhaled meaningfully right before kissing her. "What are we doing for dinner?"

Chapter Seventeen

$\mathcal{I}$T WAS OFFICIAL. LOGAN MONTGOMERY, PERSONAL trainer to the pros, was off the market. At least as far as women were concerned. He stopped making calls to other women and stopped taking them as well. Messages from old lovers piled up and were erased without his even listening to them. Texts went unanswered. He still maintained his work schedule, but every spare minute he had was dedicated to sexing Holly Brennan. Every day, as soon as his last client left and he locked the door, he would head straight for her house with a sole purpose: wanting to hear her cry out his name as she came.

He practically went underground, with only Chase and Amanda having any real clue as to his whereabouts. That first session alone with Amanda had been torture. She was on her best behavior when she came in with Chase. Chase was uninterested, his focus on getting ready for the playoffs. But she was quiet, too quiet. Her smug little smile told Logan all he needed to know. When she came in later that day for her own session, Logan cut right to it.

"Go ahead, Amanda. Get it out of your system." He sighed.

"I'm not allowed to talk about it," she told him, the smug smile fully in place.

"Tell Chase I said thank you." He winked at her, relaxing.

"But I told you so," she replied happily before launching into a full-blown diatribe, complete with planning several vacations, holidays, and a wedding.

"I'm telling on you," he finally said, pulling out his phone.

It was like having a new toy that he didn't want to share; at least that's what he told himself. Holly was different in so many new and wonderful ways. He felt like he never had enough of her. He couldn't seem to stop himself from taking her hard and fast, continuously afraid of spontaneously ejaculating the minute she touched him. Maybe it was because she told him she had never been with any other man except her late husband, which lent itself to a naïve and irresistible eagerness that drove him wild. Her soft touch across his hot skin acted like a match being struck, setting him ablaze. She cried out for him as if she was praying and he was her salvation. That first week he had trouble keeping himself from getting hard just thinking about her. It was exasperating and amazing, the ravenous desire waging war with the struggle to take back control over his own body.

He stripped her slowly and she let him, marveling at how soft she was. Each piece of clothing removed was an invitation to touch her never-ending curves and valleys. Her natural breasts, full and lush, would respond to his hands by becoming hard and jutted, not because they were designed that way by a plastic surgeon, but because of her arousal. Her dark round nipples begged to be licked and he would oblige, secure in the knowledge that she was feeling every single lap of his tongue, every nibble of his teeth. Her bottom bounced and jiggled joyfully with his kneading as well as his relentless penetration when he took her from behind. The slight roundness at her belly that remained despite the countless crunches he made her do began to remind him of a carnival ride, something he could hold on to as she willingly and without intimidation let him mold her into whatever position he chose to take her in.

But most of all, she gave, warmly, without hesitation or reservation. She was never shy about exactly who she was, laughingly telling him that she was built for endurance, not for speed. She never hid behind towels or sheets or darkness. Or ultimatums. She demanded nothing and expected nothing. Except for her kiss— her kiss demanded and expected his attention and accepted nothing less, gentle yet persistent. Every time he brought his lips to hers it was like the first time, and she responded with awe and magic and surprise. Every kiss good-bye ended up launching him back into the desire to possess her all over again.

They started sharing workouts together, making sure they locked the gym door. It always started out with the purest of intentions. They worked out diligently and seriously, paying homage to their respective body temples. But they each also secretly looked forward to watching the other's muscles in action, the rush of pheromones their sweat produced and the overpowering lust it subsequently provided. He ravished her on weight benches, in the shower room, and on his desk. He drank from between her thighs like she was an oasis in a desert and he was dying of thirst.

But when Logan was alone, his body drained and exhausted of every available ounce of testosterone, he would catch himself thinking, *How can I help her get the last of that weight off?* Or, *Maybe just a little bit of liposuction is in order.* He knew medically that she was an endomorph, that no amount of exercise and dietary changes, short of starvation, would have her reaching a single-digit size. He knew logically she was healthy and her body was as finely tuned and conditioned as any athlete's. She had followed every piece of advice he ever gave her. He preferred going to her house instead of bringing her to his to avoid any drop-bys that could lead to confrontations. He rationalized that the reason he never took her out was because she preferred a quiet existence, devoid of the hectic pace of the high-profile nightlife. He also knew he wasn't being completely truthful.

They were cuddled up in her bed late one night, their bodies entwined, mutual hands occasionally wandering. The John Mayer CD that had been playing had long since been replaced with pillow talk and then sleepy silence. Holly took her head off Logan's chest and leaned her chin on it, staring at his dozing chiseled features. As the pressure increased, he opened his eyes and gave her a thoroughly gratified smile.

"What?"

"What do you see in me?" she asked him.

"Is this a test?" He chuckled.

"Never mind. You don't have to answer that," Holly replied, discomfited, and laid her head back down on his chest, making sure he couldn't see her face. She had posed a question she didn't really want to know the answer to.

Holly felt his arm, which was resting on her shoulder, tighten around her. It moved slowly down the slope of her back and up again, his fingertips creating a sensual pattern over her skin. His hand finally rested neatly on the indent of her waist. And then he spoke.

"I see a woman who takes pleasure in a lot of the same things I do and makes me laugh. Who loves to strive and sweat and doesn't complain even though she hates leg lunges. I see a woman whose inner strength matches her outer strength, which can also be said for her beauty. I see a woman who effortlessly brings out the best in me as a man."

Holly remained with her face turned away, afraid that if she looked at him she would become overwhelmed. What he said was heartfelt and sincere, but in Holly's mind, it was also lacking. It sounded so diplomatic. Like he was enjoying everything she offered him but could easily live without it. She was positively smitten with him. He was just enjoying the time they were spending together. At least he was honest and didn't fill her head and heart with smarmy bullshit. She knew she would have to start thinking more like him, or she would be doomed when their time together was over. She took a deep breath and turned back to face him. He was smiling down at her, the same smile that still had the ability to take her breath away.

"Did I pass?" he asked as he pulled her up to bring her lips closer to his, his hands beginning to wander again.

His lips touched hers before she was forced to answer.

Chapter Eighteen

GOT A JOB," HOLLY TOLD HIM TWO WEEKS LATER AS they were snuggling up on her couch, getting ready to watch a movie.

"You did?" Logan asked, mildly surprised and then moderately concerned. He wasn't aware that she had been looking for one. "Are you in trouble? Financially?"

"No no no," she said quickly, reassuring him. "It's nothing like that. I just got to thinking it was time and an interesting opportunity came up."

"An interesting accounting opportunity? Is that even possible?" he joked.

"Not exactly," she replied tentatively, "although I will be dealing with some money. It's more like a customer-service position. I was in the Nike outlet the other day and got to talking to a guy who is the sales manager at a local gym."

"You got to talking to a guy? About a local gym?" Logan felt his irritation meter switch on. Why was Holly interested in local gyms? Why was she talking to other guys? "Which gym?"

"Bodyessy," she told him, noticing the distinct edge in his tone and that he'd gone from conversing to questioning.

"Bodyessy?" he repeated.

"Yeah. You know, like 'odyssey,' but with a 'B'? Their motto is 'We give your bod an odyssey.'"

"I'm very aware of it," Logan said with a chuckle. They were an East Coast franchise outfit of about one hundred gyms specializing in hard-sell practices with long-term loophole contracts and slowly repaired leased equipment. "And just what are you going to do for them? Sales?"

"No. I'm going to be their opener."

"Opener? He did tell you what the opener actually does, right?" he asked her in a tone more condescending that she would have considered him capable of.

"Yeah. They open the gym," she responded in kind.

"You do realize they open at five in the morning?" Logan told her, almost moping as he pictured her alarm being set for three thirty in the morning and all their late-night lovemaking flying out the window. "And calling in sick isn't really an option. Those cookie-cutter gyms live and die by the unlocking of the door. I don't think they give you three strikes to be late either; it's two and you're shit-canned. You do realize that, right?"

"Of course I do," Holly said, now starting to feel defensive and more determined than ever. "He explained the whole thing to me. I just have to turn on the lights, the music, and the equipment, get the cash register set up for the day, unlock the front door, and make sure that everyone who tries to get in is paid up. It doesn't really sound that hard. And I'm off by nine. The money isn't spectacular, but I'm guaranteed all weekends and holidays off. And they throw in a membership and a free training session once a week."

"And why exactly do you need a free gym membership or a training session?" He attempted to reverse his attitude as well as his method of persuasion by sounding lighthearted and pulled her into his lap, nuzzling her neck. "You have twenty-four-hour-a-day access to a gym. Twenty-four-hour access to a trainer, too, come to think of it."

"Well, that's just it," Holly said slowly, trying to concentrate on the topic at hand and finding it difficult with his warm lips on her throat and his hand between her legs. "I don't want you to get sick of me."

"Why don't you let me worry about that?" he said, turning the nuzzle into a nibble, this time on her earlobe.

"I don't want to get sick of you either," she murmured, wanting to choose her words carefully and realizing there was no easy way to do so.

The nibbling stopped and his head popped up. "Beg your pardon?"

She could tell by the shocked look on his handsome face that she had said it all wrong. "That didn't come out right."

"You're sick of me?" he asked her, his big brown eyes wide and disbelieving.

"Not at all," she told him quickly, climbing off him and sitting back down on the edge of the couch, wringing her hands as she tried to offer a plausible explanation. "It's just that we're spending almost all our free time together, which, don't get me wrong, is great. I'm just afraid it's going to get old really fast, especially if I'm doing all my cardio workouts around you and your other clients. I'm starting to feel like a groupie."

"I've never said or thought that, but whatever." Logan sat back in the couch, crossed his arms over his chest, and went back to moping. "I suppose the next thing you're going to do is fire me as your trainer."

"Of course not!" she gasped. "Have you lost your mind? I couldn't lose you if I wanted to! But even you've told me that every now and then, you need to shock the body by switching it up." And then she smiled, leaning back into him and placing her chin on his shoulder. "And what could shock my body more than having some mediocre trainer put me through some lame paces on some shoddy equipment?"

Logan exhaled, unmoving, but shifting his eyes downward to meet hers looking up at him from his shoulder. "You're making me sound like a petulant child that you're trying to get to eat vegetables, you know."

She batted her eyelashes dramatically up at him. "If the shoe fits, junior."

He faked a roar and tumbled her backward onto the couch, grabbing both her hands in his and restraining her at the wrists above her head. He looked down from on top of her and began to address her strictly.

"You fully realize that most of the trainers at these

chain-store gyms are nothing but hacks with dime-store educations and probably aren't qualified to hold your legs during an abdominal crunch, right?"

She made no move to escape. "Of course, my superior physical education mentor."

"And that the free session they give you is really nothing more than an opportunity to sell you an overpriced package of more sessions?"

"I'll tell them not to bother. I'll tell them I train with the legendary Logan Montgomery, although, shit, if you want to talk about overpriced . . . ," she teased.

"And because you're my grasshopper, if they try to tell you to do some crackpot exercise that you know isn't right, you won't do it?" he said, continuing to scold her while shifting both her wrists into one of his hands. With his free hand he gently traced his fingertips from the base of her throat slowly down into her shirt to where her breasts came together and lingered there.

"I'll fake an injury worthy of an Academy Award," she promised, craning her neck upward in an effort to kiss him.

He moved his head up farther, deliberately keeping her from reaching him while probing deeper within her cleavage with his middle finger. "And finally, if some 'roid-raging insomniac starts going crazy because he didn't pay his monthly dues and still wants to come in, you won't do anything stupid and will instead call the police?"

"I'll let him in like he owns the place and patiently

wait for the cops to come and Taser him," she vowed, beginning to squirm provocatively beneath him.

"That's my girl," Logan said, right before letting go of her wrists, wrapping his arms around her, and sending his mouth crashing down onto hers.

Chapter Nineteen

IN THE END, LOGAN KNEW HE HAD LITTLE CHOICE. HE
certainly didn't own Holly. They hadn't had any sort of
conversation about exclusivity. She had never pushed
the issue with him; she was always available and willing to accommodate his schedule or his mood. And he
wasn't done playing with her yet, his new fun toy. He
hadn't finished touching and tasting and arousing her
yet. It was something he had taken for granted. He took
advantage of the fact that she had no friends, except the
Walkers, so he never had to compete with anyone for
her time. Deep down, Logan knew he was being un-
reasonable, and if he was being honest, he would have
admitted he didn't like the idea of sharing his shiny
new obsession.

But as days turned into weeks and Holly began to tell
Logan more anecdotes about the people she worked

with—her regular early-bird customers and her goofy new trainer, Nick—dislike began to resemble flat-out disdain. It was when Amanda mentioned to him that *she* was joining Bodyssey for afternoon cardio dates with Holly that he realized he needed to make a change. The ensuing irrational discomfort was a clear indicator that Logan had to take back some control before his emotions got the best of him.

The first order of business, he told himself, is to know your enemy and face your fear. He played around with his schedule for a Thursday and moved all his early-morning clients to later in the day, leaving himself free until ten. Then on Wednesday night, he set his alarm for five. He awoke that morning, took a quick wake-up shower, put on his workout clothes, and made the drive to Bodyssey.

He arrived just before six. The sun was beginning to come up, but gaudy colorful spotlights illuminated the building's façade, a beacon calling out to all local gym rats. The parking lot was already half-full and he could hear the cliché hip-hop music blasting from speakers installed outside. He parked his car on the outskirts of the lot and, grabbing his towel and his water, jogged his way to the front door. He was halfway to his destination when the music suddenly stopped and was replaced by Holly's voice, sounding more like a carnival barker than anything else.

"There's three bikes left for the six A.M. spin class up for grabs," she announced. "First come, first served. And remember, I do not take threats, but I will accept cash."

Logan burst out laughing and picked up his pace.

He opened the door, stepped through a small atrium, and then was inside. She was behind a long counter, looking fresh-faced and adorable. On the other side of it, in front of her, were no less than three men, all either getting ready to go work out or already finished. They were laughing, appearing to hang on her every word. It looked to Logan as if Holly was holding court. As soon as she caught sight of him, her smile grew wide.

"Hello, handsome," she told him, beaming. "Welcome to Bodyssey." All the heads turned in his direction.

"Oh man," one of the heads, a man in his forties with red hair graying at the temples and a faded Mets shirt, announced boisterously. "We have a new guest. Shift over, everyone! Make room on the couch! Key up the music!"

"New guest!" the remaining men repeated cheerfully.

Logan stared at the group blankly, feeling left out of the joke as they moved over to allow him access to stand directly in front of her.

Holly turned her attention briefly back to the heads. "Not this one, guys. This one's a special guest. A first-timer."

"Newbie!" the heads sang in unison, laughed again, and then one by one meandered off either into the gym or out the door, telling Holly to have a great day or that they would catch up with her later.

"What's all this talk about a couch?" Logan asked warily as he approached.

"Oh, that's just Joe." She laughed, giving a haphazard wave in the general direction of where the Mets-shirt-wearing man had headed. "He likes to think of our morning front-desk conversations as the Conan O'Brien show. He's the Andy Richter. What brings you here?"

"I just wanted to check the place out," he told her truthfully, but withholding his motive. "See what I'm missing. Maybe get some new tips. What's a day pass cost?"

"Sure, like I'm going to charge you," she said, reaching behind the desk for a carbon copied piece of paper. "Here, sign this waiver. And don't hurt yourself or I'll get in trouble for not writing down your phone number and scheduling a tour for you."

"Well now, I wouldn't want to see you get in trouble," he lied, taking the pen she offered. He would've liked nothing more than to see her lovable ass fired. Let Andy Richter find a new gig.

"Hey," Holly said, switching topics excitedly. "You want to meet the personal-training manager, Michael? I'll bet he would love to meet you. He came in early today. He wanted to bring back the defibrillator. He took it home last night to replace the batteries."

Logan looked up from reading the waiver. "Replace the batteries? Just how many people nearly drop dead here?"

Holly gave him a look of reproach. "Logan. Stop it. They replace the batteries every six months whether the machine needs it or not, just like you do. You're starting to sound like a snob. Do you want to meet him or not?"

Logan smiled apologetically. "Sorry. I'll knock it off. Do you mind if I meet him next time? I just wanted to get in a quick workout, check the place out, get an idea of what you're talking about when you tell me stories."

"Sure. Of course. Not a problem. Next time," she replied, trying to mask her disappointment at his refusal. What were the odds that there was ever going to be a next time? And then she brightened. There could only be one reason that Logan would ever set foot in Bodyssey, and it would be to see her. And he was a fine-looking sight first thing in the morning, as if she needed reminding.

Logan went back to reading the waiver and other members came through the doors, greeted by cheerful good mornings from Holly and scanning their key tags. There were blatant looks of appreciation and interest at the perfect specimen of fitness in the basketball shorts and baby-blue tank top. A few of them lingered at the counter to share tidbits of information with Holly, obviously following up on prior conversations they'd had with her. Logan kept his head down, overly interested in the waiver, as he gleaned that Holly knew almost everyone who walked in by name and that they knew hers, without needing to look at the lanyard name tag dangling from around her neck. Holly gave no indication that she even knew Logan, much less that they had an intimate relationship, until they were once again left alone and she leaned over the counter to whisper in his ear, "Did you have to go with a wife beater this morning? I think we may end up needing the defibrillator after all, the way I just caught Mrs. O'Malley checking you out."

Logan looked up again, gave her one of his disarming smiles, and scribbled his signature on the paper. "Anything I need to know before I get in there?" he asked, looking casually past her and into the gym.

Holly was about to warn him that under no circumstances should he go into the sauna, because it was a badly maintained, fungus-infested sweat pit where it was rumored that several known perverts went to meet and jerk off for each other. But just then her attention was drawn to the door. Suddenly, it was as if Logan didn't exist.

"Good morning, Leslie!" Holly smiled brightly. "I'm so happy to see you. I know today's the big day."

Logan turned his head and tried not to react. Leslie wasn't just morbidly obese; she had easily passed that grade and would be considered super obese, a classification made recently by the World Health Organization to address the growing epidemic of obesity. She must have weighed close to four hundred pounds, this woman whom Holly was so happy to see. Leslie's movements were stilted, her legs struggled to bear her weight, and she lumbered from the entrance to the counter. Her outfit reminded Logan of what Holly had worn on her first day of training—sweatpants and a T-shirt that she made sure were loose fitting, although Leslie's shirt appeared to be the size of a blanket and stretched to accommodate her stomach, which hung down to the middle of her thighs. Leslie's breathing was labored and her eyes downcast. She refused to even acknowledge Logan.

"Hi, Holly." She heaved, placing her purse, towel, and

water bottle on the counter after scanning her membership key tag. "I think I'm going to be sick."

Holly continued to ignore Logan and instead walked to the section of counter where Leslie was standing and immediately laid her hand on top of hers. Logan stayed glued to his spot, resisting the professional urge to jump in and try to inspire the woman, fully aware that he wasn't even sure where he would begin. He pretended to read the fitness class schedule.

"No, you're not," Holly told her assertively, lowering her voice so that even Logan had to strain to hear the exchange. "You're going to get in there and do whatever Michael tells you, one agonizing second at a time. You're going to sweat and hurt and maybe even cry, but you are going to take this baby step and save your life. And I take back what I said before; you may actually get sick, but you won't be the first, last, or only person who ever puked in a gym. In fact, some trainers consider it a badge of honor."

"But he's going to try to kill me, I just know it," Leslie whispered back, wide-eyed and frightened.

"Michael is well aware of your limitations. And trust me, if he kills you, he loses a paying customer. No way is he going to let that happen." Holly smiled reassuringly and Leslie started smiling as well. "You can do this." Holly squeezed Leslie's hand, patted it one final time, and released it. "Now, go warm up. Remember, baby steps. You didn't get this way overnight. The only way for this to work is one minute at a time."

Leslie lifted her head up, and Holly nodded purposefully at her. Leslie nodded back, and giving Logan nothing more than a passing glance, she plodded her way into the gym.

Holly watched Leslie leave before turning back to Logan.

"That was very well done," he told her, smiling with what he could only define as genuine pride. "Who taught you to give that kind of pep talk?"

"I picked up some stuff here and there," she replied, wanting to kiss the smile right off his face.

"It's a cosmic stroke of luck that you're the first thing she sees when walking through that door. I can't help but wonder how successful she'll be if she has even half the chutzpah you do."

"She has a long road ahead," Holly responded, shaking her head, completely missing the compliment. "She's so scared and scarred. She'd been housebound for almost two years, after her husband left her, taking their three children with him. It was decided that Michael needed to handle Leslie himself, at least for a while, until she's built up some endurance and confidence."

"That's probably a good move," Logan said in agreement, and then his grin turned devilish. "And who knows? Maybe in the end, Michael will end up falling for her."

"That's not likely to happen." Holly was quick to oppose the suggestion.

"Why not?" Logan raised his eyebrows in real surprise at the thinly veiled reference to their own relationship being met with such skepticism. "Stranger things have happened."

"True," Holly responded, looking very serious, but

with merriment in her eyes. "But that would be really strange. Michael is totally gay."

"Oh." Logan pursed his lips together, once again reminded of just how out of his element he really was. "Talk about sticking my foot in my mouth."

"It's okay." Holly giggled, taking a sip of what had recently become her lifeblood, the 7-Eleven coffee she bought on her way in. "Why don't you go get your workout in? I'm sorry I'm going to miss all your flexing. By the way, I really am happy to see you."

Logan walked away from the counter and into the gym, picking a quiet corner to do a quick preworkout stretch and survey the layout of the establishment. There were two levels to the gym, with the second floor housing mostly cardio equipment that looked down onto the main gym floor. The second floor also had rooms for both yoga and spin classes. Each of the treadmills, stair climbers, stationary bikes, and elliptical machines had its own individual small television. There were multiple weight-lifting machines, each grouped in their own stations. Free weights and benches took up the entire back corner of the space, which Logan estimated to be about four thousand square feet in total. Logan had to admit, the whole setup was rather impressive.

The joint was jumping with a vast array of humanity, representing all levels of fitness. There were young people and older ones. There were the tight and sometimes vascular swollen physiques of serious bodybuilders, who were working mostly in pairs to spot for one another. There were also the neglected, overweight bodies of those just starting on the road to fitness. But the vast majority was made up of the average bodies of those who were merely serious about maintaining good health and leading a balanced life. People mingled in groups, chatting it up, and Logan felt the whole establishment had an air of cheerful morning camaraderie. With curiosity, he watched Leslie on a treadmill as she slowly yet resolutely took step after step, her hands firmly grasping the sides of the treadmill and her body virtually reverberating with every footfall. Her trainer arrived a few minutes later. It was easy to spot the personal-training manager, Michael. Not only was he wearing a lanyard much like Holly's, but he was dressed exactly the same, in the gym's standard uniform, black gym pants and the matching long-sleeved T-shirt that he'd just seen Holly in. Michael had emerged from one of the offices that lined a wall of the gym. He was short and compact, lean but muscular, and carried a clipboard. He made his way over to Leslie's treadmill and, after greeting her with an encouraging smile, checked the time elapsed on it and stood alongside her a minute or two more, chatting with her and making notes on the clipboard he had with him. He then pushed the STOP button, took her water bottle out of the holder with one hand, and offered her his other, helping her down. They ventured off into the gym and out of Logan's sight line.

By the time he finished stretching, Logan began to feel others inspecting him in much the same way he'd been doing to them. The looks he received, however, were along the lines of open stares of lust from women and competitive sizing up from men who recognized the level of Logan's dedication and training. Wishing he hadn't forgotten his iPod, Logan picked a treadmill at the end of a line alongside a wall on the main gym floor and turned it on in preparation for a run. The music from the stereo system would have to suffice, and Logan found himself beginning to pound his feet to the beat as he went from a fast walk to a full-out jog. The music was once again interrupted by the sound of Holly's voice piping through the speakers.

"Okay. You've been asking. It's horoscope time. Today's astrology is courtesy of the *New York Post*."

Logan couldn't decide if he was amused or pissed that the music had stopped. He had just begun to find his groove and now he was being forced to listen to her. He made a mental note to talk to her about it later.

"If you're a Virgo, 'It's time you realize that most things turn out better if you do them yourself. Don't believe everything you hear.'"

Logan shook his head, thinking he had a long way to go before she got to his sign—Aries—and noticed two men in their early thirties getting onto the two treadmills next to his.

Holly continued. "For Libra, 'If there's confusion in your romantic life, it's only because you aren't asking the right questions. If you feel there's more to know, you are probably right.' Well, duh."

Logan caught himself laughing, and with another quick look around saw that other people throughout the gym were chuckling as well, including Michael and Leslie, who was working on a lateral pull-down weight machine about twenty feet away. Several people even took their headphones off to listen. Apparently, Holly's show was nothing new.

Holly pressed on. "Hey, Scorpio! 'If business isn't booming right now, don't worry. The stars indicate that you are about to receive some news.' Gimme a break."

The man closest to Logan addressed his friend, louder than he probably would have liked in the effort to be heard over Holly. "Holly has issues."

Logan rolled his eyes. Jesus, was every Tom, Dick, and Harry in the building on a first-name basis with her?

Holly's voice, now with an edge of annoyance, resonated once more though the building. "Does anyone else find these things ridiculous and not the least bit helpful? They all sound the same. Let me sum it up with: Good luck with making it through the day. Stuff is going to happen to you. Now get out there and do the best you can! Anyone who absolutely needs to hear the horoscope for their own zodiac sign, stop by the front desk for your personal reading." The music switched back on.

"Thank God," the man a treadmill away turned to say to his friend. "I thought she was never going to shut up."

Logan, overhearing again, snickered, thinking he felt pretty much the same way, and picked his pace back up with the music again.

"Oh, I don't know," the man closest to Logan responded. "I think she's pretty funny. And she's not wearing a ring."

Logan's ears zeroed in on the conversation and he cast a sideways glance to get a better look at the men.

"Dude, seriously? She's kinda fat, don't you think?

She needs to spend a little less time behind that desk and a little more time on this treadmill," his companion replied with a laugh.

Logan could feel the pulse in his ears pounding in time with his feet on his treadmill, only harder. *Fucking jerk-off,* he thought as his jaw started to clench. *Try saying that to her face; you'd be spitting your teeth out like Chiclets.*

The man laughed. "You're crazy. Have you seen the muscle on her? You could bounce a quarter off her butt. Say what you want. Fat or no fat, I would wreck that chick. When I was done tapping that ass, she'd be walking like a cowboy for a week."

His friend scoffed. "As long as you don't lose your dick in her."

Logan, summoning every scrap of self-control he possessed, stopped and jumped off the treadmill. Retrieving his towel and his water bottle, he marched back up to the front of the gym to where Holly was standing, this time chatting with two middle-aged women. He pointed his finger directly at her as he stomped out the door.

"You are quitting this job!" he shouted, never breaking stride and vacating the building, leaving Holly and her customers to stare openmouthed after him.

"Who the heck was that?" one of the women asked as Holly, completely perplexed, looked from Logan's retreating form into the gym and back again, trying to figure out what had occurred to warrant such an outburst. She turned her attention back to the ladies in front of the counter.

"Ummm," Holly replied, feeling no joy at the fact that she was saying the words for the first time aloud. "I think that was my boyfriend."

"You *think*?" The other woman laughed. "Honey, if I had someone who looked like *that* ordering me around, I'd have the decency to be sure. Bravo, darling, bravo!"

Logan got into his car and took a deep breath, staggered by his own reaction, which was nothing short of rage. It was so sudden and all-encompassing. He had trouble deciding who had incensed him more—the jackass who'd cruelly made fun of Holly, or the jerk who wanted to leave her bowlegged. He pounded his steering wheel. Reacting at that level to either scenario didn't make any sense. It had always been a given in his mind that men fantasized about his other girlfriends. For Christ's sake, he'd dated several *Playboy* models. Men masturbated to their pictures with his blessing.

It was then that Logan realized why he was so furious. The woman Logan couldn't stop thinking about was fat. Maybe not to the well-experienced eye, but to society as a whole. Logan didn't jump off his treadmill to kick the shit out of that guy to defend both Holly's honor and his own. And he didn't laugh it off or ignore it as the immature malice of a nameless miserable jack-off. Instead, he stormed out of the gym in self-righteous anger, demanding that she go back to hiding within her house so he could satisfy his lust unfettered and undisturbed.

Logan laid his head on the steering wheel and released a broken sigh. He had been trying to convince himself that hiding Holly had been for her benefit. The reality was he wasn't yet willing to subject either of them to the possible judgment that would accompany the news of his making a commitment to her and settling down, especially when it was discovered she was one of his clients. This one woman had him forsaking all his prior reliable standards and ideals. All the positive thinking in the world wasn't going to change that. This was the same woman who had been perfectly fine to have tagging along with him everywhere before they were dating. Now she was supposed to be kept hidden in order for him to enjoy her company. He wanted to shake loose from his brain the idea that she was beneath him. Those two men had spoken so freely; it had never even dawned on them that the man next to them would even know her, much less be sleeping with her. This wasn't about Holly, and it wasn't about society—it was about Logan. That he was still leery of stepping away from his preconceived notions of who he should and shouldn't be seen with and attached to. He had let himself be guided by what he thought would look best on his arm to promote what he did for a living. He swallowed the sickening feeling that he had just spent the majority of his life as one big marketing ploy, one that worked.

He leaned his head back against the headrest and closed his eyes. He didn't even recognize himself anymore. He used to be balanced and detached, relaxed and easygoing. Now it seemed he was regularly clawing his way out of a constant landslide of emotion, one he was intent on hiding from Holly. If he kept it up, he would end up not only losing Holly, but losing himself as well. Sitting back up, he reached into his glove compartment and pulled out his phone.

Quickly, Logan sent out a text:

YOU AWAKE?

After a minute, he got a text in return:

I AM NOW.

Logan wrote back:

YOU IN THE MOOD FOR A WORKOUT? I COULD USE A SPOTTER.

Logan started his car and sped out of the parking lot after receiving:

COME TO THE HOUSE.

The cleaning lady opened the front door, instantly recognizing him.

"Good morning, Mr. Logan."

Logan stepped into the mansion, made a quick left turn at the living room, and hurriedly walked through the house to the back. Chase was seated at the kitchen table, fully dressed with coffee in hand, casually perusing the morning paper. He glanced up as soon as he heard Logan come into the room.

"Morning," Chase said. "Wanna hear your horoscope?"

Logan felt the pulse beat at his temple and his left eye twitch. "No thanks. I want to lift heavy stuff. Where's Amanda?"

Chase raised an eyebrow. "Sleeping. When you gave us the morning off, she felt like she'd just been paroled from prison. You okay?"

Logan tried not to express his overwhelming relief at the news that he would have his friend's undivided attention. He let out a rush of air. "I'm fine. I just need to pump some iron."

"Fair enough," Chase said mildly, putting down his coffee cup and rising from the table. "Let's get to it."

Chase led the way with Logan following closely behind through the remainder of the house to the Walkers' extensive gym room. Logan immediately set about the business of choosing the heaviest barbells and pounded out set after set of chest presses, the surest sign of pent-up aggression. He went from chest presses to the leg-press machine to dead lifts, followed by curl after curl, then crunch after crunch. Chase said nothing, even after it became apparent that he was going to be doing more spotting than lifting of his own. After twenty minutes, when Logan was fully lathered and fatigue had set in, he spoke.

"What would you do if Amanda gained a lot of weight?" Logan asked, wiping the sweat off his face with the front of his shirt.

Chase held back his smile, walked over to a nearby closet, and pulled out a towel, tossing it in Logan's direction. He appeared to give the question serious thought. "How much weight are we talking about here?"

Logan caught the towel and wiped his face again before coming up with a figure. "Let's say, fifty pounds."

Chase scoffed. "Shit. I plan to start packing that much on her the minute she tells me she's having my baby."

Logan was momentarily stunned. "Come on. I'm being serious here."

"So am I," Chase said seriously.

In exasperation, Logan tried a different tactic. "Okay, what if she wasn't getting ready to birth your fully grown linebacker and gained that much?"

"Just woke up one morning fifty pounds heavier?" Chase asked.

"Yes."

"Like she went to bed and her thyroid exploded and she gained it all overnight?"

"Yes. I mean no!" Logan tried to backtrack, realizing how ridiculous the whole matter was sounding. "Her thyroid exploding would kill her."

Chase pressed on. "I'm just trying to get some parameters here. So she's basically healthy? Like she gained it all gradually?"

"Yeah," Logan finally said, feeling his friend's overly indulgent stare bearing down on him.

Chase took a minute, his lips tightly drawn together, and considered the question before responding. "As long as she was truly healthy and it wasn't the result of a real illness or something traumatic that sent her spiraling, and she could still do all the things we enjoy doing together, I don't think I would care."

"You really mean that, don't you?" Logan asked his

friend, even though he already knew the answer was genuine.

Chase smiled. "My wife is not a small girl. Chances are it could actually happen," he said honestly and without apprehension.

"And it really wouldn't bother you?"

"When I fell in love with her, I fell in love with all of her. I've yet to meet her equal as far as beauty goes."

"You're a high-profile guy with a pretty big image to protect," Logan stated bluntly. "What about what other people might think?"

"Since when did I ever give a fuck about what other people think?" Chase laughed. "I'm rich."

"What if what they said really hurt her feelings though?" Logan asked, still probing.

Chase instantly sobered and crossed his arms over his chest. "That's an entirely different ball of wax. I would be devastated. It was the only thing about that whole video mess that I didn't think I could handle. Are you going to tell me any time soon what this is really about? You're starting to depress me."

"Holly."

Chase dropped his arms and asked, "What about her?"

"I don't know," Logan said hesitantly.

Chase smiled again. "Well, I don't know how much help I can be if you don't even know what's wrong."

"I know," Logan replied. He ran his hand through his hair and exhaled in frustration.

"Would this by any chance have anything to do with your 'morning appointment' that had you shifting all your clients around?"

Logan confirmed it miserably. "Yes."

"You went to that gym to spy on her? All covert-like?"

This time Logan could only nod before leaning his face into his hand and shaking his head.

"You still don't want people to know you're together, do you?"

"No," Logan mumbled into his own chest, still holding his head, suddenly remembering that Holly didn't make one person in Bodyssey privy to the fact that they were seeing each other. Had she done it to protect him or herself?

"You do realize this has nothing to do with Holly or her weight, don't you?"

"Yes!" Logan snapped, straightening back up. "Go ahead. Tell me it has everything to do with me being an asshole."

Chase shook his head. "I wasn't going to say that either. But I do think this is all about you."

Logan, tired of Chase's game of twenty questions and his mind-reading act, settled his hands on his hips and demanded, "Are you going to lay your knowledge on me or what?"

Chase went over to a minifridge and pulled out two bottles of water, handing one to Logan and opening the other. He tossed the cap basketball style, aiming for a small wastebasket on the other side of the room, and missed. "The way I see it, this isn't about Holly and her weight, although it's what you've chosen to hide behind. It's not about how you've deviated from your lifelong attraction to six-foot-tall blondes or the monthlong underground sex fest you've been preoccupied with. It's not even about the fact that you went to that gym and found out that at five o'clock in the morning, she's probably having a ball without you. It's about how scared you are that you've finally let somebody in. That there's someone out there you care about more than yourself."

Logan went over to Chase's bottle cap and picked it up from the floor, dropping it into the garbage can. He took a minute to fully digest Chase's theory. "You think that's it?"

"I think I'm close at any rate," Chase replied. "Everything about this relationship with Holly is a departure for you, and I'm not just talking about her looks. There was no wham-bam whirlwind involved. It was a slow building of trust and respect and finally chemistry and attraction. Sounds like the perfect setup to me."

"Hey, wait a minute," Logan interjected, feeling defensive, although he wasn't sure why. "You said that the minute you set eyes on Amanda, it was all over for you."

Chase laughed again. "Yeah, but I was always open to the possibility that it would happen like that for me. Actually, I was sure of it. But we're talking about you here. Ever since I met you, you've had this attitude that women would only gum up the works for you. You've always kept your emotional barrier up. I would go as far as to say that they always had to be so one-dimensionally beautiful so that when they figured you out, you wouldn't have to harbor any guilt that they wouldn't be able to move on to someone else. Suddenly, you're one step from becoming accountable to someone. The minute you take Holly out somewhere and make that first introduction that she's your girlfriend, it's going to be all over for you."

"I've made the girlfriend introduction before," Logan said, trying in vain to make what he thought was a valid point.

"Not contradicting a woman you're screwing when she calls herself your girlfriend is hardly the same thing," Chase replied.

"I did call Natalie my girlfriend before, and you know it."

"Which one was Natalie again?" Chase asked with sarcasm. "Oh yeah, the one you brought along to Fiji last year. I figured you just said that to lull her into believing she wasn't only your most recent plaything. We were halfway across the world. Her getting pissed would have ruined the trip for all of us."

"I fucking hate you," Logan groaned, unable to deny any part of the assertion.

"Hey, look," Chase easily replied, "this heart-to-heart crap is no picnic for me either. I could have done without playing Dr. Phil at seven in the morning. But if you're freaked out, I have to do what I can to help you get your head on straight. You've been spinning your wheels about this for weeks."

"Why can't I keep my hands off my female clients?" Logan asked, getting closer to the heart of the matter but not fully committing to it.

"Because this one isn't just a client. And why are you getting so twisted up about this? If anything, it'll look like you've finally taken your head out of your ass.

She's a great girl, probably better than you deserve," Chase joked, picking up two dumbbells and pumping out a quick set of lateral lifts. "And you're forgetting, you're really not that important. People don't give a shit about you; they give a shit about themselves. Once you let her keep her clothes on for more than five seconds and start taking her out, you'll see that. You might even enjoy breaking free of your pretty-boy-stuck-on-blondes image. It was getting sort of tired anyway."

"I made a total ass of myself in that gym this morning," Logan confessed. "I left there basically telling her she has to quit her job."

"That must have been fun to watch." Chase switched to hammer curls, not terribly concerned. "I'm sorry I missed it. You're going to have to turn that around, you know."

"You make it sound so easy."

Chase dropped the weights with a loud thud. "It is. You just tell her you had a fit of jealousy and you're sorry. Girls become putty in your hands when they hear that kind of crap. Damn, love is making you stupid."

"I never said I loved her." Logan made one final grasp at the straws of his life as he used to know it.

"You never had to," his friend replied. "But you might want to get it out of the way, so you can start to get your sanity back."

Logan left the Walkers' house only slightly less confused than before he got there, grateful that Amanda had not woken up. In his current state, he could never have withstood her taking a turn at him. He was already muddled.

Nobody knew him better than Chase did. All of this fighting what felt natural was only making Logan crazy for no good reason. He wasn't being superficial, he was just in deeper emotionally than he had ever been before, and it was easier to project the discomfort onto Holly. So what if she wasn't a Victoria's Secret model? She was adorable and she excited him. There was absolutely nothing wrong with it. In hindsight, to think anyone would give a flying fig about who he chose to spend his time with was ludicrous.

Chase had been right about many of the things he said, but not all of them. Logan was not in love. Sure, he loved Holly; he liked to believe he loved everyone. But he wasn't *in* love with her. He would never leave himself at that sort of disadvantage. Once said and out there in the airwaves, it was like some sort of noose that slowly strangled the fun out of everything. Love was an outdated concept that maybe worked for hopeless romantics like Chase, but his friend had always been the exception to every rule. Logan wasn't about to start buying into the notion that just because he was infatuated with Holly, he was in love. The only reason he was so interested was because she respected his space. He was actually doing some of the pursuing for once. She wasn't clinging to him, and it represented challenge. Good sex and common interests did not a lifetime commitment make, and Logan was not about to ruin either by taking that sort of leap. Holly didn't seem ready to take it either. It was a nonissue.

Logan got home, showered, and dressed for work, thinking no more about anything except how to get their relationship back on track. With an hour to kill before his first client arrived, he got back in his car, and as if it had a will of its own, he found himself back at Bodyssey.

When her shift was over and Holly emerged, she found Logan leaning casually against the driver's-side door of her car.

"Hi," she said, looking as puzzled as she had when he last saw her. She leaned up against the car next to hers and looked down at the ground between them. "Care to explain what happened in there before?"

He shook his head and exhaled loudly. Then he reached over and grabbed hold of her shirt where it covered her belly. He gave a tug and pulled her away from the spot where she was leaning. It achieved his desired result—unbalancing her and bringing her crashing into the solid wall of his chest. He wrapped his arms around her and kept her there despite several people walking by them to enter or exit the gym.

"It wasn't you" was all he told her, not going any farther by way of explanation. "I should be saying I'm sorry. And I am."

Holly smiled up at him. He didn't need to explain anything. He was all over her like a cheap suit and it was heavenly. It was hard to think of anything besides it. Whatever happened, he would tell her when he was ready. He was there and apologetic and that was enough for her. "It's okay."

"I-I took some antihistamines; I think I may have had a reaction to them," he stammered, knowing he had no right to her ready acceptance of his apology.

"Histamine rage," she said in agreement, nodding. "Makes perfect sense to me."

He gave her a quick kiss before standing them both up straight. "I have to get to work."

She walked him to his car, which was parked several rows away. They said nothing but intentionally kept playfully bumping into each other. When they reached it, he opened the door and turned back to her. "What are you doing tonight?"

"Waiting for you," she told him happily.

"My last client is at seven. I know that doesn't leave much time, but maybe a movie or something?"

"Netflix awaits," she said.

"No," he told her. "I want to take you out. I would suggest catching the end of the Kings game, but I know I need to have you home before you turn into a pumpkin."

Holly grinned again. "No worries there. I don't have a job anymore."

Logan's look of surprise was followed by one of barely contained joy. "You quit your job?"

Her grin grew wider and she glanced back at the building. "Sort of. I gave them my two weeks' notice and they promptly fired me. Seems they don't handle rejection very well in there. They did tell me I could remain a member though. I may do that. I met some really nice people. Guess I liked people more than I thought."

Logan's joy was short-lived as he realized his actions may have been what motivated her. "Oh my God, Holly, please tell me this didn't have anything to do with my foolishness."

"Oh hell no." Holly was quick to set him at ease, a coy smile forming on her lips. "I realized weeks ago that it was never going to work. I was getting tired of falling asleep on your shoulder at seven thirty every night, instead of in your arms."

"Be ready by eight." He kissed her before sliding into the driver's seat. "Tonight we celebrate."

Chapter Twenty

THEY STARTED DATING, WITH LOGAN SLOWLY INTEGRATING Holly into his life. And not much actually changed. They did a lot of going out with Amanda and Chase. There were charity parties, sporting events, concerts. She slipped into the man cave without him even noticing. Logan accepted every invitation in his attempt to show his newly minted status as taken. At first, Holly was shy, intimidated by the stares of the people Logan introduced her to. Logan suffered from bouts of momentary discomfort as well. He felt defensive and at times troublingly unsure when running into an ex, all long and blond, and seeing the ex's intrigued if not amused reaction as he introduced his pudgy cherub. Some of his friends and business associates weren't always so discreet about covering up their double takes.

But when Logan and Holly were alone, he was confident about his choice. She willingly went along with whatever he chose to make important, even if his choice was time alone, which had become less and less frequent, as the sex with her was still so much fun. Hell, everything attached to Holly was fun, because even the most mundane things to him were brand new to her and she embraced them fully. Still, he felt guilty for his spurts of nagging doubt.

"Hey, do you have an extra toothbrush I can borrow?" Logan asked as he entered the bathroom one evening, exhaling into his cupped hand and then bringing it up to his nose for an improvised bad-breath test. Holly was standing in front of one of the sinks, staring at herself in the mirror. He could tell with one glance at her mirrored reflection that she was troubled. "What's the matter?"

She immediately came clean. "Nothing. Everything. I can't do this."

"Do what?"

"I can't go to this party. I can't go to this party with you."

"Why not? It's a party. They're supposed to be fun. You suddenly have something against fun?"

"Sure. Fun for you. Look at you. You're gorgeous. Look at me. People will wonder what the hell I'm blackmailing you with."

Logan laughed while sneaking up behind her, wrapping his arms around her, and resting his chin on top of her head. "Stop being ridiculous, you're beautiful."

She looked at them in the mirror and tried to get the

words past the lump in her throat. "No, Logan. You're beautiful. I'm so completely not."

Logan straightened back up and grabbed her shoulders, then turned her around to face him. When she kept her eyes cast downward, he crooked his finger under her chin and lifted it, insisting she bring her eyes back up to his, and asked gently, "Holly, this isn't like you. The whole insecurity bit. What's this really about?"

She stared into his warm brown eyes and struggled to find her voice. She had never lied to him and wasn't about to start now.

The words tumbled forth. "You think I don't see the differences in us? You think I don't see the way people look at us? Like I don't deserve you? I don't really mind so much when we're out in the general public. In fact, it's flattering in a demented sort of way. But tonight is all about the beautiful people's club otherwise known as your world."

Logan was momentarily taken aback. So, she had tapped into his innermost feelings. The ones he wasn't proud of, the ones he thought he had successfully repressed, the very ones that had crossed his mind just an hour before. Tonight would be different. Tonight wasn't about a charity function; it was about the hottest ticket in town, and everyone who was anyone was sure to be in attendance. Tonight, with Holly on his arm, he would be making a statement, loud and clear, that he had never made before. She was so astute, so in tune with him, whether he wanted her to be or not. It wasn't that she wasn't worthy, just that she wasn't what he was used to. Which in turn meant that all the people he knew weren't used to her either. They would adjust, he was sure. She was so damn cute, standing before him in her pink cashmere sweater and modest black wraparound skirt. How could he possibly explain that it wasn't about her, but about his own growth?

He spoke evenly, his words measured. "Holly. I thought I had always been clear. It's not about the package, but about the *whole* package. You are easily the smartest, wittiest, most sincere person I know. Not to mention adorable and positively delectable." He placed his hands on both sides of her head and tilted her face up to him. He unhurriedly lowered his lips onto hers, effectively silencing any further retort or complaint.

After he felt her tension give way and her hands creep around his waist, he opened his mouth, probing the warm recesses of hers. His hands moved down her back to cup each of her buttocks and with one motion, he lifted and deposited her onto the wide vanity that ran the length of the bathroom wall. The loud thud and subsequent creak of the suspended marble trying to support her weight stopped them both in their tracks. Logan pulled back and saw her eyes grow wide and fill with tears of mortification.

"This thing is used to some Softsoap and a hair dryer sitting on it. Don't even go there," he told her gruffly, quickly kissing her again. Holding back the tears as well as the emotion that was behind them, she rested her hands on his shoulders and tried to focus on his warm lips, which were demanding her attention. His fingers drifted to her knees and began to pull at the hemline of her skirt until most of her leg was fully exposed. He leaned forward more, pushing, until her back was fully against the mirrored wall before his lips made their way down to her faintly perfumed neck, his hands wandering inside her skirt. He leisurely toyed with the elastic rim of her panties while she ran her hands through his hair and then stopped when he wedged his finger inside them to purposefully slide into her. She moaned with desire at the intrusion, dropping her hands, fully disposing of any lingering thoughts about anything except the feeling of his hand. He deliberately rubbed, moisture joining friction, and she spread her legs farther apart.

He suddenly withdrew, pulled her legs forward, and lifted the skirt to the middle of her full thighs. He reached beneath the now-bunched-up material, stuck his hand under her bottom, and insistently pulled at her panties. She wriggled and soon they were freed. He finished pulling them off and let them fall carelessly to the floor. He went down onto his knees and, bringing her legs forward, drew her closer to the edge of the vanity. He stuck his head beneath her skirt. The stark contrast of the cold marble against the skin on the back of her legs and his warm breath at her center was foreign and fantastic. When his lips touched the soft folds of her, she braced her hands against the marble and shifted to give him better access.

"Oh, Logan," she breathed, feeling an embarrassment of a totally different kind, which she quickly abandoned as she began to throb. His tongue sensually danced around her core, his hands determinedly at her hips to hold her in place. He greedily licked and nipped and sucked, and all the while she squirmed and ground herself against him until he felt her start to clench, and his mouth was wet with her. She moaned, deep and guttural, and he pulled away, unwilling to let her climax without him. He quickly stood and pulled her off the vanity, and they both fumbled with his belt in a race to free the raging erection from his pants. She unzipped him and he hastily removed them and his boxer briefs, not willing to waste any more time than necessary before taking her. He dropped to the floor, bringing her down with him, and lay on his back. Holly lifted her skirt, straddled him, and with his help, guided herself onto him.

"Yes, baby, yes," he groaned, filling her, and reached under her sweater, not taking the time to remove her bra and instead pushing it up to massage handfuls of breasts. He circled his thumb around taut nipples and she joined him with a groan of her own. She pulled the encumbering sweater and bra up over her head and tossed them into the neighboring bedroom, desperate to feel his hands all over her.

She rode with him deep inside her, his thick hard sex stretching her, passing all of her sensitive spots. Her rhythm sped up, matched by his pelvis moving in opposition, nearly removing himself from her, only to vigorously fill her again. His hands left her breasts to grab her roughly at the hips and hold her while he took over and glided her up and down. It was a torture that was both relentless and exquisite. Holly threw her head back and gave herself over to his torment. Before long, she felt the familiar tingle that would soon leave her breathless, the tiny tingle that would suddenly explode into an uncontrollable fit of tremors. She surrendered, unable to do anything more than say his name over and over, more pleading and gasping with each repetition. It was music to his ears and he quickened his pace just a fraction more, his own release looming. He felt her stiffen above him and then she began to writhe in orgasmic spasms. He drove in one final time before shuddering into her.

She collapsed onto him and Logan held her tight, right on the bathroom floor.

"Let's get this party over with," she purred. "So we can get back here and do this again."

Chapter Twenty-One

I T WAS THE KINGS' EXTRAVAGANT END-OF-SEASON party, being thrown at an exclusive uptown hot spot. Invitations were even more sought after than usual after the team's World Series win. Logan and Holly were already at the aptly named Bases Loaded when Amanda and her MVP husband arrived. The club was crawling with people, some Holly had met before, but most of them new faces. As Chase and Logan mingled dutifully with fans and clients, Amanda settled close by Holly's side and pointed out the famous and the infamous.

Holly and Amanda stationed themselves at a bar along the back wall. The perfect spot, Amanda called it; they could see everyone and they were close to the drinks. Holly spied Logan across the room, head cocked in conversation, eyes narrowed in concentration. She didn't think she would ever tire of watching him from afar.

"Hi, Holly." She heard the voice in her left ear and turned.

"Hi, Troy." She smiled at Troy Miller before saying, "Congratulations on a great season."

"Thanks." He smiled shyly back. "It's my first championship. It feels pretty good. I saw you at game three."

"You did?" Holly asked, surprised. She had met him several times but never thought it was memorable to either of them.

"Yeah," Troy said quietly, toying nervously with the straw in his glass. "I was going to talk to you afterward, but you got out of there pretty fast."

It was true; she had left right after that game. Logan had a six o'clock the next morning and they had made a hasty departure.

"Sorry I missed you," she told him, thinking it was the right thing to say.

"I was hoping you would be here tonight. Are you having a good time?" Troy asked politely, taking a sip of his drink.

"I am," Holly replied. "I mean we just got here a few minutes ago, but so far so good."

"Just wait. A few hours from now things should start to get interesting." He laughed.

"Are you trying to warn me about something?" She joined him with a giggle. "Should I be looking for you under a lampshade?"

"Not me," he rushed to tell her. "Club soda here. Been a twelve-stepper for the last four years. These are the kinds of nights I can't wait to be over."

You and me both, Holly thought.

"Still, it will be nice to have a little time off," Troy said. "I'm a Southern boy and by October, I'm usually longing for home, even if it is only for a few months."

"Not to mention you get to escape the cold winters here," Holly added. "I thought I recognized your twang."

"Is it that bad?" He chuckled.

"Not at all," she told him honestly. "Hadn't you heard? Most girls find Southern accents irresistible."

"I'll try to remember that." He smiled.

"The whole being-a-baseball-player thing probably isn't hurting you either," Holly teased.

Troy hesitated a moment, gathering his nerve. He took another sip of his drink, then asked, "I was wondering, though, if before I left, maybe you would like to join me for dinner one night."

Holly blinked, taking a quick look around. Was he talking to her? She looked back and figured that he was by the way his gaze remained on her; he was obviously waiting for her answer.

"I'm sorry, Troy. I guess you didn't know. I'm seeing Logan," she told him gently.

His look of surprise was palpable. "Logan Montgomery?"

Holly didn't know whether to feel flattered or offended. "I guess you hadn't heard."

Troy tried to recover from his error but still looked shocked by her statement. "No. I hadn't."

Holly couldn't help feeling defensive. "It's sort of new."

"I understand," he told her quickly, embarrassed. "I really should've known. I'm sorry if I offended you with my invitation. But listen, if it doesn't work out, my offer stands. I'm here till the end of the month. You can get my number from Amanda."

"Thanks," Holly said stiffly. Obviously Troy wasn't seeing Holly's relationship with Logan as long-term. It wasn't the first time she'd had to deal with that attitude and she realized she would probably never get used to it. "I'll keep that in mind."

Troy promptly excused himself and walked away, leaving Holly to stare after him.

While the exchange between Holly and Troy was taking place, Amanda was craning her neck in their direction to nonchalantly get a better listen. She congratulated herself on her ability to bring people together. It was apparent that if things hadn't turned out with Logan and Holly, Troy would have been the correct choice. She was scanning the room when in her peripheral vision she caught sight of potential trouble. A group of three women were clustered together, a trio of Versace wearers on the prowl. At the center was Natalie Kimball, Logan's last serious girlfriend. They'd lasted four months at the most. As soon as Natalie caught sight of her, she broke away from her friends and floated up beside Amanda in all her supermodel glory, flaxen mane flowing, lips perfectly glossed, fingernails as long as her arms. She ordered a drink.

"Hi, Amanda. Another year, another party."

"Nice to see you again, Natalie." Amanda tensed. If

Natalie was going out of her way to say hello, Amanda was pretty sure what would follow. "I heard you were in California awhile."

"I was. I don't stay long. I get in and get out. It's too weird out there," Natalie replied, then got right to the point. "I thought I saw Logan when I got here."

Amanda had a choice to make. Natalie was not your average bimbo. She hadn't been happy when Logan called her bluff and ended the relationship. Too proud to try reconciliation on her own, she'd called Amanda for days on end in the hopes of getting Amanda to plead her case, something that Amanda politely but steadfastly refused to do. The calls finally ceased and Amanda made a mental note to never again give her cell phone number to any of Logan's women. And for a while, Natalie remained persistently in the background, readily available, as she waited for Logan to come to his senses. And then he fell for Holly, the kind of woman who could make someone like Natalie go ballistic.

Amanda glanced over to Holly, taking note of her exchange with Troy. She wondered whether she should even introduce Holly and Natalie. The better plan would be to get Natalie's questions answered so that Natalie would move on. If Logan was unfortunate enough to encounter her, he could deal with her himself.

"He's here somewhere," Amanda replied casually.

Natalie didn't waste any more time on formalities. "Rumor has it he settled on one of his protégées. She with him?"

"I don't know that I'd call her a protégée," Amanda said, keeping her voice as low as possible.

"What magazine did he first see her in?" Natalie snickered, scanning random faces around the club.

"You make it sound like he picked her out of a catalog," Amanda snapped, a feeling of dread taking root. "He does have a life, you know. Why don't you just get over him, Natalie? Move on."

Hearing the distinct edge in Amanda's tone, Holly turned her attention to her. She instantly recognized the woman standing next to Amanda. It was the woman in the pictures with Logan in Fiji, she was certain.

"Amanda, relax," Natalie said, giggling. "Why so uptight? I realize Logan's your favorite big-brother charity case; I was just making conversation. She must be really something if you're making this much of a fuss. I bet part of you isn't ready to see him settled down either."

Holly felt as if she'd just been handed her cue. Refusing to be spoken about like a figment of someone's imagination and almost itching for the altercation that would follow, she piped up. "He settled on me," she said. "Hi, I'm Holly."

Natalie's mouth dropped open, unbelieving, even though she had heard the rumors. Nobody had ever been outright rude in describing Logan's new girl, but the word "hot" was never used either. Natalie didn't know how to compete with a woman like this, a chubby, average kewpie doll. And this was what the woman looked like after seven months of his tutelage. Natalie could only imagine what Holly must have looked like when Logan first got hold of her. There was no way it could have been love at first sight, nor could it be a passing fancy. There was also no way for Natalie to compete. What was she supposed to do? Gain sixty pounds, abandon her makeup bag, and stop wearing heels? It took her a nanosecond to size up the situation. If this brood mare was Logan's choice, he had to be one step from going down the aisle. She no longer had anything to lose, did she? With a dazzling smile and a calculated risk, Natalie smoothly extended her claws.

"So it's true then. Hi. Or shall I say, 'quack'?"

Amanda paled and her eyes grew wide, confirming to Natalie that the risk had paid off. Logan had used his "beautiful swan" line on her, too. Holly turned toward Amanda to share a look that said, "I just blew this bitch's mind," and saw that Amanda was shooting daggers with her gaze at Natalie. Holly felt the hair on the back of her neck rise. The look on Amanda's face indicated there was surely a hidden meaning to the word that only she and Natalie knew about. Holly was the butt of some inside joke. She just knew it. Holly grabbed Amanda's arm before turning briefly back to Natalie.

"Pardon us. I have to go blow my beak."

Holly weaved Amanda through the crowd to the ladies' room and rounded on her before the door closed. "Why did that woman just quack at me?"

"How should I know? She's crazy." Amanda was never good at pretending under pressure, especially without Chase as her wingman.

"I'm the one who's crazy if I believe that. I saw your face. Tell me." Holly could feel her insides beginning to twist into knots.

Amanda's teeth bit into her lower lip. It was painfully obvious that Holly knew nothing of Logan's favorite comparison. Logan had really dug a hole with this—it was so unlike him to let such a disparaging remark get out. "It's not a big deal. Really it isn't. When you first started training with Logan, he just gave you a nickname, that's all."

"A nickname? About a duck? Tell me. Now." If it wasn't so bad, why was Amanda making such a fuss to conceal it? Holly was sick to her stomach. Unless the next word out of Amanda's mouth was "Daffy," her heart was about to break. Amanda could only shake her head, her lips tightly drawn together, and then she became unreasonably fixated on the hand dryer. It hit Holly like a painful brick wall falling down upon her. Holly whispered it herself. "It's 'ugly,' isn't it?" She swallowed hard, her throat feeling as if it had been filled with concrete. "He called me an ugly duckling."

As soon as Amanda heard it, she hastened to soften the blow, panic-stricken. "He says it about all the women he trains. He tries to motivate them by getting them to imagine themselves as the swan, you know, the 'after' picture. He even said it to me when I started training with him. But look at you now, Holly. You really *are* a beautiful swan."

Calling Amanda an ugly duckling was like referring to that diamond from *Titanic* as costume jewelry. Besides, if what Amanda was saying was true, Holly would have heard Logan use the term during their workouts, even once. She wouldn't be hearing it for the first time at a party full of his friends. But clearly, that's what she really was to him. She would never be beautiful enough to be his equal. She would always be the duck. It certainly explained why he'd begged off from her side as soon as they arrived, to leave her to be ridiculed by his prior conquests.

Holly smiled a smile that didn't quite reach her eyes. "Oh yes. You're right. That really is nothing. Knew about it all along. That nasty bitch just threw me. We better get back out there before the boys think we've left."

Every face Holly saw after that seemed mocking. The eyes of every person Logan introduced her to held insinuation. Natalie kept her distance from them and left early, but not before spending quality time staring at her smugly from across the bar. She watched the whole night unfold as if she was looking through the lens of a camera. She was present but detached, pleasant but monotone. What she didn't realize was that while she was indeed being stared at, it had very little to do with her. It had everything to do with the fact that Logan Montgomery, the most aloof, standoffish opponent of public displays of affection, was spending more than half the night with his hand securely holding hers.

She told him on the way home she had a headache, hinting that she needed to take some Tylenol and lie down. Logan admitted that she seemed off but didn't push it, although he conveyed his disappointment that he wouldn't be spending the night. He dropped her off at the house. As soon as she got through the front door, she went to the phone and dialed.

"Hello?" Tina answered sleepily.

"You were right." As soon as Holly heard her voice, the tears started to fall.

"Holly? Right about what? Are you okay?" Tina asked, instantly recognizing the emotion in Holly's voice and waking up immediately.

"About Logan, about everything," Holly choked out.

"That rotten snake. He dumped you?"

"Worse." Holly sniffled loudly, hating the fact that she was crying at all. "He made a fool of me, a complete and utter fool of me."

"Holly, calm down. You're not making any sense. You told me things were going fine with you two. What did he do?"

Holly took a deep breath, grabbing a tissue out of a box on the counter and wiping her nose with it. "He's been calling me his ugly duckling. I found out about it from some bitch he used to date. At a party we went to tonight. Can you imagine? If she knew about it, everyone must know."

"What is this, some kind of joke?" Tina was virtually speechless. "Are you sure?"

Holly felt fresh tears starting to build and she impatiently dashed at them with a new tissue. Tina's quiet astonishment only served to drive home just how despicable it sounded. "I wish it was a joke. Even Amanda couldn't deny it."

"M-maybe it's a hot, buff guy thing? Borderline-insulting terms of endearment?" Tina stammered in the attempt to come up with a positive spin.

"Then the hot buff guy thing is not for me!" Holly practically shouted before blowing her nose. Weeping again, she added, "I guess I should be congratulating myself. I must have gotten down to a weight where it's worth letting people see his great work. He could at least have had the decency to say it to my face, so that when I heard it, it didn't come out of left field."

"You just used a baseball term there." Tina suddenly smirked.

"Why wouldn't I? I live sports all day long," Holly snorted, ramping up again. "I watch ESPN twenty-four hours a day, just to have a clue what he's talking about. I made everything that was important to him important to me. And for what? So I can be his best buddy until he gets tired of playing with me? He never once made a plan based on anything I like to do. Like botanical gardens or modern art or opera."

"Since when do you have an interest in opera?"

"That's not the point," Holly snapped. "The point is I lost myself in him. I was so blown away by the fact that he was interested in me, all I could think about was how to keep him. Like I should consider myself so fucking lucky to have him. I'd had misgivings all along that something wasn't right about the whole relationship, but he made me feel paranoid for thinking it. All the while he's been looking at me like some sort of testament to how fabulous he is. And whose side are you on here?"

"I'm on your side, but you have to admit, before it got all messed up, it sure did sound like you were having a blast."

Holly stopped, took a deep breath. "What are you saying?"

Tina waited before answering. "I'm just suggesting, maybe it isn't all that bad. I haven't seen the two of you together, and in the beginning I had my reservations, but from everything you've told me, he seems nice enough. You always sounded like you were having so much fun with him. Who cares if you were doing all the things he likes to do? When you first met him, you didn't give a crap about anything anyway."

"It almost sounds like you're defending him." Holly sniffed again.

Tina clarified. "No way. I'm pro-Holly and you know it. I'm just wondering if maybe you're not a better fit with him than you think. Okay, so the guy made a bonehead move and said something unflattering about you. Maybe he did it before he really knew you. It's not like he consistently refers to you as the troll living under his bridge."

"Neither one of us knows that. Maybe he does. And you don't understand," Holly said, her eyes welling up again. "It's not that he said it, it's that he never said it to me. Which means it holds a ring of truth for him. I can't stay with him. Not if thinks he's better than me."

"So did you tell him to get lost?" Tina asked, switching gears. By the sound of Holly's voice, trying to change her mind was futile. Tina knew Holly's quiet determination when she heard it.

"No." Holly scoffed at her own stupidity. "I stood there like an idiot the whole night, knowing that they were all laughing behind my back, not saying a word."

"That doesn't make you an idiot, Holly. It makes you tough. And the better person."

"You know what, Tina?" Holly sighed desolately. "I can't keep doing this. Not if ten pounds means he's going to be finished with me. Now that I know this is out there, I feel like he's not into me, but his own creation. Every time I see him, I'm going to ask myself if it's in the back of his mind. I went along with everything that man wanted, afraid if I didn't, he would walk away. I catered to him and never once made him even work for it, thinking the whole time he was better than I deserved. Turns out he was thinking it, too. I can't do it anymore. I don't want to."

"And you shouldn't have to. It was him that didn't deserve you. None of them deserve you. This whole thing just breaks my heart," Tina said sadly. "I knew he was too good to be true. People like him are never held accountable for acting like assholes."

Holly sniffled loudly. She took a moment before saying, "But what if they were?"

"Were what?"

"You know, held accountable." There was another pause and Holly asked, "Do you think you can get any time away?"

"I guess so," Tina answered slowly, then asked suspiciously, "Holly? Why do I get the feeling you're up to something?"

"Because I am. There'll be a ticket waiting for you at the JetBlue counter. Let me know when you're going to arrive."

Chapter Twenty-Two

NEARLY A WEEK LATER, WHILE DRESSING FOR THEIR Halloween party, Amanda mentioned to Chase how relieved she was that Natalie wasn't invited to the party and hoped she wouldn't be crashing it.

"Why do you care if she shows up or not?" Chase asked. "It's for charity. As long as she brings her checkbook, I say let her in!"

"I just don't think Logan or Holly needs the aggravation."

"Stay out of it," he growled playfully. "Logan knows how to handle his exes, and Holly has always seemed to take them in stride."

"I guess so," Amanda said apprehensively. "But Natalie really takes pleasure in going for the jugular. After what happened last week at Bases Loaded, I wouldn't care if I never saw her again. She can keep her money."

"What happened?" he asked indulgently. "Did I miss a good old-fashioned catfight?"

"Hardly." Amanda sniffed with distaste. "It was more of a sucker punch and a hasty exit."

"Amanda." Chase stopped what he was doing to regard her with his eyes narrowing. "Why are you speaking to me in metaphors?"

"Forget it," Amanda said hastily, feeling the weight of his stare. "It's nothing. Everything's fine. I just don't like her."

"What aren't you telling me?" he asked, this time not quite so indulgently. "Spill it."

"They had a little altercation is all," Amanda said quickly. "Natalie quacked at her and she demanded to know why. I told her about Logan's penchant for bird references, and we laughed, sort of, and moved on. See? Not even worth telling you about."

"You did *what*?!" Chase resumed putting the finishing touches on his costume, laying the green wig flat over his own hair while scolding her. "Mandy, how could you tell her? Holly's your friend. What got into you?"

"What was I supposed to do? Lie to her face, point-blank? Strangle Natalie in the middle of a nightclub? Why don't you ask Logan that question? He's the one who gave her the stupid nickname, then blabbed it to enough people for Natalie to hear about it. Why aren't you directing this lecture at him?" She finished applying her red Betty Boop lipstick, gave her cleavage a heave, and checked to make sure her dress covered her bottom. By the way her Jolly Green Giant sounded, Amanda wasn't sure how long it would stay covered.

But they were twenty minutes from meeting a house full of people, so she figured she was safe for the moment. Besides, if he spanked her now, he'd get green body paint all over her, and that was a little too obvious, even for them. He shook his head at her reprovingly and put on his big green feet, and they went downstairs.

The mansion had been transformed into a haunted castle. From the entrance gate on, jack-o'-lanterns and shadowy ghouls graced the lawn. Creepy music started at the bottom of the driveway and led all the way to the front door, which was covered in would-be cobwebs and mist. At the entrance to the Walkers' ballroom were two dry-ice machines that blasted eerie clouds of fog as each guest passed by them. The great room was also theatrically decorated and forebodingly dim, with the exception of strobe lights that flashed to the bass of the DJ-driven dance music. In half-hour intervals, the house lights came on for ten minutes so that guests could better mingle, eat, and admire other partygoers' costumes.

An hour into the party, Holly still had not shown up. Logan arrived, alone, assuring Amanda that he'd spoken to Holly and everything was fine. "She's just running late. She's been fighting a cold," he told his hostess through the wads of cotton in his cheeks, the glue on his Godfather mustache pulling slightly.

Amanda had no choice but to believe Logan and move on. She had guests to mingle with, caterers to supervise. It felt good to have something to do again that she could take credit for. Chase had originally balked at the idea of a costume party, but one look at him stomping around in his big green feet and leafy toga made all the finagling worth it. They were posing for a photographer from the *Daily News* when Holly walked through the door.

Luckily, they had just taken the picture, so the smiles were already pasted on their faces. With perfect timing, Holly came in just before the DJ's set was over and the lights went up. When she spotted Logan, she ignored all others and made her way over to him. As people started to notice her, a path began to clear.

Logan's pleasure at seeing Holly changed as soon as he got a good look. She was wearing a dress not unlike Björk's infamous Academy Awards gown. It was far too small; Holly was nearly busting out of it, folds of skin spilling over the top and sides of the bodice. Cellulite dimples abounded on her bare thighs. The hideous swan boa, complete with head and beak, was threaded through a plastic six-pack holder with a couple of Coke cans still dangling from the rings. The bird's eyes had big X's on them. A cardboard slice of pizza with real pepperoni pasted on was duct-taped to its beak. Unwrapped Twinkies and Devil Dogs hung from the dress hem, some of them crushed within the feathers. Other feathers were dipped in chocolate. People were beginning to stare. Cameras flashed. She was a messy sight. But Holly was oblivious to the attention. Her eyes were locked on Logan, her mouth frozen in the same spiritless smile that she'd been wearing for the better part of a week when she was forced to come into contact with any of them.

Logan felt the heat rise up his neck, took a quick look

at the people around him, and spoke to Holly as a very shaky Vito Corleone.

"What's with the getup, babe?"

"I'm a swan. Get it?"

And then in front of all Logan's friends, his colleagues, and the press, Holly hauled off and clocked him. And all hell broke loose.

A deafening "*Oh*" erupted and the room brightened like a giant flashbulb. From the corner of his rapidly swelling eye, Logan caught a brief glimpse of the Jolly Green Giant and Betty Boop, their jaws slack. Various versions of shock on other partygoers' faces became a whirling blur. And as the birds started to sing and stars swirled around his head, he saw the remnants of a retreating fudge-encrusted tail waddling away, back into the fog from where it came. Before completely losing his balance, Logan said:

"She coulda been a contender."

Chapter Twenty-Three

THE PARTY WAS OVER, IN EVERY SENSE OF THE PHRASE. Holly already knew the layout of the house, so when she disappeared through a side door, she seemed to magically vanish. She left bits of broken cake and pure pandemonium in her wake and was gone before security could get their hands on her. Logan never actually lost consciousness, so when they questioned him, he insisted the situation go no farther. Chase and Amanda wanted it left alone as well. Word of the incident spread like a quick-moving brushfire. But it happened so fast and there were so many guests coming and going that by the time the night was over, the story had morphed into Logan's walking in on some woman dressed like the devil's dog trying to make off with the silverware and a fight ensuing.

At least he got to sound like a hero and not the jerk he really felt like.

Now there were three of them left: Logan, Chase, and Amanda. They were in the den, Chase pouring them all well-deserved, stiff drinks from behind the bar. Logan sat on the couch holding an ice bag to his eye. Amanda sat beside him, concern evident on her heavily made-up face. He looked so pitiful, and it wasn't just because of the impending shiner that would be following him around for the next week. He knew he had fucked up. Hell, they all had.

"I think the swelling has gone down." She tried to sound optimistic.

"Twenty-four to thirty-six hours, but thanks anyway." Logan shifted the bag of ice.

"Thank God you didn't go with calling her Franken-stein; she might have broken a bone." Amanda gave a halfhearted smirk, and then the three of them exchanged silent meaningful looks, pondering the validity of the statement.

Chase came from around the bar with all three drinks and set two of them down on the table, holding on to his own. "What do you think that was, a right hook?"

"Nah. Her left foot was out. Definitely a cross, and I have to admit, perfectly executed. I think I even saw her hand twist right at the end. I knew all those kick-boxing drills would come back to haunt me." Logan laughed at his own joke, despite the added throbbing it caused. He sighed. "You know, all the references to birds and animals are supposed to be very Zen. The whole man-being-one-with-nature thing."

Amanda sat back, kicked off her shoes, and put her feet up on the coffee table. She took a swallow of bourbon. "Logan, I'm really sorry I didn't tell you," she said earnestly. "And she really seemed fine when she found out. You could have tried to cut this off at the pass. At the very least, taken your beating in private."

"Speaking of which, you and I have an appointment to keep." Chase tipped his drink toward her and downed it.

"Are you insane? Can't you see we are in the middle of a crisis here?" she instantly protested, shooting Logan a look. "And that we have a guest?"

Logan rolled his one good eye.

A crisis brought on courtesy of your meddling. And Logan isn't a guest." Chase pointed toward the door. "Upstairs, Betty."

Amanda didn't move a muscle, in full rebellion. "I don't think so. Take it down a notch, slugger."

"No? Did you just tell me no?" He took a menacing step toward her—as menacing as a green giant got, at any rate. "I guess you feel comfortable enough to make this a spectator sport?"

Amanda tilted her head to one side and peered up at him from the couch, completely unaffected. "Why not? Considering how ridiculous you sound, I guess I should be grateful you didn't go all dom in the middle of the party. Not to mention, it's like you don't even care that Logan is clearly suffering."

"Hey, that's right," Logan interjected. "Thanks for being there for me, buddy."

"Trust me," Chase remarked sardonically with a touch of defensiveness, "I probably could have. With the *Swan Lake* spectacle taking place, no one was looking at us."

Both Amanda and Logan continued to stare at Chase, nonplussed, from their respective spots on the couch.

"Amanda Cole Walker." Chase's voice got louder, infuriated and threatening. "You have exactly three seconds to be up and on your way to that bedroom, or by all that's holy, I'm going to spank you all around this house!"

That got her off the couch. She marched right up to him and stood on her tiptoes, face-to-green-streaked-face, and gave his chest several meaningful pokes.

"Don't you dare try to bully me in front of our friends, Chase."

"Will you two just shut the fuck up?!"

Chase and Amanda stopped, midshout, and turned to look at Logan, who threw the ice bag on the table. He stood. "Good God. The two of you are certifiable, you know that? Amanda, I love you, I really do, but you just don't know when enough is enough. Heaven forbid you should let me find my own girlfriend in my own time. And, Chase, this is just as much your fault. You and your rose-colored glasses and romantic notions. You want to talk about meddling? Nobody worked harder than you to push the two of us together. Why I ever listened to you in the first place is a mystery. Oh yeah, now I remember: because you started telling her to find someone else! Then you convinced me to assault her, which pretty much sent the message that all bets were off when it came to creativity!" His fury at the whole fiasco was building—fury with them, with Holly, and mostly with himself. "Thanks to all the really wonderful advice from the both of you, I just managed to screw myself out of the first real relationship of my life." He clapped his hands together, signaling the grand finale. "Our work here is done. The three of us have collectively turned the most beautiful swan I ever knew into the ugliest duck around!"

Chase didn't miss a beat. "That was very poetic. Wouldn't you agree, Mandy?"

"I certainly would, honey. I would also add corny. Is this where we applaud, or do we wait for the encore?"

They both looked at Logan as if the punch had given him brain damage, and Chase continued. "We could wait for the encore, but we'd just have him wasting more time before going to get her back." They waited patiently for Logan to realize the obvious.

Logan took one sweeping bow, and without another word, he ran for the door.

And then there were two.

Silence lingered, and then Amanda clucked her tongue.

"Oh my God, you totally meddled," she sang, her face a mask of pure delight. When Chase caught on to her insinuation, a moment later, he threw his jolly green head back and laughed. He wagged a finger at her.

"Don't even think about it, little girl."

Amanda sauntered out of the room, humming a little tune. Chase watched her leave and smiled, shaking his head. She might never be able to turn the spanking tables on him, but he had a pretty good idea his Amex card wouldn't be sitting down for a week. He followed after her, whistling a little song of his own.

Chapter Twenty-Four

HOLLY WENT HOME AND STOOD UNDER THE SHOWER for twenty minutes. She wouldn't cry. Not anymore. Not for anyone. She looked down at her swollen knuckles, the water washing over them, and allowed herself a bitter laugh. She almost wished she could have stayed around to see their faces. It didn't matter now. Tomorrow she would start anew, wiser, stronger. Chase had been right about her; she really did have potential. Who would have thought it would be the potential to create mayhem for all of them?

She was curled up on the living room couch when the doorbell rang. She wasn't scared. She wasn't anything. If the police were coming to take her to the big house for assault, they could have her. Holly got up and looked through the peephole.

Tina came out of the kitchen and found Holly standing at the closed door, pale and impassive. "Who is it?" she mouthed.

"Logan." Holly shrugged, then shook her head. "I wasn't expecting him. Not tonight."

Tina poked a long slender finger at her own chest with vigor. "I've got this. Go make yourself scarce."

Holly went up the stairs and Tina went to the door. She opened it and looked him up and down with disdain. Even disheveled and thrashed, he was every bit as spectacular as his pictures. The pictures she caught Holly staring at sorrowfully day after day. This was the man she'd watched her friend cry over for the better part of a week. Tina was ready for him. Her eyes finally settled on his bemused face.

"I need to see Holly," Logan said without any preamble.

"If she wanted to see you, she'd be standing here."

Logan blinked. Who was this tall wispy woman with long brown hair and cold dark eyes. "I'm Logan Montgomery. Who the hell are you?"

Tina raised an unimpressed eyebrow. "I know exactly who you are. Who am I? The person you better start being a whole lot nicer to if you have any hope of getting past this door."

Logan stared, dumbfounded. He could forget about trying to be intimidating; hostility was practically radiating out of her. It was plain to see charm wasn't going to work on her either. Whoever this woman was, she was taking her role of bulldog seriously. He continued to stand on the front porch staring blankly, racking his brain trying to figure out just who she was and how to get past her without muscling his way in. Then it dawned on him.

"You must be Tina." He gave her a lopsided grin.

"You're very perceptive. You can add it to your list of attractive attributes."

"Welcome to New Jersey," Logan muttered, feeling the slap of her sarcasm.

"And so polite, too! But you're a little late on that one. I've been here all week."

Logan felt his ire pitch and his jaw start to clench. "I guess you'd be the person I should thank for Holly's outstanding performance this evening."

Tina threw back her head and laughed before answering coolly, "You're giving me way too much credit. All I did was run some errands, give some moral support, and drive the getaway car. You really are a piece of work. Why don't you thank yourself? If you weren't such a shallow spoiled narcissist, my best friend would've never felt the need to do something so drastic."

Logan's teeth began to grind. All of this was getting him nowhere. It was obvious Tina had already made up her mind about him and wasn't going to budge from her preconceived notion.

"What's the matter?" Tina asked. "Not used to the labeling and name-calling?"

Logan shook his head slowly and released a single chuckle. "You've got it all wrong, you know. You both do. I guess you never heard the phrase 'There are three sides to every story'?"

"I couldn't care less about your side. And Holly's side

is usually the truth, because I've known her long enough to know she's honest. That's good enough for me."

"She's hurt and confused. If you'll just let me in, I can explain."

"Explain? What's to explain? Did you or did you not tell all your highfalutin friends she was your ugly duckling? Have you or have you not been taking all the credit for her hard work? You don't even need to answer; the guilt is written all over your jacked-up face. Whatever you want to tell her you can tell me from right where you are; I'll be sure to pass it along."

"I'm not leaving until I see her," Logan stated with resolve.

"I'll bet the cops would have a different take on that."

"Tina." Holly broke in quietly from behind her. "It's okay. You can let him in."

Tina turned briefly from her spot at the door to look at Holly, who was now standing at the bottom of the stairs, calm but wide eyed. "You're sure?"

Holly met Tina's eyes. "It's okay." Then she added, "Stay close."

Tina turned back to Logan, gave him one more disapproving snort, and opened the door. Logan stepped into the foyer.

"Thank you," he said, overly polite.

"Not my idea," Tina retorted, closing the door behind him and resuming her post beside it.

Holly took one look at him and wiggled her bruised fingers. No wonder her hand hurt so much. Even she was surprised at the damage she had inflicted, but she refused to give him the satisfaction of displaying any remorse. Besides, she didn't feel any.

"What do you want?" She was as emotionless as stone.

"I really need to talk to you." He took one more fleeting look in Tina's direction. "Do you think we can go someplace private?"

"No." She stood at the staircase, leaning on the banister. "Tina isn't going anywhere. Whatever you have to say, just say it."

She waited. It sure was easier to deal with having only one of those sad puppy eyes staring back at her. And it disgusted her that even with the swollen, half-closed, bruising eye, he was still absolutely magnificent.

"I never meant to hurt you when I called you an ugly duckling." He got right to the point, for the first time acutely conscious of how unkind the words sounded as he spoke them.

"If you're using it as a pickup line, you might want to reconsider." Her face remained expressionless.

He continued miserably, throwing his hands up in surrender. "It was never my intention to pick you up. I don't even know why I ever used the term."

She didn't bother holding back the hollow laugh. "I do. You said it yourself. Because it was never your intention to pick me up. You and Amanda and Chase and all of your friends—you beautiful people would never let a fat loser like me get close enough to your circle to worry what goes on within it. You go on, from day to perfect day, blinded by spotlights, living your perfect lives, surrounding yourselves with other perfect people. You were only willing to let me in because I busted my ass twenty-four-seven for the privilege. I don't know if I could make it in a world like yours, but I sure as hell don't think I want to spend the rest of my life trying." Her genuine overwhelming sadness was beginning to show and Holly made no attempt to conceal it.

He ineffectively tried to rationalize. "That's not true, Holly. You are part of my world. It didn't mean anything. I say it all the time."

"You *never* said it to me but you said it to others, which can only mean it rang true to you in my case," she stated with unaffected calm. "Go ahead, Logan, tell me I'm wrong."

"It's not true!" he said emphatically, desperate to be understood, all thought of Tina's witnessing the exchange forgotten. "I never thought of you in that way at all. When I said it to Natalie and all the others before her, I would do it to provoke them. People would rave to them about their beauty all the time. When exactly should I have said it to you? While you were grieving the loss of your husband? While you were trying to overcome your food issues? When I realized—" His stopped short of finishing the sentence, the one that would have ended with "I loved you."

Holly was unimpressed. She shook her head. "Shame on me. I trusted you. Like I trusted my husband, when he tore me away from everything and everyone I knew and locked me away in this tower, only to leave me stranded. You know, the first time I laid eyes on you, I hated you. But the more we talked, the more I got to know you, I started to feel like you might really be my knight in shining armor. The biggest joke of all was that you totally looked the part. And isn't *that* ironic? When all is said and done, I'm really no different from the rest of you—worshipping physical perfection."

Logan said nothing, the impact of her words heavier than any weight he'd ever lifted.

Holly stood there, tears threatening but refusing to fall. His silence was the confirmation that everything she said was true. She turned and went up the stairs.

"You know the way out," she said without looking back.

Logan waited 'til he heard the slam of her bedroom door before turning to leave. Tina was standing at the now-reopened door with her arms crossed, ready to close it behind him.

Their eyes met. Her look had softened, was no longer hostile. There may have even been some pity thrown in. Her mouth was slightly open, as though she wanted to say something but had thought better of it. She believed him. Her gaze drifted to the staircase and then settled back on him. After her single nod, he turned away from her and took the stairs two at a time. She didn't follow.

He stood outside Holly's bedroom door.

"You're right, you know," he said loudly through the wood that separated them. "About almost everything. Everything except the part where you said you're like me. I'm an idiot, Holly, a first-class idiot."

When he got no response, he laid his ear against the door, his fingers gently tracing along the lines of the frame. His voice was low and pleading. "Don't you see, Holly? That day on the plane? I thought I was going to teach you something. But in the end, it was *you* who taught *me*. Taught me not to judge a book by its cover. Taught me about real strength, and endurance, and beauty, and all the other things I used to consider my specialty. I'm not done learning, Holly." He lightly banged his forehead on the door and whispered, hoarse: "If you leave me now, it'll be a real loss. A real loss."

As soon as he heard the door begin to open, he burst through, giving her no opportunity to change her mind. He swept her up into the middle of the room and kissed her. And kissed her. And kissed her. With each kiss he pulled her closer, hugged her tighter. He stole breath after breath and squeezed her until she felt dizzy. When he finally set her at arm's length, she felt like she'd just ridden a roller coaster.

"Does this mean we get another chance?" Logan inhaled and then held his breath.

Holly looked at him with deep sadness, so deep she was afraid she might actually drown in it. This was supposed to be her crowning moment, where she would emerge triumphant, having finally and completely freed herself from the hold he had over her. Maybe it was because his delicious kiss was still fresh on her lips or she was still light-headed from his crushing embrace, but suddenly she didn't want to say the cruel things she'd planned. Holly slowly shook her head. "No. It means I didn't want to have any bad feelings between us when I said good-bye."

His look of relief was replaced with one of confusion,

and his grip tightened on her shoulders. "What do you mean 'good-bye'?"

"I mean that as of tomorrow morning, I'm packing it in and going home."

Logan released her and looked around the room. Two suitcases were situated near the doorway, the confirmation of her statement. He returned his befuddled gaze to her. "You're going back to Toronto?"

"Oregon," she stated simply.

"Oregon?" he repeated, fully aghast. "That's a terrible idea. You were miserable there!"

She gave him a sad little smile. "Your time for telling me what is and isn't a good idea has passed, Logan. Besides, I think I'm ready to go back there, be part of a family again."

"A family that you told me didn't want you for anything more than a nurse and maid," he told her. "Where they have an illness that can't be cured without active participation. You can't save them if they don't want saving."

She shrugged. "No family is perfect. They don't even know I'm coming. And I'm not that same girl anymore, thanks in part to you. I'm stronger, focused. I'm going to stay with Tina for a while, till I find a place to live. Once I'm settled, I'll make the call. They're starting to deteriorate, my father rapidly. I don't want to have any regrets about whether or not I was a lousy daughter."

"What about this place?" he asked her, still trying to reconcile the words that were coming out of her mouth with the meaning behind them.

"It goes on the market tomorrow. No matter how long

it takes, I can wait it out," Holly said. *If it takes too long, I'm willing to take a bath on it,* she added to herself, anything to get away.

"I don't want you to do this," he said.

"What you want no longer matters," she told him quietly. "And it's going to be okay, for both of us. I'm sure of it. You'll be ringing in the New Year saying, 'Holly who?' I guarantee it."

There was nothing more to say. Logan took a step back and turned, making his way to the door. Before exiting, he turned back to her with his single beautiful eye, the one that wasn't swelling. "I'm really sorry I hurt you, Holly."

"I'm really sorry I gave you a black eye, Logan. But if it makes you feel any better, I was aiming for your nose," she said.

"Thanks for missing. That would've really sucked," he told her, wanting desperately to kiss her again one last time and knowing it wouldn't make any difference. It would only prolong the agony. "I hope you know what you're doing."

She nodded and he left the room. Holly listened to the sounds of his footsteps going down the stairs, a brief quiet exchange of voices, and the sound of the front door closing. She threw herself on the bed and began to sob.

Chapter Twenty-Five

LOGAN DIDN'T BOTHER ACKNOWLEDGING THE IN-
trigued look on the doorman's face when he entered
his apartment building. What was he supposed to tell
him, that he hadn't been mugged? That yes, it hurt
every bit as much as it appeared to? Lowering his head,
Logan opted not to make direct eye contact and walked
briskly to the elevator. He pushed the UP button and
offered a prayer of thanks when the doors immediately
opened. He selected his floor and leaned against the
wall, waiting for the doors to close, staring at the floor.
It felt good to not have to look the world in the face,
although he wasn't accustomed to feeling the weight
of guilt heavy on his shoulders. Just before the elevator doors closed, a woman entered, taking her place on
the other side of the elevator. The doors closed and the
elevator ascended.

He recognized the perfume even before his gaze drifted from her designer shoes up her long legs to finally settle on her face. It was a face that was smiling slightly.

Just when he thought his night couldn't get any worse. "Jesus Christ, news travels fast," he muttered.

"This sort of news does anyway," she replied cautiously, testing the waters of his mood. "Bet a hickey doesn't seem so bad now."

Logan refused to answer and instead sighed, returning his stare to the floor. "What are you doing here, Natalie?"

"I was waiting for you in the lobby, but you blew right by me. I came to see if you're all right. And see for myself if it was actually true."

The elevator dinged and came to a stop at his floor, the doors opening. Logan got out with Natalie following behind him.

"You have a lot of nerve showing up here," he said over his shoulder as he walked briskly down the hall.

"I wanted to try to explain."

"So explain," he replied, never breaking his stride.

"I wanted to explain what really happened. How badly Holly overreacted," she told him, quickening her pace in the effort to keep up with him.

"That sounds more like accusation than explanation." Logan stopped in front of his door, pulling his keys out of his jacket pocket. Natalie caught up to him and placed her hand over his before he could unlock the door.

"I know you're probably furious with me. I don't blame you. Please hear me out," Natalie said.

Even with his pounding headache, her beauty was remarkable. So graceful, so delicate, it was hard to believe she could be so completely malicious. Still, she seemed sincere. With all the fight in him depleted and depression setting in, he exhaled loudly before relenting.

"Sure. Come on in."

Logan unlocked the door and went inside, instinctively holding it open for her. He turned on several lights and made straight for the couch, taking a seat. Resting an elbow on his knee, he placed his good eye directly into his palm, applying pressure to his eye socket in the hopes of relieving his headache. Without looking up, he could feel the shifting of the couch as Natalie took a seat beside him.

"She really did a number on you," Natalie finally said.

"Is that what you came to talk to me about?" Logan replied into his forearm, his eyeball still firmly ensconced within his palm.

Natalie settled back on the couch. "You didn't deserve this, Logan. You didn't deserve to be made a fool out of. When I got the phone call that this happened, I couldn't believe my own ears."

"Just out of curiosity, who told you?" Logan asked, not really wanting to know.

"Cliff Caldwell from the *Post*," she told him as gently as she could. 'It's going to be on Page Six."

"Great," Logan said blandly, lifting his head out of

his hand and sitting back against the couch with another sigh. He looked at Natalie and resisted the urge to laugh. Her concern was evident. He thought he also recognized a touch of remorse.

"He said the picture's not very good though, and they probably won't use it. It's nothing more than a blurb. They're not even using names other than Chase's." She gave him a small contrite grin before continuing. "Once he told me what she was wearing, I knew right away what happened. I'm so sorry, Logan. I swear, I only said five words to her—of course, one of them being 'quack.' I had no idea she was that unstable."

The urge to laugh won out as soon as he heard the word "quack" and it started the replay of the night's events in his head. A chuckle of irony escaped. "You know what? I totally believe you."

Natalie breathed a sigh of relief. "You do? Thank you. I really did feel awful, even if I wasn't the one to push her over the edge."

Logan said nothing, disinclined to reveal anything more about Holly than Natalie already knew. If Natalie wanted to believe that Holly was irrational or insane, so be it. There was little to be gained by Natalie's knowing her words had had the desired effect, or why. The fact was, he had nothing to say, about anything. He wasn't interested in making Natalie feel any worse or any better. His only interest was the woman a town over who was hours away from leaving.

Natalie continued to watch him. All traces of the lothario she'd previously known were gone. There was no hint of his easygoing wit or his playful smile. He looked not only battered but broken. She was uncomfortable, began to doubt her reasoning for showing up. At first, she was certain the timing couldn't have been more perfect. He would be supremely pissed off at having that sort of attention drawn to him. But he would also probably want to move on as quickly as possible, even if he was admitting he missed the psychopath who had done this to him. The Logan sitting beside her was a man she didn't recognize. He looked disheartened and not ready to move on anywhere. He wasn't even going through the motions of trying to hide it. She finally said, "You really do look awful. Can I get you a couple Advil or some ice?"

Eager for a few moments of solitude, he nodded. "Advil would be great. I think I have some in the medicine cabinet."

Natalie hurriedly stood up to retrieve the pain reliever and get him a glass of water to take it with, leaving him alone in the living room. There was no doubt in his mind that what Natalie told him was the truth. There was also no doubt that Holly was clever enough to piece the whole scenario together with only one word to go by, especially after Amanda confirmed Holly had reacted to hearing it. Nobody could have predicted the kind of scene Holly would create. It would be easy to lay the blame on Natalie, but deep down he knew the culpability was his alone. Tina was right. It was bound to happen. He had been so careless, thoughtless even. If it hadn't been Natalie, eventually it would have been someone else. Still, he couldn't stop from grinning, thinking how entertaining Holly's display must have been to watch for those with no emotional stake in it.

Natalie came back and handed him the capsules and a glass of water, sitting back down next to him. She waited for him to knock the Advil back with a hearty slug of water.

"Thanks," he said, adding, "Forgive my manners. Help yourself to anything you want."

Natalie waited before quietly asking, "Anything?"

Logan looked at her curiously for a moment before shaking his head. "Come on, Nat, you don't really want to be my rebound skank."

She slammed back against the couch, crossing her arms over her chest, clearly put off. "Not when you put it like that. Anyone ever tell you that you have a way with words?"

He waited for her to look at him before pointing to his eye and saying sarcastically, "Yeah. I did get a memo." And then he laughed. Natalie couldn't stop her smile from forming either. He took a deep breath before settling his gaze on her, shaking his head again. He said with sincerity, "I'm sorry. I'm not sure when my mouth became my worst enemy, but you know what I mean here. I'd fuck you tonight, because you're here and you're offering and I'm a putz like that, but it'd be all about her."

Her. Natalie crossed her legs and tilted her head, continuing to study him. This time she noticed he was actually untidy. The collar was sticking up from his pin-striped suit jacket. His shirt was wrinkled and unbuttoned, his tie loose. He looked miserable. If he would just give her a chance, she could fix it, all of it. They belonged together, they were a much better fit; surely he would see that now. She smiled again. "I can see you haven't completely lost your touch. You can still make the most repugnant things sound positively charming."

"It's a gift," he replied with no real conviction.

She continued to stare at him, weighing the risks, before confessing, "I really missed you, Logan. And I'd like to think I've grown a lot. You were good for me in so many ways. I'm not saying we try to pick up where we left off. I'm still traveling anyway. We can go back to enjoying each other's company. Keep it casual. And I get your no-strings-attached thing, especially after what you've just been through. I've kissed a lot of frogs since I stopped seeing you. Maybe you kissed a couple, too?"

If she was trying to convey through subtle wordplay any slight at Holly, he wasn't biting. Instead, Logan said wearily, "I'm sort of laying off all the animal references for now."

Natalie giggled, encouraged by his remark and general nonreaction to her disclosure. She sat up straight and licked her lips nervously. She leaned her head in slightly toward his. When he made no move to pull away, she brought her head in closer and tentatively placed her mouth over his.

Her lips were soft and warm, just as he remembered them. Her breath was sweet. But there was just no magic. No awe or surprise. No wide-eyed wonder triggering his hunger. His own lips responded, but without enthusiasm. His hands remained limply at his sides. Natalie detected his hesitation. She opened her eyes to find his lifeless ones looking vacantly ahead. She slowly pulled her head away and leaned back on the couch. Demurely, she folded her hands neatly in her lap.

"I didn't mean to be pushy. We just always had chemistry. You're right. Maybe you just need some time."

He threw his hands in the air, landing them on his knees. "And that's what I've been trying to tell you. It won't matter tomorrow or a week from now; it's still going to be all about her. This girl isn't going to be out of my system any time soon." He looked up from his hands and at her. "You deserve to be worshipped."

"Worshipped?" Natalie snickered. "Once again, you leave me feeling insultingly flattered. I'd like to think I'm slightly less demanding."

Logan smiled sadly at her. "There's no insult of any kind attached. You're a beautiful girl who deserves a guy's full attention. A guy who's willing to do backflips to get you to notice him and dotes on you to keep it. I'm not that guy. I wish I could be."

It was in that moment that Natalie knew she had made a mistake in coming. Her plan, while it had worked, had also backfired. Logan wanted for her all the things he was doing for someone else. All her initial suspicions were confirmed. Logan's playboy days were over. He had fallen, and hard. If she wasn't seeing it for herself she wouldn't have believed it. She had just chosen to ignore it. But she couldn't any longer. Natalie nodded at him, reaching for her purse. She started to rise. "Why the hell do you have to be so nice? You even make a brush-off sound sweet. I would say lose my number, but I get the feeling it's already gone."

Logan didn't respond to that, but he did stand up. Together they made their way to the door. "Thanks, Natalie, for coming by, clearing things up. For understanding that right now I'm a hot mess."

When they reached the door, Natalie turned around to face him one more time. "She must have been crazy to risk losing you."

"I'll be sure to tell her, if she ever speaks to me again," Logan replied, thinking that if he didn't get Natalie out the door in the next thirty seconds, she might see him start to melt down.

He was unmistakably distraught. She stared at him a second more. Then Natalie started to laugh, uncontrollably. She couldn't help it.

"You find something about that funny?" he asked her irritably.

"I do," Natalie replied, catching her breath. "I find it hilarious that she's the most average, run-of-the-mill woman I've ever seen in my life. She has no glamour and certainly no refinement. She humiliated you publicly, and in a pretty major way. Now the only thing you can think of is how to get her back." Natalie started giggling again, right into Logan's red frustrated face, before turning to walk out the door.

"But the best part?" she said with infuriating glee. "She's making you sweat it."

Chapter Twenty-Six

HOLLY WOKE UP THE NEXT MORNING TO THE SOUND of her cell phone's alarm. It was just before five. She felt lethargic and worn out, having spent most of the night crying. Once again she was mourning the loss of a man who had stepped in and changed her world. Only this time, she was left in a world she was now confident she could conquer without him.

"Oh hell no!" she said out loud as she sat up, rubbing the salty crust her tears had formed from her eyes. "This is *not* the way you are going to start the first day of the rest of your life!"

She got out of bed and headed for the bathroom, disrobing and lecturing herself on the way. After a quick shower, she dressed and took her suitcases down to the front door to await the car service that would be picking her and Tina up at six to take them to the airport. Tina's suitcase was already there. Holly could hear the sound of the television coming from the living room. She found Tina fully dressed, sitting cross-legged on the couch, watching CNN.

Tina looked up and said excitedly, pointing to the television, "You made the news."

Holly froze. "What are you talking about?"

"Well, not you exactly," Tina said while still bouncing on the couch in amusement. "They just had a story about a skirmish at Chase Walker's house last night. I'm guessing you're the 'unidentified assailant' who broke into their charity party and started a melee resulting in one minor injury. You'll be happy to know that you're still on the loose."

The grip of fear was immediate. Holly had been so wrapped up in plotting her scheme that she had forgotten there could be that kind of fallout. Chase had never been anything but nice to her. She'd repaid that kindness by giving him bad publicity. She slowly shook her head.

"That is so not funny," Holly said, bringing her finger to her mouth. "I hope they at least mentioned the charity."

"Sorry, they didn't. What a bunch of bullshit; I'd hardly call it a melee. And you didn't break in, you had an invitation."

Holly began chewing on her fingernail. Her mind began to race. It was too early in the morning for this. She said distractedly, "They probably said that to save my ass."

Tina watched Holly from her spot on the couch and asked, "Holly? Are you having second thoughts?"

"No," Holly replied quickly before moving on to another fingernail. "Suddenly I'm thinking I can't get out of town fast enough."

"What are you so worried about?" Tina giggled. "Afraid Walker's going to show up here and put you over his knee?"

"Don't believe everything you hear. He's not like that," Holly replied irritably, dropping her hand and taking a deep breath. Tina's jokes weren't helping. Last night she didn't care what happened, but with the new day came logic and regret and a sense of self-preservation. She hadn't only done this to Logan; she'd essentially stabbed Chase and Amanda in the back as well. She felt the panic start to mount. "But what if the only reason they didn't tell the police it was me was because of Logan? What if by now they know I kicked Logan to the curb? They don't need to protect me out of loyalty to him anymore. What if now they decide they want to get justice?"

Tina stood up and joined Holly, who had begun to pace around the foyer and wring her hands. She grabbed Holly's forearm to halt her as she passed and spoke calmly. "Whoa. Holly, relax. It wasn't all that late when he left here last night. Trust me; no one is coming to get you. They know."

Holly stopped pacing and looked at Tina with wide frightened eyes.

"Come on, we have about fifteen minutes before our pickup. You need to hold it together for just a little while longer," Tina said gently in an effort to get Holly refocused. "Do you have our tickets?"

"They're in my pocketbook," Holly replied, worrying her lower lip. She went over to a small table next to the door where her purse was sitting and pulled them out, showing them to Tina.

"Keys to the house and the car?" Tina asked.

"With the Realtor," Holly replied. The real estate agent had frowned at the suggestion that the car could be part of the deal for the house, but Holly had asked anyway. If she had to, she would make arrangements later to ship the car once Holly was situated. "What would I do without you? You're a lifesaver. Along with being so bright eyed and bushy tailed at the crack of dawn."

"Are you kidding?" Tina laughed. "I'm always up at five in the morning. I have three kids; it's the only time I get any peace and quiet."

Together they took the time to quickly look around, making sure Holly hadn't forgotten anything. The refrigerator was empty, the cupboards bare. The lights were all on timers to give the appearance that someone still lived there. All papers were gone, shredded and disposed of, with the exception of the important ones that were tucked away within one of her suitcases. She had done every single thing she could think of to avoid making any return to Jersey that would require more than the briefest of stays.

It had worked; Holly was once again composed. Tina was probably right; if there were going to be any repercussions, they would have happened already. Still, she wouldn't be able to completely relax until she was in the sky, and she never in a million years would have thought she would feel safer at thirty thousand feet than she did on the ground. She really had come such a long way. And she had already begun to view the house as nothing more than a shell. Bruce's ghost had long since departed. Wherever he was, he was probably laughing his ass off, proud that she had stood up for herself, and in such a grand fashion. She shook her head and swallowed any lingering sadness. She didn't have to worry about being that pliant, accommodating girl anymore. She was steady, focused, and in control. Bruce had seen to it that she could have any sort of life she wanted. Logan had seen to it that she was strong enough to know how to make the most of it. If she could just get to the airport and on the plane without a felony assault charge, she'd be home free. She heard the faint sound of a car horn outside and breathed a sigh of relief.

A kindly gray-haired gentleman in his early sixties was waiting outside when Holly opened the front door, and he wished them a good morning, introducing himself as Gus. He took their bags to place them in the car's already opened trunk. Satisfied that both the suitcases and the passengers were secure within the car, he took his position behind the steering wheel and shifted the nondescript black Crown Victoria into gear. The car began to stealthily make its way down her driveway.

"Would you like me to stop somewhere so we can pick up some coffee?" he asked politely, glancing at her reflection in his rearview mirror.

"No, thanks," Holly told him. "I'm a slightly nervous flyer to begin with. No point in adding octane to that mix."

"Understood," the chauffeur replied, chuckling. "Then let's get you two to the airport."

Tina and Gus engaged in small talk, leaving Holly to her own thoughts. She watched from her window in the backseat as she passed by the streets that used to be her neighborhood. It was like she was seeing much of it for the first time. Sort of a shame, she mused; so much had happened in the relatively short time she was here that she never got a chance to really explore all the state had to offer. She had never even gotten to go to Atlantic City or the beach. By the time they hit the highway she felt a lump start to form in her throat. In the distance, with the sun only just beginning to rise, she could see from her window an overly bright glow reaching out. She had little doubt it was the glow of the spotlights shining from the front of Bodyssey. There were people in there she would actually miss. She childishly refused to turn her head in the direction of either Logan's gym or his apartment.

Logan. She'd never expected him to search her out so soon. And he hadn't even been angry, just contrite. Beyond contrite; he was downright wretched. He had ruined the final part of her plan, the getaway, with his sad soulful eye and his apologetic declaration. It left a rotten taste in her mouth.

Tina broke into Holly's thoughts. "Are you feeling any better? I brought your Xanax."

Holly turned to her with an absent smile. "I'm fine. You know I'm not going to take them."

"It looks like it's going to be a nice day for flying, if that makes you feel any better," Gus commented.

"It does," Holly replied. "I was hoping it would be. Every little bit helps. Let's hope our Portland landing is as cooperative."

"Well, I can't speak for Oregon, but the weather in Maine is probably similar," Gus said, taking a quick look up into the sky through the windshield.

"If we were going to Maine, I probably would have tried to get a later flight, but thanks for trying," Holly told him. "We're going to Oregon."

"Oregon, huh?" he remarked. "Been there a few times fishing. Some beautiful country out there."

"There sure is," Tina replied, full of pride, then laughed. "Although I can only imagine what sort of 'beauty' awaits me in my house after being away all week."

"How long are you staying?" he politely inquired, making eye contact with Holly in the mirror again. "Did you schedule a pickup? I can do that for you if you need me to."

"My ticket is one-way," Holly said. "And Tina already lives there."

"Had enough of the East Coast rat race, eh?"

"Something like that. I have family there." Holly closed her eyes tight for a moment, to keep out of her mind the implications that came with the word "family."

The conversation was minimal after that, with Gus returning his attention to the congested traffic on the New Jersey Turnpike. Holly and Tina were quiet also, each lost in her respective thoughts. He pulled up to the front of their terminal, opened the trunk, and handed over their bags to a porter, who accompanied Holly and Tina to the check-in counter. Holly confidently handed their coach boarding passes and both her and Tina's driver's licenses to the ticket agent. There would be no disputes this time about how many asses she had or how many seats she would need. But Holly's confidence began to falter as the agent took several long, drawn-out moments looking from the ticket to the identification to her computer screen to Holly.

"Is something wrong?" Holly asked nervously.

"No, Mrs. Brennan, not at all," the agent said amiably while typing out several keystrokes on her computer. "These tickets have been upgraded."

"Upgraded?" Tina piped up. "Did I just make it to the big time?"

"Both of them?" Holly asked, her shock evident. "I didn't think I had enough flyer miles for that."

The ticket agent handed Holly back the licenses and the newly printed boarding passes with a smile. "I'm sorry; I don't know anything about that. If you're a frequent flyer and you have the most miles of any of the ticketed flyers, they upgrade you automatically. If you want to wait a minute I can confirm that's what happened."

"No, that's fine. You don't need to go through the trouble," Holly said quickly, noticing Tina's thinly veiled excitement and the line of people gathering behind them. Even if they ended up charging her, it was the least she could do to repay Tina for all she had done to see her through this past week. Still, she was mildly disappointed. She had actually been looking forward to sliding smoothly into the smaller seat. It would have been another victory in her life's story. *No matter,* she thought as they made their way to their gate. Surely she would have to return for the finalization of the house sale; she could try out her new ass then. Today she would consider it a stroke of luck, a positive omen that she was indeed heading in the right direction. She should have thought of treating Tina to the upgrade in the first place.

Holly let Tina have the window seat and took her seat beside her, leaving the aisle seat empty. There was still plenty of room. The early-morning flight wasn't crowded and business class was nearly empty. Maybe she would move around later. For now it was comforting to have her best friend right beside her. She buckled herself in and began her mental preparation for takeoff. The new Holly was not going to be afraid to fly and she wasn't going to assuage that fear by gorging herself on whatever junk food was offered to her. The new Holly was going to placidly nap and enjoy the royal treatment. She leaned her head back and closed her eyes, considering whether or not she should ask for a blanket.

"Whew! That was close! I thought for a minute there I wasn't going to make it."

Holly didn't need to open her eyes. Her pulse raced with the immediate recognition of the voice. But she did open them, speechless, just as Logan Montgomery slid into his seat beside her. He was scruffy from not having taken the time to shave, and it was the closest to disheveled she had ever seen him. He was smiling at her, his beautiful captivating smile, which offset the horror that was his eye. Everything around the socket was painted various shades of purple, and the white of his eye was tinged red. What she could see of the white, anyway. His eye was approaching the state of what looked like a permanent wink.

"Good morning, gorgeous," he said to Holly before leaning past her and adding, "Hi, Tina."

"Morning, Logan," Tina said, way too friendly for Holly's liking.

"What are you doing here?" she sputtered incredulously when she finally found her voice.

"What does it look like I'm doing here?" He smiled while buckling himself in. "I'm flying to Portland."

"B-but why?" She continued to stammer. "How?"

He released an energized rush of air. "You didn't really think I was just going to let you go without a fight, did you? At first I was just going to show up at your house early this morning with flowers and a boom box playing some goofy love song, John Cusack style. But then I had a little chat with your friend here."

Holly turned her head away from Logan long enough to level a cold, disbelieving glare at Tina.

"Traitor," she hissed.

Tina grinned apologetically and gave a small shrug. Holly shook her head, her mouth a thin tight line, before turning back to Logan, and he continued. "She told me everything I needed to know in regard to your flight. Then I called and switched your tickets, and booked the seat next to you. We figured it was a much better idea. Now you're a captive audience. And I have witnesses in case you decide to go all ninja on me again, not that it would really stop you. The way I see it, I have six hours to win you over. I hope it's enough. I know just how tough you are." His smile grew so wide the bloodshot eye completely disappeared within the swollen purple flesh surrounding it.

"I'm not doing this. I'm switching my seat," Holly replied hotly. She unbuckled and rose, climbing over him, careful not to make contact with him and failing when he grabbed her around the waist to help her safely into the aisle. His hands were warm and strong and she could feel them through her clothing. She gave Tina one more furious glare. "You and Benedict Arnold here can compare some more notes."

Holly went to the other side of the plane and several rows down, taking a window seat. A minute later, Tina arrived and took the seat beside her. Holly crossed her arms and stared out the window, refusing to look at her. The plane began to taxi to its runway and the flight crew went through the emergency procedures protocol. She seethed. The audacity, the unmitigated gall of him to merrily announce his arrival and reveal his plot and think she'd be anything other than incensed. And then to incorporate her best friend into the plan! She was too irate to be afraid. As the plane took off all she could think about was how good it would feel to push both Logan and Tina out of it—with anvils strapped to their chests. It seemed only minutes later when the flight attendant appeared, asking them if they would like some coffee or anything else to drink and whether she could take their breakfast orders. Holly could feel her skin start to crawl when she overheard the distinct giggle and syrupy quality of the attendant's voice once she got to Logan. Typical. She added it to the list of crap she wouldn't miss when she finally was rid of him. She rounded on Tina.

"I can't believe you did this," Holly said fiercely. "I can't believe you did this to me. I don't think I can ever forgive you. I hope you're proud of yourself. And that you realize that all you did was fall under his spell, like all the rest of the women who get in his crosshairs. I really thought you were made of stronger stuff."

Tina waited patiently while Holly ranted and then asked, "Are you done?"

"No, I'm not done. Thanks for letting me spend the last two hours freaking out about how I'd look in an orange jumpsuit with numbers on the back!" Holly snapped. Once again, she felt utterly alone. Only yesterday Tina had detested Logan on her behalf; now she was his co-conspirator. It was overwhelming, too much to bear. It was impossible to comprehend the betrayal. She shook her head, running a hand through her hair. "There. Now I am. I just need to know why. Why would you do this?"

"Because I was there," Tina said by way of explanation. "I heard you. And I heard him."

The way she said it made Holly pause. She felt her shoulders loosen from up around her earlobes as the tension began to drain out of her. "All he did was play you, Tina, like he played me," Holly said dispassionately, resuming her gaze out the window. "It's his specialty."

"I don't think so. And if you can stop being pissed

off for a second, I'll tell you why," Tina said. When Holly remained staring out the window, she continued quietly. "I've heard that sort of voice before."

What was Tina getting at? Her quiet confidence was unexpected. Holly turned back from the window.

"I was so jealous of you the day you left for college," Tina said. "Jealous that you were actually able to do what you always said you were going to do: escape our small insignificant town. It didn't matter that I knew all the reasons you were desperate to get out. Every time I got an e-mail from you, it got worse. There you were, across the country, beginning a life I could only dream about. I was determined to save up my money and try to apply to college the next year. Maybe not the likes of Brown, 'cause you were always smarter than me, but someplace where I could live in a dorm room, really be on my own, have a college experience."

"I never knew you felt that way," Holly murmured, her defenses starting to slip. "I was miserable that first year, just so you know."

Tina chuckled a little. "Trust me, you weren't nearly as miserable as I was when I found out I was pregnant with Danny. I saw any hope of college or even a good job passing me by with that stupid EPT test. And then I realized I didn't have to let it stop me. It was the twenty-first century. I could solve the problem with one trip to a clinic. I could have an abortion without anyone even knowing about it."

Holly stifled a gasp. She remembered holding Danny right after he was born that first summer she was home from college. He was so small and pink and precious.

It had been nearly impossible to wipe the beaming smiles off Tina and Tommy's faces. It was hard to believe that Tina would have even considered termination an option.

"But I knew I could never keep what I was going to do from Tommy. He was already suspicious. He had seen me get sick a couple times and I was acting strangely in general. I figured he would be happy anyway since I was letting him off the hook and everything."

Holly nodded, saying nothing. Tina's voice became softer.

"But he wasn't happy. In fact, he started to cry. He begged me not to go through with it. He told me that he'd loved me since the second grade. That he had a prayer answered the first time I said I loved him. He told me that he wanted to marry me and have a family, and if I would just give him the chance, he would spend the rest of his life making sure I didn't regret it. And he's lived up to that promise." Tina smiled. "So far."

Holly found herself smiling as well. The Blakes' relationship was as strong as it ever had been. Tina had spoken with Tommy and the kids every day while at Holly's. Those conversations were full of affection. It was the same sort of rapport they'd shared back in high school.

Tina continued, her eyes bright. "The point of this story is that until the day I die, I will never forget the look on Tommy's face or the raw emotion in his voice that night. Some people go a whole lifetime and never see someone act that way over them. My heart still skips a beat when I think about it."

Holly stared at Tina and began biting into her lower lip. This story was certainly leading up to something. Something Holly didn't think she wanted to face.

"Holly," Tina said quietly. "My heart skipped a beat last night, only this time for you."

Holly continued to stare, only now with her mouth slightly agape and fresh tears starting to burn her eyelids. *Damn it,* she thought. She had been sure she didn't have any tears left.

Holly began to protest. "I don't think you know what the hell you're talking about."

"I know what I saw. And what I saw last night was a man who would do anything to keep you from leaving him. And has."

Holly closed her eyes and leaned her head back. It felt like the world was spinning around her and she didn't know how to make it stop.

"You know what else I think?" Tina asked, and then said bluntly, "I think the truth is you'd rather have a root canal than go back to Fairview. You've just spent so much of your life settling and trying to make the most of rotten situations that you honestly don't believe you deserve anything better. I think it's time to stop all your bullshit and put on your big-girl panties."

Holly's head snapped back up, insulted. "I beg your pardon?"

"You heard me. Wipe that offended look off your face; this past week proved to me you're no delicate flower. Listen, no one was more surprised than me when I got off the plane and saw you. You're a completely different person, which isn't saying all that much considering the last time I saw you was Bruce's funeral. But the fire was back in your eyes and I don't think it was only because you were plotting the big get-even. It's so much deeper. No one wanted to hate Logan or have your plan work more than I did. Even Tommy was jazzed up, thinking about you sticking it to the man. But now I'm not so sure this guy is the villain I thought he'd be, or that you'd be better off without him. When he called your cell phone late last night and I answered it, all he could talk about was how to keep you from getting on this plane."

"You answered my phone?" Holly asked indignantly, trying to even the playing field. Tina was really letting her have it.

"Well, it kept ringing!" Tina laughed, completely unrepentant. "Like every twenty minutes. You had already cried yourself to sleep and I was already having serious reservations. He's genuine and deeply cares for you; it's so goddamn obvious. Guys don't talk like that unless they mean it. Not to mention he's gorgeous as sin. Something tells me your reaction was disproportionate to what he did to you. Not that I blame you; even he thinks he could have handled it better. He's scared, too, you know. I would be the worst friend ever if I let you walk away from this. I hope you can see past blaming me for helping him."

"What if you're wrong?" Holly asked weakly, Tina's speech ringing in her ears. She seriously doubted that Logan had ever been scared of anything in his life.

Tina grinned. "There's only one way to find out, and it's sitting right behind you."

Holly turned around and casually peeked over the back of her seat. Her eyes immediately locked on Logan's. It was as if he had been staring at her seat, unmoving, from the moment she sat down in it, willing her to look at him. His elbow was on the armrest, his thumb under his chin, his finger curled over his upper lip. His eyes bore into hers; even the swollen one. She quickly sat back down.

"He's staring at us." Holly gulped.

"No," Tina responded with a giggle. "He's staring at *you*. Now, get over there and find out exactly what he came for."

"Come with me?" Holly asked feebly.

"No way," Tina replied, leaning back in her seat. "This is something you need to do on your own. I don't think you really want me there anyway; it's your moment. I'm going to stay here and order the flight attendants around, make the most of my upgraded status. Who knows when I'll get another chance to be treated like a big shot?"

Holly squared her shoulders and stood. Taking great pains to avoid looking directly at him, she crossed over to where Logan was sitting.

"Benedict Arnold convinced me to come talk to you," she mumbled at his muscular thighs. She watched his legs shift to the side, making room for her to pass him. She sat down in the seat next to him and folded her hands tightly on her lap. She stared at them. She didn't know where to begin, what to say to start the exchange he was determined to have and she would have done anything to avoid. His hand came into her line of vision to rest on top of hers. His strong fingers tried to coax her hands apart and she let them. Then he began to faintly trace her discolored knuckles, the knuckles she'd bruised when they forcefully made contact with his face. He was so gentle, so caring in his touch; it was as if he were examining them to see if she had injured herself while clobbering him. Her throat tightened. She continued to stare into her lap when he took her hand and it left her sight line. She could feel his lips placing a feathery kiss on each of the three affected knuckles before he entwined his fingers in hers. Then he settled both their hands in his lap. It was a gesture so tender, her eyes began to burn with sentiment she didn't want to give in to. He was waiting for her to look up and deal with him, she could tell. She swallowed hard and brought her face up to meet his. He was looking at her earnestly.

"If I had known all the trouble you were going to cause me, I would have stayed an extra night in Toronto," he said with only a hint of teasing.

"You and me both. You should be ashamed of yourself, trying to garner sympathy and support from my oldest friend. Don't you have enough friends of your own?" she said, trying to maintain her posture of anger and trying to ignore the familiar warmth spreading throughout her whenever he looked at her like that.

"Desperate times call for desperate measures," Logan replied, a small grin playing at the corners of his mouth. "I hope you went easier on her than you did on me."

"She didn't embarrass the shit out of me by making me a laughingstock."

"You punched me out in a room full of people who used to respect me. I'm going to spend the next week walking around looking like Popeye. Let's call us even," he retorted, all playfulness gone despite the joke. He was staring at her intently.

"Is that why you're doing all this, Logan? Is that what this is about? Getting even?" she asked, still unwilling to believe what he'd told her the night before. Guys like Logan didn't settle down. They played the field; they enjoyed counting notches on bedposts. Her mouth felt dry. She felt the tears of frustration beginning to build. Why did he insist on torturing her? Why couldn't he just thank her for making it easy for them both and move on, like she was doing?

"I told you. I'm not letting you go without a fight," he said soberly. "But please remember, I currently only have one eye left to see out of."

"This has nothing to do with me," she choked out, her voice raspy with unexpressed sorrow. "It has to do with you getting the upper hand or the last word or whatever else it is you think you're owed."

"You're wrong, Holly. It has everything to do with you. If I'd gotten what I wanted, I would have never met you. I would have continued with my perfectly happy life. I would have steered clear of the woman who would make me question every aspect of my very existence and shred my world piece by piece."

"You did the same thing to me," she said desolately. "Except for the prior-happy-life part."

He continued, his voice low and heavy with emotion, his eyes melting into hers. "You are the woman who came out of nowhere and made me feel the most intense feelings possible in the most fun and amazing ways, in spite of your history full of misery and disappointment. You gave yourself to me so freely, in every single way a person can. I had your complete and unwavering trust. And even though I know I sometimes took it for granted, we had a good thing. And I refuse to believe you stopped caring about me over a stupid misunderstanding with a jealous petty ex-lover who was determined to try to take all that away from us. You're way too smart for that. This is about you, all right, and the leap of faith it's going to take for you to believe that you're worthy and deserve love and to be loved, for you to take the chance of being hurt or left again. I'm onto you, and your days of hitting and running are over."

Holly had to look away, staring blankly out the plane's small oval window at the fluffy clouds below in the distance. So much of what he said was the truth she didn't want to admit. She had been waiting for him to leave her from the moment their affair started. A wave of shame came out of nowhere and washed over her. She'd never let him defend or explain himself. She went straight to thinking the worst of him. She let the feeling of betrayal fester into one of vengeance in record time, and ultimately the only way she thought she could hurt him was by ruining his physical perfection. Where just a day ago she had felt vindication and righteous anger, she now felt humiliation. A tear slipped from the corner of her eye, followed by another.

He let her indulge in her moment of withdrawal and

let his words sink in before gently taking her chin and turning her face back to his again.

"I love you, Holly. You're the most beautiful person I've ever known," Logan said softly, stroking his thumb across her cheek. "When I think of my life moving forward without you in it, my soul hurts."

"Why didn't you tell me all this last night?" she asked, her voice shaking and her chin trembling.

Logan gave her a weary smile and squeezed her hand before kissing it again. "I wanted to, but by the time I found the right words, you had handed me my walking papers. You had a real creepy calm about you. I wasn't sure how mad you still were and I wasn't willing to risk a kick in the jewels."

A giggle escaped, in contrast to her swimming eyes. They shared small knowing smiles as a flight attendant showed up with their breakfast, having been told by Tina that her friend had once again switched her seat. It was impossible to miss the admiration in the attendant's eyes when she looked at Logan. Or the poorly masked envy when she saw his hand securely wrapped around Holly's. Only this time Holly didn't feel intimidated by either. In fact, she quite enjoyed them.

Suck it up, wench. He's taken . . . by a Barbie doll's worst nightmare, she thought with satisfaction.

They sat in silence, picking at their food. It wasn't an uncomfortable silence. It was contemplative.

Holly finally broke the stillness. "Logan? What do you see in me?"

She had him asked that question once before. Before he knew life with her would be so much better than going it alone. Before he knew that commitment wasn't a trap, but a treasured gift. This time he was determined to get the answer right.

"I see the woman who taught me how to love. And I have no intention of letting her go."

"Good answer," she murmured, blushing.

"Glad you approve." He smiled devilishly at her. "I'll stand up and shout it if you need me to."

"This doesn't mean I'm taking you back, you know. Don't get too comfortable and sure of yourself. I might want to actually see that," she fibbed, wanting to curtail some of his swagger.

"I've got about another five hours before my clock runs out. Be careful what you wish for," he replied, popping a strawberry in his mouth. "I'm ready, willing, and able to profess my love for you to the other six or seven people here, complete with the sad story of just how I got this black eye. I might take my show on the road and head into coach. Maybe even the cockpit."

They went back to giving each other some quiet space. But he took the opportunity to touch her, and he took it often. He leaned his leg against hers, a tender brush against her arm or hand with his. Each and every contact made Holly more aware of just how much pleasure she took from it and how much she would really miss it if they weren't together. When breakfast was over and their trays were cleared, he reclined his seat and began to doze.

Holly watched him. She thought about all he'd said and a touch of guilt bubbled to the surface. She had taken him out of his comfort zone to make him look as ridiculous as humanly possible; he had taken her out of hers to save her life and then change it, in all the best ways. There was nothing she could do about any of that now; all she could do was spend the rest of her life trying to make it up to him. It sounded like a wonderful proposition. She caught Tina peeking around her seat from several rows in front of her. They made eye contact and smiled at each other before Tina gave her an enthusiastic thumbs-up and turned around to settle back in her seat. Holly continued watching Logan a moment more, then reached out and gently ran her fingertips along his cheekbone, just below the swelling, and he stirred.

"You okay?" he asked her, opening his eyes.

"Does it hurt?"

"Only when I blink," he teased, closing them again.

"It must be quite a shock when you look in the mirror," she said seriously.

"Nah," he replied drowsily, reaching out for her hand. "I think it makes me look tough. I plan on telling people I got pistol-whipped breaking up a robbery."

"You look tired," she said, noting the dark circle under his good eye.

"It takes a lot out of a guy to get his ass kicked and hatch a devious plot in less than twelve hours." He opened his eyes and turned his head to gaze at her before saying gently, "We can stop in on your parents, if you like?"

Holly instantly paled and looked away. "I can't make you do that. I don't know what's there."

Logan took her by the chin to face him, then cradled her head in his hand. He tilted his head to lock his eyes on hers. "My beautiful swan. Whatever's there, you're strong enough to face. And I'll be right there, spotting for you. Because whatever this thing is, we're in it together. We'll do what we can. We don't have to stay. We don't have to go at all."

She blinked up at him, glassy-eyed and wordless. He brushed her cheek with his thumb before kissing the other and releasing her.

"Decide when we land," he said confidently, resuming his grasp of her hand.

He went back to napping and she went back to looking at him, only this time Holly was sure she could see beyond the spectacular physicality straight down to his heart. And in the end, she decided it was really just as beautiful as the rest of him. And he wanted her to have it. He had gotten that message across, and in a way that rivaled any romance movie she had ever seen. He was her real-life hero. With that realization, her own heart swelled with the love she'd had for him all along. And she didn't want to run or ignore it or dispute it anymore. She wanted to enjoy feeling it and share it with him, for however long it lasted.

"I love you, Logan." Holly said it so softly, it was barely a whisper. But she could tell he heard it when the corners of his mouth turned up ever so slightly and his fingers tightened around hers.

"I guess the tickets back to New Jersey are on me," she finally said, assuring him his plan had worked.

"Not necessary," Logan replied easily, eyes still closed, giving her hand another squeeze. "Chase's jet is waiting for us at the airport in Portland."

Chase. An uneasy giggle blurted. She could almost
hear the stammering that would take place when she
saw him again. After all, it was the Walkers' party
she'd ruined. Once she was on the plane she had completely forgotten about facing that music. That was one
apology she wasn't looking forward to.

Logan read her mind. "You should be way more concerned about Amanda." He chuckled, cheered by the
prospect of seeing Amanda make someone else miserable for a change. "She's going to run you through the
wringer."

"Chase has a plane?" she asked, ignoring his comment. She would worry about them later.

He opened his eyes and smiled at her. "Chase has
everything. When I told him what I was planning to do,
he offered it up and I accepted."

"You consulted with him on all this mess? Needed
his approval, did you?" She felt irked and embarrassed.

"Well, I did have to cancel his appointment for
today," he said, taking the time to remind her of all the
sacrifices that were made on her behalf. "And lots of
others."

"A tad presumptuous, don't you think?" She tried to
sound miffed, to cover up another pang of guilt. "Guess
you all were pretty confident of the outcome here?"

"Not at all." Logan explained, bringing his seat back
up, stretching out his legs, and bestowing a wry grin
on her. "You know he's a hopeless romantic. I think he
felt partially responsible, that he got way too involved
in my affairs. And he was kind enough to point out that
if my plan didn't work, it wouldn't be fair to subject the

general public to my devastation. I could brood and cry all the way home in private."

"I don't know why I should be surprised; Chase thinks of everything," she said, marveling.

"He does," Logan said readily before yawning, then added nonchalantly, "He also mentioned that if I did manage to win you back, there was still the business of our dealing with the aftermath of what you did last night. We would certainly want privacy for that."

It took only a moment for what he meant to register. Chase's idea of retribution for antics like Holly's was singular. She had put Logan through quite a bit. She would never be able to match Logan's strength or overpower him if he was focused and intent. Even she couldn't honestly say she didn't have it coming. "I'm getting the Chase Walker treatment soon as you get me alone on that plane?" she asked, striving to sound casual but still concerned.

Logan laughed out loud. "No worries, kid," he replied, completely relaxed. "Totally not my style. Although if I have my way, there will be plenty of smacking going on."

There was a pregnant pause.

"So? What? You're going to punch me in the eye?" she queried, becoming more and more suspicious of his open-ended statement and overly laid-back demeanor.

He took note of her anxiousness and straightened back up to gaze at her affectionately. "Not even close. The smacking I plan on doing to you involves your lips against mine, all the way back to Jersey. And maybe, if we're lucky, by the time we're somewhere over Saint

Louis, other parts of our bodies will be smacking together as well. But I promise you, it won't hurt a bit."

Holly didn't think she could stand waiting that long and leaned over to place a warm, lingering kiss on his lips. Suddenly, the thought of an airplane takeoff seemed like the best idea in the world, and she couldn't wait to do it again. She settled back down in her seat and rested her head on his strong, broad shoulder. She let him resume his dozing. And then curiosity got the best of her.

"Speaking of what is and isn't your style, I can't believe you're just going to let what happened last night go, no matter how badly you want me back." Her voice was full of warranted skepticism.

"Oh, I never said that." He chuckled, supremely self-assured. "I will have my payback."

Logan could sense her fidgeting and then felt her remove herself from his shoulder. He opened his good eye and saw her wringing her hands, worrying her lower lip in that way he adored. Her brow was furrowed and her eyes narrowed as if she was deep in thought. She was ignorant of his watching her, busy concentrating on trying to figure out what he might have in store for her. He grinned and stretched again. He clasped his hands behind his head and left them there, savoring the moment. He exhaled in ultimate victory before saying under his breath:

"You thought you hated leg lunges before . . ."

Here's an exciting sneak peek at

the sweet spot,

the new novel by

Stephanie Evanovich!

Available now from William Morrow

The Sweet Spot

AMANDA RETURNED TO THE COLD CREEK GRILLE just in time for opening. She had gone home, showered again, and redressed. She redid her makeup but didn't have time to blow-dry her hair, so the result was curly instead of straight, not the sophisticated look she would have gone for, but it would have to do. While there, she'd also checked the reservation list from her own computer and had seen that one of the parties was friends of her parents'. After a slightly awkward phone call on her end and the promise of their next meal being on the house, the couple politely gave up their reservation to accommodate the special mystery guests Amanda had begun to refer to as "the nuisances." She didn't bother telling anyone about the phone call that resulted in her order to roll out the red carpet. Being distracted by it was bad enough. It was probably an actor; they usually thought the world revolved around them. Maybe it was a politician, though that was unlikely. Her parents knew every major politician in the tristate area and the reservation call would have reflected that. Odds were it wasn't a musician, which was something to be grateful for. They tended to bring entourages.

Alan Shaw arrived promptly at 6:50. He was everything Amanda imagined he would be, right down to his overpriced suit, his prematurely receding hairline, and his creepy flagrant once-over. She was surprised he wasn't twirling a cigar. Amanda seated him at a booth in a quiet back corner, which seemed to meet with his approval. He dismissed her with the order of a Red Bull and vodka while pulling out his smart phone. She was more than happy to remove herself, not bothering to tell him she'd send his server. Her smile was starting to feel forced and unnatural. Fussy customers she could handle, but feeling manipulated by obnoxious superiority in her own establishment was a different story. The timing only added to her general feeling of dread. She spent the next ten minutes awaiting the arrival of the mystery man she had spent the better part of the afternoon referring to as "the king."

She had no idea just how close to the truth she was.

It started precisely at seven o'clock, with a flurry of activity at the entrance. Patrons waiting for the rest of their parties to arrive and those lingering with their good-byes cleared a path when three exceeding large figures seemingly filled all the remaining space at the front of the restaurant. Two of the men looked nearly identical: burly and clean shaven with short hair, matching blue suits, and serious expressions.

The third man was instantly recognizable.

His charisma had entered ten seconds before he did, spreading to everyone within its vicinity. And at its nexus was well over six feet of stacked muscle and magnetism presented casually in gray tailored slacks and a teal cashmere sweater. The corners of a button-down shirt politely pointed up at the collar and the ensemble was completed with ten-thousand-dollar Louis Vuitton shoes. His movie-star good looks only added to it, from the perfectly mussed sandy blond hair right down to the cleft in his chiseled chin. It was a heady combination and the room began to buzz.

Great Caesar's ghost! The Golden Boy was *hot* . . . and then some. Amanda and her friends had been to their fair share of Kings games over the years. There may have even been a whistle or two in his direction from their seats when they were in attendance. They may have also referred to him as "steamy hot," "fig-leaf-wearing-in-the-garden hot," and "fry-an-egg-on-his-left-pec hot."

"Hi. I'm Chase Walker," he said before he reached her.

Amanda stared at him for a moment. Chase didn't introduce himself in a way that was different than anyone else would. But her rotten day dictated that she heard him announcing his arrival as the final straw. It reeked of ego. Everyone on the planet knew who he was, even if they didn't know a thing about baseball. He was one of those extraordinary specimens that became a national treasure, probably against the greater good. You couldn't swing a dead cat without hitting something that had Chase Walker's name on it. He probably just

liked to hear the sound of his own name even if he was
the one having to say it.

In that moment, for reasons she couldn't begin to explain, Amanda chose to stand up for every person that
was ever forced to cater to the perpetually pampered.
Even on the best days, people like him were difficult
for her to take. But she had the luxury of not having
to worry about getting fired—she was the boss. Her
day already stunk; she might as well make a total hash
of it. When he and his goons left in a huff, she could
have the added pleasure of tossing Alan Shaw out on
his keister. Amanda looked from one security guard
to the other and then tilted her head at Chase, looking
thoughtful.

"Mr. Walker, has anyone ever told you that your
name is an oxymoron?" she asked and then blinked
at him with the subtle dare that he wouldn't make the
connection and she'd have to explain.

He raised his eyebrows for a moment before breaking
out into the most boyishly genuine smile she had ever
seen. "Not since the fifth grade." He chuckled, playing right into her observation. "Very funny. You can't
really chase anyone when you're a walker. Thanks for
bringing it up. My therapist can probably start picking
out his new car now."

His smile was disarming and his voice even more so.
Both were warm and magnetic and terribly engaging.
His reaction was completely unexpected. Suddenly she
felt ashamed for acting so immature. She had just taken
the well-mannered route to calling him a moron, and
he had good-naturedly called her out on it. He didn't

seem insulted, nor did he seem ready to leave. She started to blush.

Chase leaned backward a bit, turning his head, and one of the suits immediately rushed over. He whispered something in the suit's ear. The man nodded and then the two security guards left the building. Chase straightened back up and returned his attention to Amanda, leaning closer. Because of his height, he could've come clear across the podium and breathe into her ear, but he stopped just short of it.

"I'm guessing my agent worked you over pretty good?" he said pleasantly. "Because back in fifth grade, I think I beat that kid up on the playground. I'd hate to think you really want to pick a fight."

"He does seem to bring out the worst in people," she murmured, trying to stand her ground and not apologize, but also feeling guiltier for having been so unprofessional. He had made her feel downright childish.

"He's a legend in his own mind," Chase agreed, all mirth and amusement. "He bullies me into bringing the security. He can be insufferable. But he acts that way so I don't have to. Can we start over?"

Amanda looked up into his sparkling green eyes and felt her breath catch. He was already towering over her and had moved in so close. His subtle hint of cologne and pure raw masculinity was intoxicating. It was hard to believe that Chase Walker could be bullied by anyone. And he was going out of his way to make her comfortable. He was being a perfect gentleman. She blinked up at him, flabbergasted again, but this time for entirely different reasons.

"What's your name, darlin'?" His casual use of arbitrary endearments had the opposite effect of his agent's use of them. His voice sounded sweet and smooth, like honey.

"I'm Amanda Cole." She instantly played along and extended her perfectly manicured hand with a more relaxed smile. "Welcome to the Cold Creek Grille, Mr. Walker. Your party is already waiting."

Then her hand completely disappeared within his grip. His hand was huge, in keeping with the rest of him. It was also surprisingly gentle.

"It's a pleasure to meet you, Amanda. Please call me Chase," he replied, refraining from telling her that her smile was radiant for fear it would sound condescending. They had already started off on the wrong foot. In fact, he noticed, she was beautiful in every way. As soon as he'd walked in, he'd been drawn to her. Her big round eyes were so blue, her lashes long and inviting, a pure contrast with the shoulder-length ebony curls that framed her face. She had a pert little nose that looked adorable even when she wrinkled it up just prior to insulting him. He could picture himself nibbling on her rosy bottom lip. All brought about by the kinetic energy of her placing her hand in his.

Chase finally released the handshake and she turned to lead him to his table.

Amanda Cole wasn't thin, he noted—she was robust and buxom. She had curves, lots of them, and in all the right places. Making sure she was several steps ahead of him, he pulled out his phone as he walked. The action served a dual purpose. If he looked focused on something, people were less likely to try to stop him. It was all about avoiding eye contact. He could also discreetly look her up and down without looking like a letch as he followed her. And he could tell in one sweeping glance that beneath the lines of her royal blue Halston dress, Amanda Cole was a brick house, right down to her bodacious booty. He idly guesstimated how much of it his hand could cover in one shot. She had certainly given him reason to want to. She had a brat switch and he had tripped it the minute she saw him. If she had spoken any louder, she would've cut him to the quick in front of half a dozen people, including his own employees. But she had been careful to make sure that he was the only one to hear it. She wasn't flirting with him. She resorted back to acting professional and moving things along. Thanks to his agent, she had probably already hated him for hours.

In too short a stroll, they arrived at where Alan Shaw was waiting. Chase took a seat. Amanda wished them both a lovely dinner and left. He allowed himself one more thorough glance as she walked away.

"You had a good day," Alan said, taking another swallow of his drink as Chase settled into his side of the booth.

"All my days are good," Chase replied, gearing up for the onslaught that always came at dinner with Alan Shaw. He picked up his menu as Alan snapped his fingers even though Nicki was already hurrying over.

"Mr. Walker." Nicki tried to stifle the giggling, "What can I get you to drink?"

"Please call me Chase," he said, thinking that that

particular phrase was starting to sound like a broken record. "And I'll take a Heineken."

"Right away . . . Chase." Nicki giggled again and scurried off.

"I should have demanded a waiter," Alan muttered before waving his own glass and calling after her, "I'll take another one too."

"I'm so glad you didn't," Chase replied, playfully casting another glance at Amanda, "but I could have done without you pissing off the hostess. If she wasn't so cute and you weren't so obnoxious, I'd seriously consider complaining."

Alan turned his head briefly to follow Chase's gaze back to the front of the restaurant.

"That's not the hostess," Alan said indifferently. "She owns the place. She has no trouble turning on the bitch, but I hear the food is excellent."

Chase immediately bristled at the use of the word *bitch* to describe any woman, much less the one that he currently had his eye on. But if that was as bad as Alan got in his description of women this evening, he'd consider it a win. "Know anything else about her?"

"Oh, great," Shaw griped, "I can already tell where this is going. If I answer your question, can we get down to business?"

Chase held up his hand. "Scouts honor."

"She's got a rich daddy."

"Daddy as in sugar?" Chase asked, disappointed that such a beauty might be going home to some shriveled-up geezer. But it would explain why she was a bit cantankerous.

"Daddy as in father," Alan clarified, and Chase brightened.

"There's a rumor that he's going after next year's Senate seat. Her mother is the Essex County DA," Alan continued. "And she's single, which I'm sure is the only thing you really want to know anyway."

So she had breeding, Chase thought, not bothering to confirm or deny. "How do you find out all this stuff?"

"I'm only as good as the knowledge I hold," Shaw scoffed.

"You always sound so shady," Chase said, "like you just came up with something from the seedy underbelly."

"I'll take that as a compliment," Alan remarked before switching topics. "Where's your security?"

"I told them to go get my car and bring it back. The crowd doesn't look too rowdy here and I want to take off as soon as we're done."

"Take off where?" Alan questioned suspiciously.

"Wherever I feel like," Chase replied easily, knowing it would aggravate Alan further. "It's my day off tomorrow."

"When are you going to learn you just can't venture off alone anymore?"

"Watch me," Chase said. "I don't have to always live in a bubble. And I like it when you don't know where I am. Keeps you on your toes. What's the agenda this evening?"

"I heard from Trojan again," Alan began.

"I told you, I'm not doing a condom ad," Chase cut him off heatedly, "and if that's our only business tonight, I'm leaving right now."

"Relax, it's not." Alan was quick to defuse the conversation before adding, "But it's an incredible amount of money. And they don't just sell condoms."

Chase didn't bother responding. He leaned back against the booth, crossing his arms and raising an eyebrow, signifying there would be no further discussion on the topic.

Nicki returned with their drinks, took their order, and left to go place it.

"Thank you, thank you, thank you," Nicki gushed to Amanda, who was standing with Eric at the bar. "I've never been so happy to wait on someone in my life. He called me 'darlin'.' It sounded like something out of one of those Hallmark movies."

Amanda rolled her eyes and considered telling her he had called Amanda the same thing. But then she might end up confessing that, at least for a moment, it had produced the same giddy effect. It also proved that it was a term he probably threw out to countless women.

"He looks like he's made of plastic. Why on earth would you want to get involved with someone who's more Ken doll than actual person?" Amanda asked.

"Do you know what someone like Chase Walker could do for my career?" Nicki couldn't contain her excitement.

"Make you forget all about it?" Amanda quipped, and Eric snickered. "Let me guess, they both want steak?"

"How did you know?" Nicki asked.

"A little bird told me," Amanda replied, fully appreciating the irony.

Chase periodically studied Amanda throughout his meal. His agent droned on and he listened for key words signaling for his full attention, a trick he had learned from being pulled in too many directions at once. He watched her go about her business in the bustling atmosphere. She was graceful, moving fluidly from table to table. She took a vested interest in every single one, sitting down at some of them with a wholesome familiarity. She seemed diligent and serious about her work, but with an appealing smile always at the ready. Not the fake, stretched smile she'd first given him, but the one that showed she knew how to work a room. He looked around the restaurant, which seated about a hundred. It was tastefully decorated without being ostentatious. There was a cozy ambience without it being too dark. It was also spotless. And the employees working seemed relaxed and happy enough to be there. It proved that she knew how to run a smooth operation. It all added up: Amanda Cole had gotten his attention.

Chase also noticed that she left his table alone. The service was still impeccable, but it wasn't Amanda doing the serving. He liked that she wasn't impressed with him, even if his ego did take a hit. She may have been fresh, but she was also clearly intelligent—class and sass, all perfectly packaged. Now he just needed to figure out if she was playing hard to get.

When they finished eating, Chase convinced Alan to leave with the promise that he was going to stay put for a while, have a few drinks, let security drive him home. After a snide remark that if some tail was going to keep him from wandering off, he would take it, Alan left, although not without casting a smug grin in Amanda's direction. When he was gone, Chase took a seat at the bar, ordered another beer, and started chatting with Eric. Soon customers began to approach him and camera phones started to come out.

Amanda tried not to notice—to focus on doing her job—but his charisma had started swirling all around her again. She could feel him watching her, in between polite conversation he made with any and all comers. He didn't make any attempt to hide it. Whenever she glanced in his direction, he would give her a little wink, not the least bit concerned that she had caught him staring.

"You're going to sit here all night and remind me of my bad manners, aren't you?" Amanda said from behind him once the commotion had died down.

He turned around on his barstool to take her all in, appreciating what he saw. "I'm just waiting for security to come back with my car. I hope you don't mind if I hang out."

"They've been standing watch over a very nice Jaguar double-parked out front for the last half hour."

"In that case, I'm just an oxymoron fishing for a date," he said with a note of pure swagger.

"You know, one of those security guards is smaller than you," she continued, deliberately ignoring his attempt to extend an invitation. "That seems counterproductive."

"He's the one I use when random women poke fun of me in public."

"That hurt."

"Guilty enough to join me for dinner?"

"You just ate."

"Not tonight, tomorrow."

"Sorry, I can't. I have a business to run."

"Then let's do lunch? Or breakfast?"

"That's a bit presumptuous, don't you think?" she found herself teasing back.

"That's what I'm talking about. What time are we getting off?" He was so annoyingly easygoing, not to mention attractive.

"Sorry, I don't date guys I can see half naked with a Google search."

"Jeez, does that leave anyone else?"

"It leaves lots of people, Mr. Walker," she retorted snippily as if she was engaging in a political debate. "It leaves teachers and doctors and policemen. Men who are a little choosier about whom they let into their private lives, who can go out for a hamburger without it making Page Six of the *New York Post*."

"I'm about as choosy as they come when it's about my privacy. It's not my fault I can't even spit dirt out of my mouth without someone taking a picture of it."

"You really don't spit all that much," she mused before catching herself. Dagnamit, it sounded like she knew too much about him.

He smiled again. "I promised my mother I would try to curb it. So you watch baseball?"

"Occasionally," she fibbed, attempting to take another swipe at his swagger. "It's hard to turn off Derek Jeter, he's pretty dreamy."

But he only grinned at her. "You can meet him at our wedding."

"That's laying it on a bit thick."

"Maybe, but I'm just trying to illustrate how confident I am."

"More like stubborn. Don't worry, your interest in me will pass," Amanda told him, disappointed deep down that she knew she was speaking the truth. He was just killing time between models and debutantes. Soon this superstar would go back to his world of pomp and accolades. She wasn't interested in the dubious distinction of sleeping with him just to claim the honor of having done so.

"I don't think so, angel," he replied. "I'm a little more one-track-minded than that. All you have to do is say yes. It'll make it easier for both of us."

"I beg to differ, Mr. Walker," she corrected him. "The way I see it, all I have to do is make it through to closing while dodging your cheesy advances."

But she had been wrong. The next day Chase came back. Soon after opening, before the dinner rush, he arrived alone, dressed in jeans and a button-down with his shirttail out, and took the same seat he had at the bar the night before. Then he proceeded to stay until closing.

"This is ridiculous," Amanda told him a little after eight, when he'd been there for over three hours. She wanted to sound annoyed, but secretly she was flattered. Not only was he pleasant and wonderful to look at, he was just so good with the banter. They had developed an easy rapport that she was beginning to find irresistible.

"I know." Chase even managed to gripe with delight. "I can't believe you're making me do this. But at least I'm getting the lowdown on you from your staff."

Eric took that precise moment to find his way to the other end of the bar after an apologetic shrug and a sheepish "It was all good." Amanda crossed her arms over her chest and narrowed her eyes at him as he walked away before going back to Chase.

"Their opinions might be biased. They work for me."

"Then you better let me take you out, so I can draw my own conclusions. If you'd just give me your digits, I'd be on my way."

"Then what?" she asked him.

"You're going to have to say yes to find out." He smiled.

"And if I don't?"

"Then I'm going to have to keep coming back here until I change your mind."

Amanda laughed. "I almost want to see that."

"Be careful what you wish for," he warned her.

And after she politely rebuffed him again, Chase went about the business of doing just that. Every day he was in town, he found his way to the Cold Creek Grille. She started keeping his table open. He began having all his dinners there. He sometimes dined with his security, sometimes they discreetly sat at the bar or a nearby table while he hosted Kings players or held other meetings.

He became a permanent fixture at the Cold Creek. After the first week, word started to spread and there was a constant influx of people going there to dine in the hopes of seeing Chase Walker. And they weren't disappointed. He had dozens upon dozens of pictures taken; he signed napkins and random pieces of paper. He even autographed a few body parts. All with one single purpose: trying to score a date with Amanda Cole. The bar stayed crowded the whole time he was there. He learned the names of all the employees and went out of his way to engage them. If he was faking the average joe routine, he was an exceptional actor. After the third week, it became apparent he wasn't going to go away.

"For Pete's sake," Eric eventually said one unusually quiet Sunday night while Chase was in the men's room, "he's starting to tell people that he's eaten everything on the menu twice. The guy is really starting to get our sympathy vote. If you don't say yes soon, you're going to look like you're shooting him down to build up your clientele."

Eric wasn't far off. Her staff was making her feel like saying no to Chase was akin to burning the American flag.

"He's got you batting for him now?" Amanda asked. She had started to find all the good-natured teasing a bit intimidating. She never expected Chase to make good on his threat to become a pest. She couldn't throw him out now. By the sound of it, her entire staff would start a mutiny if she did. And when all was said and

THE SWEET SPOT

done, she didn't want to. When he took a four-day road trip, she started to miss him.

"Yeah, what are you waiting for?" Nicki chimed in, joining them to pick up her drink order. "He's not perfect enough for you?"

Amanda didn't take it personally. Nicki had tried her best to hide her disappointment when it became apparent that Chase was indeed interested in someone at the Cold Creek and it wasn't her. It was a tough pill to swallow. Amanda knew that pill all too well. The current pill didn't feel much different. Letting a man like Chase Walker get too close was asking for a one-way ticket to Heartbreak City. The real dilemma was in getting him to see her reasoning.

"No one is perfect," Amanda stated firmly. "There's always that fatal flaw and I'll bet his is a doozy."

"Fatal flaw?" Nicki repeated with interest.

"Yeah," Amanda explained. "It's a theory we figured out back in college. When you first start dating a guy, he's busy saying all the right words and acting like Prince Charming, trying to get you naked. Then if he likes the outcome, it's all about trying to get you to stay naked, but the flaw is there, lying dormant, until you're hooked. By then, it's usually too late, you're all wrapped up in the memory of when you first met and everyone was on their best behavior. Then you ride the break-up make-up carousel until you both can't stand yourselves. Our final analysis was, until you find the flaw in your potential partner, the relationship can't ever be real."

"That's stupid," Eric retorted. There were times when Amanda was a boss and there were times when Amanda was a friend. Most of the time, she was both. "People are always changing. What's a flaw in some-one who's twenty-five could be a nonissue five years later."

"So what happens when you find it?" Nicki asked curiously, ignoring Eric. Boys knew nothing of the sisterhood.

"Then you decide if it's something you can live with and if the good makes the flaw worth it," Amanda continued. "Like maybe you can take a guy that enjoys his free time with the boys, but one that spends every weekend drunk is a no go. Maybe he's a real cheapskate when it comes to showering you with gifts and expensive dates, but he's all about you when you hit the sheets. Or you don't mind that he doesn't have a real great job as long as while you're working he's not at home cheating on you."

"You realize that every situation you just described has nothing to do with the guy that's trying to get your attention," Eric pointed out. "For crying out loud, you babes are always jumping the gun. He just wants to take you to dinner."

"Guys like that don't just want dinner." Amanda shook her head. Besides, Chase was not just a guy. He was more of a stalker who just happened to win every-body over, a drop-dead sexy stalker with electric eyes, a teen-idol smile, and a butt worthy of an underwear model. "I'm telling you, he's only pushing because I had the nerve to shoot him down. And how do you know he isn't a cheater? For all we know, he's the biggest philanderer on the planet."

"Oh, sure." Eric snorted, rolling his eyes and shaking his head, "'Cause all the best womanizers sit alone at a bar being shot down for nights on end."

"He's like your own personal Norm from *Cheers*"— Nicki giggled—"except he's gorgeous."

"And he has a job," Eric added.

"And a million women want to have his baby," Amanda concluded as Chase came back to the bar.

Chase took one look at the three guilty faces and raised an eyebrow. "You were all talking about me," he said suspiciously, retaking his seat. Both Eric and Nicki hustled back to work, leaving Amanda to deal with Chase.

"Guilty as charged," she admitted. "But they were just telling me what a fool I am for making you sit here every night."

"I knew I liked them," Chase said.

"I told them that if you were the one doing the sitting, then maybe the fool was actually you," she teased.

"As long as I get what I want in the end. And I can be very patient."

Why did he have to be so impossibly easygoing?

"I'm not going to get you to give this up, am I?" Amanda asked.

"Of course you are, just as soon as you say yes."

Amanda hesitated. For a long moment she debated the pros and cons one more time of saying the word that once was out there she couldn't take back and would probably end up regretting.

"Yes," she said quietly.

Chase shook his head dramatically, as if he couldn't believe what he'd heard, then broke out into a full-blown grin.

"See?" he asked happily. "Was that so hard?"